TREASURE OF KHAN

A DIRK PITT NOVEL

**Center Point
Large Print**

**This Large Print Book carries the
Seal of Approval of N.A.V.H.**

TREASURE OF KHAN
A DIRK PITT NOVEL

CLIVE CUSSLER
AND
DIRK CUSSLER

CENTER POINT PUBLISHING
THORNDIKE, MAINE

This Center Point Large Print edition
is published in the year 2007 by arrangement with
G. P. Putnam's Sons, a member of Penguin Group (USA) Inc.

The text of this Large Print edition is unabridged. In other
aspects, this book may vary from the original edition.
Printed in the United States of America.
Set in 16-point Times New Roman type.

ISBN-10: 1-58547-878-4
ISBN-13: 978-1-58547-878-1

Library of Congress Cataloging-in-Publication Data

Cussler, Clive.
    Treasure of Khan : a Dirk Pitt novel / Clive Cussler and Dirk Cussler.--Center Point large print ed.
        p. cm.
    ISBN-13: 978-1-58547-878-1 (lib. bdg. : alk. paper)
        1. Pitt, Dirk (Fictitious character)--Fiction. 2. Oceanographers--Fiction. 3. Oil
industry--Fiction. 4. Mongols--Fiction. 5. Genghis Khan, 1162-1227--Fiction.
6. Treasure troves--Fiction. 7. Mongolia--Fiction. 8. Russia (Federation)--Fiction.
9. Large type books. I. Cussler, Dirk. II. Title.

PS3553.U75T74 2007
813'.54--dc22

2006026342

For Kerry, with my love.
D.E.C.

THE
EMPEROR'S
TEMPEST

AUGUST 10, 1281 A.D.
HAKATA BAY, JAPAN

ARIK TEMUR PEERED INTO THE darkness and tilted his head toward the side rail as the sound of oars dipping through the water grew louder. When the noise closed to within a few feet, he slouched back into the shadows, pulling his head down low. This time the intruders would be welcomed aboard warmly, he thought with grim anticipation.

The slapping of the oars ceased, but a wooden clunk told him the small boat had pulled alongside the larger vessel's stern. The midnight moon was a slim crescent, but crystal clear skies amplified the starlight, bathing the ship in a cottony luminance. Temur knelt quietly as he watched a dark figure climb over the stern rail, followed by another, then another, until nearly a dozen men stood on the deck. The intruders wore brightly colored silk garments under tunics of layered leather armor that rustled as they moved. But it was the glint of their razor-sharp katanas, single-edged dueling swords, that caught his eye as they assembled.

With the trap set and the bait taken, the Mongol commander turned to a boy at his side and nodded. The boy immediately began ringing a heavy bronze bell he cradled in his arms, the metallic clang shattering the still night air. The invaders froze in their tracks, startled by the sudden alarm. Then a hidden mass of thirty armed soldiers sprang silently from the shadows. Armed with iron-tipped spears, they flung themselves at the invaders, thrusting their weapons with deadly fury. Half of the boarders were killed instantly, struck by multiple spear tips that skewered their body armor. The remaining invaders wielded their swords and tried to fight back but were quickly overpowered by the mass of defenders. Within seconds, all of the boarders lay dead or dying on the ship's deck. All, that is, except a lone, standing dervish.

Clad in an embroidered red silk robe with baggy trousers tucked into bearskin boots, he was clearly no peasant soldier. With devastating speed and accuracy, he surprised the attacking defenders by turning and running right into them, deflecting spear thrusts with quick waves of his sword. In an instant, he closed on a group of three of the ship's defenders and quickly dropped them all to the deck with a flash of his sword, nearly cutting one man in two with a single swipe of the blade.

Watching the whirlwind decimate his soldiers, Temur jumped to his feet and unsheathed his own sword, then leaped forward. The swordsman saw Temur charge at him and deftly parried a spear thrust aside before whirling around and plunging his bloodied sword in the path of the oncoming warrior. The Mongol commander had killed more than twenty men in his lifetime and calmly sidestepped the swinging blade. The sword tip whisked by his chest, missing the skin by millimeters. As his opponent's sword passed, Temur raised his own blade and thrust it tip first into the attacker's side. The invader stiffened as the blade tore through his rib cage and bisected his heart. He bowed weakly at the Mongol as his eyes rolled back, then he fell over dead.

The defenders let out a cheer that echoed across the harbor, letting the rest of the assembled Mongol invasion fleet know that the guerrilla attack this night had failed.

"You fought bravely," Temur complimented his soldiers, mostly Chinese, who gathered around him. "Throw the bodies of the Japanese into the sea and let us wash their blood from our decks. We may sleep well and proud tonight." Amid another cheer, Temur knelt next to the samurai and pried away the bloodstained sword clasped in the dead man's hands. In the dim light of the ship's lanterns, he carefully studied the Japanese weapon, admiring its fine craftsmanship and razor-sharp edge, before sliding it into his own waist scabbard with a nod of satisfaction.

As the dead were unceremoniously dumped over the side, Temur was approached by the ship's captain, a stern Korean named Yon.

"A fine battle," Yon said without empathy, "but how many more attacks on my ship must I endure?"

"The land offensive will regain momentum once the South of the Yangtze Fleet arrives. The enemy will soon be crushed and these raiding attacks will cease. Perhaps our entrapment of the enemy tonight will prove to be a deterrent."

Yon grunted in skepticism. "My ship and crew were to have been back in Pusan by now. The invasion is turning into a debacle."

"While the arrival of the two fleets should have been better coordinated, there is no question as to the ultimate outcome. Conquest shall be ours," Temur replied testily.

As the captain walked away shaking his head, Temur cursed under his breath. Reliant on a Korean ship and crew and an army of Chinese foot soldiers with which to do battle was like having his hands tied behind his back. Land a division of Mongol cavalry, he knew, and the island nation would be subdued in a week.

Wishing would not make it so, and he begrudgingly considered the validity of the captain's words. The invasion had in fact started off on a shaky footing, and, if he was superstitious, he might even think there was a curse on them. When Kublai, emperor of China and khan of khan's of the Mongol Empire, had requested tribute from Japan and been rebuffed, it was only natural to send an invasion fleet to subdue their insolence. But the invasion fleet sent in 1274 was much too small. Before a secure beachhead could be established, a severe gale battered the Mongol fleet, decimating the warships as they stood out at sea.

Now, seven years later, the same mistake would not be made. Kublai Khan called for a massive invasion force, combining elements of the Korean Eastern Fleet with the main battle group from China, the South of the Yangtze Fleet. Over one hundred fifty thousand Chinese and Mongol soldiers would converge on the southern Japanese island of Kyushu to overrun the ragtag warlords defending the country. But the invasion force had yct to be consolidated. The Eastern Fleet sailing from Korea had arrived first. Pining for glory, they tried landing forces north of Hakata Bay but quickly ground down. In the face of a spirited Japanese defense, they were forced to pull back and wait for the second fleet to arrive.

With growing confidence, the Japanese warriors began taking the fight to the Mongol Fleet. Brazen raiding parties on small boats would sneak into the harbor at night and assault the Mongol ships at anchor. The gruesome discovery of decapitated bodies told the story of yet another attack by samurai warriors, who took the heads of their slain victims home as war trophies. After several guerrilla strikes, the invasion fleet began tying their ships together for protective safety. Temur's entrapment ploy of mooring his ship alone at the edge of the bay had worked as anticipated, enticing a Japanese boarding party to their death.

Though the late-night attacks caused little strategic harm, they dampened the fading morale of the invading forces. The soldiers were still stationed aboard the cramped Korean ships nearly three months after departing Pusan. Provisions were low, the ships were rotting, and dysentery outbreaks were cropping up across the fleet. But Temur knew that the arrival of the South of the Yangtze ships would turn the tables. The experienced and disciplined force from China would easily defeat the lightly organized samurai warriors, once they were landed in mass. If only they would arrive.

The next morning broke sunny and clear, with a stiff breeze blowing from the south. On the stern of his *mugun* support ship, Captain Yon surveyed the crowded confines of Hakata Bay. The fleet of Korean ships was an impressive sight in its own right. Nearly nine hundred vessels stretched across the bay in an assortment of shapes and sizes. Most were wide and sturdy junks, some as small as twenty feet, others like Yon's stretching nearly eighty feet long. Almost all had been constructed purposely for the invasion. But the Eastern Fleet, as it was known, would be dwarfed by the forces to come.

At half past three in the afternoon, a call rang out from a lookout, and soon excited cries and the sound of banging drums thundered across the harbor. Out to sea, the first dots of the southern invasion force appeared on the horizon crawling toward the Japanese coast. Hour by hour, the dots multiplied and grew larger until the entire sea seemed to be a mass of dark wooden ships with blood red sails. More than three thousand ships carrying one hundred thousand additional soldiers emerged from the Korea Strait, comprising an invasion fleet the likes of which would not be seen again until the invasion of Normandy almost seven hundred years later.

The red silk sails of the war fleet flapped across the horizon like a crimson squall. All night and well into the following day, squadron after squadron of Chinese junks approached the coast, assembling in and around Hakata Bay as the military commanders calculated a landing strike. Signal flags rose high on the flagship, where Mongol and Chinese generals planned a renewed invasion.

Behind the defenses of their stone seawall, the Japanese looked on in horror at the massive fleet. The overwhelming odds seemed to heighten the determination in some of the defenders. Others looked on in despair and desperately prayed for the gods to help through heavenly intervention. Even the most fearless samurai recognized that there was little likelihood they would survive the assault.

But a thousand miles to the south, another force was at work, more powerful even than the invasion fleet of Kublai Khan. A percolating mix of wind and sea and rain was brewing together, welding into a wicked mass of energy. The storm had formed as most typhoons do, in the warm waters of the western Pacific near the Philippines. An isolated thunderstorm set off its birth, upsetting the surrounding high-pressure front by causing warm air to converge with cold. Funneling warm air off the ocean's surface, the churning winds gradually blew into a tempest. Moving unabated across the sea, the storm grew in intensity, exuding a devastating force of wind. Surface winds raged higher and higher, until exceeding one hundred sixty miles per hour. The "super typhoon," as they are now branded, crept almost straight north before curiously shifting directions to the northeast. Directly in its path were the southern islands of Japan and the Mongol Fleet.

Standing off Kyushu, the assembled invasion force was focused only on conquest. Oblivious to the approaching tempest, the joint fleets assembled for a combined invasion.

"We are ordered to join the deployments to the south," Captain Yon reported to Temur after signal flags were exchanged within his squadron. "Preliminary ground forces have landed and secured a harbor for unloading the troops. We are to follow portions of the Yangtze Fleet out of Hakata Bay and prepare to land our soldiers as reinforcements."

"It will be a relief to have my soldiers on dry land again," Temur replied. Like all Mongols, Temur was a land warrior used to fighting on horseback. Attacking from the sea was a relatively novel concept for the Mongols, adopted only in recent years by the emperor as a necessary means of subjugating Korea and South China.

"You shall have your chance to land and fight soon enough," Yon replied as he oversaw the retrieval of his ship's stone anchor.

Following the main body of the fleet out of Hakata Bay and along the coastline to the south, Yon looked uncomfortably at the skies as they blackened on the horizon. A single cloud seemed to grow larger and larger until it shaded the entire sky. As darkness fell, the wind and seas began to seethe, while sprays of rain slapped hard against the ship's surface. Many of the Korean captains recognized the signs of an approaching squall and repositioned their ships farther offshore. The Chinese sailors, not as experienced in open-water conditions, foolishly held their positions close to the landing site.

Unable to sleep in his rollicking bunk, Temur climbed above deck to find eight of his men clinging to the rail, seasick from the turbulence. The pitch-black night was broken by dozens of tiny lights that danced above the waves, small candlelit lanterns that marked other vessels of the fleet. Many of the ships were still tied together, and Temur watched as small clusters of candlelight rose and fell as one on the rolling swells.

"I will be unable to land your troops ashore," Yon shouted to Temur over the howling winds. "The storm is still building. We must move out to sea in order to avoid being crushed on the rocks."

Temur made no effort to protest and simply nodded his head. Though he wanted nothing more than to get his soldiers and himself off the pitching ship, he knew an attempt to do so would be foolhardy. Yon was right. As miserable as the prospect sounded, there was nothing to do but ride out the storm.

Yon ordered the lugsail on the foremast raised and maneuvered the ship's bow to the west. Tossing roughly through the growing waves, the sturdy vessel slowly began fighting its way away from the coastline.

Around Yon's vessel, confusion reigned with the rest of the fleet. Several of the Chinese ships attempted to put troops ashore in the maelstrom, though most remained at anchor a short distance away. A scattering of vessels, mostly from the Eastern Fleet, followed Yon's lead and began repositioning themselves offshore. Few seemed to believe that yet another typhoon could strike and damage the fleet as in 1274. But the doubters were soon to be proven wrong.

The super typhoon gathered force and rolled closer, bringing with it a torrent of wind and rain. Soon after dawn the sky turned black and the storm reared up with its full might. Torrential rains blew horizontally, the water pellets bursting with enough force to shred the sails of the bobbing fleet. Waves crashed to shore in thunderous blows that could be heard miles away. With screeching winds that exceeded a Category 4 hurricane, the super typhoon finally crashed into Kyushu.

On shore, the Japanese defenders were subject to a ten-foot wall of storm surge that pounded over the shoreline, inundating homes, villages, and defense works while drowning hundreds. Ravaging winds uprooted ancient trees and sent loose debris flying through the air like missiles. A continuous deluge of rain dumped a foot of water an hour on inland areas, flooding valleys and overflowing rivers in a deadly barrage. Flash floods and mud slides killed untold more, burying whole towns and villages in seconds.

But the maelstrom on shore paled in comparison to the fury felt by the Mongol Fleet at sea. In addition to the explosive winds and piercing rains came mammoth waves, blown high by the storm's wrath. Rolling mountains of water belted the invasion fleet, capsizing many vessels while smashing others to bits. Ships anchored close to shore were swiftly blown into the rocky shoals, where they were battered into small pieces. Timbers buckled and beams splintered from the force of the waves, causing dozens of ships to simply disintegrate in the boiling seas. In Hakata Bay, groups of ships still lashed together were battered mercilessly. As one vessel foundered, it would pull the other ships to the bottom like a string of dominoes. Trapped inside the fast-sinking ships, the crew and soldiers died a quick death. Those escaping to the violent surface waters drowned a short time later, as few knew how to swim.

Aboard the Korean *mugun,* Temur and his men clung desperately to the ship as it was tossed like a cork in a washing machine. Yon expertly guided the vessel through the teeth of the storm, fighting to keep his bow to the waves. Several times, the wooden ship heeled so far over that Temur thought she would capsize. Yet there was Yon standing tall at the rudder as the ship righted itself, a determined grin on his face as he did battle with the elements. It wasn't until a monster forty-foot wave suddenly appeared out of the gloom that the salty captain turned pale.

The huge wall of water bore down on them with a

thunderous roar. The cresting wave swept onto the ship like an avalanche, burying the vessel in a froth of sea and foam. For several seconds, the Korean ship disappeared completely under the raging sea. Men belowdecks felt their stomachs drop from the force of the plunge and oddly noted the howl of the wind vanish as everything went black. By all rights, the wooden ship should have broken to pieces by the wave's pounding. But the tough little vessel held together. As the giant wave rolled past, the ship rose like an apparition from the deep and regained her position on the frenzied sea.

Temur was tossed across the deck during the submersion and barely clung to a ladder rung as the ship flooded. He gasped for air as the vessel resurfaced and was distraught to see that the masts had been torn off the ship. Behind him, a sharp cry rang out in the water off the stern. Glancing about the deck, he realized with horror that Yon and five Korean seamen, along with a handful of his own men, had been swept off the ship. A chorus of panicked cries pierced the air momentarily before it was washed out by the howl of the wind. Temur caught sight of the captain and men struggling nearby in the water. He could only watch helplessly as a large wave carried them from his sight.

Without masts and crew, the ship was now at the complete mercy of the storm. Pitching and wallowing feebly in the seas, pounded and flooded by the high waves, the ship had a thousand opportunities to founder. But the simple yet robust construction of the

Korean ship kept her afloat while around her scores of Chinese ships vanished into the depths.

After several intense, buffeting hours, the winds slowly died down and the pelting rains ceased. For a brief moment, the sun broke clear, and Temur thought the storm had ended. But it was just the eye of the typhoon passing over, offering a brief reprieve before the assault would continue again. Belowdecks, Temur found two Korean sailors still aboard and forced them to help man the ship. As the winds picked up and the rains returned, Temur and the sailors took turns tying themselves to the rudder and battling the deadly waves.

Lost as to position or even the direction they sailed, the men bravely focused on keeping the ship afloat. Unaware that they were now absorbing the counter-clockwise winds that swirled from the north, they were pushed rapidly through open water to the south. The brunt of the typhoon's energy had been expended as it struck Kyushu, so the battering was less intense than before. But gusts over ninety miles per hour still buffeted the vessel, blasting it roughly through the seas. Blinded by the pelting rain, Temur had little clue to their path. Several times the ship nearly approached landfall, inching by islands, rocks, and shoals that went unseen in the gloom of the storm. Miraculously, the ship blew clear, the men aboard never realizing how close they came to death.

The typhoon raged day and night before gradually losing its power, the rain and winds fading to a light squall. The Korean *mugun,* battered and leaky, held fast and clung to the surface with gritty pride. Though the captain and crew were lost and the ship was a crippled mess, they had survived all that the killer storm could throw at them. A quiet sense of luck and destiny settled over them as the seas began to calm.

No such luck befell the rest of the Mongol invasion force, which was brutally decimated by the killer typhoon. Nearly the entire Yangtze Fleet was destroyed, smashed to bits against the rocky shoreline or sunk by the vicious seas. A jumbled array of broken timber from huge Chinese junks, Korean warships, and oar-driven barges littered the shoreline. In the water, the cries of the dying had long since echoed over the shrieks of the wind. Many of the soldiers, clothed in heavy leather body armor, sank immediately to the bottom upon being cast in the waves. Others fought through the throes of panic to stay afloat, only to be pummeled by the endless onslaught of massive waves. The lucky few who crawled ashore alive were quickly cut up by marauding bands of samurai roving the shoreline. After the storm, the dead littered the beaches like stacked cords of wood. Half-sunken wrecks lined the horizon off Kyushu in such numbers that it was said a man could walk across the Imari Gulf without getting wet.

The remnants of the invasion fleet limped back to Korea and China with the unthinkable news that Mother Nature had again spoiled the Mongol plans of conquest. It was a crushing defeat for Kublai Khan.

The disaster represented the worst defeat suffered by the Mongols since the reign of Genghis Khan, and showed the rest of the world that the forces of the great empire were far from invincible.

For the Japanese, the arrival of the killer typhoon was nothing less than a miracle. Despite the destruction incurred on Kyushu, the island had been spared conquest and the invading forces defeated. Most believed it could only have come as a result of the eleventh-hour prayers to the Sun Goddess at the Shrine of Ise. Divine intervention had prevailed, a sure sign that Japan was blessed with heavenly protection to ward off foreign invaders. So strong was the belief in the Kami-Kaze, or "divine wind" as it was called, that it permeated Japanese history for centuries, reappearing as the appellation for the suicide pilots of World War II.

ABOARD THE Korean troopship, Temur and the surviving crew had no idea as to the devastation suffered by the invasion fleet. Blown out to sea, they could only assume that the invading force would regroup after the storm passed and continue the assault.

"We must rejoin the fleet," Temur told the men. "The emperor is expecting victory and we must fulfill our duty."

There was only one problem. After three days and nights of severe weather, tossed about without mast and sails, there was no telling where they were. The weather cleared, but there were no other ships in sight.

Worse for Temur, there was nobody aboard capable of navigating a vessel at sea. The two Korean sailors who survived the storm were a cook and an aged ship's carpenter, neither possessing navigation skills.

"The land of Japan must be to the east of us," he conferred with the Korean carpenter. "Construct a new mast and sails, and we shall use the sun and stars to guide us east until we reach landfall and relocate the invasion fleet."

The old carpenter argued that the ship was not seaworthy. "She is battered and leaking. We must sail northwest, to Korea, to save ourselves," he cried.

But Temur would have none of it. A temporary mast was hastily constructed and makeshift sails raised. With a fresh determination, the Mongol soldier-turned-sailor guided the waylaid ship toward the eastern horizon, anxious to put ashore again and rejoin the battle.

TWO DAYS passed, and all Temur and his men could see was blue water. The Japanese mainland never materialized. Thoughts of changing course were dispelled when yet another storm crept up on them from the southwest. Though less intense than the earlier typhoon, the tropical storm was widespread and slow moving. For five days, the troopship battled the throes of high winds and heavy rains that pitched them wildly about the ocean. The beaten ship seemed to be reaching its limits. The temporary mast and sails were again lost overboard to the gales, while leaks below the waterline kept the carpenter working around the clock. More disconcerting, the entire rudder broke free of the ship, taking with it two of Temur's soldiers, who clung to it for dear life.

When it seemed that the ship could bear no more, the second storm quietly passed. But as the weather eased, the men aboard became more anxious than ever. Land had not been sighted in over a week and food supplies were beginning to dwindle. Men openly pleaded with Temur to sail the ship to China, but the prevailing winds and current, as well as the lack of a ship's rudder, made that impossible. The lone ship was adrift in the ocean with no bearings, no navigation aids, and little means to guide the way.

Temur lost track of time, as the hours drifted into days, and the days into weeks. With their provisions depleted, the feeble crew resorted to catching fish for food and collecting rainwater for drinking. The gray stormy weather was gradually replaced by clear skies and sunny weather. As the winds tapered, the temperature warmed. The ship seemed to grow stagnant along with the crew, drifting aimlessly under light winds over a flat sea. Soon a death cloud began to hover over the vessel. Each sunrise brought the discovery of a new corpse as the starving crewmen began to perish in the night. Temur looked over his emaciated soldiers with a feeling of dishonor. Rather than die in battle, their fate was to starve on an empty ocean far from home.

As the men around him dozed in the midday sun, a

sudden clamor erupted on the port side deck of the ship.

"It's a bird!" someone cried. "Try to kill it."

Temur lurched to his feet to see a trio of men attempting to surround a large, dark-billed seagull. The bird hopped around spastically, eyeing the hungry men with a wary look. One of the men grabbed a wooden mallet with a gnarled sunburned hand and flung it swiftly at the bird, hoping to stun or kill it. The gull deftly sidestepped the flying mallet and, with a loud squawk of indignation, flapped its wings and rose lazily into the sky. While the disgruntled men cursed, Temur quietly studied the gull, his eyes following the white bird as it flew south and gradually melted into the horizon. Squinting at the far line of blue where the water met the sky, he suddenly arched a brow. Blinking forcefully, he looked again, tensing slightly when his eyes registered a small green lump on the horizon. Then his nose joined in on the fantasy. Temur could smell a difference in the air. The damp salt air that his lungs had become used to now had a different aroma. A sweet, slightly flowery fragrance wafted through his nostrils. Taking a deep breath, he cleared his throat and grumbled to the men on the deck.

"There is land before us," he said in a parched voice, pointing toward the path of the gull. "Let every man who is able help guide us to it."

The exhausted and emaciated crew staggered to life at the words. After straining their eyes at the distant speck on the horizon, the men gathered their wits and went to work. A large deck-support beam was sawed loose and manhandled over the stern, where, secured with ropes, it would act as a crude rudder. While three men wrestled the beam about to steer the ship, the remaining men attacked the water. Brooms, boards, and even sabers were used as makeshift oars by the desperate men in a struggle to row the battered vessel to land.

Slowly the distant spot grew larger, until a shimmering emerald island materialized, complete with a broad, towering mountain peak. Approaching the shoreline, they found heaving waves battering a rocky coastline, which rose up vertically. In a panicked moment, the ship became caught in a crosscurrent that drove them toward an inlet surrounded by jagged boulders.

"Rocks ahead!" the old ship's carpenter cried, eyeing the protrusions off the bow.

"Every man to the left side of the ship," Temur bellowed as they bore down on a dark wall of rock. The half-dozen men on the starboard railing ran, scampered, and crawled to the port side and frantically slapped the water with their makeshift oars. Their last-second surge nosed the bow away from the rocks, and the men held their breath as the port hull scraped against a line of submerged boulders. The grinding ceased, and the men realized that the ship's timbers had held together once more.

"There is no place to put ashore here," the carpenter shouted. "We must turn and go back to sea."

Temur peered at the sheer rock cliff rising above the shore. Porous black and gray rock stretched in a high jagged wall in front of them, broken only by the small black oval of a cave, cut off their port bow at the waterline.

"Bring the bow around. Row again, men, at a steady pace."

Clawing at the water, the drained men propelled the boat away from the rocks and back into the offshore current. Drifting along the landmass, they saw that the towering shoreline eventually softened. Finally, the carpenter spat out the words the crew waited to hear.

"We can land her there," he said, pointing to a large crescent-shaped cove cut into the shoreline.

Temur nodded, and the men guided the vessel toward shore, a final gust of energy flowing from their limbs. Paddling into the cove, the exhausted men drove the ship toward a sandy beach, until its barnacle-encrusted hull ground to a halt a few feet from shore.

The weary men were nearly too spent to climb off the ship. Grabbing his sword, Temur painfully staggered ashore with five men to search for food and fresh water. Following the sound of rushing water, they cut through a thicket of tall ferns and found a freshwater lagoon, fed by a waterfall that rushed down a rocky ledge. In jubilance, Temur and his men plunged into the lagoon and happily gulped down mouthfuls of the cool water.

Their enjoyment was short-lived when a sudden pounding broke the air. It was the boom of the signal drum aboard the Korean ship, thumping out a cry to battle. Temur sprung to his feet in a single motion and called immediately to his men.

"Back to the ship. At once."

He didn't wait for his men to assemble but vaulted ahead in the direction of the ship. Whatever pain and weakness his legs had felt before vanished under the replenishment of fresh water and the surge of adrenaline rushing through his body. Bounding through the jungle, he could hear the drumbeat's decibels rise in his ears as he moved closer until he finally burst past a cluster of palm trees and onto the sandy beach.

The veteran soldier's eyes quickly scanned the surrounding waters and immediately spotted the source of the alarm. Midway across the cove, a narrow canoe sailed toward the grounded ship. Seated inside, a half dozen shirtless men rhythmically muscled spade-shaped wooden paddles through the water, driving the canoe swiftly toward shore. Temur noted the men's skin was colored a deep bronze, and most had curly black hair kept shorter than his own. Several of the men wore necklaces with a hook-shaped bone dangling across their chests.

"Your orders, sir?" asked a frail soldier who had been banging the drum, finally ceasing the alarm.

Temur hesitated before answering, knowing that a harem of old maids could defeat his emaciated crew in their present state.

"Arm with spears," he ordered calmly. "Defensive line behind me on the beach."

The surviving remnants of his command staggered off the boat and out of the jungle, lining up behind Temur with the few remaining spears still aboard. The ragged force had little strength left, but Temur knew they would die fighting for him if necessary. He felt for the grip of the Japanese samurai sword he now wore at his belt and wondered if he would die with its blade in his hand.

The canoe made its way directly toward the men on the beach, its rowers silent as they propelled the boat to shore. When the bow scraped the sand at the water's edge, the occupants jumped out and quickly dragged the canoe onto the beach, then stood solemnly alongside the craft. For several seconds, the two parties eyed each other suspiciously. Finally, one of the men from the canoe crossed the sand and stood before Temur. He was short, barely five foot tall, and older than the rest, with long white hair wrapped with a bark strip into a ponytail. He wore a string of shark's teeth around his neck and gripped a wooden staff made from twisted driftwood. His brown eyes sparkled with luster, and he smiled broadly at the Mongol, displaying a crooked row of bright white teeth. In a melodic language, he spoke rapidly, offering what seemed to be a nonthreatening greeting. Temur simply nodded slightly, keeping a sharp eye on the other men by the canoe. The old man jabbered for several minutes, then abruptly returned to the canoe and reached inside.

Temur tightened his grip on the Japanese sword and gave his men a knowing look of caution. But he relaxed when the old man stood and held up a fat thirty-pound yellowfin tuna. The other natives reached into the canoe and retrieved other fish and shellfish carried in reed baskets, which they placed at the feet of Temur's men. The famished soldiers anxiously waited for approval from the Mongol leader, then voraciously attacked the food, smiling thanks to the native hosts. The old man strode up to Temur and offered him a drink of water from a pigskin bag.

Having gained mutual trust, the natives pointed into the jungle and motioned for the shipwrecked men to follow. Hesitantly leaving their ship, Temur and his men followed the natives through the jungle, hiking for a mile or two before entering a small clearing. Several dozen small thatch-covered huts surrounded a fenced corral where small children were playing with a herd of pigs. On the opposite side of the clearing, an even larger hut with a high roof served as the home of the village chief, who Temur was surprised to learn was none other than the old white-haired man.

The residents of the village gawked at the strangers as a feast was hastily prepared and the Asian warriors were welcomed into the community with great honor. The ship, clothes, and weapons of the strangers were evidence of great knowledge, and the men were prized surreptitiously as new allies against potential enemy combatants. The Chinese and Korean warriors were simply glad to be alive and welcomed the generous offers of food, housing, and female companionship that the friendly villagers extended. Only Temur accepted the hospitality with reservation. As he chewed on a slab of grilled abalone with the village chief, his men around him enjoying themselves for the first time in weeks, he silently wondered if he would ever see Mongolia again.

OVER THE next few weeks, the men of the Mongol invasion force took up residence in the village, gradually assimilating into the community. Initially, Temur refused to settle in the camp, sleeping in the rotting ship each night. Only when the storm-ravaged hull timbers finally gave way and the battered remains of the ship slid to the bottom of the cove did he reluctantly move to the village.

Thoughts of his wife and four children played in his mind, but, with the ship ruined, Temur began to give up hope of returning home. His crew had gladly accepted their new lives on the tropical outpost, viewing their station as far preferable to the bleak life in China as soldiers of the Mongol emperor. It was an attitude Temur could never accept. The scrappy Mongol commander was a loyal servant to the khan and knew it was his duty to return to service at the first opportunity. But with his ship in pieces at the bottom of the cove, there was no viable means of returning home. With a bitter reluctance, Temur gradually resigned himself to a castaway's life on the large island.

THE YEARS trickled by and gradually softened the

resolve of the old warrior. Over time, Temur and his men had learned the lyrical native tongue of the island community, and the Mongol commander enjoyed swapping adventure tales with the white-haired chief. Mahu, as he was called, bantered on about how his ancestors had sailed an epic voyage across the great sea just a few generations before in mammoth sailing ships. The island had called to them, he said, with a rumble and a billow of smoke from the mountaintop, a sign of welcome from the gods to come and prosper. The gods had smiled on them ever since, providing a land of temperate weather and abundant food and water.

Temur chuckled at the description, wondering how the primitive natives who barely traversed to neighboring islands in small canoes could find their way to crossing the ocean itself.

"I would like to see one of these majestic sailing ships," he chided the old man.

"I will take you to one," Mahu replied indignantly. "You will see for yourself."

The amused Temur saw that the old chief was serious and took him up on the offer. After a two-day trek across the island, he was beginning to regret his curiosity when the weathered jungle path they followed suddenly opened onto a small sandy beach. Temur stopped when his feet touched the sand, and the old man silently pointed toward the far end of the beach.

Temur didn't recognize it at first. Gazing across the

beach, he saw only a pair of large tree trunks lying perpendicular to the shore. The rest of the beach appeared barren. As his eyes fell back to the fallen trees, he suddenly realized that they were more than just dead wood; they were the support frames for a massive raft that lay half buried in the sand.

The Mongol warrior ran toward the object, not believing his eyes. With each step, he became more mesmerized. Though obviously sitting on the beach for years, perhaps even decades, the ancient sailing craft was still intact. Temur could see it was a double-hulled design, with a single flat deck supported by the two large logs. The vessel stretched over sixty feet but carried only a large single mast, which had rotted away. Though the plank deck had disintegrated, Temur could see that the massive support timbers looked as sturdy as when they were felled. There was no doubt in Temur's mind that the boat had been an oceangoing vessel. Mahu's fanciful tale was true after all. Temur excitedly gazed at the remains of the vessel, eyeing a means to escape the island.

"You shall return me to my home and emperor," he muttered wistfully to the wooden mass.

With a native work crew under the direction of the Korean ship's carpenter put to the task, Temur set about refitting the old sailing vessel. Deck planking was cut and fit from nearby hardwood trees. Coconut husk fibers were braided into sennit cord and tied to the hull timbers and supports. A large reed sail was woven and fitted to the replacement mast, cut from a

young tree near the beach. In just a few short weeks, the nearly forgotten ocean voyager was reclaimed from the sands and made ready to ply the waves again.

To sail the craft, Temur could have ordered his old crew aboard, but he knew that most were afraid to risk their lives again in a daring sea voyage. Many of the men now had wives and children on the island. When he asked for volunteers, just three men stepped forward, along with old Mahu. Temur could ask for no more. It would be barely enough to sail the old craft, but the Mongol commander accepted without question the decision of those who elected to stay.

Provisions were stocked, and then the men waited until Mahu declared that the time was right.

"The goddess Hina will offer us safe passage to the west now," he finally told Temur a week later, when the winds shifted direction. "Let us be away."

"I shall report to the emperor of his new colony in this distant land," he shouted to the men assembled on the beach as the twin canoe hull broke through the surf and an offshore breeze launched them briskly out to sea. Loaded with plenty of water, dried fish, and fruit from the local landscape, the ship set sail with enough stores for the crew to survive for weeks at sea.

As the lush verdant island disappeared in the waves behind them, the men aboard the catamaran felt a moment of insecurity and foolishness. Their deadly struggles on the sea more than a decade earlier came flooding back and they all wondered whether the forces of nature would allow them to survive again.

Yet Temur was confident. His trust lay in the old man, Mahu. Though the native chief had little sailing experience, he had read the stars with ease and tracked the sun's movements by day while studying the clouds and sea swells. It was Mahu who knew that the winds to the south of the island turned west in the fall months, which would fill their sails with a steady breeze in the direction home. It was Mahu who also knew how to catch tuna with a line and bone hook using flying fish for bait, which would supplement their diet during the long voyage.

After landfall disappeared from sight, the sailing came surprisingly easy for the inexperienced crew. Fair skies and calm seas greeted the men each day for a fortnight as they sailed with the wind. Only an occasional squall tested the boat's sturdiness, and it also gave the crew a chance to collect fresh rainwater. All the while, Mahu calmly issued the sailing orders while constantly tracking the sun and stars. Studying the clouds on the horizon several days later, he noticed an unusual clustering to the southwest.

"Land to the south, two days' sailing," he proclaimed.

Relief and excitement flowed through the crew at the prospect of reaching land again. But where were they, and what lands were they approaching?

The next morning, a dot appeared on the horizon, which grew larger with each passing hour. It was not land, however, but another sailing vessel crossing their path. As the ship drew near, Temur could see it sported a low stern and captured the wind with triangular white

sails. She was not a Chinese vessel, he knew, but looked to be an Arab merchant ship. The trader drew alongside the island catamaran and dropped its sails as a thin dark-skinned man in a brightly colored robe shouted a greeting from the rail. Temur studied the man for a moment, then, reading no threat, climbed aboard the small sailing ship.

The trading vessel was from Zanzibar, its captain a jovial Muslim merchantman with considerable experience trading goods with the royal court of the Great Khan. The ship was bound for Shanghai with a cargo of ivory, gold, and spices, to be traded for fine Chinese porcelain and silk. Temur's tiny crew was welcomed aboard and sadly watched as their sturdy double-hulled canoe was cut loose, left to drift the Pacific alone.

The Muslim captain shrewdly guessed that saving the life of a Mongol commander would result in a more favored trading status and he wasn't disappointed. Landing at the port city of Shanghai, the vessel ignited an immediate uproar. News of the soldiers' appearance thirteen years after the aborted invasion of Japan spread across the city like wildfire. Representatives from the government met Temur and his men and whisked them up to the Imperial City at Ta-tu for a briefing with the emperor. Along the way, Temur quizzed his escorts about news of war and politics during his absence.

Much of the news was dispiriting. The invasion of Japan had been an unmitigated disaster, he learned, the typhoon having wiped out over two thousand ships and nearly one hundred thousand men. Temur was saddened to learn that his commander and many of his comrades had not returned with the remnants of the surviving fleet. Equally disturbing was the revelation that the islands of Japan still lay unconquered. Though Kublai Khan wished to attempt a third invasion, his advisers had wisely quelled the notion.

In a little over a decade, the dominance of the entire empire had been shattered. After defeat in Japan, an expedition to suppress unrest in Vietnam had also met with failure, while the expense of expanding the Grand Canal to Chung-tu had nearly caused the economy to collapse. Questions about the emperor's health created apprehension about his successor. A simmering resentment already resided in the people over the fact that a Mongol ruled the Yuan Empire. There seemed to be little dispute. Since defeating the Song Dynasty in 1279 and uniting China under a single rule, Kublai Khan's empire was now withering in a slow decline.

Arriving in the capital city of Ta-tu, Temur and his men were led to the Imperial City and escorted into the private chambers of the emperor. Though Temur had seen Kublai Khan many times in earlier years, he was shocked at the sight of the man before him now. Stretched out on a padded chaise lounge and clad in yards of silk robing was a fat haggard man who stared through sullen black eyes. Despondent over the recent death of his favorite wife and the loss of his second son, Kublai had turned to food and drink for solace, consuming both in excess. Though he'd reached the startling age of eighty, the dietary excesses were now wreaking havoc on the revered leader's health. Temur noted that the overweight Khan rested a gout-inflamed foot on a pillow, while jugs of fermented mare's milk stood at arm's length.

"Commander Temur, you have returned from a considerable absence to resume your duty," the Khan stated in a raspy voice.

"As the emperor commands," Temur replied, bowing deeply.

"Tell of your voyages, Temur, and the mysterious land on which you were shipwrecked."

Carved chairs were brought for Temur and his men to sit, as the Mongol commander described the fierce typhoon that blew his ship away from the Japanese mainland and their subsequent plight adrift at sea. As cups of the alcoholic liquid were passed around, he described their luck at landing on the lush island and being welcomed by the local inhabitants. Introducing Mahu, he told of the old man's aid in sailing the large double-hulled vessel across the sea before they met up with the Muslim merchant.

"A remarkable journey," Kublai lauded. "The lands you fell upon, they were rich and fertile?"

"Exceedingly. The soil is bountiful, and, with a temperate climate subject to much rainfall, an abundance of wild and cultivated plants flourish there."

"Congratulations, my emperor," said a wrinkled man with a long white beard standing at the Khan's side. The Confucian adviser to the throne was clearly unimpressed with the tale or the audience before him. "You have once again added new lands to the empire."

"It is true you have left a garrison behind?" Kublai asked. "The lands are now under Mongol rule?"

Temur silently cursed the Confucian adviser's ploy to fabricate glory for the emperor. He knew that the men he left behind had long ago ground their swords for domestic life. Their loyalty to the khan had been a question well before they even shipwrecked.

"Yes," Temur lied. "A small contingent rules the land in your name." He looked at the old village chief Mahu with shame, but the old man simply nodded back, understanding the politics of the empire.

Kublai gazed past the men across the room, his eyes seeing an image far beyond the walls of the palace. Temur wondered if the Mongol ruler was intoxicated from the drink.

"I should like to see this wondrous place, this land where the sun first shines on my empire," Kublai finally whispered dreamily.

"Yes, it is a near paradise on earth. As beautiful as any lands under the reign."

"You know the route back, Temur?"

"I do not know the ways of navigation at sea, but Mahu can read the sun and the stars. He could find the way back to his home in a stout ship, I believe."

"You have served the empire well, Temur. Your loyalty to the empire shall be well rewarded," Kublai gasped, coughing up a mouthful of liquid that sprayed over his silk tunic.

"Thank you, my emperor," he replied, bowing again. A pair of palace guards suddenly materialized and escorted Temur and his men out of the Khan's chamber.

The Mongol commander felt remorse as he left the palace. The great Kublai Khan was but a tired and ancient shell of the old leader who ruled one of the largest empires in world history. Much more than a bloodthirsty conqueror like his grandfather, Kublai had ruled with an enlightenment not seen before. He welcomed traders and explorers from distant lands, imposed laws that fostered religious tolerance, and promoted scientific research into geography, astronomy, and medicine. He was now near death, and the empire couldn't help but become a less inspired land without his visionary leadership.

As Temur exited the grand palace grounds, he suddenly noticed than Mahu was not by his side. Oddly, he realized that the old villager had remained behind in the emperor's chamber. Temur waited for him to emerge, but after several hours gave up and proceeded out of the capital city to his home village and family. He never again saw the old man who had led him home and often wondered of the fate of his foreign friend.

JUST TWO months later, the somber news was announced of the death of the great emperor. Kublai Khan had finally succumbed to the ravages of age and alcoholism. An elaborate farewell ceremony to honor the emperor's life was held in Ta-tu, the city he had selected to be his primary capital. An altar would later be constructed in his honor south of the city, now known as Beijing, which still stands today. After the public services, a funeral caravan left the city toting the coffin of the Great Khan in an ornate carriage. Followed by a thousand horses and soldiers, the solemn procession marched slowly north into Mongolia and the homeland of Kublai. At a secret spot in the Khentii Mountains, the tomb of Kublai Khan was laid to rest with a cortege of animals, concubines, and valued riches from the across the empire. To ensure a peaceful afterlife, the burial region was trampled with horses to disguise the site. Construction laborers tasked with digging the tomb were executed outright and the procession commanders sworn to secrecy under penalty of death. In a few short years, the burial site of the Mongol leader was lost to history, and the memory of Kublai Khan cast to the winds that whip tirelessly down the slopes of the green-forested mountain range.

A THOUSAND miles to the south, a large Chinese junk slipped out of its dock at Shanghai before dawn and silently drifted down the Yellow River toward the Pacific Ocean. One of just a handful of oceangoing trade ships in the emperor's fleet, the massive junk stood over two hundred feet long, carrying a dozen sails on four tall masts. With the Yuan Empire still in mourning, the vessel didn't fly its usual state banners, and, in fact, carried no identifying flags at all.

Few people on shore wondered much about the early

departure of the large ship, which normally set sail with great fanfare. Only a handful of onlookers noted that the vessel was manned with half its normal crew. And fewer still noticed the odd sight at the ship's helm. An old dark-skinned man with flowing white hair stood next to the captain pointing to the clouds and rising sun. In a strange tongue, he directed the path of the majestic vessel as it departed civilization and entered the waters of the vast blue ocean for a distant and uncharted destination.

TRACE
OF A
DYNASTY

AUGUST 4, 1937
SHANG-TU, CHINA

THE MUFFLED BOOMS IN THE distance echoed with the pall of a tribal war drum. First a subtle pop would waft through the air, followed by an inevitable jarring thud a few seconds later. The lazy pause between each beat led to a false hope that the acoustic barrage had finally come to an end. Then another quiet pop would ring through the air, unnerving all within earshot as they waited for the impact to follow.

Leigh Hunt stood up from a freshly dug earthen trench and stretched his arms skyward before carefully setting a hand trowel atop a nearby mud-brick wall. The Oxford-educated field archaeologist for the British Museum was dressed for the part, clad in long khaki pants and matching dual-pocket shirt, both of which were coated in a fine layer of dust and sweat. Instead of the classic pith helmet, he wore a battered fedora to shield his head from the rays of the summer sun. Through tired hazel eyes, he peered east down a wide valley toward the source of the thundering noise. For the first time, small puffs of smoke could be seen on the horizon through the shimmering heat of the morning sun.

"Tsendyn, it would appear that the artillery is moving closer," he spoke nonchalantly in the direction of the trench.

A short man wearing a thin woolen shirt with a red sash tied around his waist climbed quietly out of the pit. Beyond him in the trench, a crew of Chinese laborers continued digging through the dry soil with heavy spades and hand trowels. Unlike the Chinese workers, the small but broad-shouldered man had slightly rounded eyes, which were imbedded in a face of dark leathery skin. They were features that the local Chinese knew at a glance belonged to a Mongolian.

"Peking is falling. Already the refugees are fleeing," he said, pointing toward a small dirt road a mile away. Rolling through the dust, a half dozen ox-drawn carts toted the life possessions of several Chinese families escaping to the west. "We must abandon the excavation, sir, before the Japanese are upon us."

Hunt instinctively felt for the .455 caliber Webley Fosbery automatic revolver holstered at his hip. Two nights before, he had shot at a small gang of marauding bandits that attempted to steal a crate of excavated artifacts. In the environment of China's collapsing infrastructure, bands of thieves seemed to roam everywhere, but most were unarmed and unsophisticated. Fighting his way past the Japanese Imperial Army would be an entirely different matter.

China was rapidly imploding under the juggernaut of the Japanese military might. Ever since the renegade Japanese Kwantung Army had seized Manchuria in 1931, Japan's military leaders had set their sights on colonizing China in the manner of Korea. Six years of thrusts and parries and staged incidents finally erupted in the summer of 1937 when the Japanese Imperial Army invaded northern China, in fear that the Nationalist forces of Chiang Kai-shek were growing too strong.

Though the Chinese forces vastly outnumbered the Japanese Army, they were no match for the superior equipment, training, and discipline that the Japanese forces brought to the field. Utilizing his resources as best he could, Chiang Kai-shek battled the Japanese by day, then retreated at night, in an attempt to slow the Japanese advance in a war of attrition.

Hunt listened to the crack of the approaching Japanese artillery that now signaled the loss of Peking and he knew that the Chinese were in trouble. The capital city of Nanking would be next, resulting in yet a further pullback to the west of Chiang Kai-shek's army. With an impending sense of his own defeat, he glanced at his wristwatch then spoke to Tsendyn.

"Have the coolies cease all excavations at noon. We'll secure the artifacts and complete final documentation of the site this afternoon, then join in the growing caravan heading west." Glancing at the road, he noted a ragtag band of Chinese Nationalist soldiers filtering into the evacuation route.

"You will be leaving on the aircraft to Nanking tomorrow?" Tsendyn asked.

"Assuming the plane shows up. But there's no sense in flying to Nanking under these hostile conditions. I intend to take the most important artifacts and fly north to Ulaanbaatar. You'll have to manage the remaining items, equipment, and supplies with the packtrain, I'm afraid. You should be able to catch up with me in Ulaanbaatar in a few weeks. I'll wait for you there before catching the Trans-Siberian railway west."

"A wise move. It is evident that the local resistance is failing."

"Inner Mongolia offers little strategic value to the Japanese. They are likely just chasing the remnants of the defensive forces out of Peking," he said, waving an arm toward the distant artillery barrage. "I suspect they will pull back shortly and enjoy a few days or even weeks pillaging Peking before renewing the offensive. Plenty of time for us to be on our way."

"It is unfortunate that we must leave now. We are nearly finished with the excavation of the Pavilion of Great Harmony," Tsendyn said, surveying a maze of excavated trenches that stretched around them like a World War I battlefield.

"It's a bloody shame," Hunt said, shaking his head in anger, "though we've proven that the site has already been well-ransacked."

Hunt kicked at some excavated fragments of marble and stone piled near his feet and watched as the dust settled over the remnants that had once constituted an imposing imperial structure. While most of his archaeological contemporaries in China were chasing prehistoric burial tombs loaded with bronze artifacts, Hunt's focus was on the more recent Yuan Dynasty. This was his third summer on the grounds of Shang-tu, excavating the remains of the royal summer palace built in 1260. Staring at a barren hillside dotted with mounds of fresh dirt, it was difficult to imagine the former grandeur of the palace and grounds that would have stood before him nearly eight hundred years earlier.

Though surviving Chinese historical records provide scant detail, Marco Polo, the Venetian adventurer who vividly documented thirteenth-century China and the Silk Road in his book *The Travels*, provided a striking description of Shang-tu at its zenith. Built on a huge mound at the center of a walled city, the original palace was surrounded by a forest of transplanted trees and lapis lazuli stone paths, which lent a magical blue hue to the estate. Exquisite gardens and fountains weaved

45

through a series of government buildings and residences that encircled the Ta-an Ko, or "Pavilion of Great Harmony," which stood as the imperial palace. Constructed of green marble and stone and gilded with gold, the great structure was inlaid with glazed tiles and decorated with breathtaking paintings and sculptures from China's most skilled artisans. Used primarily as a summer residence by the emperor to escape the heat of Peking, Shang-tu quickly developed into a scientific and cultural hub. A medical center and astronomical observatory were constructed, and the city became a haven for scholars both foreign and domestic. A constant breeze across the hilltop cooled the emperor and his guests, as he administered over an empire that stretched from the Mediterranean to Korea.

But it was the emperor's adjacent hunting ground that perhaps gave the summer palace its most renown. It was a vast enclosed park of trees, streams, and thick grass, encompassing sixteen square miles. The park was stocked with deer, boar, and other game for the hunting pleasure of the emperor and his guests. Elevated paths circled through the preserve, to keep the hunters' feet dry. Surviving tapestries show the emperor hunting in the park on a favorite horse, with a trained hunting cheetah at his side.

Centuries of abandonment, neglect, and looting had reduced the palace to little more than scattered rubble. It was nearly impossible for Hunt to picture the lush grounds of gardens, fountains, springs, and trees as they existed centuries ago. The landscape was now barren. A wide, grassy plain stretched empty to the distant brown hills. The area was void of life, the city's past glory just a whisper on the wind that ruffled through the tall grass. Xanadu, the romantic name of Shang-tu popularized by the Samuel Taylor Coleridge poem, existed now only in the imagination.

With approval from the Nationalist government, Hunt had begun excavations three years before. Trowel by trowel, he had been able to piece together the boundaries of the Palace of Great Harmony, identifying a grand hall, a kitchen, and a dining hall. An assortment of bronze and porcelain artifacts recovered from the earth told the tale of daily life at the palace. But, to Hunt's disappointment, there were no dazzling artifacts uncovered, no terra-cotta armies or Ming vases that would make a name for himself. The dig was nearly completed, just the remains of the royal bedroom chamber remained to be excavated. Already, most of his colleagues had fled the eastern regions of China, not wanting to get caught up in a civil war or foreign invasion. Hunt seemed to perversely enjoy the turmoil and pending danger from the site in Northwest China, not far from Manchuria. With a love of antiquity and drama, he knew that he was standing thick in the middle of history in the making.

Hunt also knew that the British Museum would be pleased with whatever artifacts he would provide them for their planned exhibit of Xanadu. The chaos and danger created by the Japanese invasion was actually a benefit. Not only did it add to the allure of the artifacts that he transported west, it actually made the process easier. Local authorities had already fled the nearby villages, and the government antiquities officials had not been seen in weeks. He would have an easy time removing the artifacts from the country. That is, assuming he could extricate himself as well.

"I guess I've kept you from your family long enough, Tsendyn. I doubt the Russians will allow the Japanese to pussyfoot around in Mongolia, so you should be safe from this craziness."

"My wife shall welcome my return." The Mongol smiled through a yellowing set of sharply pointed teeth.

The faint drone of a nearby aircraft halted their conversation. To the south of them, a small gray speck grew larger in the sky before banking to the east.

"Japanese reconnaissance aircraft," Hunt mused. "Not a good sign for the Nationalist chaps if the Japanese own the skies." The archaeologist pulled out a pack of Red Lion cigarettes and lit one of the unfiltered smokes as Tsendyn peered at the fading aircraft with a nervous look.

"The sooner we are away, the better, I think," he said.

Behind them, a sudden commotion erupted from one of the excavation trenches. One of the Chinese laborer's heads popped up over the edge, his grimy jaws jabbering at a rapid clip.

"What is it?" Hunt said, setting down his tea.

"He says he's found some lacquered wood," Tsendyn replied, stepping toward the trench.

48

Both men walked to the edge and peered down. The chattering laborer excitedly pointed his trowel toward the ground as the other laborers crowded around. Barely exposed through the dirt at his feet was a flat square yellow object the size of a serving platter.

"Tsendyn, you handle the excavation," Hunt barked, waving away the other laborers. As the Mongolian jumped into the trench and carefully began scraping the dirt away with a trowel and brush, Hunt retrieved a notebook and pencil. Thumbing to a hand-drafted sketch of the localized area and trench, he neatly outlined the object in its discovered location. Flipping to a blank sheet, he then began sketching the artifact while Tsendyn gently dug around it.

As the dirt and dust fell away, Hunt could see that the object was in fact a yellow lacquered wooden box. Every square inch was painted with delicate images of animals and trees in elaborate detail, trimmed with inlaid mother-of-pearl. Hunt noted with curiosity that an elephant was depicted on the lid. Carefully scraping the dirt away to its base, Tsendyn gently lifted the box out of the sediment and placed it on a flat stone outside the trench.

The Chinese laborers all stopped their digging and crowded around the ornate box. Most of their discoveries to date consisted of little more than broken shards of porcelain and the occasional jade carving. This was easily the most impressive item uncovered in their three years of digging.

Hunt studied the box deliberately before taking it in

his hands and lifting it. Something heavy was inside, which shifted as he moved the box. With his thumbs, he could feel a seam midway around the shallow sides and gently tried to separate the lid. The box, sealed for nearly eight hundred years, protested at first and then slowly opened. Hunt set the box down and gingerly worked his fingers around the entire edge, then pulled on the lid until it creaked off. Tsendyn and the laborers all leaned in as if in a football huddle, peering to see what was inside.

Two objects were nestled in the box and Hunt removed them for all to see. A spotted animal skin, colored black and yellow in the camouflage pattern of a leopard or cheetah, was rolled up like a scroll, the ends tied together with leather straps. The other item was a patinated bronze tube, sealed at one end, but with a removable cap at the other end. The Chinese workers all grinned and chuckled at the sight of the objects, not knowing what significance they held, but assuming correctly that they had some importance.

Hunt set down the cheetah skin and examined the heavy bronze tube. It had aged a deep green color, which only enhanced the elaborate image of a dragon that stretched along its length, the tail of the imaginary beast curled around the capped end of the tube like a coil of rope.

"Go ahead, open it up," Tsendyn urged with excited impatience.

Hunt easily pried off the end cap, then held the tube up to his eye, peering in. He then turned the open end toward the ground and carefully shook the tube, catching with his open left palm the contents as it slid out.

It was a rolled-up bolt of silk, dyed a pale blue. Tsendyn shook clean a nearby blanket and spread it across the ground at Hunt's feet. The archaeologist waited for the dust to clear, then knelt down over the blanket and carefully unfurled the silk roll to its full length of nearly five feet. Tsendyn noticed the normally unflappable archaeologist's hands trembled slightly as he smoothed out the creases in the silk.

A picturesque landscape scene was painted on the silk, portraying a mountaintop with deep valleys, gorges, and streams depicted in beautiful detail. But the silk was obviously much more than an ornamental work of art. Along the left border was a sizeable section of text that Hunt recognized as Uighur script, the earliest Mongolian written language adopted from early Turkish settlers to the Asian Steppes. On the right margin was a sequence of smaller images, depicting a harem of women, herds of horses, camels, and other animals, and a contingent of armed soldiers surrounding several wooden chests. The landscape portion of the painting was bare of life except for a lone figure at the very center of the silk roll. Standing on a small mountain rise was a Bactrian camel draped with a saddlecloth inscribed with two words. Oddly, the camel was painted weeping, shedding oversized tears that fell to the ground.

As he studied the silk painting, a band of sweat

formed across Hunt's forehead. He suddenly felt his heart thumping loudly in his chest and he had to force himself to take a deep breath of air. It just couldn't be, he thought.

"Tsendyn . . . Tsendyn," he muttered, nearly afraid to ask. "It is Uighur script. Can you read what it says?"

The Mongol assistant's eyes grew to the size of silver dollars as he, too, grasped the meaning of the image. He stuttered and stumbled as he tried to translate for Hunt.

"The wording on the left is a physical description of the mountainous region in the painting. 'At home atop Mount Burkhan Khaldun, nestled in the Khentii Mountains, our emperor sleeps. The Onon River quenches his thirst, between the valleys of the doomed.'"

"And the inscription on the camel?" Hunt whispered, pointing a shaky finger at the center of the painting.

"Temujin khagan," Tsendyn replied, choking the words out in a hushed tone of reverence.

"Temujin." Hunt repeated the word as if in a trance. Though the Chinese laborers failed to comprehend, Hunt and Tsendyn realized with shock that they had made a discovery of astounding proportions. A wave of emotion surged over Hunt as he digested the enormity of the silk painting. Though he tried to mentally question its content, the power of the description was just too overwhelming. The weeping camel, the offerings depicted on the side, the locale description. Then there was the name on the camel's back. Temujin. It was the birth name of a tribal boy who became the world's greatest conqueror. History would remember him by his royally appointed moniker: Genghis Khan. The ancient silk painting before them could be nothing other than a diagram of the hidden burial site of Genghis Khan.

Hunt collapsed to his knees as the realization of the find sunk in. The grave of Genghis Khan was one of the most sought-after archaeological sites in history. In an amazing tale of conquest, Genghis Khan had united the Mongol tribes of the Asian Steppes and expanded on a march of conquest the likes of which have never been matched since. Between 1206 and 1223 A.D., he and his nomadic horde captured lands as far west as Egypt and as far north as Lithuania. Genghis died in 1227 A.D. at the height of his power, and was known to have been secretly buried in the Khentii Mountains of Mongolia, not far from his birthplace. In the Mongol tradition, he was buried secretly with forty concubines and untold riches, the grave site carefully concealed by his subjects after interment. Ordinary foot soldiers who accompanied the cortege were put to death, while their commanders were sworn to silence upon threat of similar punishment.

Any hint as to the location of the grave site vanished as those in the know expired, keeping their loyal vow of silence to the very end. Only a camel, or so the legend went, tipped off the location a decade or so later. A Bactrian pack camel, known to be the mother of a camel interred with the great leader, was found weeping at a spot in the Khentii Mountains. The camel's owner realized it was crying for its lost son buried beneath its feet, in the same location where Genghis Khan must be entombed. Yet the fable ended there, the secret kept with the herder, and the grave of Genghis Khan left undisturbed in the Mongolian mountains of his birth.

Now the legend was whisked to life in the silk painting before Hunt's eyes.

"This is a most sacred find," Tsendyn whispered. "It will lead us to the tomb of the Great Khan." Tsendyn spoke with a reverence that bordered on fright.

"Yes," Hunt gasped, imagining the fame that would sweep his way if he led the discovery of Genghis Khan's grave.

Suddenly fearful of exposing the significance of the silk to the Chinese laborers, one of whom might have an eager bandit in the family, Hunt hastily rerolled the fabric into the tube and replaced it in the lacquered box with the cheetah skin. He then wrapped the box in a cloth and secured it in a large leather satchel, which stayed clasped in his left hand for the rest of the day.

After riddling the earth where the box was recovered and finding no other artifacts, Hunt reluctantly ordered a halt to the dig. The laborers quietly stowed their picks, shovels, and brushes into a wooden cart, then stood in line for their meager salary. Though paid just pennies a day, several of the men had actually fought over the physically demanding jobs, which were a rare commodity in the poverty-stricken Chinese provinces.

With the equipment and artifacts secured in a trio of wooden carts and the Chinese laborers dismissed, Hunt retired to his canvas tent after dinner with Tsendyn and packed up his belongings. For the first time, an uneasiness fell over him as he documented the day's events in his personal journal. With the last minute discovery of the valued artifact, he suddenly became more cognizant of the dangers around him. Looters and bandits had wantonly robbed other excavations in Shaanxi Province, and a fellow archaeologist had been beaten and pistol-whipped by marauders seeking three-thousand-year-old bronze artifacts. Then there was the Japanese Army. Though they might not harm a British citizen, they could very well appropriate his work and artifacts. And who knows? Would the discovery of Genghis Khan's grave prove to be a curse for him, as many claimed it was for Lord Carnarvon and the crew that discovered the grave of King Tut?

With the satchel containing the wooden box safe under his cot, he slept fitfully, the myriad of thoughts banging around his head like a blacksmith's hammer. The night was made more ominous by the howl of a shrieking wind that rocked the tent till dawn. Rising groggily at daybreak, he was relieved to find the satchel safe and sound under his cot, while, outside, there were no Japanese militants to be seen. Tsendyn was standing nearby, cooking some goat meat over an open fire with a pair of Chinese orphan boys who assisted the Mongol.

"Good morning, sir. Hot tea is at the ready." Tsendyn

smiled, handing Hunt a cup of steaming brew. "All of the equipment is packed, and the mules are hitched to the carts. We can depart at your desire."

"Jolly good. Stow my tent, if you would, and take a good mind of that satchel under the cot," he said, taking a seat on a wooden crate and watching the sunrise as he enjoyed his tea.

The first distant artillery shell sounded an hour later as the remaining excavation party rolled away from the Shang-tu site aboard three mule-drawn wagons. Across the windswept plains stood the tiny village of Lanqui, just over a mile away. The caravan continued past the dusty town, joining a small trail of refugees headed west. Near noon, the mules clopped into the aged town of Duolun, where they stopped at a roadside hovel for lunch. Downing a tasteless bowl of noodles and broth that was sprinkled with dead bugs, they made their way to a large flat meadow at the edge of town. Sitting atop one of the wagons, Hunt peered overhead into a partly cloudy sky. Almost like clockwork, a faint buzz broke the air, and the archaeologist watched as a tiny silver speck grew larger against the clouds as it approached the makeshift airfield. As the airplane neared, Hunt pulled a handkerchief from his pocket and tied it to a stick, thrusting it into the ground as a primitive wind sock for the pilot to gauge the breeze.

With a gentle touch, the pilot circled the metal-sided aircraft in a wide, low turn, then set the noisy plane down onto the turf in a quick motion. Hunt was relieved to see the plane was a Fokker F. VIIb trimotor, a safe and able aircraft aptly suited to flying over remote stretches of barren landscape. He noted with curiosity that the name *Blessed Betty* was painted beneath the pilot's cockpit window.

The motors barely gurgled to a stop when the fuselage door burst open and out jumped two men in worn leather jackets.

"Hunt? I'm Randy Schodt," greeted the pilot, a tall man with a rugged yet friendly face who spoke with an American accent. "My brother Dave and I are here to fly you to Nanking, or so the contract says," he added, patting a folded paper in his jacket pocket.

"What's a pair of Yanks doing way out here?" Hunt mused.

"Beats working in the shipyard back home in Erie, Pennsylvania," grinned Dave Schodt, an affable man like his brother who was quick with a joke.

"Been flying for the Chinese Ministry of Railroads, supporting rail extensions on the Peking–Shanghai line. Though work has come to a sudden halt with this unpleasantness by these Japanese folks," Randy Schodt explained with a smirk.

"I have a slight change in destination," Hunt said, sidestepping the banter. "I need you to fly me to Ulaanbaatar."

"Mongolia?" Schodt asked, scratching his head. "Well, as long as we're headed away from the neighborhood of the Nippon Army, I guess it's okay with me."

"I'll plot it out, see if we have the range to get there," Dave said, walking back to the plane. "Hopefully, they'll have a gas station when we arrive," he laughed.

With Schodt's help, Hunt supervised the loading of the more important artifacts and tools into the fuselage of the Fokker. When the wooden crates had nearly filled the interior, Hunt took the satchel with the lacquered box and carefully placed it on the front passenger's seat.

"That will be a hundred fifty miles less than the flight to Nanking. But we'll need return mileage, which exceeds what your British Museum people contracted me to fly," Schodt explained, spreading a map of the region across a stack of crates. Ulaanbaatar, the capital of Mongolia, was marked with a star in the north-central region of the country, over four hundred miles from the Chinese border.

"You have my authorization," Hunt replied, handing the pilot a handwritten request for the change in route. "I assure you, the museum will honor the additional expense."

"Sure they will, they don't want your artifacts to end up in the Tokyo Museum," Schodt laughed. Sticking the note in his pocket, he added, "Dave has the route to Ulaanbaatar laid in and promises we can make it in one hop. Since we'll be flying over the Gobi Desert, you're lucky the *Blessed Betty* has extra fuel tanks. Whenever you're ready."

Hunt walked over and surveyed the two remaining mule carts still packed with equipment and artifacts.

Tsendyn stood holding the reins of the lead mule, stroking the animal's ears.

"Tsendyn, we have had a difficult but fruitful summer. You have been invaluable in the success of the expedition."

"It has been my honor. You have done a great service to my country and heritage. My heirs shall be particularly grateful."

"Take the remaining equipment and artifacts to Shijiazhuang, where you can catch the rail to Nanking. A representative from the British Museum will meet and arrange shipment of the items to London. I will wait for you in Ulaanbaatar, where we will investigate our latest find."

"I look forward to the next search with great anticipation," Tsendyn replied, shaking the archaeologist's hand.

"Farewell, my friend."

Hunt climbed aboard the loaded Fokker as the plane's three 220-horsepower Wright Whirlwind radial engines roared to life. Tsendyn stood and watched as Schodt turned the plane into the wind, then shoved the throttles to their stops. With a deafening roar, the aircraft jostled across the meadow, bouncing up and down several times before slowly lumbering into the air. Turning in a graceful arc low above the field, Schodt swung the big plane northwest toward the Mongolian border as it gradually gained altitude.

Tsendyn stood in the meadow and watched as the

plane grew smaller on the horizon and the throbbing of the motors dissolved from his ears. Not until the aircraft had completely vanished from sight did he reach into the vest pocket of his coat for a reassuring touch. The bolt of silk was still there, as it had been since the early hours of the night before.

IT WAS two hours into the flight when Hunt reached for the satchel and pulled out the lacquered box. The boredom of the flight mixed with the excitement of the find was too much to bear and he was drawn to run the silk painting through his fingers one more time. With the box in his hands, he felt the familiar weight of the bronze tube rolling around inside in a reassuring manner. Yet something didn't feel right. Prying off the lid, he found the cheetah skin tightly rolled up and stuffed to one side, as it had been before. The bronze tube sat next to it, appearing secure. But picking the tube up, he noticed it felt heavier than he remembered. With a shaking hand, he quickly pulled off the cap, releasing an outpouring of sand that dribbled onto his lap. As the last grain tumbled out, he peered in and saw that the silk scroll had vanished.

His eyes bulged at the sudden realization that he'd been duped and he struggled to catch his breath. The shock quickly turned to anger and regaining his voice, he began screaming at the pilots.

"Turn back! Turn the airplane around! We must return at once," he cried.

But his plea fell on deaf ears. In the cockpit, the two

pilots suddenly had something more troubling of their own to contend with.

THE MITSUBISHI G3M bomber, known in the west as a Nell, was not on a bombing mission at all. Flying casually alone at an altitude of nine thousand feet, the twin-engine aircraft was flying reconnaissance, probing the aerial resources of Russia that were rumored to have surfaced in Mongolia.

With its easy conquest of Manchuria and successful advance into northern China, the Japanese had sharpened their sights on the important seaports and coal mines of Siberia to the north. Leery of the Japanese intent, the Russians had already bolstered their defensive forces in Siberia, and recently signed a defense pact with Mongolia that allowed for the deployment of troops and aircraft in that mostly barren country. Already the Japanese were busy gathering intelligence, testing and probing the defensive lines in preparation for an outright northern offensive that would be launched from Manchuria in mid-1939.

The Nell had come up empty on its foray into eastern Mongolia, finding no sign of troop deployments or runway construction on behalf of Russian aircraft. If there was any Russian military activity in Mongolia, it would be much farther north, the Japanese pilot concluded. Below him was nothing but the occasional nomadic tribe, wandering the empty expanse of the Gobi Desert with their herd of camels.

"Nothing but sand out here," the Nell's copilot, a

youthful lieutenant named Miyabe, said with a yawn. "I don't know why the wing commander is excited over this real estate."

"As a buffer to the more valuable territory to the north, I suspect," Captain Nobuji Negishi replied. "I just hope we get repositioned to the front when the northern invasion occurs. We're missing all the fun in Shanghai and Peking."

As Miyabe stared at the flat ground beneath the plane, a bright glint of sunlight briefly flashed out of the corner of his eye. Scanning across the horizon, he tracked the source of the light, squinting at what he saw.

"Sir, an aircraft ahead and slightly below us," he said, pointing a gloved hand toward the object.

Negishi peered ahead and quickly spotted the plane. It was the silver Fokker trimotor, flying northwest toward Ulaanbaatar.

"She's crossing our path," the Japanese pilot noted with a rise in his voice. "At last, a chance for battle."

"But sir, that's not a combat plane. I don't think it is even a Chinese airplane," Miyabe said, observing the markings on the Fokker. "Our orders are to engage only Chinese military aircraft."

"The flight poses a risk," Negishi explained away. "Besides, it will be good target practice, Lieutenant." No one in the Japanese military was getting reprimanded for aggressive behavior in the Chinese theater, he well knew. As a bomber pilot, he would be afforded few opportunities to engage and destroy other aircraft in the skies. It was a rare chance for an easy kill and he wasn't about to pass it by.

"Gunners at your stations," he barked over the intercom. "Prepare for air-to-air action."

The five-man crew of the attack bomber were immediately energized as they manned their battle positions. Rather than play the quarry of smaller and quicker fighter aircraft, as was their lot in life, the bomber crew suddenly became the hunter. Captain Negishi mentally computed a dead-reckoning line of the trimotor's path, then eased back on the throttles and banked the bomber in a wide slow turn to the right. The Fokker slipped by beneath them until Negishi eased out of the turn, which brought the bomber around and behind the silver trimotor.

Negishi eased the throttles forward again as the Fokker loomed ahead. With a top speed of two hundred sixteen miles per hour, the Mitsubishi was nearly twice as fast as the Fokker and easily closed the gap.

"Ready with the forward guns," Negishi ordered as the unarmed plane grew larger in the gunsights.

But the trimotor was not going to pose like a sitting duck. Randy Schodt had seen the bomber first and tracked it as it curled around onto his tail. His hopes that the Japanese plane was just making a harmless flyby vanished when the Mitsubishi took up position squarely behind him and hung on his tail, rather than fly alongside. Unable to outrun the faster military aircraft, he did the next best thing.

The Japanese plane's turret gunner just squeezed the

first round from his 7.7mm machine gun when the tri-motor banked sharply left and seemed to stall in the air. The gunner's bullets sprayed harmlessly into the sky as the bomber quickly overshot the Fokker.

Negishi was caught completely off guard by the sudden maneuver and cursed as he tried to muscle the bomber back toward the smaller plane. The rattle of machine-gun fire echoed through the fuselage as a side gunner tracked the sudden juke by the Fokker and sprayed a long burst in its direction.

Inside the Fokker, Hunt swore louder at the pilots as crates of artifacts began tumbling around the interior of the plane. A loud crash told him that a crate of porcelain bowls was suddenly smashed by the plane's violent turns. It wasn't until the Fokker banked sharply right and Hunt caught a glimpse out the side window at the Japanese bomber that he realized what was happening.

In the cockpit, Schodt tried every trick in the book to shake the Mitsubishi, hoping that the bomber would abandon the pursuit. But the Japanese pilot was angered by the earlier rebuff and pursued the Fokker relentlessly. Time and again, Schodt would stunt and stall his aircraft to throw the bomber off his tail, causing the Japanese plane to circle around and reacquire the trimotor in its gunsights. The hunter would not give up the chase, and Schodt would soon find the Mitsubishi back on his tail again, until finally one of the gunners found his mark.

The Fokker's rear stabilizer was the first to go,

shredded in a hail of lead. Negishi licked his chops, knowing the plane could no longer turn left or right without the control from the stabilizer. Grinning like a wolf, he brought the bomber in close for the kill. As the gunner fired again, he was shocked to see the Fokker once again juke to the right, then pull up in a stall.

Schodt wasn't through yet. With Dave jockeying the throttles on the two wing-mounted engines, Randy was still able to duck and weave away from the Mitsubishi. Once again, the gunfire burst harmlessly into the fuselage, Hunt grimacing as another crate of artifacts was decimated.

Wise to his opponent's tactics, Negishi finally swung the bomber around in a wide arc and approached the Fokker from the side. This time, there was no escaping the gunfire and the Fokker's right wing engine disintegrated under a fury of bullets. A plume of smoke burst from the engine as Schodt shut down the fuel line before the motor caught fire. Jockeying the remaining two engines, he continued to fight with all his skills to keep the Fokker airborne and out of harm's way, but his hourglass finally ran out. A well-placed shot by the Mitsubishi's topside gunner severed the Fokker's elevator controls and effectively ended the flight of the *Blessed Betty*.

Without the ability to control altitude, the wounded trimotor began a flat descent toward the ground. Schodt watched helplessly as the Fokker plunged toward the dusty ground with its wings ajar. Amazingly, the airplane held its balance, gliding downward, with its nose bent just a fraction forward. Shutting down the remaining engines just before impact, he felt the left wingtip clip the ground first, throwing the plane into a clumsy cartwheel.

The crew of the Japanese plane watched with minor disappointment as the Fokker rolled across the ground, failing to explode or burst into flames. Instead, the silver trimotor simply flipped twice, then slid inverted into a sandy ravine.

Despite the difficulty in downing the civilian plane, a cheer rang out aboard the Mitsubishi.

"Well done, men, but next time we must do better," Negishi lauded, then banked the bomber back toward its base in Manchuria.

On board the Fokker, Schodt and his brother were killed instantly when the cockpit was crushed on the first roll of the aircraft. Hunt survived the crash, but his back was broken and his left leg nearly severed. He painfully clung to life for nearly two days before perishing in the jumbled wreckage of the fuselage. With his last gasp of energy, he pulled the lacquered box close to his chest and cursed his sudden turn of luck. As his last breath left him, he had no idea that still clutched within his arms, he held the clue to the most magnificent treasure the world would ever see.

PART I

Seiche

~ 1 ~

T HE STILL WATERS OF THE world's deepest lake radiate the deep translucent blue of a polished sapphire. Fed by cold ancient streams that are free of silt and sediments, Lake Baikal possesses remarkably crystalline clear waters. A tiny crustacean, *Baikal epishura,* aids the cause by devouring algae and plankton growths that degrade most freshwater lakes. The combination produces such a stunning clarity to the water that on a calm day, a silver coin can be seen from the surface at a one-hundred-foot depth.

Surrounded by craggy snowcapped peaks to the north and dense taiga forests of birch, larch, and pine to the south, the "Blue Pearl of Siberia" stretches as a beacon of beauty across an otherwise hostile landscape. Situated in the dead center of lower Siberia, the four-hundred-mile-long crescent-shaped lake curves south to north just above the border with Mongolia. A massive body of water, Lake Baikal is nearly a mile deep in some spots and holds one-fifth of all the fresh water on the planet, more than all of North America's Great Lakes combined. Just a few small fishing villages dot the lake's shore, leaving the enormous lake a nearly vacant sea of tranquillity. Only at its southern end does the lake sprawl toward any significant population centers. Irkutsk, a modestly hip city to a half million Siberian residents, sits forty-five miles west, while the ancient city of Ulan-Ude lies a short distance from its eastern shoreline.

Theresa Hollema glanced up from a laptop computer and briefly admired the purple mountains at the edge of the lake, crowned by cotton-ball clouds that grazed their peaks. The Dutch geophysicist delighted in the clear blue skies that so seldom graced her home outside of Amsterdam. Drawing a deep breath of the crisp air, she subconsciously tried to absorb the scenery through all her senses.

"It is an agreeable day on the lake, no?" asked Tatiana Borjin. She spoke with a deep voice in the emotionless manner endemic to Russians speaking English. Yet the gruff tone and a businesslike personality didn't match her appearance. Although she resembled the local ethnic Buryats, she was, in fact, Mongolian. With long black hair, bronze skin, and almond-shaped eyes, she possessed a natural and robust beauty. But there was a deep intensity behind her dark eyes that seemed to take everything in life with harsh seriousness.

"I had no idea that Siberia was so beautiful," Theresa replied. "The lake is breathtaking. So calm and peaceful."

"She is a calm jewel at the moment but can turn wicked in an instant. The Sarma, sudden winds from the northwest, can burst onto the lake with the force of a hurricane. The local graveyards are filled with fishermen who failed to respect the forces of Baikal."

A slight chill ran up Theresa's spine. The locals seemed to constantly speak of the spirit of the lake. Baikal's pristine waters were a proud cultural resource to the Siberians, and protecting the lake from industrial pollutants had fostered an environmental movement that had grown globally. Even the Russian government was surprised at the widespread outcry when it had first decided to build a wood-cellulose-processing plant on its southern shores fifty years earlier. Theresa just hoped that a Greenpeace rubber boat armada would not appear to assail their presence on the lake.

At least her involvement was relatively harmless, she convinced herself. Her employer, Royal Dutch Shell, had been contracted to survey a section of the lake for reported oil seeps. Nobody said anything about drilling or exploratory wells, and she was confident that would never happen on the lake anyway. The company was just trying to cozy up to the owners of some exploratory Siberian oil fields in hope of landing more significant business.

Theresa had never heard of the Avarga Oil Consortium before traveling to Siberia but knew there were a variety of oil companies clamoring in the Russian marketplace. A few of the government-sponsored companies, like Yukos and Gazprom, grabbed all the headlines, but, like anywhere in the world, there were always some little wildcatters owning a smaller piece of the pie. From the looks of what she'd seen so far, the Avarga Oil Consortium didn't even have a piece of the crust.

"They're obviously not pumping their revenues into R & D," she joked to the two Shell technicians that accompanied her as they climbed aboard the leased survey boat.

"Clever how they designed her to resemble a decrepit fishing boat," cracked Jim Wofford, a tall, friendly geophysicist from Arkansas who wore a thick mustache and a ready smile.

The high-prowed black fishing boat looked like it should have been scuttled years earlier. The exterior paint was peeling everywhere and the whole vessel reeked of wood rot and dead fish. It had been decades since the brightwork had been polished, and only the occasional rainstorm accounted for any washing of the decks. Theresa noted with unease that the bilge pump ran continuously.

"We do not possess our own sea vessels," Tatiana said without apology. As the representative from Avarga Oil, she had been the sole interface with the Shell survey team.

"That's all right, for what it lacks in space it makes up for in discomfort." Wofford smiled.

"True, but I bet there's some caviar hiding aboard someplace," replied Wofford's partner, Dave Roy, a fellow seismic engineer who spoke in a soft Boston accent. As Roy knew, Lake Baikal was the home to enormous sturgeon that could carry up to twenty pounds of caviar.

Theresa helped lend a hand as Roy and Wofford lugged aboard their seismic monitors, cable, and tow-fish, organizing the equipment on the cramped stern deck of the twenty-eight-foot fishing boat.

"Caviar? With your beer tastes?" Theresa chided.

"As a matter of fact, the two make an excellent combination," Roy replied with mock seriousness. "The sodium content of caviar produces a hydration craving that is perfectly fulfilled by a malt-based beverage."

"In other words, it's a good excuse to drink more beer."

"Who needs an excuse to drink beer?" Wofford asked indignantly.

"I give up." Theresa laughed. "Far be it for me to argue with an alcoholic. Or two."

Tatiana looked on without amusement, then nodded toward the boat's captain when all the equipment had been stowed aboard. A dour-faced man who wore a jacquard tweed hat, the captain's most notable feature was a wide bulbous nose tinted red from a steady consumption of vodka. Ducking into the small wheelhouse, he fired up the boat's smoky diesel engine, then released the dock lines. In calm waters, they chugged away from their berth at the small fishing and tourist village of Listvyanka, located on the lake's southwest shoreline.

Tatiana unrolled a map of the lake and pointed to an area forty miles north of the town.

"We shall survey here, at Peschanaya Bay," she told the geologists. "There have been numerous surface oil slicks reported by the fishermen in this area, which would seem to indicate a hydrocarbon seepage."

"You're not going to take us sniffing around in deep water, are you, Tatiana?" Wofford asked.

"I understand the limitations of the equipment available to us. Though we have a number of potential seeps in the center of the lake, I realize the depths are too great for us to survey in those regions. Our research objective is focused on four locations in the south of Lake Baikal that are all near the shoreline, presumably in shallow water."

"We'll find out easy enough," Roy replied as he plugged a waterproof data cable into a three-foot-long yellow towfish. In addition to providing an acoustically derived image of the lake bed, the side-scan sonar sensor would also indicate the relative bottom depth when towed.

"Are the sites all located on the western shoreline?" Theresa asked.

"Only the target area in Peschanaya Bay. We must cross the lake to the other three sites, which are on the eastern shore."

The old fishing boat motored past the docks of Listvyanka, passing a hydrofoil ferry slicing into port on its return from a transport run to Port Baikal on the opposite shore of the Angara River. The sleek enclosed passenger ferry looked out of place beside the small fleet of aged wooden fishing boats that filled Listvyanka's waters. Escaping the small harbor, the fishing boat turned north, hugging the craggy western shore of the cold lake. Deep, rich forests of taiga marched down to the shoreline in a carpet of green, interspersed with rolling meadows of thick grass. The rich colors of the landscape against the crystal blue lake made it difficult for Theresa to picture the stark bitterness of the region in the dead of winter, when a layer of ice four feet thick covered the lake. A shiver at the thought made her glad she was visiting when the days were longest.

It was of little matter to Theresa, though. The petroleum engineer's true love was traveling and she would have gladly visited the lake in January just for the experience. Bright and analytical, she had chosen her career less for the intellectual challenge than for the opportunity to travel to remote places around the globe. Extended stints in Indonesia, Venezuela, and the Baltic were broken up by the occasional two-week assignment like this one, where she was sent to survey an offbeat prospective oil field. Working in a man's field proved to be no setback, as her vivacious personality and humorous outlook on life easily broke down barriers with men who weren't already attracted to her athletic build, dark hair, and walnut eyes.

Forty miles north of Listvyanka, a shallow bay called

Peschanaya cut into the western shoreline, protecting a narrow sandy beach. As the captain nosed the boat's prow into the bay, Tatiana turned to Theresa and proclaimed, "We will start here."

With the engine thrown into neutral and the boat drifting, Roy and Wofford lowered the side-scan sonar towfish over the stern as Theresa mounted a GPS antenna onto the side rail and plugged it into the sonar's computer. Tatiana glanced at a fathometer mounted in the wheelhouse and shouted, "Depth, thirty meters."

"Not too deep, that's good," Theresa said as the boat moved forward again, towing the sensor a hundred feet behind. A digitally enhanced image of the lake bed scrolled by on a color monitor that captured the processed sound waves emitted from the towfish.

"We can acquire meaningful results as long as the depth stays under fifty meters," Wofford said. "Anything deeper and we'll need more cable and a bigger boat."

"And more caviar," Roy added with a hungry look.

Slowly the fishing boat swept back and forth across the bay, its hardened captain spinning the ship's wheel lightly in his hands as the four visitors on the stern hunched over the sonar monitor. Unusual geological formations were noted and their positions marked, as the experienced oil surveyors looked for lake bed features that might indicate a hydrocarbon seep. Further studies, using core sampling or geochemical analysis of water samples, would still need to be undertaken to verify a seep, but the side-scan sonar would allow the surveyors to zero in on future geological points to examine.

As they reached the northern edge of the bay, Theresa stood and stretched as the captain swung the boat around and aligned it for the last survey lane. Toward the center of the lake, she noticed a large dirty-gray ship sailing north. It appeared to be some sort of research vessel, with an old-style helicopter wedged on the stern deck. The rotors on the helicopter were sweeping in an arc, as if preparing to take off. Scanning above the bridge, she noted oddly that the ship's mast appeared to be flying both a Russian and an American flag. Likely a joint scientific study, she mused. Reading up on Lake Baikal, she was surprised to learn of the West's scientific interest in the picturesque lake and its unique flora and fauna. Geophysicists, microbiologists, and environmental scientists migrated from around the world to study the lake and its pure waters.

"Back on line," Roy's voice shouted across the deck. Twenty minutes later, they reached the southern edge of the bay, completing their multilane sweep. Theresa determined that there were three lake bed structures seen with the sonar that would warrant further examination.

"That wraps it up for the opening act of today's program," Wofford said. "Where to next?"

"We will cross the lake to a position here," Tatiana said, tapping the map with a slender finger. "Thirty-five kilometers southeast of our current position."

"Might as well leave the sonar in the water. I don't think this boat can go much faster than our survey speed anyway, and we'll get a look at the water depths as we cross over," Theresa said.

"No problem," Wofford said, taking a seat on the deck and stretching his legs up onto the side railing. As he casually watched the sonar monitor, a quizzical expression suddenly appeared on his face. "That's odd," he muttered.

Roy leaned over and studied the monitor. The shadowy image of the lake bottom had abruptly gone haywire, replaced by a barrage of spiked lines running back and forth across the monitor.

"Towfish bouncing off the bottom?" he asked.

"No," Wofford replied, checking the depth. "She's riding forty meters above the lake floor."

The interference continued for several more seconds, then, as abruptly as it started, it suddenly ceased. The contours of the lake bottom again rolled down the screen in clear imagery.

"Maybe one of those giant sturgeon tried to take a bite out of our towfish," Wofford joked, relieved that the equipment was working properly again. But his words were followed by a low, deep rumble that echoed across the water.

Far longer and lower pitched than a clap of thunder, the sound had an odd muffled quality to it. For nearly half a minute, the strange murmur echoed across the lake. All eyes on the boat scanned north in the direction of the noise, but no visible source was evident.

"Some sort of construction?" Theresa asked, searching for an answer.

"Maybe," Roy replied. "It's a long ways off, though."

Glancing at the sonar monitor, he noticed a brief spate of noise that minimally disrupted the image before a clean contour of the lake bed reappeared.

"Whatever it is," Wofford grimaced, "I just wish it would stop messing with our equipment."

─ 2 ─

TEN MILES TO THE NORTH, Rudi Gunn walked onto the bridge wing of the gray-hulled Russian research vessel *Vereshchagin* and looked up at the azure sky overhead. Removing a thick pair of horn-rimmed glasses, he carefully cleaned the lenses and then peered upward again. Shaking his head, he walked back onto the bridge and muttered, "Sounds like thunder, but there's hardly a cloud in the sky."

A hearty laugh erupted at his words, flowing from a portly man with black hair and matching beard. Dr. Alexander Sarghov resembled a circus bear, his large frame softened by a jovial demeanor and warm ebony eyes that twinkled with life. The geophysicist from the Russian Academy of Sciences Limnological Institute enjoyed a good laugh, especially if it was at the expense of his newfound American friends.

"You Westerners are very amusing," he chuckled in a heavily accented voice.

"Alexander, you'll have to excuse Rudi," answered a warm, deep voice from the opposite side of the bridge. "He's never lived in an earthquake zone."

The green opaline eyes of Dirk Pitt sparkled with mirth as he helped heckle his deputy. The head of the National Underwater and Marine Agency stood up from a bank of video monitors and stretched his six-foot-three frame, his palms scraping against the deckhead. Though more than two decades of undersea adventures had exacted a toll on his rugged body, he still had a lean and fit form. Just a few more wrinkles around the eyes and a growing tussle of gray at the temples indicated a wavering battle with age.

"An earthquake?" Gunn speculated. The brainy deputy director of NUMA, an Annapolis graduate and former Navy commander, stared out the bridge in wonder. "I've only been in one or two, but those were felt and not heard."

"Puny ones just rattle the dishes, but larger quakes can sound like a string of locomotives running by," Pitt said.

"There is a great deal of tectonic activity under Lake Baikal," Sarghov added. "Earthquakes occur frequently in this region."

"Personally, I can do without them," Gunn said sheepishly, retaining his seat by the monitor bank. "I hope they don't disrupt our data collection of the lake's currents."

The *Vereshchagin* was engaged in a joint Russian-American scientific survey of Lake Baikal's uncharted current flows. Not one to stay confined in NUMA's Washington headquarters, Pitt was leading a small team from the government research agency in collaboration with local scientists from the Limnological Institute at Irkutsk. The Russians provided the ship and crew, while the Americans provided high-tech sonobuoys and monitoring equipment which would be used to paint a three-dimensional image of the lake and its currents. The great depth of Lake Baikal was known to create unique water-circulation patterns that often behaved unpredictably. Tales of swirling vortexes and fishing boats getting pulled underwater by their nets were common stories among the local lakeside communities.

Starting at the northern tip of the lake, the scientific team had deployed dozens of tiny sensors, packaged in orange colored pods that were ballasted to drift at varying depths. Constantly measuring temperature, pressure, and position, the pods relayed the data instantaneously to a series of large underwater transponders that were positioned in fixed locations. Computers onboard the *Vereshchagin* processed the data from the transponders, displaying the results in 3-D graphic images. Gunn glanced at a bank of the monitors in front of his seat, then focused on one in particular, which depicted the midsection of the lake. The image resembled a pack of orange marbles floating in a bowl of blue ice cream. Nearly in unison, a vertical string of the orange balls suddenly jumped rapidly toward the top edge of the screen.

"Whoa! Either one of our transponders is going tilt or there's a significant disturbance at the bottom of the lake," he blurted.

Pitt and Sarghov turned and studied the monitor, watching as a flood of orange dots raced toward the surface.

"The current is uplifting, at a dramatic rate," Sarghov said with a raised brow. "I find it difficult to believe the earthquake was severe enough to produce that kind of effect."

"Perhaps not the earthquake itself," Pitt said, "but a resulting side effect. A submarine landslide set off by a minor quake might create that sort of uplift."

A hundred and thirty miles north of the *Vereshchagin* and two thousand feet beneath the surface, Pitt was exactly right. The rumblings that first echoed across the lake were the shock waves from a strong earthquake, measuring 6.7 on the Richter scale. Though seismologists would later determine that the quake's epicenter was near the lake's northern shore, it created a devastating effect midway down the western flank, near Olkhon Island. A large, dry, barren landmass, Olkhon sat near the center of the lake. Directly off the island's eastern shoreline, the lake floor dropped like an elevator down a steep slope that ran to the deepest part of the lake.

Seismic studies had revealed dozens of fault lines running beneath the lake floor, including a cut at

Olkhon Island. Had an underwater geologist examined the fault line before and after the quake, he would have measured a movement of less than three millimeters. Yet those three millimeters were sufficient enough to create what the scientists call a "fault rupture with vertical displacement," or an underwater landslide.

The unseen effects of the quake sheared off a mountain-sized hunk of alluvial sediments nearly twenty meters thick. The runaway chunk of loose sediments slid down a subterranean ravine like an avalanche, accumulating mass and building momentum as it went. The mountain of rock, silt, and mud fell a half mile, obliterating underwater hills and outcroppings in its path before colliding with the lake bottom at a depth of fifteen hundred meters.

In seconds, a million cubic meters of sediment was dumped on the lake floor in a dirty cloud of silt. The muffled rumble of the massive landslide quickly fell away, but the violent energy produced by the slide was just unleashed. The moving sediment displaced a massive wall of water, driving it first to the bottom ahead of the landslide and then squeezing it up toward the surface. The effect was like a cupped hand pushing under the surface of a bathtub. The force from millions of gallons of displaced water had to be redirected somewhere.

The submarine landslide had fallen in a southerly direction off Olkhon Island and that was the direction that the mounting swell of water began to move. To the north of the slide, the lake would remain relatively undisturbed, but to the south a rolling wave of destructive force was released. At sea, the moving force of water would be labeled a tsunami, but in the confines of a freshwater lake it was called a seiche wave.

An upsurge of water punched the surface in a ten-foot-high rolling wave that drove south along the lake's lower corridor. As the wave pushed into shallower depths, the upswell squeezed higher, increasing the size and speed of the surface wave. To those in its path, it would be a liquid wall of death.

On the bridge of the *Vereshchagin*, Pitt and Gunn tracked the development of the killer wave with growing alarm. An enlarged three-dimensional map of the lake south of Olkhon Island showed a swirl of orange dots jumping in rapid succession across an expanding line.

"Dial up the surface pods only, Rudi. Let's find out exactly what's going on up top," Pitt requested.

Gunn typed a short command into the computer and a two-dimensional image suddenly appeared on the monitor, showing an array of surface pods bobbing over a five-mile stretch of the lake. All eyes on the bridge focused on the screen as one orange pod after another visibly jumped in a slow line of progression from north to south.

"It's a rolling wave, all right. The sensors are getting kicked up almost five meters as it passes," Gunn reported. He double-checked his measurements, then nodded silently to Pitt and Sarghov with a grim look on his face.

"Of course, a landslide would produce such a wave," Sarghov said, comprehending the electronic images. The Russian pointed to a map of the lake pinned to the bulkhead. "The wave will pass through the shallow delta of the Selenga River as it moves south. Perhaps that will dilute its force."

Pitt shook his head. "As the wave moves into shallower water, it will likely have the opposite effect and increase its surface force," he said. "How fast is she moving, Rudi?"

Gunn toggled the computer mouse and drew a line between two pods, measuring their distance apart. "Based on the spikes in the sensors, the wave looks to be traveling about one hundred twenty-five miles per hour."

"Which will put it upon us in about fifty minutes," Pitt calculated. His mind was already racing in overdrive. The *Vereshchagin* was a stout and stable vessel, he knew, and stood a good chance of steaming through the wave with minimal damage. The greater harm would be to the lake's prevailing marine traffic, small fishing boats and transport vessels not designed to withstand the onslaught of a ten-foot wave. Then there were the shoreline inhabitants, who would be subject to an unexpected flooding of the low-lying areas around the lake.

"Dr. Sarghov, I suggest you have the captain issue an immediate emergency warning to all vessels on the lake. By the time anyone catches sight of the wave, it will be too late to get out of its way. We'll need to contact the authorities on shore to evacuate all residents at risk to flooding. There's no time to lose."

Sarghov beat a path to the ship's radio and issued the warning himself. The radio hummed with chatter as a myriad of respondents called back to confirm the emergency. Though Pitt didn't speak Russian, he could tell by the tone of skepticism in the replying voices that at least some thought Sarghov was either drunk or crazy. Pitt could only smile when the normally jovial scientist turned red and spat a series of obvious obscenities into the microphone.

"Idiot fishermen! They're calling me a fool!" he cursed.

The warnings took heed when a fishing boat in the protected cove of Aya Bay barely survived capsizing as the fringe of the wave passed by and its captain hysterically reported the event. Pitt scanned the horizon with a pair of binoculars and could make out a half dozen black fishing boats motoring toward the safety of Listvyanka, in addition to a small freighter and a hydrofoil ferry.

"I guess you got their attention, Alex," Pitt said.

"Yes," Sarghov replied with some relief. "The Listvyanka Police Department has issued alerts to all stations around the lake and is going door-to-door to evacuate risky areas. We've done all we can do."

"Perhaps you would be kind enough to have the captain apply full speed and move us toward Listvyanka and the western shore of the lake as quickly as possible," Pitt said, smiling that Sarghov had neglected their own plight.

As the *Vereshchagin* turned toward Listvyanka and increased speed, Gunn eyed the map of Lake Baikal, rubbing his finger across the lower toe of the lake, which angled to the west.

"If the wave holds its southerly track, we should be positioned away from its primary force," he remarked.

"That's what I'm banking on," Pitt replied.

"We are eighteen miles from Listvyanka," Sarghov said, peering out the bridge window toward the western shoreline. "We will be cutting it close, as you say."

At Listvyanka, an old air-raid alarm was sounded as the panic-stricken residents pulled ashore their small boats, while larger vessels were secured tightly to the docks. Schoolchildren were sent home with warnings for their parents, while dockside shops were swiftly closed. En masse, the residents around the lake moved to high ground and waited for the mountain of water to wash through.

"It resembles the Irish Derby out here," Sarghov said, peering out the bridge window with a humorless grin. Nearly a dozen vessels dotted the horizon ahead of them, driving toward Listvyanka at top speed as if pulled by a magnet. The *Vereshchagin*'s captain, a quiet and steady man named Ian Kharitonov, gripped the ship's wheel tightly, silently urging his vessel to sail faster. Like the others on the bridge, he periodically took sneak peeks toward the northern section of the lake, looking for signs of the impending wave.

Pitt studied the ship's radar, noting a stationary object lying ten miles to the southeast of their position.

"Apparently, someone still didn't get the word," he said to Sarghov, motioning toward the radar target.

"The fool probably has his radio turned off," Sarghov muttered as he trained a pair of binoculars out the portside window. In the distance, he could just make out a faint black speck moving slowly across the lake to the east.

"Heading right for the middle of the tempest," Sarghov said, grabbing the radio microphone again. Hailing the lone vessel several times brought only silence.

"Their ignorance will mean their death," he said slowly, shaking his head as he hung up the microphone. His anguish was broken by the approach of a loud thumping noise that rattled the windows of the bridge.

Skimming low above the water, a small helicopter swooped directly toward the *Vereshchagin*'s bridge before suddenly pulling up and hovering off the starboard wing. It was a Kamov Ka-26, an old Soviet civilian helicopter that saw its heyday in the 1960s as a utilitarian light transport craft. The chopper sported a faded coat of silver paint garnished with a seal from the Limnological Institute plastered prominently on the fuselage. The thirty-five-year-old helicopter dipped closer to the boat as its cigar-chomping pilot tossed a genial wave toward the men on the bridge.

"Have released all of the survey pods. Permission to

park this whirlybird and get her tied down before surf's up," crackled the deep voice of Al Giordino over the radio.

Sarghov stood and stared out the bridge, looking aghast at the movements of the adjacent helicopter.

"That is a valuable asset of the institute," he said hoarsely to Pitt.

"Don't worry, Alexander," Pitt said, suppressing a grin. "Al could fly a 747 through a doughnut hole."

"It might be best if he parked that thing on shore, rather than risk getting it tossed off the deck," Gunn said.

"Yes . . . of course," Sarghov stammered, just wishing the helicopter would move away from the bridge.

"If it's all the same to you, I'd like to fly by that wayward fishing boat first and try and alert them," Pitt said.

Sarghov looked into the markedly calm eyes of Pitt and then nodded in agreement. Pitt quickly reached for the radio microphone.

"Al, what's your fuel status?" he asked.

"Just fueled up ashore at the Port Baikal airfield. Should have about three and a half hours of remaining flight time, if I keep off the gas. But this pilot's seat wasn't exactly manufactured by La-Z-Boy, I feel compelled to mention." After the better part of the afternoon deploying survey pods across the lake, Giordino was weary from flying the physically demanding craft.

"Go ahead and set her down on the pad, but keep her

wound up. We've got an emergency call to make."

"Roger," the radio squawked. The helicopter immediately rose and slipped to the rear of the ship, where it gently set down on a rickety platform built above the stern deck.

"Rudi, keep us advised over the radio as to the wave's progress. We'll take the chopper to shore after we head off the fishing boat," Pitt directed.

"Aye, aye," Gunn responded as Pitt dashed out of the bridge. Sprinting to the rear of the ship, Pitt ducked down a level to his cabin, emerging seconds later with a red duffel bag flung over his shoulder. Shooting up a stairwell and down the center passageway, he exited onto the open stern deck, where he edged past a bulbous white decompression chamber. The helicopter thumped loudly above him and he felt a blast of air from its rotors as he climbed a narrow flight of steps onto the helipad and ducked toward the Kamov's passenger door.

The odd little helicopter reminded Pitt of a dragonfly. At first glance, the thirty-foot-long helicopter was little more than a high-framed fuselage. The small cockpit appeared to have been sheared in half behind the twin flight controls, the result of a detachable passenger cabin that had been removed. The vintage helicopter had been designed with versatility in mind, and the dead space could be fitted with a tank for agricultural spraying, an ambulance or passenger cabin, or, in the case of the institute's craft, an open cargo platform. A large rack of tubes was fastened to the platform, which had housed the marine-current survey pods. Above the rack and mounted high on the fuselage was a pair of radial piston engines, which drove the helicopter's two separate contrarotating blades, one fixed above the other. A spindly forked tail led to a large stabilizer and elevator flaps, but no tail rotor. The Ka-26, or "Hoodlum" as it was known in the West, was built as a practical multiuse lifting system. Put to marine use, it was perfect for operating off small shipborne platforms.

As Pitt sprinted to the right side of the cockpit, the passenger door popped open and a young Russian technician wearing a ZZ Top baseball cap jumped to the deck. Nodding at Pitt to take his seat, he handed the tall American his radio headset, then quickly scrambled off the platform. Pitt wedged his duffel bag into the footwell and climbed in, glancing toward his old friend in the pilot's seat as he slammed the door shut.

Albert Giordino hardly cut the figure of a suave aviator. The stocky Italian with jackhammer arms stood nearly a foot shorter than Pitt. A shock of unruly black hair curled around his head, while an ever-present cigar protruded from a hard face that hadn't seen a razor in days. His mahogany brown eyes glistened with intelligence and a hint of the sardonic wit that sparkled at even the most trying of times. Pitt's lifelong friend and the director of underwater technology for NUMA was more at home piloting a submersible, but had acquired a silken touch with most types of flying aircraft as well.

"I heard the distress warning. You want to go track that roller as it pounds Listvyanka?" Giordino asked through his headset.

"We've got a social call to make first. Get us airborne and head southeast, and I'll fill you in."

Giordino quickly lifted the Kamov off the moving ship and climbed to an altitude of two hundred feet, swinging east across the lake. As the helicopter accelerated to eighty-five miles per hour, Pitt provided a description of the seiche wave and the unsuspecting fishing boat. The black hull of the boat soon appeared on the horizon and Giordino adjusted his direction toward the vessel as Pitt radioed back to the *Vereshchagin*.

"Rudi, how's our wave rolling?"

"Gaining more power by the minute, Dirk," Gunn's voice replied soberly. "The wave is now topping thirty feet in height at its center, with velocity on the increase as it squeezes past the Selenga River delta."

"How much time before she reaches us?"

Gunn paused as he keyed in a command on the computer. "ETA to the *Vereshchagin* is approximately thirty-seven minutes. We'll be shy of Listvyanka by about five miles."

"Thanks, Rudi. Keep the hatches battened down. We'll be overhead for the show once we get the fishing boat alerted."

"Roger," Gunn replied, suddenly wishing he could trade seats with Pitt.

The wave was still forty miles away and the hills of

Listvyanka were now plainly visible to the men on the *Vereshchagin*. The ship would safely be out of the main force of the wave when the tempest arrived, but there was no protecting the shoreline. Counting the minutes to go, Gunn peered out the bridge window and silently wondered what the picturesque lakeside community would look like in another hour.

— 3 —

L OOKS LIKE WE'VE GOT SOME company," Wofford said, pointing off the fishing boat's stern toward the horizon.

Though Theresa had already spotted the aircraft, Wofford's words made everyone else aboard the boat stop and look. The stubby silver helicopter was approaching from the west and there was no mistaking its beeline path directly toward them.

The fishing boat was cruising toward the eastern shore with its survey gear tailing behind, the crew oblivious to any impending danger. No one aboard had noticed the sudden disappearance of all other surface boats, though an absence of vessel sightings was hardly unusual on the huge lake.

All eyes turned skyward as the ungainly helicopter roared up to the small boat, then pivoted and hovered off the port beam. The survey crew gazed up at an ebony-haired figure in the passenger's seat who waved a microphone toward the window and pointed a finger at his headset.

"He's trying to call us on the radio," Wofford observed. "Do you have your ears on, Captain?"

Tatiana translated to the annoyed captain, who shook his head and spoke indignantly back to the Russian woman. He then grabbed a radio microphone from the wheelhouse and held it up toward the helicopter while slicing his free hand horizontally across the front of his throat.

"The captain says his radio has not operated for two years," Tatiana said, reporting the obvious. "He states that there is no need for one, he sails efficiently without it."

"Now why does that not surprise me?" Roy said, rolling his eyes.

"He obviously wasn't in the Boy Scouts," Wofford added.

"It looks like they want us to turn around," Theresa said, interpreting new motions from the helicopter copilot. "I think they want us to return to Listvyanka."

"The helicopter is from the Limnological Institute," Tatiana noted. "They have no authority. We can ignore them."

"I think they are trying to warn us," Theresa protested, as the helicopter dipped its rotors several times, while the passenger continued making motions with his hands.

"We're probably intruding on an insignificant experiment of theirs," Tatiana said. Shooing her arms at the helicopter, she yelled, "*Otbyt', otbyt'* . . . go away."

GIORDINO PEERED out the cockpit windshield and grinned in amusement. The crusty captain of the fishing boat appeared to be yelling obscenities at the helicopter, while Tatiana stood shooing them away.

"Apparently, they don't like what we're selling," Giordino remarked.

"I think their captain is either short on brains or long on undistilled vodka," Pitt replied, shaking his head in frustration.

"Could be your lousy Marcel Marceau imitation."

"Take a look at the waterline on that bucket."

Giordino studied the portside hull of the fishing boat, noting that it rode low in the water.

"Looks like she's sinking already," he said.

"She won't have much chance against a thirty-foot wave," Pitt remarked. "You're going to have to put me on the deck."

Giordino didn't bother questioning the wisdom of the request or protesting the danger to Pitt. He knew it would be a futile gesture. Pitt was like an overgrown Boy Scout who wouldn't take no for an answer when helping an old lady across the street. He would put his own safety last in order to help others, regardless of the risk. With a steady hand on the controls, Giordino inched the helicopter in a tight circle around the boat, searching for a spot he could touch down and offload Pitt. But the old vessel would not cooperate. A tall wooden mast ran up from the wheelhouse a dozen feet, shielding the boat like a lance. With its forty-two-foot-diameter rotors, there wasn't a place on the boat the helicopter could hover without striking the mast.

"I can't get in tight enough with that mast. You'd have to swim it or risk a twenty-foot drop without breaking a leg," Giordino said.

Pitt surveyed the derelict black boat with its crowd of occupants who still stared up in confusion. "I'm not ready for a swim just yet," he said, contemplating the frigid lake water. "But if you can put me on that mast, I'll do my best fireman's imitation."

The thought seemed crazy, Giordino thought, but he was right. If he could maneuver the helicopter up tight to the mast from above, Pitt could grab hold and slide down to the deck. A tough enough maneuver over land, Giordino knew the attempt over a moving and rocking boat could knock the chopper out of the sky if he wasn't careful.

Pulling the Kamov up till its wheels hung ten feet above the mast, Giordino gently inched the helicopter forward until its passenger door was directly above the mast. Lightly stroking the throttle control, he adjusted the chopper's speed until it precisely matched that of the moving boat. Satisfied he was tracking together, he slowly lowered the helicopter until it hung just three feet above the mast.

"With the boat rocking, I'll have to take just a quick dip to get you down," Giordino said through the headset. "Sure you can climb back up, so I can pull you off?"

"I'm not planning on coming back," Pitt replied

matter-of-factly. "Give me a second, and I'll guide you down."

Pitt took off his headset, then reached down and pulled out the red duffel bag at his feet. Opening the cockpit door to a rush of air from the rotors, he casually tossed the bag out, watching it land with a bounce on the wheelhouse roof. Pitt then dangled his feet out the door and motioned with one hand for Giordino to hold steady. The mast swung brusquely back and forth from the rocking motion of the boat, but Pitt quickly got a feel for the rhythm. When it slowed between swells, Pitt dropped his palm to Giordino. The pilot instantly dipped the helicopter three feet and, in a flash, Pitt was gone out the door. Giordino didn't wait to see if Pitt had successfully connected with the mast but immediately lifted the helicopter up and away from the fishing boat. Gazing out the side window in relief, he saw Pitt with his arms grappled to the top of the mast, slowly sliding his way down.

"*Vereshchagin* to airborne unit, over," burst the voice of Rudi Gunn through Giordino's ears.

"What's up, Rudi?"

"Just wanted to give you a status on the wave. It's now traveling at one hundred thirty-five miles per hour, with a wave height cresting at thirty-four feet. It has passed the Selenga River delta, so we expect no further increases in velocity before it reaches the southern shoreline."

"I suppose you call that the good news. What's the current ETA?"

"For your approximate position, eighteen minutes. The *Vereshchagin* will turn to align itself to the wave in ten minutes. Suggest you stand by for emergency relief."

"Rudi, please confirm. Eighteen minutes to arrival?"

"Affirmative."

Eighteen minutes. It was nowhere near enough time for the dilapidated fishing boat to reach safe haven. Staring at its black hull skimming low in the water, he knew that the old boat had no chance. With a gnawing sense of dread, Giordino realized he might have just given his old friend a death warrant by dropping him to her decks below.

PITT CLUNG to the mast cross-member momentarily, eyeing a pair of worn GPS and radio antennas sprouting just inches from his face. Once Giordino pulled the helicopter away and the air deluge from its rotors subsided, he casually slid down the mast, using his feet as brakes to slow his descent. Grabbing his duffel bag, he stepped across the wheelhouse roof and down a stepladder at its stern edge. Dropping to the deck, he turned and faced the group of shocked people staring at him with open mouths.

"Privet." He grinned disarmingly. "Anyone here speak English?"

"All of us but the captain," Theresa replied, surprised like the others that Pitt was not Russian.

"What is the meaning of this intrusion?" Tatiana demanded tersely. Her dark eyes surveyed Pitt with a look of distrust. Behind her, the fishing boat's captain stood in the wheelhouse door and launched an equally contemptuous tirade in his native tongue.

"Comrade, tell your captain that if he ever wants to hoist another vodka, he had better get this tub turned toward Listvyanka at full speed and right now," Pitt replied in a commanding tone.

"What's the trouble?" Theresa asked, trying to thaw the tension.

"An underwater landslide has triggered a large freak wave near Olkhon Island. A thirty-foot wall of water is bearing down on us as we speak. Emergency radio broadcasts were issued across the lake, but your good captain was incapable of hearing the warning."

Tatiana had an ashen look on her face as she spoke rapidly to the captain in a hushed tone. The captain nodded without saying a word, then climbed into the wheelhouse. A second later, the boat's old motor whined in protest as the throttle was pushed to its stops and the bow eased around toward Listvyanka. On the stern deck, Roy and Wofford were already yanking in their survey gear as the boat slowly accelerated.

Pitt looked up and was disturbed to find that Giordino had flown away from the fishing boat, the silver helicopter now skimming west rapidly toward the horizon. If the boat couldn't outrun the wave to safety, which was a certainty, then he wanted Giordino standing by above them. Silently, he cursed himself for not bringing a handheld radio with him.

"Thank you for flying out to warn us," Theresa said,

approaching Pitt with a nervous smile and a hand-shake. "That was a dangerous way to come aboard." She had a warm honesty that reminded Pitt of his wife Loren and he decided that he liked the Dutch woman immediately.

"Yes, we are grateful for the alert," Tatiana said, apologizing for the earlier inquisition in a slightly warmer tone. Making quick introductions, she asked, "You are from the Limnological Institute research ship, no?"

"Yes. They're headed to Listvyanka, along with the other vessels at this end of the lake. Yours was the only one we couldn't alert by radio."

"I told you there was something wrong with this boat," Wofford whispered to Roy.

"Something wrong with the captain, too," Roy replied with a shake of the head.

"Mr. Pitt, it appears that we will be riding the wave out together. How much time do we have before it will reach us?" Tatiana asked.

Pitt glanced at his orange-faced Doxa dive watch. "Less than fifteen minutes, based on the rate it was traveling when I left the *Vereshchagin*."

"We'll never make it to Listvyanka," Tatiana quietly assessed.

"The lake broadens at the southern end, which will dissipate the wave toward the west. The closer we get to Listvyanka, the smaller the wave we'll have to nav-igate."

But standing on the deck of the leaky fishing boat,

Pitt secretly had doubts whether they could navigate a puddle. The old boat seemed to ride lower in the water by the minute. Its engine sputtered and coughed as if it would die at any moment. Wood rot was evident every-where, and that was just what was visible above decks. Pitt could only imagine the feeble state of the timbers hidden below.

"We better prepare for a wild ride. Life jackets on everyone. Anything you don't want lost over the side should be secured to the deck or gunwales."

Roy and Wofford quickly tied down their survey equipment with Theresa lending a hand. Tatiana rummaged around in the wheelhouse a few minutes, then returned on deck with an armful of aged life pre-servers.

"There are only four life jackets aboard," she announced. "The captain refuses to wear one, but we are still short a jacket," she said, eyeing Pitt as the odd man out.

"Not to worry, I brought my own," Pitt replied. While the survey team fastened their life jackets, Pitt kicked off his shoes and outer clothes and immodestly slid into a neoprene dry suit he pulled from his duffel bag.

"What's that noise?" Theresa asked.

Almost imperceptibly, a distant rumble echoed lightly across the lake. To Pitt, it sounded like a freight train rounding a faraway mountain curve. The rumble held constant, however, and grew ever so slightly louder.

Pitt knew without looking that their reprieve was over. The wave must have increased speed—and, with it, power—as it raced toward them, bearing down earlier than Rudi had estimated.

"There it is!" Roy yelled, pointing up the lake.

"It's huge," Theresa gasped, shocked at the sight.

The wave wasn't a cresting white-capped breaker of the kind that surfers relish but, rather, an oddly smooth cylinder of liquid that rolled from shore to shore like a giant rolling pin. Even from a distance of twenty miles, the men and women on the fishing boat could see that the wave was massive, standing nearly forty feet high. The surreal image of the moving wall of water accompanied by its odd rumble caused everyone to freeze and stare in awe. Everyone but Pitt.

"Tatiana, tell the captain to turn the bow into the wave," he ordered. The crusty captain, his eyes the size of a pair of hubcaps, quickly swung the wheel over. Pitt knew the odds were stacked against the aged and waterlogged vessel. But as long as there was hope, he was determined to try to keep everyone alive.

The first challenge was to keep everyone aboard. Scanning the deck, Pitt zeroed in on an old fishing net coiled against the starboard side gunwale.

"Jim, give me a hand with that net," he asked of Wofford.

Together, they dragged the coiled net across the deck and pushed it against the back bulkhead of the wheelhouse. As Wofford wrapped one end around the starboard railing, Pitt secured the opposite end to a port stanchion.

"What is that for?" Theresa asked.

"When the wave approaches, everyone lie down and grab a tight hold of the net. It will act as a cushion and hopefully keep everyone from taking an undesired swim in the lake."

As the captain nosed the bow toward the approaching wave, the three men and two women took up positions in front of the net. Roy sided up to Pitt and whispered out of earshot of the others.

"A game effort, Mr. Pitt, though we both know this old derelict isn't going to make it."

"Never say die," Pitt whispered back with an odd look of confidence.

The rumbling bellow from the moving water grew louder as the wave approached within five miles. There were just minutes to go before it would strike the boat. The occupants all braced for the worst, some praying silently while others contemplated death with grim determination. Against the roar of the water, nobody detected the sound of the approaching helicopter. The Kamov was barely a hundred yards off the port flank when Wofford looked up and blurted, "What the heck?"

All eyes darted from the approaching wave to the helicopter and back and then did a double take. Dangling beneath the chopper on a twenty-foot cable was a white cylindrical object that swayed just a few feet above the waves. The object was clearly taxing the lifting ability of the helicopter, and everyone but Pitt figured that the helicopter pilot had lost his mind. At this dire point in time, why would he be trying to transport some machinery to the fishing boat?

A broad grin spread over Pitt's face as he recognized the bulky object twisting beneath the helicopter. He had nearly tripped over it while leaving the *Vereshchagin* just a short time ago. It was the research ship's decompression chamber, on board as a security measure in case of a diving accident. Giordino had hastily realized it could act as a submersible for the fishing boat's crew to take haven in. Jumping to his feet, Pitt waved at Giordino to lower the chamber to the boat's stern deck.

With the seiche wave bearing down on the boat, Giordino moved in rapidly, hovering high over the stern until the swaying chamber stabilized. With a sudden dip and a crunch, the one-ton chamber descended from the sky and collided with the deck. The four-person hyperbaric chamber took up the entire rear deck space and pushed the boat's stern down several inches deeper into the water.

Pitt quickly unhooked the attached cable then jumped to the side rail and waved a thumbs-up gesture toward the helicopter. Giordino immediately swung the helicopter up and away from the boat, settling in a hover a short distance away to observe the impact.

"Why did he dump that here?" Tatiana asked.

"That big ugly bobber is your ticket to safety," Pitt replied. "Everybody in, there's no time to lose."

Glancing forward, Pitt could see that the fast-moving wave was just a mile away. He quickly unhinged the sealed lock and swung open the heavy circular door to the chamber. Theresa was the first to climb in, followed by Wofford and Roy. Tatiana hesitated, grabbing a leather satchel before stepping in behind Roy.

"Hurry up," Pitt prompted. "There's no time to check luggage."

Even the brash captain, staring awestruck at the looming wall of water, abandoned the wheel and scrambled into the chamber after the others.

"Aren't you joining us?" Tatiana asked as Pitt began to close the door.

"It will be tight enough with five people in there. Besides, someone's got to seal the chamber," he replied with a wink. "There's blankets and padding in the rear. Use them to protect your heads and bodies. Brace yourselves, it will be here quick."

With a metallic clang, the door clapped shut and Pitt twisted the locking mechanism closed. A strange silence suddenly enveloped the occupants, but it lasted for less than a minute. Then the wave was upon them.

Theresa sat opposite a thick porthole window and looked out at the mysterious man who had arrived from nowhere to save them. She saw Pitt reach into his duffel bag and remove a dive faceplate and backpack with a small tank attached. Quickly strapping the equipment on, he stepped up onto the side gunwale before a deluge of water obscured the viewport.

The chartered fishing boat was still fifteen miles

from Listvyanka and the western shoreline when the seiche wave hit. Those aboard had no way of knowing that they were struck by the leading force of the rolling wave, its peak cresting as high as a three-story building at impact.

From his perch two hundred feet in the air, Giordino looked on with a sickening helplessness as the wave piled into the black fishing boat. Its throttle was still set at full, and Giordino watched as the aged boat tried valiantly to climb up the vertical wall of water. But the rolling force of the water overpowered the rotted hull timbers and the old wooden boat seemed to melt away, disappearing completely under the tall wave.

Giordino desperately scanned the surface for signs of Pitt or the decompression chamber. But as the waters fell to a subtle calm again, only the bow section could be seen floating on the surface. The old fishing boat had split in two from the force of the wave and only the bow section had survived the initial onslaught. The stern deck, with the compression chamber, had vanished from sight. The black-hulled wreckage of the bow bobbed only momentarily, its masthead swaying across the sky before it, too, disappeared in a gurgle of bubbles to the bottom of the frigid lake.

— 4 —

H ANG ON!" THERESA CALLED OVER the sudden roar
from the wall of water.

Her words echoed in the chamber as its occupants
were violently tossed about. The entire chamber jerked
upright as the striking wave lifted the fishing boat on
end. The three men and two women clung frantically
to the welded railings of twin bunks, trying to keep
their bodies from becoming flying missiles inside the
chamber. Time seemed to stand still as the boat stalled
in its attempt to climb the face of the wave. Then a
loud cracking noise reverberated beneath their feet as
the fishing boat broke in two. Free of the lighter and
more buoyant bow, the stern section slowly slid back
vertically into the trough of the wave just as the brunt
of its force rolled onward.

For Theresa, the impact seemed to occur in slow
motion. The initial sensation of sinking on end pre-
dictably gave way to the tumbling force of the wave
thrusting the chamber over on its back. Arms, legs, and
torsos flailed about the chamber as it flipped over amid
a chorus of cries and gasps. The minimal light that
flared through the view port quickly dimmed, then
vanished altogether, thrusting the interior into a frightening blackness.

Unseen by its victims, the wave had flipped over the
entire stern section of the fishing boat, pinning the

chamber beneath it. The flooded engine compartment, aided by the weight of the engine and driveshaft, easily drove the inverted chamber toward the lake bed. Though the force of the wave surged past above them, the wreckage and chamber continued to descend under its own weight. Instead of becoming a life preserver, the decompression chamber had turned into a coffin, plunging its victims toward the cold depths of the Siberian lake.

The heavy steel chamber was built to withstand the force of thirty atmospheres, or the pressure found at a depth of one thousand feet. But the lake depths exceeded three thousand feet where the fishing boat broke up, which would cause the chamber to implode before ever reaching the lake floor. Under its own weight, the encapsulated chamber would float freely on the surface and would be still buoyant even with five people inside. But pinned against the inverted stern section, the chamber was headed to the bottom.

As the light dimmed from the view port, Theresa knew that they were sinking deeper into the lake. She recalled Pitt's words at the last minute, calling the chamber a "bobber." It must float, she deduced. There was no apparent water leakage in the chamber, so another force must be driving them to sink.

"Everybody to this end of the chamber, if you're able," she shouted to the others after groping her way to one end. "We must shift the weight."

Her dazed and battered companions crawled their way to Theresa, huddling together quietly while trying to aid one another's injuries in the dark. The thousand pounds of shifted weight alone might not have set them free, but Theresa had guessed right and placed everybody adjacent to what had been the stern edge of the boat. Above their heads now was the boat's engine, the heaviest part of the stern section. The combined concentration of weight was focused just off of dead center, and slight enough, to create an angular imbalance in the sinking wreckage.

As the plunging boat drove deeper, the pressure from the depths increased. Creaking sounds wafted through the chamber as the pressure limits were approached in its welded seams. But the shift in ballast gradually weighed on the angle of descent, tipping the stern section of the boat slightly steeper. Inside the chamber, nobody could feel the shift, but a slight scraping sound was heard as the chamber began sliding across the angled deck. The movement accelerated the imbalance until the chamber perceptively tipped upward. The gradient increased to almost forty degrees before the decompression chamber finally rattled off the stern edge and broke free of the sinking wreckage.

To those inside the chamber, it felt like a rollercoaster ride in reverse, as the buoyant capsule shot to the surface like a bullet. To Giordino, who scanned the lake surface high above in the Kamov, the sight reminded him of a Trident missile being launched from a submerged Ohio-class nuclear submarine. After watching the wave pass and the bow section sink, he'd noticed a large surge of bubbles nearby. At a depth of eighty feet, he perceived, the white decompression chamber accelerating toward the surface. Released from the depths at a tilted angle, the chamber broke the surface nose first and shot completely out of the water before slamming down violently onto the surface. Hovering closer, Giordino could see that the chamber appeared airtight and floated easily in the light choppy waves.

Despite a severe battering, Theresa could hardly contain her relief at seeing blue sky again out the chamber's porthole window. Peering out the view port, she could see that they were floating steadily on the water. A shadow passed by overhead, and she caught a reassuring glimpse of the silver helicopter. With new-found light illuminating the interior again, she turned and surveyed the tumbled mass of bodies crowded around her.

The tumultuous ride had bruised and battered everyone, but amazingly there were no serious injuries. The fishing boat's captain bled from a nasty gash to the forehead, while Wofford grimaced over a wrenched back. Roy and the two women managed to escape lasting injuries. Theresa wondered how many concussions and broken bones would have occurred had they not insulated themselves with the bed mattresses just before the wave struck. As she regained her senses, her thoughts drifted back to Pitt, wondering whether the man who had rescued them had himself survived the maelstrom.

The veteran head of NUMA had figured he could

best beat the wave in open water. An experienced body surfer since his childhood days growing up in Newport Beach, Pitt knew that diving under the approaching wave would let it roll over him with minimal surge. After securing the survey team inside the decompression chamber, he'd quickly strapped on his faceplate attached to a Dräger rebreather system and dropped over the side of the fishing boat. Hitting the water, he kicked and pulled hard, attempting to swim away from the fishing boat and dive beneath the wave before it struck. But he'd been just a few seconds too late.

The seiche wave broke over him just as he cleared the surface. Rather than escape under the passing wave, he was positioned too shallow and found himself being drawn up the face of the wave. The sensation was of riding an ascending elevator at high speed and Pitt felt his stomach drop as his body was sucked upward. Unlike the fishing boat, which rode the external surface of the wave before breaking up, Pitt was embedded within the mass of water and became part of the wave itself.

His ears rang from the rush of the mammoth wave while the turbulence of the roiling water dropped the visibility to zero. With the rebreather system on his back, he was able to breathe normally through his faceplate despite the tempest around him. For a moment, he felt like he was flying though air and a part of him actually enjoyed the ride, though the danger of being crushed under the wave gnawed at his senses. Trapped in the uplift, he realized there was no sense in fighting the overpowering force of water and relaxed slightly as he was pushed higher. He had no sensation of any forward motion, despite the fact he had already been carried several hundred yards from the point he entered the water.

As he zoomed upward, he suddenly felt a leg break free of the water, then a flash of light burst through his faceplate as his head broke the surface. His momentum shifted, and now he felt his body getting tugged forward. He instantly realized that he had been pushed to the very top of the wave and was in danger of getting hurled over the wave's leading edge. Just inches away, the peak of the wave dropped over thirty feet in a vertical wall of water to the lake surface. A torrent of white foamy water curled around him as the wave began showing signs of cresting. Pitt knew that if he fell over the precipice and the wave crested on top of him, he could be crushed to death under a mass of falling water.

Pivoting his body perpendicular to the wave front, he flung his arms through the water and kicked with all his might to swim over the top of the wave. He could feel himself being pulled backward from the momentum of the wave and willed his legs to kick harder against the water. With the frenzy of a sprint swimmer, he lunged over the wave crest, arms and legs flailing at a supersonic rate. The rushing water continued to pull at his body, trying to suck him into the morass, but he willed himself on desperately.

Then suddenly the grip released and the wave

seemed to let go beneath him. He felt himself falling headfirst, which meant he had made it to the backside of the wave. The elevator ride zipped down this time, but in a controlled free fall. He consciously tensed for an impact, but it never arrived. The rushing force of water eased, then dissipated to nothing. In a froth of clearing bubbles, Pitt found himself floating freely underwater. As the loud rush of the wave diminished, he glanced at a depth gauge affixed to his harness and found that he was twenty feet under the surface.

Reorienting himself in the water, he eyed the shimmering lake surface above him and lazily kicked with tired legs until his head broke the water. Gazing toward the still-thundering rumble, he watched as the massive wave rolled rapidly toward its destructive rendezvous with the south shoreline. The roar slowly faded, and Pitt's ears detected the rotor-thumping sound of a helicopter take its place. Turning in the water, he saw the Kamov helicopter low in the sky making a beeline toward him. Scanning the lake, he saw no sign of the fishing boat on the horizon.

Giordino brought the Kamov right alongside Pitt, hovering so low that waves washed over the helicopter's landing wheels. Pitt swam to the cockpit as the passenger door was flung open above his head. Climbing up the landing skid, he hauled himself through the door and onto the passenger's seat. Giordino immediately elevated the helicopter as Pitt removed his faceplate.

"Some guys will do anything to hang ten," Giordino

grinned, relieved to have found his friend in one piece.

"Turned out to be a lousy pipeline," Pitt gasped in exhaustion. "The fishing boat?"

Giordino shook his head. "Didn't make it. Snapped in two like a twig. Thought we lost the decompression chamber, too, but she finally shot to the surface a short time later. I could see someone waving through the view port, so hopefully everyone inside that soda can is okay. I radioed the *Vereshchagin* and she's on her way to fish them out."

"Nice thinking, bringing the chamber over at the last minute. The crew wouldn't have made it otherwise."

"Sorry I didn't have a chance to yank you out before the surf hit."

"And spoil a good ride?" Pitt nodded at his good fortune in surviving the punishing wave, then thought of the *Vereshchagin*. "How did the institute ship fare?"

"The wave was down to fourteen feet near Listvyanka. The *Vereshchagin* apparently rode it through without a hitch. Rudi says a few of the deck chairs got rearranged, but otherwise they're fine. They expect that the village incurred a fair amount of damage."

Pitt looked down at the blue water below the cockpit and was unable to spot the decompression chamber.

"How far did I travel?" he asked, finally catching his breath. The battering ride was catching up to him and he began to feel a dozen sore spots across his body.

"About three miles," Giordino replied.

"Covered in gold medal time, if I do say so myself,"

he said, wiping a bead of water off his brow.

Giordino accelerated the helicopter north, skimming low over the now-calm lake. A white object materialized in the water ahead, and Giordino slowed the Kamov as they reached the bobbing chamber.

"Bet the air in that tank is starting to get a little foul," he said.

"They'd need several more hours before any real danger of carbon dioxide poisoning," Pitt replied. "How long before the *Vereshchagin* arrives?"

"About ninety minutes. But I'm afraid we can't hang around and keep them company until then," Giordino said, tapping a fuel dial that was heading low.

"Well, if you'd kindly return to the deck, I'll let them know they haven't been abandoned."

"You just can't get enough of the cold lake water, can you?" he asked, lowering the helicopter till it hovered just a few feet above the water.

"Sort of like your affinity for pure Rocky Mountain springwater," Pitt countered. "Just make sure Alexander doesn't run us over," he said, pulling the faceplate back over his head.

With a short wave, he leaped out of the door, splashing into the water just a few feet from the chamber. As Giordino swung the helicopter toward the approaching research ship, Pitt swam over to the chamber and pulled himself up to the view port and peered inside.

Theresa let out a gasp when she saw Pitt's faceplate pressed up against the view port.

"He's still alive," she said with amazement after recognizing the green eyes.

The others crowded around the porthole and waved at Pitt, not knowing he had been washed away nearly three miles before returning via the helicopter.

Pitt pointed a gloved finger at the occupants, then curled it toward his thumb and held it to the view port.

"He's asking if we're okay," Roy deciphered.

Tatiana, sitting closest to the view port, nodded yes and returned the gesture. Pitt then pointed toward his wristwatch and held up his index finger.

Tatiana nodded again in understanding. "One hour," she said to the others. "Help is on the way."

"Guess we might as well get comfortable," Wofford said. Together with Roy, they rearranged the mattresses on the angled floor, allowing everyone to sit comfortably.

Outside, Pitt swam around the chamber, checking it for damage and signs of leakage. Satisfied that the chamber wasn't sinking, he climbed aboard the exposed top section and waited. In the clear afternoon air, Pitt easily spotted the *Vereshchagin* in the distance and tracked its progress as it steamed toward them.

Giordino already had a large crane positioned over the side when the research ship pulled alongside a little over an hour later. The original transport cables were still attached to the decompression chamber, so Pitt had only to gather them together and slide them over the crane's hook. Pitt sat straddled atop the chamber as if riding a giant white stallion while it was hoisted onto the stern of the *Vereshchagin*. When its skids kissed the deck, Pitt jumped down and spun open the locked entry hatch. Gunn ran up and poked his head in, then helped pull out Theresa and Tatiana, followed by the three men.

"Man, does that taste good," Wofford said as he sucked in a deep breath of fresh air.

The Russian fisherman, climbing out last, staggered to the ship's rail and peered over the side, searching for his old fishing boat.

"You can tell him she's at the bottom, crushed by the wave," Pitt said to Tatiana.

The captain shook his head and sobbed as Tatiana translated the news.

"We couldn't believe you appeared after the wave passed," Theresa marveled at Pitt. "How did you survive?"

"Sometimes, I'm just lucky," he grinned, then he opened his duffel bag to reveal the dive equipment inside.

"Thank you again," Theresa said, joined by a chorus of praise from the other survey crew members.

"Don't thank me," Pitt said, "thank Al Giordino here and his flying decompression chamber."

Giordino stepped over from the crane and bowed in mock appreciation. "Hope the ride wasn't too rough in that tin can," he said.

"You saved our lives, Mr. Giordino," Theresa said, shaking his hand gratefully and not letting go.

"Please, call me Al," the gruff Italian said, softening

under the gaze of the pretty Dutch woman.

"Now I know what that steel ball in a pinball machine feels like," Roy muttered.

"Say, you don't suppose they'd have any vodka aboard?" Wofford groaned, rubbing his back.

"Does it rain in Seattle?" Gunn replied, overhearing the comment. "Right this way, ladies and gentlemen. We'll have the ship's doctor check you over, and then you can rest and relax in a cabin or have a drink in the galley. Listvyanka's a mess, so we probably won't be able to put you to shore until tomorrow anyway."

"Al, why don't you lead the way to sick bay. I'd like a word with Rudi first," Pitt said.

"My pleasure," Giordino said, holding Theresa's arm and guiding her and the others along the port passageway to the ship's tiny medical station.

Rudi stepped over to Pitt and patted him on the shoulder. "Al told us about your sojourn in the water. If I'd known you were going to be one with the wave, I would have strung some current-measuring devices on your back," he grinned.

"I'll be happy to share my experience in fluid dynamics with you over a tequila," Pitt replied. "What is the extent of damages around the shoreline?"

"From what we could see at a distance, Listvyanka weathered the storm in one piece. The docks are chewed up and there are a couple of boats sitting on the main street now, but the rest of the damage appeared to be confined to a few commercial shops along the waterfront. We've heard of no reported fatalities over

116

the radio, so the advance warning apparently did the trick."

"We'll need to stay on our toes for potential after-shocks," Pitt said.

"I've got an open satellite line to the National Earthquake Information Center in Golden, Colorado. They'll give us a shout if they detect a subsequent quake the second they see it."

As dusk settled over the lake, the *Vereshchagin* steamed into the port village of Listvyanka. On the forward deck of the research ship, the crew lined the rails to observe the ruin. The wave had struck like a hammer, flattening small trees and shredding the smaller buildings that had stood along the water's edge. But most of the town and port had survived with minimal loss. The research ship dropped anchor in the dark a mile from the damaged shoreline docks, which glistened under a battery of temporary lights strung along the shore. The hum of an old Belarus tractor drifted over the water as the townspeople began working late into the night to clean up the flood damage.

In the ship's galley, Roy, Wofford, and the fishing boat captain sat in a corner chugging shots with a Russian crewman who generously shared his bottle of Altai vodka. Pitt, Giordino, and Sarghov sat across the room, finishing a dinner of baked sturgeon with Theresa and Tatiana. After their dishes were cleared away, Sarghov produced an unmarked bottle and poured a round of after-dinner drinks.

"To your health," Giordino said, toasting both ladies, his glass meeting a clink from Theresa's.

"Which is much improved on account of you," Theresa replied with a laugh. Taking a sip of the liquid, her smile waned as her eyes suddenly bugged out.

"What is this stuff?" she rasped. "Tastes like bleach."

Sarghov laughed with a deep bellow. "It's samogon. I acquired it in the village from an old friend. I believe it is similar to a liquid in America called moonshine."

The rest of the table laughed as Theresa pushed the half-filled glass away from her. "I believe I shall stick to vodka," she said, now grinning with the others.

"So tell me, what are a couple of gorgeous young ladies doing out hunting for oil on big, bad Lake Baikal?" Pitt asked after downing his glass.

"The Avarga Oil Consortium possesses oil and mining rights to territories east of the lake," Tatiana replied.

"Lake Baikal is a cultural treasure. It has United Nations World Heritage status and is an icon for environmentalists around the globe," Sarghov said, clearly disdainful at the prospect of seeing an oil rig on the pristine lake's waters. "How can you possibly expect to drill on the lake?"

Tatiana nodded. "You are correct. We respect Baikal as sacred water, and it would never be our intent to establish oil-pumping structures on the lake. If oil prospects are proven and deemed reachable, we would drill from the eastern territories at a high angle beneath

118

the lake to reach the potential deposits."

"Makes sense," Giordino stated. "They angle drill in the Gulf of Mexico all the time, even drill horizontally. But that still doesn't explain the presence of this lovely Dutch angel from Rotterdam," he added, smiling broadly at Theresa.

Flattered by the comment, Theresa blushed deeply before answering. "Amsterdam. I'm actually from Amsterdam. My intoxicated American coworkers and I work for Shell Oil." As she spoke, she hooked her thumb toward the far corner, where an inebriated Roy and Wofford were loudly sharing dirty jokes with their Russian companions.

"We are here at the request of Avarga Oil," she continued. "They are not equipped for marine surveys, for obvious reasons. My company has performed survey work in the Baltic as well as the western Siberia oil fields of Samotlor. We are exploring a joint-development opportunity with Avarga Oil for some regional lands that show promise. It was a natural fit for us to come here and perform the lake survey together."

"Had you confirmed any petroleum deposits before the wave struck?" Pitt asked.

"We were searching for structural indications of hydrocarbon seeps only and did not have the seismic equipment necessary to gauge any potential deposits. At the time we lost the boat, we had failed to survey any significant characteristics normally associated with a deposit seep."

"Oil seeps?" Sarghov asked.

"Yes, a common if somewhat primitive means of locating petroleum deposits. In a marine setting, oil seeps show up as leakages from the seafloor that rise to the surface. In the days before boomer trucks and other seismic devices that ping the sedimentary depths and produce a visual geological image of the ground, oil seeps were the primary means of locating hydrocarbon deposits."

"We have had fishermen report the sightings of oil slicks on the lake where no surface traffic was evident," Tatiana explained. "We realize, of course, they could represent releases from small deposits that are not economical to drill."

"A potentially costly venture, given the depths of the lake," Pitt added.

"Speaking of ventures, Mr. Pitt, what are you and your NUMA crew doing here aboard a Russian research ship?" Tatiana asked.

"We're guests of Alexander and the Limnological Institute," Pitt replied, tipping his glass of samogon in the direction of Sarghov. "A joint effort to study current patterns in the lake and their effect on the endemic flora and fauna."

"And how was it that you became aware of the seiche wave well in advance of its appearance?"

"Sensor pods. We've got hundreds of sensor pods deployed in the lake, which measure the water temperature, pressure, and so on. Al's been dropping them like bread crumbs from the helicopter all over the lake. We just happened to be surveying the area of lake near

Olkhon Island and had a heavy concentration of sensors in the water there. Rudi quickly picked up the indicators of an underwater landslide and the resulting seiche wave as it formed."

"A fortunate thing for us, as well as many others, I imagine," Theresa said.

"Al just has a nose for catastrophes," Pitt grinned.

"Coming to Siberia without a bottle of Jack Daniel's was the real catastrophe," Giordino said, sipping the glass of samogon with a sour look on his face.

"It is a shame that our base current data was disrupted by this unexpected event," Sarghov said, contemplating the scientific impact, "but we will have some exciting data on the formation and movement of the wave itself."

"These sensor pods, can they reveal where the earthquake originated?" Tatiana asked.

"If it occurred under the lake," Pitt replied.

"Rudi said he would massage the computers tomorrow and see if he can pinpoint an exact location from the sensors. The seismologists he talked to placed the epicenter somewhere near the northwest corner of the lake," Giordino said. Scanning the galley and finding no sign of Gunn, he added, "He's probably up in the bridge conversing with his computers as we speak."

Tatiana downed the last of her samogon, then glanced at her watch. "It has been a trying day. I'm afraid I must turn in for the evening."

"I'm with you," Pitt said, suppressing a yawn. "May

I escort you to your cabin?" he asked innocently.

"That would be satisfactory," she replied.

Sarghov joined them as they rose to their feet and declared good night to all.

"I trust you two are waiting for the baked alaska to be served?" Pitt smiled at Theresa and Giordino.

"Tales of the Netherlands await my hungry ears," Giordino grinned at Theresa.

"And anecdotes of the deep await in return?" she laughed back.

"There certainly is something deep around here," Pitt laughed as he bid good night.

Pitt politely escorted Tatiana to her cabin near the stern, then retired to his own stateroom amidships. The day's physical demands had consumed his body and he was glad to ease his aching limbs into his bunk. Though physically exhausted, he fell asleep with difficulty. His mind stubbornly replayed the day's events over and over until a black veil of sleep thankfully washed over him.

~ 5 ~

PITT HAD BEEN ASLEEP FOR four hours when suddenly he sprang awake, bolting upright in his bunk. Though all was quiet, his senses told him something was wrong. Flicking on a reading light, he swung his feet to the floor and stood up but nearly fell over in the process. Rubbing the sleep from his eyes, he realized that the ship was listing at the stern, at an angle of almost ten degrees.

Dressing quickly, he climbed a stairwell to the main deck, then moved along its exterior passageway. The passageway and open deck before it were completely deserted, the whole ship strangely quiet as he walked uphill toward the bow. The silence finally registered. The ship's engines were shut down and only the muted hum of the auxiliary generator in the engine room throbbed through the late night air.

Climbing another set of stairs to the bridge, he walked in the doorway and gazed around the compartment. To his chagrin, the bridge was entirely deserted. Wondering if he was the only man aboard the ship, he scanned the bridge console before finding a red toggle switch marked TREVOGA. Flicking the toggle, the entire ship suddenly erupted in a clamor of warning bells that shattered the night silence. Seconds later, the *Vereshchagin*'s sinewy captain charged onto the bridge like an angry bull from his cabin below.

"What is going on here?" the captain stammered, fighting to recollect his English in the middle of the night. "Where is the watch, Anatoly?"

"The ship is sinking," Pitt said calmly. "There was no watch aboard the bridge when I entered just a minute ago."

A wide-eyed grimace appeared on the captain's face as he noticed the ship's list for the first time.

"We need power!" he cried, reaching for a phone to the engine room. But as his hand gripped the receiver, the bridge suddenly fell black. Mast lights, cabin lights, console displays—everything—went dark throughout the ship as the electrical power vanished in an instant. Even the alarm bells began dying with a wounded bellow.

Cursing in the dark, the captain fumbled with his hands along the bridge console until finding the emergency battery switch, which bathed the bridge in low-level lighting. As the lights flickered on, the *Vereshchagin*'s chief engineer burst onto the bridge, gasping for air. A heavyset man with a neatly trimmed beard, he gazed through sky-blue eyes that were tinged with panic.

"Captain, the hatches to the engine room have been chained shut. There's no way to gain entry. I fear she may well be half flooded already."

"Someone has locked the hatches? What has happened . . . Why are we sinking while moored at anchor?" the captain asked, shaking away the cobwebs in search of an answer.

"It appears that the bilges have flooded and the lower deck is taking on water quickly at the stern," the engineer reported, his breath finally slowing.

"You better prepare to abandon ship," Pitt advised in a logical tone.

The words still cut the captain to the bone. For a ship's captain, the order to abandon ship is like volunteering to give away one's own child. There is no order more searing on the soul. The pain of answering to the shipowners, the insurance companies, and the maritime inquiry boards after the fact would be difficult enough to face. But harder still was seeing the crew scramble off in fear, then watching as that inanimate mass of wood and steel actually vanishes before one's eyes. Like a favorite family car, most ships take on a persona of their own for the captain and crew, with nuances, quirks, and personality traits unique to that vessel. Many a captain has been accused of having a love affair with the vessel he commanded, and so it was with Captain Kharitonov.

The tired captain knew the truth but still couldn't utter the words. With a grim look, he simply nodded at the chief engineer to pass the order.

Pitt was already out the door, his mind churning over solutions to keep the ship afloat. Retrieving his dive gear and accessing the engine room was his first temptation, but he would have to defeat the chained hatch first and then what? If the flooding was from a gash to the hull beneath the engine room, there would be little he could do to stem the tide anyway.

The answer struck him when he ran into Giordino and Gunn on the suddenly bustling middeck.

"Looks like we're about to get wet," Giordino said without alarm.

"The engine room is locked and flooding. She's not going to stay afloat a whole lot longer," Pitt replied, then gazed down the sloping aft deck. "How quickly can you get that whirlybird warmed up?"

"Consider it done," Giordino replied, then sprinted aft, not waiting for Pitt's reply.

"Rudi, see that the survey team we picked up is safely on deck and near a lifeboat. Then see if you can convince the captain to release the anchor line," Pitt said while Gunn stood shivering in a light jacket.

"What's up your sleeve?"

"An ace, I hope," Pitt mused, then disappeared aft.

THE KAMOV bounded into the night sky, hovering momentarily above the stricken research vessel.

"Aren't we forgetting 'Women and children first'?" Giordino asked from the pilot's seat.

"I sent Rudi to round up the oil survey team," Pitt replied, reading Giordino's real concern about Theresa. "Besides, we'll be back before anyone gets their feet wet."

Gazing out the cockpit, they observed the full outline of the ship illuminated more from the shore lights than the emergency deck lights, and Pitt silently hoped his words would hold true. The research ship was clearly going down at the stern and sinking fast. The waterline had already crept over the lower deck and would shortly begin washing over the open stern deck. Giordino instinctively flew toward Listvyanka, while Pitt turned his gaze from the foundering *Vereshchagin* to the scattered fleet of vessels moored off the village.

"Looking for anything in particular?" Giordino asked.

"A high-powered tug, preferably," Pitt replied, knowing no such vessel existed on the lake. The boats whisking by beneath them were almost exclusively small fishing vessels of the kind that the oil survey team had leased. Several were capsized or washed ashore from the force of the seiche wave.

"How about that big boy?" Giordino asked, nodding toward a concentration of lights in the bay two miles away.

"She wasn't around when we came in last night, maybe she's on her way in. Let's go take a look."

Giordino banked the helicopter toward the lights, which quickly materialized into the outline of a ship. As the chopper zoomed closer, Pitt could see that the ship was a cargo ship of roughly two hundred feet. The hull was painted black creased with brown patches of rust that dripped to the waterline. A faded blue funnel rose amidships, garnished with the logo of a gold sword. The old ship had obviously plied the lake for decades, transporting coal and lumber from Listvyanka to remote villages on the northern shores of Baikal. As Giordino swung down the ship's starboard side, Pitt noted a large black derrick mounted on the stern deck. His eyes returned to the funnel, then he shook his head.

"No good. She's moored here, and I see no smoke from her stacks, so her engines are probably cold. Take too long to get her in play." Pitt tilted his head back toward the village. "Guess we'll have to go for speed over power."

"Speed?" Giordino asked as he followed Pitt's nod and aimed the helicopter back toward the village.

"Speed," Pitt confirmed, pointing to a mass of brightly colored lights bobbing in the distance.

• • •

ABOARD THE *Vereshchagin*, an orderly evacuation was already under way. Two lifeboats had been loaded with half the crew and were in the process of being lowered to the water. Gunn threaded his way past the remaining crowd of scientists and ship's crewmen toward the rear quarters, then dropped down a deck. Incoming water had risen above the deckhead at the far end of the passageway but sloshed only to ankle depth at the higher point where Gunn stood. The guest cabins were closest to him, where, to his relief, the water had yet to rise much higher.

Gunn shuddered as he approached the first cabin shared by Theresa and Tatiana, the icy water swirling about his calves. Shouting and pounding loudly on the door, he turned the unlocked handle and pressed against it. Inside, the cabin was bare. There were no personal effects about, which was to be expected, since the women had come aboard with little more than the clothes on their back. Only the ruffled blankets on the twin bunks indicated their earlier presence.

He closed the door and quickly moved aft to the next cabin, grimacing as the cold water sloshed around his thighs. Again he shouted and knocked on the door before forcing it open against the resistance of the water. Roy and Wofford were sharing this cabin, he recalled as he stepped in. Under a dim emergency light he could see that the cabin was empty like the first, though both beds looked as if they had been slept in.

As the frigid water stung his legs with the pain of a

thousand needles, Gunn satisfied himself that the survey crew had made it above decks. Only the cabin of the fishing boat's captain was unchecked, but the water was chest high to reach it. Foregoing the opportunity to acquire hypothermia, Gunn turned and made his way up to the main deck as a third lifeboat was lowered into the water. Scanning what was now just a handful of crewmen left on deck, he saw no sign of the oil survey team. There was only one conclusion to make, he thought with relief. They must have made it off on the first two lifeboats.

IVAN POPOVICH was asleep, buried in his bunk, lost in a dream that he was fly-fishing on the Lena River when a deep thumping noise jolted him awake. The ruddy-faced pilot of the Listvyanka hydrofoil ferry *Voskhod* slithered into a heavy fur coat, then staggered half asleep out his tiny cabin and climbed up onto the ferry's stern deck.

He immediately came face-to-face with a pair of bright floodlights that seared his eyes, while a loud thumping from the blinding force sent a blast of cold air swirling about his body. The lights rose slowly off the deck, hovered for a moment, then turned and vanished. As the echo of the helicopter's rotors quickly receded into the night air, Popovich rubbed his eyes to vanquish the parade of spots dancing before his retinas. Reopening his eyes, he was surprised to see a man standing before him. He was tall and dark-haired, with white teeth that were exposed in a friendly smile.

In a calm voice, the stranger said, "Good evening. Mind if I borrow your boat?"

THE HIGH-SPEED ferry screamed across the bay, riding up on its twin forward hydrofoil blades for the brief journey to the *Vereshchagin*. Popovich charged the ferry directly toward the bow of the sinking ship, then deftly spun about as he killed the throttle, idling just a few feet off the research vessel's prow. Pitt stood at the stern rail of the ferry, looking up at the foundering gray ship. The vessel was grotesquely tilted back on its stern, her bow pointing toward the sky at a twenty-degree angle. The flooded ship was in a precarious state, liable to slip under the surface or turn turtle at any moment.

A metallic clanking suddenly erupted from overhead as the ship's anchor chain was played out through the hawsehole. A thirty-foot length of the heavy chain rattled across the deck and over the side, followed by a rope line and float to mark where the anchor line had been cut. As the last link dropped beneath the surface, Pitt could detect the ship's bow rise up several feet from the reduced tension and weight of the released anchor line.

"Towline away," came a shout from above.

Looking up, Pitt saw the reassuring sight of Giordino and Gunn standing near the bow rail. A second later, they heaved a heavy rope line over the side and played it out to the water's edge.

Popovich was on it instantly. The veteran ferry pilot

promptly backed his boat toward the dangling line until Pitt could manhandle the looped end aboard. Quickly securing the line around a capstan, Pitt jumped to his feet and gave Popovich the thumbs-up sign.

"Towline secured. Take us away, Ivan," he yelled.

Popovich threw the diesel engines in gear and idled forward until the towline became taut, then he gently applied more throttle. As the ferry's propellers thrashed at the water, Popovich wasted no time being cautious and smoothly pushed the throttles to FULL.

Standing on the stern, Pitt heard the twin engines whine as their revolutions peaked. The water churned in a froth as the props dug into the water, but no sense of forward momentum could be felt. It was akin to a gnat pulling an elephant, Pitt knew, but this gnat had a nasty bite. The ferry was capable of cruising at thirty-two knots, and its twin 1,000-horsepower motors produced a blasting force of torque.

Nobody felt the first movement, but inch by inch, then foot by foot, the *Vereshchagin* began to creep forward. Giordino and Gunn watched from the bridge with the captain and a handful of crewmen, holding their breath as they edged toward the village. Popovich wasted no effort, taking the shortest path to shore, which led to the heart of Listvyanka.

The two vessels had crept a half mile when a succession of creaks and groans began echoing from the bowels of the *Vereshchagin*. A battle waged between the flooded aft and the buoyant bow of the ship for control of the vessel, a fight that tested the structural integrity of the aged ship. Pitt stood tensely near the towline watching the gray ship shudder, knowing he would have to quickly release the rope if the *Vereshchagin* plunged beneath the waves, lest the ferryboat be dragged along with her.

The minutes seemed to slow to hours as the *Vereshchagin* crawled closer to shore, its stern sinking lower and lower under the lake surface. Another metallic groan rumbled from deep within the ship and the whole vessel shuddered. With agonizing slowness, the vessel inched closer, a warm yellow glow now bathing it from the village lights. Popovich ran the shallow-draft ferry directly toward a small rocky beach beside the damaged marina docks. To those watching, it looked as if he was trying to drive his ferry aground, yet everybody prayed he would keep coming. With the roar of his motors echoing off the town's buildings, Popovich kept charging forward until, just a few yards from shore, a muffled grinding sound affirmed that the *Vereshchagin*'s hull had finally run aground.

In the hydrofoil ferry's cabin, Popovich felt rather than heard the grounding of the research vessel and quickly shut down his boat's overheated engines. A deathly still enveloped both vessels as the echo from the dying motors fell away. Then a loud cheer burst forth, first from the ship's crew who had landed the lifeboats ashore nearby, then from a crowded throng of villagers watching along the beachfront, and, finally, from the remaining men aboard the *Vereshchagin*, all applauding the heroic efforts of Pitt and Popovich. Popovich let go two blasts from an air horn in acknowledgment, then walked to the ferry's stern and waved toward the men in the *Vereshchagin*'s bridge.

"My compliments, Captain. Your skill at the helm was as artistic as Rachmaninoff on the piano," Pitt said.

"I couldn't bear the thought of seeing my old ship go down," Popovich replied, staring at the *Vereshchagin* nostalgically. "I started out scrubbing decks on that babushka," he grinned. "Captain Kharitonov is also an old friend. I would hate to see him get in trouble with the state."

"Thanks to you, the *Vereshchagin* will sail the waters of Baikal again. I trust that Captain Kharitonov will be in command when she does."

"I pray so as well. He told me over the radio that it was an act of sabotage. Perhaps it was one of these environmental groups. They act like they own Baikal."

For the first time, Pitt considered the thought. Sabotage it appeared to be, but by whom? And for what purpose? Perhaps Sarghov would know the answer.

In Listvyanka, a flurry of activity roused the town in the late hour as the locals rushed to offer assistance following the near tragedy. Several small fishing boats acted as shuttles, running crew members to shore and back, while others assisted in tying up the grounded ship for safety. An adjacent fish-packing plant, its floors still damp from minor flooding only hours earlier, was opened up for the crew and scientists to gather and rest. Coffee and vodka were served with zeal by the local fishing wives, accompanied by fresh smoked *omul* to those with a late-night appetite.

Pitt and Popovich were welcomed with a cheer and applause as they entered the warehouse. Captain Kharitonov gratefully thanked both men, then, with uncharacteristic emotion, threw a bear hug around his old friend Popovich in appreciation.

"You saved the *Vereshchagin*. I am most grateful, comrade."

"I am glad to have been of help. It was Mr. Pitt who wisely recognized the worth of utilizing my ferry, however."

"I just hope next time I won't need to call on you in the middle of the night, Ivan." Pitt smiled, glancing down at the bedroom slippers Popovich still wore on his feet. Turning to Captain Kharitonov, Pitt asked, "Has all the crew been accounted for?"

An unsettled look crossed the captain's face. "The bridge watchman Anatoly has not been seen. And Dr. Sarghov is also missing. I had hoped he might be with you."

"Alexander? No, he was not with us. I haven't seen him since we turned in after dinner."

"He was not aboard any of the lifeboats," Kharitonov replied.

A subdued-looking Giordino and Gunn approached Pitt with their heads hung down.

"That's not all who's missing," Giordino said, over-hearing the conversation. "The entire oil survey team that we rescued has vanished. Not a one made it into any of the lifeboats, and they were not in their cabins."

"I was able to check all of their cabins but the fisherman's," Gunn added with a nod.

"No one saw them leave the ship?" Pitt asked.

"No," Giordino said, shaking his head in disbelief. "Gone without a trace. It's as if they never existed."

~ 6 ~

WHEN THE SUN CRAWLED UP the southeast horizon several hours later, the precarious state of the *Vereshchagin* became clearly apparent in the dawn's light. The engine room, stern hold, and lower-berth cabins were completely submerged, while water sloshed over nearly a third of the main deck. Just how many more minutes the ship would have stayed afloat had she not been towed ashore was a game of pure conjecture, but the answer was obvious to all: Not very long.

Standing near the remains of a tourist kiosk that was leveled by the seiche wave, Pitt and Captain Kharitonov surveyed the grounded research ship. Off her stern, Pitt watched as a pair of shiny black nerpa popped to the surface and swam over the stern rail. Small doe-eyed seals that inhabit the lake, they floated lazily about the flooded stern deck before vanishing under the water in search of food. As Pitt waited for the nerpa to resurface, he gazed at the ship's waterline, noting a small smudge of red paint amidships that had rubbed off a dock or small boat.

"A salvage repair crew from Irkutsk will not arrive until tomorrow," Kharitonov said with a grim expression. "I will have the crew activate the portable pumps, though I suppose there is little purpose until we can determine the exact cause of the damage."

"More pressing is the disappearance of Alexander and the oil survey team," Pitt replied. "Since they have not been found ashore, we must assume they didn't make it out alive. The flooded portion of the ship must be searched for their remains."

The captain nodded with reluctant acceptance. "Yes, we must locate my friend Alexander. I am afraid we will have to wait for a police dive team to give us the answer."

"I don't think you'll have to wait that long, Captain," Pitt said, nodding toward an approaching figure.

Fifty yards away, Al Giordino marched along the waterfront toward the two men, toting a red-handled pair of bolt cutters over his shoulder.

"Found these at a garage sale in town," Giordino said, hoisting the bolt cutters off his shoulder. The long handles stretched half his height from the ground to his waist.

"Should allow us access to the verboten portions of the ship," Pitt said.

"You? You will investigate the damage?" Kharitonov asked, surprised at the Americans' initiative.

"We need to find out if Alexander and the others are

still aboard," Giordino said with a stern look.

"Whoever tried to sink your vessel may have had an interest in halting our research project," Pitt added. "If so, I'd like to find out why. Our dive gear is stowed in the forward hold, so we have access to all of our equipment."

"It may not be safe," Kharitonov cautioned.

"The only difficult part will be to convince Al to dive before breakfast," Pitt said, trying to lighten the morbid task at hand.

"I have it on good authority that the local IHOP is having an all-you-can-eat special on sturgeon pancakes," Giordino replied with a raised brow.

"We'll just have to hope they don't run out."

Gunn joined Pitt and Giordino as they motored up to the grounded ship in a borrowed Zodiac. Climbing the sloped deck to the forward hold, Gunn lent a hand as the two men pulled on black dry suits and weight belts, then hooked up the lightweight rebreather systems. Before they pulled on their faceplates, Gunn pointed a finger up toward the deckhead.

"I'm going to check the computers up in the bridge and get an update on regional seismic activity. Don't run off with any mermaids without me," he said.

"They'd be too blue to swim in this frigid water anyway," Giordino grunted.

Foregoing fins, the two men trudged down the deck in the rubber-soled feet of their dry suits and waded into the water. When the water level reached his shoulders, Pitt reached up and flicked on a small light strapped to his head, then ducked underwater. A starboard side stairwell was just a few feet ahead and Pitt walked toward it like Frankenstein's monster, plodding slowly against the water's resistance. A bouncing beam of light to his rear told him Giordino was following just a few feet behind.

Dropping down the stairs in a series of hops, Pitt passed the lower cabin level and continued down to the orlop deck and engine room. Distancing himself from the surface daylight, a cloud of darkness quickly enshrouded him. The water itself was as clear as a swimming pool, though, and Pitt's small headlight cut a bright white path through the gloom. With negative buoyancy, it was easier to walk than swim and he moon-hopped his way to the starboard engine-room hatchway. As the chief engineer had reported, the heavy steel door was sealed closed. An old, rusty chain was wrapped around the latch and fastened to the bulkhead, locking the hatch shut. Pitt noted that a gold-colored padlock, which secured the chain, appeared to be new.

Pitt watched the glow from Giordino's light illuminate the hatch, then the snips from the bolt cutter slipped in front of him and grasped a link of chain near the padlock. Pitt turned and watched as Giordino cut the link as if cracking a walnut, the Italian's thick arms easily brandishing the cutter. As it sliced through the second half of the link, Pitt unwound the chain and pulled open the hatch, then stepped inside.

Though the *Vereshchagin* was more than thirty years

old, the engine room was neat and spotless, the hallmark of a meticulous chief engineer. The ship's large diesel generator occupied most of the room, centered in the middle of the bay. Pitt slowly circled the bay, searching for obvious signs of damage to the deck and bulkheads, as well as the engine itself, but none was evident. Only a large steel-grated footplate was out of place, pulled up from the rear deck and left leaning against a tool bin. Peering inside, Pitt recognized it as an opening to the bilge. A four-foot drop led to a crawl space that ran under the enclosed deck. At its base was the curved steel plate of the ship's hull.

Lowering himself into the hole, Pitt dropped to the hull plate and knelt down, examining the compartment toward the stern. As far as his light would shine, the hull plates appeared smooth and intact. Spinning slowly around, he backed into a metal object as Giordino's light-dispensing head poked into the compartment. Under the beam of Giordino's spotlight, Pitt noticed a thick pipe running forward from the object at his back. Turning to examine the protrusion, he noted Giordino was nodding his head up and down in affirmation.

The object was a squat valve that rose a foot above the trailing pipe. Adjacent to it was a small red placard that proclaimed in bold white letters PRE-DOSTEREZHENIYE!, which Pitt could only assume meant "Caution!" Pitt placed his gloved hands on the valve and twisted it counterclockwise. The valve wouldn't budge. He then reversed pressure and tried turning it clockwise. The valve turned freely under a light touch until Pitt pushed it to its stops. He glanced at Giordino, who nodded back with a knowing look. It was as simple as that. The valve opened the ship's sea cock, which would flood the bilge—and, ultimately, the entire ship—when opened at sea. Somebody had entered the engine room, opened the sea cock, disabled the bilge pumps, and then sealed off access to the bay. A quick and easy way to sink a ship in the middle of the night.

Pitt swam out of the bilge compartment and crossed the engine room. On the opposite side, he found an identical grated floor plate, this one properly positioned in the deck. Yanking the grate off, he climbed down and inspected the portside sea cock, finding it too had been turned to the open position. Closing the valve, he reached for the open hand of Giordino, who helped yank him out of the compartment and onto the engine-room deck.

Half of their objective was complete. They had accessed the engine room and determined the cause of the flooding. But there was still the question of Sarghov, Anatoly, and the missing oil survey team. Glancing at his watch, Pitt noted that they had been submerged for nearly thirty minutes. Though they had plenty of air and bottom time left, the cold water was beginning to sap at his bones, despite the insulating dry suit. In his younger days, he would dive nearly oblivious to the cold, but Father Time was offering yet another reminder that he was no longer a kid.

Shaking off the thought, he led Giordino out of the room, then quickly checked the other flooded compartments around the engine bay. Finding nothing out of sorts, they ascended the stairwell a level to the lower cabin berths. The passageway led amidships then turned fore and aft, with cabins on either side of the hall that extended to the ship's beam.

With hand gestures, Pitt directed Giordino to check the portside cabins while he searched the starboard berths. Moving aft, he felt like a prowler as he entered the first cabin, which he knew to be Sarghov's. Despite being completely submerged, Pitt was surprised to find that the contents of the room had remained largely in place. Only a few sheaves of typewritten papers and sections of a local newspaper drifted lazily about the flooded cabin. Pitt saw a laptop computer sitting open on a desk, its screen long since shorted out from the immersion. A foul-weather jacket, which Sarghov had with him at dinner, was draped over the desk chair. Peeking into the small cabin closet, Pitt found an assortment of Sarghov's shirts and pants hanging neatly on a rack. It was not the reflection of a man who had planned to depart the ship, Pitt observed.

Exiting Sarghov's cabin, he quickly searched the next three cabins before reaching the final starboard berth. It was the one cabin Gunn had been unable to reach when he searched for the oil survey team. Across the passageway, Pitt saw the flickering light from Giordino, who had moved ahead of him and was searching the last port cabin.

Pitt turned the latch and leaned his body against the door to force it open against the invisible force of the water. Like the other cabins he searched, its interior appeared orderly, with no obvious disruptions from the flooding. Only, from the doorway, Pitt could see that there was something different about this cabin. It still contained its occupant.

In the restrictive light, it might have been a duffel bag or a couple of pillows lying on the bunk, but Pitt had a feeling otherwise. Taking a step closer, he could see it was a man lying on the bunk, a pale and very dead man at that.

Pitt slowly approached the prone figure and cautiously leaned over the body, illuminating the corpse with the beam from his spotlight. The open eyes of the surly fishing boat captain stared up at him without blinking, a confused look permanently etched upon the dead man's face. The old fisherman was clad in a T-shirt, and his legs were tucked snugly under the covers. The tight blanket had kept him from floating off the bunk until the air in his lungs had slowly purged.

Shining his light closely at the fisherman's head, Pitt rubbed a finger across the man's hairline. Two inches above his ear, a slight indentation creased the side of his head. Though the skin had not broken, it was obvious that a heavy blow had cracked the man's skull. Pitt morbidly wondered whether the old fisherman had been done in by the blow itself or had drowned while unconscious when the cabin flooded.

As Giordino's light suddenly appeared in the

doorway, Pitt took a careful look around the floor of the bunk. The carpeted deck was bare. He saw no porcelain pitchers, lead paperweights, or bottles of vodka that could have fallen off a shelf and struck the man by accident. The entire room was bare, a spare cabin given to the fisherman who brought no belongings of his own.

Pitt took another look at the old man and knew his initial instincts were right. From the first the minute he saw him, Pitt knew the old fisherman had not died by accident. He had been murdered.

~ 7 ~

IT'S GONE," GUNN SPAT, HIS face flushed with anger. "Someone systematically yanked out our database hardware and disappeared with it. All of our data collection points, everything we've gathered in the last two weeks, it's all gone."

Gunn continued to fume as he helped Pitt and Giordino out of their dry suits beneath the bridge.

"What about backups, Rudi?" Pitt asked.

"That's right. As a good computer geek, I know you save everything on backup disks, probably in triplicate," Giordino admonished as he hung up his dry suit on a hook.

"Our rack of backup DVDs is missing, too," Gunn cried. "Somebody had an idea of what to take."

"Our buddy Sarghov?" Giordino asked.

"I don't think so," Pitt replied. "His cabin didn't have the look of an impending escape artist."

"I don't understand. The research data would be of value only to the scientific community. We've shared everything with our Russian counterparts. Who would want to steal the information?" Gunn asked, his anguish slowly cooling.

"Perhaps the intent was not to steal the data. Perhaps they just didn't want us to discover something in the data," Pitt reflected.

"Could be," Giordino agreed. "Rudi, that means your beloved computer is probably at the bottom of Lake Baikal snagging lures about now."

"Is that supposed to be a consolation?" he muttered.

"Don't feel bad. You still made out better than the old fisherman."

"True. He did lose his boat," Gunn said.

"He lost more than that," Pitt replied, then told Gunn of the discovery in the cabin.

"But why murder an old man?" Gunn gasped, shaking his head in disbelief. "And what of the others? Were they abducted? Or did they leave willingly, after killing the fisherman and destroying our scientific data?"

The same questions percolated through Pitt's mind, only there were no answers.

BY MIDDAY, an overhead city utility line was tapped from shore and wired to the *Vereshchagin*, providing electrical power to the grounded ship and activating

144

the bilge pumps that had been disabled. Auxiliary water pumps were deployed on the aft deck, helping pump dry the flooded compartments under the whine of their attached generators. Slowly but surely, the submerged stern began to creep out of the water at a pace far too sluggish for the few remaining crew members watching from shore.

Around Listvyanka, residents continued the cleanup from the flood-ravaged waters. The town's celebrated open-air fish market was quickly pieced back together, with several vendors already offering an aromatic assortment of fresh-smoked fish. The sounds of sawing and hammering filled the air as a row of tourist kiosks, taking the brunt of the wave's carnage, were already being rebuilt.

Word gradually filtered in about other destruction around the lake caused by the quake and wave. Extensive property damage had occurred along the southern shores of the lake, but remarkably no loss of life was reported. The Baikalsk paper mill, a landmark facility on the south coast, suffered the most costly damage, its operations forced to close for several weeks while debris was cleared and its flooded structures restored. At the opposite end of the lake, there were reports that the earthquake had severely damaged the Taishet–Nakhodka oil pipeline that skirted the northern shore. Ecologists from the Limnological Institute were already en route to assess the potential environmental damage should an oil spill approach the lake.

Shortly after lunch, Listvyanka's police chief

boarded the *Vereshchagin,* accompanied by two detectives from Irkutsk. The police authorities climbed up to the ship's bridge, where they greeted Captain Kharitonov in a formal manner. The Listvyanka chief, a slovenly man in an ill-fitting uniform, dismissed with a glance the three Americans who sat reconfiguring their computer equipment on the opposite side of the bridge. A self-important bureaucrat impressed with his own power, the chief enjoyed the perquisites, if not the actual work, required of the job. As Kharitonov relayed the missing crewmen and the discovery of the dead fisherman in the flooded cabin below, a flash of anger crossed the chief's face. The missing persons and attempted sinking of the *Vereshchagin* might be explained away as an accident, but a dead body complicated matters. A potential murder would mean extra paperwork and state officials looking over his shoulder. In Listvyanka, the occasional stolen bicycle or barroom brawl was the extent of his normal criminal dealings, and that was the way he preferred it.

"Nonsense," he retorted in a gravelly voice. "I knew Belikov well. He was a drunken old fisherman. Drank too much vodka and passed out like an old goat. An unfortunate accident," he casually explained away.

"Then what about the disappearance of the two crewmen and the survey team that was rescued with the fisherman, as well as the attempted sinking of my ship?" Captain Kharitonov added with rising anger.

"Ah yes," the police chief replied, "the crew members who opened the sea cocks by mistake. Ashamed of their mechanical error, they have probably fled in embarrassment. They will turn up eventually at one of our fine drinking houses," he said knowingly. Realizing that the two Irkutsk men did not appear to be buying his rationale, he continued. "It will, of course, be necessary to interview the crew and passengers for an official accounting of the incident."

Pitt turned from the egotistical police chief and studied the two lawmen at his side. The detectives from the Irkutsk City Police Criminal Investigation Division were clearly not cut from the same cloth. They were hardened men who wore suits rather than uniforms and carried concealed weapons. No ordinary beat cops, they had an air of quiet confidence that suggested experience and training derived from someplace other than the local police academy. When the three men began a quick round of inquiries aboard ship, Pitt curiously noted that the Irkutsk men seemed more interested in Sarghov's absence than the missing survey team or the dead fisherman.

"Who says Boris Badenov isn't alive and well?" Giordino muttered under his breath after a brief interrogation.

When the interviews were completed, the lawmen returned to the bridge, where the police chief gave Captain Kharitonov a last stern admonition, for effect. The *Vereshchagin*'s captain glumly announced that at the direction of the Listvyanka police, all crew members would be required to return to the ship at once, where they were to remain in confinement until the completion of the investigation.

"They could have at least let us make a beer run first," Giordino moaned.

"I knew I should have stayed in Washington," Gunn grumbled. "Now we're exiled to Siberia."

"Washington is a miserable swamp in the summertime anyway," Pitt countered, admiring the panoramic lake view from the bridge window.

A mile and a half away, he noticed the black freighter that he and Al had flown over the night before. The ship had moved ashore and was docked at an undamaged pier at the far end of town, its stern cargo hold being picked at by a large wharf-side crane.

A pair of binoculars dangled from a hook near the bridge window and Pitt unconsciously pulled them to his eyes while studying the ship. Through the magnified lenses, he saw two large flatbed trucks and a smaller enclosed truck parked on the dock adjacent to the ship. The crane was off-loading items onto the trucks, a little unusual in that Listvyanka was primarily an outgoing port that provided goods to the rest of the lakefront communities. Focusing on one of the flatbed trucks, he could see that it held a strange vertically shaped item on a wooden pallet that was wrapped in a canvas tarp.

"Captain?" he asked of Kharitonov while pointing out the window. "That black freighter. What do you know about her?"

Captain Kharitonov stepped over and squinted in the direction of the ship. "The *Primoski*. A longtime scullion on Lake Baikal. For years, she made a regular run from Listvyanka to Baikalskoye in the north, carrying steel and lumber for a rail spur being built up there. When the work was completed last year, she sat dead at her moorings for several months. Last I heard she was under short-term lease to an oil company. They brought in their own men to sail her, which upset her old crew. I do not know what they're using her for, probably to transport pipeline equipment."

"An oil company," Pitt repeated. "Wouldn't by chance be the Avarga Oil Consortium, would it?"

Kharitonov looked up in thought for a moment. "Yes, now that I think about it, I believe it was. Forgive a tired man for not recalling that earlier. Perhaps they know something of our missing oil survey team. And the whereabouts of Alexander and Anatoly," he added with a cross tone.

The Russian captain reached for the radio and issued a call to the freighter whose name, *Primoski*, was taken from a mountain range on Lake Baikal's western shore. A grunt voice answered almost immediately and replied in short, clipped responses to the captain's questions. As they conversed, Pitt played the binoculars over the old freighter, focusing a long gaze on the freighter's bare stern deck.

"Al, take a look at this."

Giordino ambled over and grabbed the binoculars, studying the freighter carefully. Noting the covered cargo being unloaded, he said, "Being rather secretive with their cargo, wouldn't you say? Though I'm sure if we asked, they'd say it's nothing more than used tractor parts."

"Take a look at the stern deck," Pitt prompted.

"There was a derrick on that deck last night," Giordino observed. "It has disappeared, like our friends."

"Granted it was dark when we flew over the ship, but that derrick looked to be no Tinkertoy piece."

"No, it wasn't something that could be disassembled in short order without an army of mechanical engineers," Giordino said.

"From what I've seen through the glasses, it's a skeleton crew working that ship."

The hearty voice of the captain interrupted as he hung up the radio microphone.

"I'm sorry, gentlemen. The captain of the *Primoski* reports that he has taken on no passengers, has not seen or heard from any oil survey team or, in fact, was even aware of their activities on the lake."

"And I bet he doesn't know who's buried in Grant's tomb, either," Giordino said.

"Did he happen to reveal his ship's manifest?" Pitt asked.

"Why, yes," Kharitonov replied. "They are transporting agricultural equipment and tractor components from Irkutsk to Baikalskoe."

T HE ROOKIE POLICEMAN TASKED WITH ensuring that no one left the ship quickly grew bored with his assignment. Pacing the shore tirelessly a few yards from where the *Vereshchagin*'s bow had ground into the lake bed, he had alertly monitored the vessel as the sun went down. But as the evening hour waned without event, his attention began to wander. Loud thumping noises from a bar up the street gradually seized his senses and it wasn't long before he had swiveled around to face the bar's entrance, hoping to catch sight of an attractive tourist or college coed visiting from Irkutsk.

Sufficiently distracted, he had almost no chance of spotting two men dressed in black who quietly slid a small Zodiac over the *Vereshchagin*'s stern rail, then silently dropped themselves into the rubber boat.

Pitt and Giordino eased the Zodiac away from the *Vereshchagin*, careful to keep the research ship between them and the shore guard.

"A couple of nice friendly drinking establishments are just a short paddle away, and you want to take us on a fishing expedition," Giordino whispered.

"Overpriced tourist traps that hawk warm beer and stale pretzels," Pitt countered.

"Alas, a warm beer is still better than no beer," he replied poetically.

Though they quickly melted into the dark night, Pitt had them row almost a mile from shore before pulling on the starter rope to the boat's 25-horsepower outboard motor. The small engine quickly coughed to life, and Pitt turned the boat parallel to shore as they putted forward at slow speed. Once the boat was moving, Giordino lifted a three-foot-long sonar towfish from the floorboard and slipped it over the side, feeding it out to nearly the full length of its hundred-meter electronic tow cable. Securing the line to the gunwale, he flipped open a laptop computer and initiated the side-scan sonar's operating software. Within minutes, a yellow-tinted image of the lake bed began scrolling down the screen.

"The picture show has started," Giordino announced, "featuring an undulating sandy bottom one hundred seventy feet deep."

Pitt continued running the boat parallel to shore until he was even with the black freighter. He held his course for another quarter mile before turning the Zodiac around and running back in the opposite direction, a few dozen meters farther into the lake.

"The *Primorski* looked to be parked in this neighborhood when we flew over her last night," Pitt said, waving an arm toward the southeast. His eyes turned and studied the landmarks on shore to the north, which he tried to recall sighting from the helicopter.

Giordino nodded. "I agree, we should be in the ballpark."

Pitt pulled a compass from his pocket and took a

heading, then set it on the bench in front of him. Tracking the bearing with the occasional flash of a penlight, he held a steady course until he passed a half mile in the other direction, then turned and back-tracked again farther to the south. For the next hour, they continued the search, moving farther offshore as Giordino monitored the bottom contours on the laptop computer.

Pitt turned his eyes to shore, preparing to turn at the end of an imaginary lane when Giordino said, "Got something."

Pitt held his course, leaning forward to examine the image on the laptop. A dark linear object began scrolling down the screen, followed by another thin line that angled toward it. The image slowly evolved into a large A shape that had grown a few additional cross-members.

"Length is about forty feet," Giordino said. "Sure looks like the structure we saw sitting on the poop deck of the *Primorski* last night. Shame on them for littering the lake."

"Shame on them, indeed," Pitt replied, staring off toward the black freighter. "The question is, my dear Watson, why?"

When Pitt leaned over and shut off the outboard motor, Giordino knew they were going to seek the answer. Something had bothered Pitt about the black freighter the first time he saw it. Finding out it was leased by the Avarga Oil Consortium had just sealed the deal. He had little doubt that there must be some connection to the ship and the disappearance of Sarghov and the oil survey team. As he studied the ship from afar, Giordino quickly pulled in the sonar fish and closed the laptop computer, then retrieved the oars for the rowing ahead of them.

The *Primorski* sat dark and quiet at its still berth near the end of the village waterfront. The large trucks were still parked on the adjacent pier, the two flatbed rigs loaded with their concealed cargo. A tall chain-link fence secured the dock from passing villagers and was enforced by a pair of security guards lounging in a hut at the entrance. Around the trucks, a couple of men milled about studying a map splayed across one of the fenders, though the ship itself appeared devoid of life.

Pitt and Giordino approached the ship's stern silently, drifting slowly under the shadow of its high fantail. Pitt reached up and grabbed the freighter's stern mooring line, which ran down to the water, and used it to pull them alongside the dock. As Giordino tied a line around a splintered pylon, Pitt climbed from the Zodiac and crept onto the wooden dock.

The trucks were parked at the opposite end near the ship's bow, but Pitt could still hear the voices of the men wafting across the empty pier. Spotting a pair of rusty oil drums, he crept up and kneeled behind them near the dock's edge. A second later, Giordino silently appeared behind him.

"Empty as a church on Monday," Giordino whispered, eyeing the ghostly quiet ship.

"Yes, a little too peaceful."

Pitt peered around the drums and spied a gangway at the far end that ran up to the ship's forward hold. He then studied the freighter's side deck railing, which stood eight feet above the dock.

"Gangplank might be too grand an entrance," he whispered to Giordino. "I think we can step over from these," he said, pointing to the drums.

Pitt gingerly rolled one of the drums to the edge of the dock, then climbed on top. Bending his knees, he sprang off the drum and across three feet of water, reaching out and grabbing hold of the ship's lower side railing. He hung there for a second before swinging his body to the side, using the momentum to slip himself through the railing and onto the deck. It was a harder jump for the shorter Giordino, who nearly missed the rail and hung by one hand for a moment until Pitt jerked him aboard.

"Next time, I take the elevator," he muttered.

Catching their breath, they hung to the shadows and examined the silent ship. The freighter was small by oceangoing standards, stretching just over two hundred thirty feet. She was built of the classic cargo ship design, with a central superstructure surrounded by open deck fore and aft. Though her hull was steel, her decks were made of teak and reeked of oil, diesel fuel, and a candy store assortment of chemicals spilled and absorbed into the wood fibers over four decades of use. Pitt surveyed the stern deck, which was dotted with a handful of metal containers congregated near a single hold. Moving silently across the deck, he and Giordino crept toward the shadow of one of the containers, where they stopped and peered into the open stern hold.

The deep bay was stacked at either end with bundles of small-diameter iron pipe. The center of the hold was empty, but even in the darkness, the scarred markings where the feet of the mystery trestle had recently stood was etched into the hold's decking. More intriguing was a six-foot-diameter deck cap that sealed an access hole through the deck at the exact center of the footing markers.

"Looks like a string hole for a North Sea drill ship," Pitt whispered.

"And the drill pipe to go with it," Giordino replied. "But this sure ain't no drill ship."

It was a salient point. A drill ship contains the pipe and storage apparatus to drill into the earth for petroleum and collect the liquid aboard. The old freighter might have been able to set drill pipe, but obviously wasn't capable of collecting a drop of oil, if that was indeed the intended goal.

Pitt didn't stay to contemplate the point but moved quickly toward the portside passageway. Reaching the corner edge, he stopped and pressed himself against the bulkhead then peeked around the corner. There was still no sight of any shipboard inhabitants. Moving forward slowly with Giordino on his heels, he breathed easier now that they were out of sight of the dock.

They crept forward until reaching a cross-passageway that bisected the superstructure from beam to beam. A lone overhead light illuminated the empty passageway in a dull yellow glow. Somewhere in the distance, an electrical generator hummed like a swarm of cicadas. Pitt walked underneath the light and tugged his sweater down over his right hand, then reached up and unscrewed the bulb until the saffron glow was extinguished. Shielded from the dock lights, the passageway fell nearly pitch-black.

Standing at the corner of the crossways, the latch to a cabin door suddenly clicked behind them. Both men quickly turned into the side passage, moving out of sight of the opening door. A dimly illuminated open compartment beckoned on Pitt's left and he stepped into it, followed by Giordino, who closed the door behind them.

As they stood by the door listening for footsteps, their eyes scanned the room. They stood in the ship's formal mess, which doubled as a conference room. The bay was a plush departure from the rest of the shabby freighter. An ornate Persian carpet buoyed a polished mahogany table that stretched across the room, surrounded by rich leather-backed chairs. Thick wallpaper, a smattering of tasteful artwork, and a few artificial plants made it resemble the lobby of the Waldorf-Astoria. At the opposite end, a set of double doors led to the ship's galley. On the bulkhead next to Pitt, a large video screen was mounted at eye level to accept satellite video feeds.

"Nice atmosphere to chow down fish soup and borscht," Giordino muttered.

Pitt ignored the comment as he stepped closer to a series of maps pinned to one wall. They were computer generated, showing enlarged sections of Lake Baikal. At various locations around the lake, red concentric circles had been drawn in by hand. A map of the northern fringe of the lake showed a thick concentration of the circles, some overlapping the shore where an oil pipeline was depicted running from west to east.

"Target drill sites?" Giordino asked.

"Probably. Not going to make the Earth First! crowd too happy," Pitt replied.

Giordino listened at the door as the outside footsteps descended a nearby stairwell. When the footfalls faded away, he cracked the door slightly and peeked into the now-empty passageway.

"No one about. And no sign of any passengers aboard."

"It's the shore boat I want to get a look at," Pitt whispered.

Inching the door open, they crept into the side hall and back to the portside passageway. Moving forward, the freighter's superstructure quickly gave way to the open forward deck, which encompassed a split pair of recessed holds. Along the port rail near the bow sat a beat-up tender, stowed in a block cradle affixed to the deck. A nearby winch with cables still attached to the tender offered evidence that it had recently been deployed.

"She's in plain sight of the bridge," Giordino said, nodding up toward a fuzzy light that shined from the forward bridge window twenty feet above their heads.

"But only if someone's looking that way," Pitt replied. "I'll zip over and take a quick look."

While Giordino hung to the shadows, Pitt crept low and scurried across the open deck, holding close to the port rail. Lights from the dock and the bridge itself bathed the deck in a dull glow, which cast a faint shadow of Pitt's steps as he moved. Out of the corner of his eye, he caught a glimpse of the trucks on the dock and a handful of men milling about them. Dressed in black pants and sweater, he would be almost invisible to the men at that distance. It was the occupants of the bridge that concerned him most.

Nearly sprinting as he reached the small boat, he ducked around its bow and kneeled in its covering shadow beside the rail. As his heart rate slowed, he listened for sounds of detection, but the freighter remained silent. Only the muffled sounds of activity from the nearby village echoed across the deck. Pitt peered up at the bridge and could see two men through the window talking with each other. Neither paid the slightest attention to the ship's forward deck.

Crouching down, Pitt pulled out his penlight and held it against the hull of the shore boat, then flicked the switch on for just a second. The tiny beam illuminated a battered wood hull that was painted a crimson red. Rubbing his hand along the hull, flakes of the red paint chafed onto his fingers. As Pitt had suspected, it was the same shade of red that had rubbed off against the starboard side of the *Vereshchagin*.

Rising to his feet, he moved toward the tender's bow when something in the interior caught his eye. Dropping his hand to the floorboard, he again flicked on the penlight. The brief flash of light illuminated a worn baseball cap with a red emblem of a charging hog sewn on the front. Pitt recognized the razorback mascot of the University of Arkansas and recalled that it was Jim Wofford's hat. There was no doubt in his mind now that the *Primorski* was involved with the attempted sinking of the *Vereshchagin* and disappearance of the crew.

Replacing the penlight, he stood and glanced at the bridge again. The two figures were still engaged in an animated conversation, paying no attention to the deck below. Pitt moved slowly around the tender's bow, then stopped in his tracks. A sudden warning rang out in his brain, he senses detecting a nearby presence. But it was too late to act. A second later, a halogen flashlight burst on in his face and a screeching Russian cry of *"Ostanovka!"* split the air.

~ 9 ~

UNDER THE GLOW FROM THE dock lights, a man emerged from the shadows and walked to within five feet of Pitt. He was slightly built, with oily black hair that matched the color of his work overalls. He nervously swayed back and forth on the balls of his feet, but there was nothing nervous in the way he held a Yarygin PYa 9mm automatic pistol aimed rock steady at Pitt's chest. The gunman had been sitting quietly in the forecastle behind the capstan, Pitt now realized, where he had a clear view of the gangplank. From that forward position, he had caught sight of Pitt's penlight and had crept over to investigate.

The guard was barely past his teens, and stared at Pitt through darting brown eyes. Professional guard was not his first duty, Pitt surmised, noting the grease-stained fingers of a mechanic wrapped around the handgun. Yet he held the gun perfectly trained on Pitt and there was little doubt he would pull the trigger if pressed.

Pitt found himself in an awkward position, squeezed between the tender and the side rail, with open deck between him and the guard. As the guard pulled a handheld radio to his lips with his left hand, Pitt decided to act. It was either lunge at the guard and risk getting shot in the face or slip over the rail and take a chance in the cold lake water below. Or he could hope that Giordino would appear. But Giordino was fifty feet away and would be in immediate sight of the guard the second he stepped on the forward deck.

As the guard spoke briefly into the transmitter, his eyes remained locked on Pitt. Pitt stood perfectly still, contemplating the penalty for trespassing in Russia and dryly noting that an exile to Siberia wouldn't require any traveling. He then thought of the dead fisherman aboard the *Vereshchagin* and wondered if a Siberian gulag wasn't too rosy an assumption.

He subtly bent his knees while waiting for the radio to squawk back, which would create a slight distraction to the guard. When a deep voice blared back through the handset, Pitt inched his left hand to the side rail and tighten his legs for a springing vault over the side. But that's as far as he got.

The muzzle flash flared with a simultaneous bark from the Yarygin as the gun bucked slightly in the guard's hand. Pitt froze as a baseball-sized chunk of teak splintered off the wood rail inches from his hand and splashed into the water below a moment later.

Pitt made no further movements as a series of shouts erupted on the dock, inspired more from the gunshot than the radio call. Two men stormed up the gangway, each brandishing the same type Yarygin pistol carried by the Russian military that had nearly blown away Pitt's left hand. Pitt immediately recognized the second man as the missing helmsman from the *Vereshchagin*, a humorless icicle named Anatoly. A third man soon emerged from the bridge companionway and approached with an authoritative air. He had long ebony hair and surveyed the scene through a pair of callous brown eyes. Under the dock lights, Pitt could see a long scar running down his left cheek, the tattoo from a youthful knife fight.

"I found this intruder hiding behind the tender," the guard reported.

The man eyed Pitt briefly, then turned to the other two crewmen. "Search the area for accomplices. And no more gunfire. We do not need to attract attention."

The two men from the dock jumped at his words and quickly fanned through the forward deck, searching the shadows. Pitt was led to the center of the deck, where an overhead light illuminated the scene.

"Where is Alexander?" Pitt asked calmly. "He told me to meet him here."

Pitt didn't expect the bluff to work but studied the man in charge for a reaction. A slight arch of the brow was all he offered.

"English?" he finally said without interest. "You would be from the *Vereshchagin*. A pity you have lost your way."

"But I have found those responsible for trying to sink her," Pitt responded.

Under the dim lights, Pitt could see the man's face flush. He checked his anger as Anatoly and the other crewman approached, shaking their heads.

"No companions? Then put him with the other and quietly deposit them over the side where no one will find them," the man hissed.

The guard stepped forward and thrust the barrel of his pistol into Pitt's ribs and nodded toward the port-side passageway. Pitt grudgingly walked toward the shadows where he had left Giordino and turned down the passageway, followed by the guard and two crewmen. Out of the corner of his eye, he saw the scar-faced boss return to the bridge via a side stairwell.

Marching past the crossways, he half expected to see Giordino lunge out of the shadows at his assailants, but his partner was nowhere to be seen. Reaching the stern deck, he was prodded toward one of the rusty cargo containers lining the rail. Acting calm and nonresistant, he waited until one of the crewmen fumbled with a padlock on the container before taking the offensive. The guard still poked him in the ribs with a pistol, standing off balance in the process. In a lightning-quick move, Pitt bumped the muzzle away from his body with a flick of his left elbow. Before the guard realized what was happening, Pitt had swung at him, carrying the full weight of his right fist with the momentum. The roundhouse hammered the guard's chin, coming within a hair of knocking him unconscious. Instead, he staggered backward into the arms of Anatoly as the gun clanked to the deck.

The other crewman was still occupied holding the padlock in his hands, so Pitt gambled and dove for the loose gun. As he hit the deck, his outstretched right hand just snared the Yarygin's polymer grip when a one-hundred-seventy-pound mass landed on his back. With calm callousness, Anatoly had wisely pushed the punch-drunk guard back at Pitt, the dazed man landing in a heap on Pitt's back. As Pitt tried to roll the guard off, he felt the cold steel muzzle of an automatic pistol suddenly pressed into the side of his neck. Pitt knew the order not to shoot would only go so far and dropped his gun to the deck.

Pitt was held at gunpoint on his knees until the padlock was freed and the double doors of the twenty-foot-long container were flung open. Shoved roughly in the back, Pitt staggered into the container, falling against a soft object. Under the dim light he realized that he had fallen against a human form, lying crumpled on the container floor. The body moved, the torso pulling up on an elbow as its hidden face turned to Pitt.

"Dirk . . . it's good of you to drop in," rasped the weary voice of Alexander Sarghov.

WHEN PITT was apprehended on the bow, Giordino silently cursed from the shadows. Without a weapon at hand, his options were limited. He considered charging the gunman from afar, but there was just too much open deck to cross in plain view. Watching the guard fire a warning shot at Pitt dispelled the thought of conspicuous heroics altogether. Then hearing the men from the dock running aboard, he decided to backtrack and skirt through the cross-passageway to the starboard side. Perhaps he could fall in place behind the men boarding the gangplank and make a move on the guard with the approach of the other men.

Moving silently along the bulkhead, he quick-stepped down the port deck and turned into the cross-passageway. Just as he turned the corner, a black-clad figure running from the opposite direction collided head-on with him. In a scene out of a Keystone Kops silent movie, both men bounced off each other like rubber balls and fell flat on their backs. Agile as a cat and quickly shaking off the blow, Giordino sprang to his feet first and lunged at the other man as he scrambled to stand up. Grabbing him by the torso, Giordino slammed the other man headfirst into the bulkhead. A soft clang echoed as the man's skull met the steel wall and his body instantly fell limp in Giordino's arms.

No sooner was the man out cold than the sound of footsteps resonated down the port deck. A glance to the lighted forward deck revealed Pitt being escorted aft. Quickly dragging the unconscious man down the cross-passageway, Giordino ducked back into the conference room. Hoisting the limp body onto the conference table, he noticed that the crewman was his same height and dressed in the same black overalls that the deck guard wore. A quick search turned up no weapons on the man, who was actually the ship's radio operator. Giordino stripped off the overalls and slipped them over his own pants, then pulled on a dark wool fishing cap that the man had been wearing. Satisfied he could in the dark pass as a crewman, he stepped back into the corridor and moved aft, completely unsure of his next move.

SARGHOV'S CLOTHES were rumpled, his hair askew, and his left brow glistened a midnight blue. Though his face was weary, his eyes sparkled with life as he recognized Pitt.

"Alexander, how bad are you hurt?" Pitt asked, helping Sarghov to a sitting position.

"I'm all right," he replied in a stronger voice. "They just roughed me up a little after I laid one of their men down." A slight smile of satisfaction creased his lips.

Behind them, the double doors of the container slammed shut, casting the interior into complete darkness. The hum of a diesel generator kicked to life as one of the crewmen took the controls of a nearby shipboard crane. The operator swung the boom across the deck, jerking it to a stop above the container as its dangling steel hook swung wildly about. Releasing the cable, he let the hook drop until it landed on the container with a metallic clang, then killed the controls.

Inside, Pitt turned on his penlight for illumination as Sarghov regained his strength.

"They tried to sink the *Vereshchagin*," the Russian said. "Pray tell, your presence here indicates they failed?"

"Not by much," Pitt replied. "We were able to tow the ship ashore before she sank in the bay. The oil survey team is missing. Did they come aboard with you?"

"Yes, but we were separated when we came aboard the freighter. I heard a commotion in the passageway outside my cabin and was met with the muzzle of a pistol when I went to investigate. It was the deck officer, Anatoly. He and the woman Tatiana marched us to a waiting tender at gunpoint and brought us here. Their purpose for doing so is a complete mystery," he added, shaking his head.

"That's less important at the moment than how we get out of here," Pitt said, climbing to his feet. Scanning the container, he found it was empty but for a few scattered rags on the floor.

Outside its steel walls, Anatoly collected a pair of looped cable strands and wrapped them around the base of the container. The other crew member, a thin man with greasy hair, climbed atop the container and pulled the cables together, then slid them over the crane hook. The guard who had taken the punch from Pitt staggered back to his feet, retrieving his gun while watching the spectacle from a distance.

Jumping from the container roof, the thin crewman returned to the crane controls in a darkened corner a few yards away. Tapping his fingers on the lift lever, he elevated the boom until the cables went taut, then slowly raised the container off the deck until it swung loosely in the air. With his eyes focused on the dangling container, he failed to notice a figure creep silently across the deck and approach from the side. He additionally failed to see the balled fist that suddenly materialized out of the darkness and struck him below his ear with the kinetic energy of a wrecking ball. Had he not immediately blacked out from the blow to his carotid artery, he would have looked into the face of Al Giordino as he was dragged from the controls like a wet noodle and dumped on the deck.

Giordino had no time to study the controls as he took the man's place. Pulling at a lever with his right hand, he guessed right, and watched as the boom rose, elevating the container a few more inches. Testing the lateral controls with his left hand, he swung the boom amidships a foot or two before reversing directions and swinging the container out over the port side of the ship, the metal box just barely clearing the railing. Giordino held the crane steady for a minute, the container twisting back and forth perilously over the water. As he had hoped, Anatoly and the guard followed the path of the container and stood at the port rail to watch the impending drowning. Though the night temperature was cool, a bead of sweat trickled down Giordino's brow as he calmly waited with his hands on the controls until Anatoly waved at him to drop the boom. Giordino slowly swung the crane a few more feet away from the ship, then waited until the container had swayed to its farthest point in the pendulum, then reversed the controls and jammed the boom back over the stern deck as hard as he could.

The two men at the rail watched with a confused look as the boom swung overhead while the container hung in midair for a split second, then its momentum shifted and the two-ton steel box suddenly came barreling right toward them.

The unsteady guard managed to teeter back on his heels, cursing as the flying container skimmed by just inches from his face. Anatoly was not so lucky. Rather than duck, he tried to sidestep the hurling box in the other direction. But he had too far to jump and took only a short step before the swinging container was on top of him. A gurgled cry from his crushed lungs was the only sound he made as his body was tossed across the deck like a rag doll.

The dazed guard at the rail peered at the crane controls and cursed like a madman, then fell silent as he realized the man operating the boom was not his colleague. As he reached for his gun, Giordino whipped the lateral boom controls back to the right and the crane mechanism began marching again toward the port rail. Giordino ducked as the guard aimed and fired a shot, the bullet whizzing close over his head. Even crouching low, he still kept his hands on the crane controls.

The swinging container had reached its shipside apex and now arced toward the port rail. Stepping into its path to fire his gun, the guard ducked low to let it pass over him. But as the flying container approached the gunman, Giordino yanked down on the elevation controls, lowering the boom to the deck. The container followed suit, plunging the short distance to the deck just ahead of the gunman.

A piercing shriek wailed across the stern as the container struck the deck, then rolled onto one side from the momentum. Careening over, the container clipped the left leg of the guard as he scrambled to get clear. Pinned under the massive container with a smashed leg, the guard howled in agony. Giordino sprinted over and stepped on the man's wrist, grabbing the pistol that fell out of his clenched grip. He then yanked off his borrowed wool cap and jammed it in the man's mouth, temporarily stemming the guard's cries.

"Beware of flying objects," Giordino grunted at the man, who stared back through glassy eyes that cringed with pain.

Taking aim at the padlock, Giordino ripped off two point-blank shots, then tore away the demolished device. Grasping the release lever, he threw open one of the doors, which fell flat to the deck from the tilted container. Pitt and Sarghov tumbled out like a pair of rolled dice, staggering to their feet, rubbing aching body parts.

"Don't tell me, you spent a previous life as a carnival ride operator?" Pitt said with a crooked smile.

"Naw, just practicing my bowling," Giordino replied. "If you boys are able, I suggest we vacate the premises posthaste."

On the forward part of the ship, a thunder of footfalls mixed with loud shouts could be heard storming up the gangplank. Pitt scanned the stern deck, noting the unconscious bodies lying there, before turning his gaze to Sarghov. The beat-up Russian scientist was moving slowly and appeared in no condition to be outrunning anyone that night.

"I'll get the boat. Take Alexander and get off down the stern line," Pitt directed.

Giordino barely nodded a reply when Pitt took off at a sprint toward the starboard rail. Climbing over the rail, he bent his knees and sprang toward the dock. Without a running start, he nearly missed the pier, managing to catch a foot and propel himself forward, landing in a self-cushioning ball on the dock.

More voices yelling aboard the ship, now moving closer following a spray of flashlight beams. Pitt abandoned any attempt at stealth and sprinted back to the Zodiac as a drumbeat of footsteps tailed him down the dock. When he leaped into the small boat, his prayers were answered when the worn outboard motor fired on the first pull of the rope. Gunning the motor, he aimed the Zodiac toward the freighter's stern, charging ahead until the rubber boat's bow bounced off the steel transom.

Pitt cut the throttle and looked up. Directly overhead, Sarghov plunged into view, clinging to the stern rope line with a tenuous grip.

"Let go, Alexander," he urged.

Pitt stood and half caught the heavy Russian as he dropped into the boat with all the finesse of a sack of flour. Above their heads, an automatic handgun suddenly barked, spraying a half dozen shots about the ship and dock. A second later, Giordino appeared on the stern line, quickly lowering himself hand over hand until he dangled a few feet above the boat. As the shout of voices resumed on the deck above them, Giordino dropped silently into the boat.

"Exit stage left," he urged.

Pitt was already gunning the throttle, steering under the ship's stern and around to the port beam before turning into the lake. The small boat quickly planed up on its fiberglass hull, raising the buoyancy tubes above the waterline, which provided an added surge of acceleration. For several seconds, they remained in clear view of the ship and dock and the three men ducked low in the boat to avoid gunfire.

Yet no one fired. Pitt glanced back to see nearly a half dozen men surge to the ship's port rail, but they just stood and watched as the little boat disappeared into the darkness.

"Odd, they went pacifist on us at the last minute," Giordino noted, observing the sight.

"Especially since you already woke up the neighborhood with your exhibition of quick-draw shooting," Pitt agreed.

He made no effort to disguise their course, running a direct path to the *Vereshchagin*. Approaching the research vessel a few minutes later, Pitt motored alongside a lowered stairwell on the starboard beam. On shore, the police rookie suddenly noticed their arrival and shouted for them to stop. Sarghov stood up in the boat and yelled back in Russian. The policeman visibly shrank, then quickly turned and hightailed it into the village.

"I told him to go wake the chief," Sarghov explained. "We're going to need some muscle to search that freighter."

Rudi Gunn, who had nervously paced the deck during their absence, heard the shouts and ran from the bridge as the three men staggered aboard.

"Dr. Sarghov . . . are you all right?" Gunn asked, staring at his swollen face and bloodied clothes.

"I am fine. Please find the captain for me, if you would be so kind."

Pitt shepherded Sarghov to the *Vereshchagin*'s sick bay while Gunn roused the ship's doctor and Captain Kharitonov. Giordino located a bottle of vodka and poured a round of shots while the doctor examined Sarghov.

"That was a close call," the Russian scientist

declared, regaining color and strength once the vodka surged through his bloodstream. "I am indebted to my friends from NUMA," he said, hoisting a second shot of vodka toward the Americans before downing it in a casual gulp.

"To your health," Pitt replied before kicking back his shot.

"Vashe zdorovie!" Sarghov replied before downing his drink.

"Do you know what became of Theresa and the others?" Giordino asked, concern evident on his heavy brow.

"No, we were separated once we boarded the ship. Since it was apparent they were going to kill me, they must have wanted them alive for some reason. I would presume they are still aboard the ship."

"Alexander, you are safe!" bellowed Captain Kharitonov as he barged into the cramped sick bay.

"He has a sprained wrist and a number of contusions," the doctor reported, applying a bandage to a cut on Sarghov's face.

"It is nothing," Sarghov said, waving away the doctor. "Listen, Ian. The Avarga Oil Consortium freighter . . . there is no doubt that they were responsible for attempting to sink your ship. Your crewman Anatoly was working for them, and possibly the woman Tatiana as well."

"Anatoly? I had just hired him on at the beginning of the project when my regular first officer fell ill with severe food poisoning. What treachery!" the captain cursed. "I will call the authorities at once. These hoodlums will not get away with this."

The authorities, in the form of the chief of police and his young assistant, arrived nearly an hour later, accompanied by the two Irkutsk detectives. It had taken that long for the impertinent chief to rise, dress, and enjoy an early breakfast of sausages and coffee before casually making his way to the *Vereshchagin*, retrieving the two detectives from a local inn along the way.

Sarghov retold his tale of abduction, while Pitt and Giordino added their search for the missing derrick and their escape from the freighter. The two Irkutsk men gradually took over the interrogation, asking more probing and intelligent questions. Pitt noted that the two detectives seemed to show an odd deference to the Russian scientist, as well as a hint of familiarity.

"It will be prudent to investigate the freighter with our full security force," the police chief announced with bluster. "Sergei, please round up the Listvyanka auxiliary security forces and have them report immediately to police headquarters."

Nearly another hour passed before the small contingent of local security forces marched toward the freighter's berth, the pompous chief leading the way. The first light of dawn was just breaking, casting a gray pall over a damp mist that floated just above the ground. Pitt and Giordino, with Gunn and Sarghov at their sides, followed the police force through the dock gate, which was now open and unguarded. The dock was completely deserted, and Pitt began to get a sick feeling in his stomach when he realized that all three trucks parked by the ship had now vanished.

The bossy police chief charged up the freighter's gangplank, calling out for the captain, but was met by only the sound of a humming generator. Pitt followed him to the empty bridge, where the ship's log and all other charts and maps were noticeably absent. Slowly and methodically, the police team searched the entire ship, finding an equally purloined and empty vessel. Not a shred of evidence was uncovered as to the ship's intent, nor a person around to tell its tale.

"Talk about abandoning ship," Giordino muttered, shaking his head. "Even the cabins are empty of personal effects. That was one quick getaway."

"Too quick to have been carried out unexpectedly in the short time we were gone. No, they had finished their work and were already sneaking out the door when we stopped by. I'll bet there weren't any personal effects or links to the crew brought aboard in the first place. They planned on walking away from an empty ship."

"With a kidnapped oil survey team," Giordino replied, his mind centered on Theresa. After a long silence, he returned to the bridge, hopeful to find some sort of clue as to where the departed trucks had gone.

Pitt stood on the bridge wing, staring down at the stern deck and its array of empty containers. His mind whirred with puzzlement over the motive for the abductions and the fate of the survey team. The pink glow of the rising sun bathed the ship in a dusky light and illuminated the gouge marks imbedded in the deck where the sunken derrick had stood the night before. Whatever secrets the ship possessed had departed with the crew and cargo that vanished quietly in the night. But the sunken derrick was something they had not been able to hide. The significance was lost on Pitt, but, deep inside, he suspected it was an important clue to a bigger mystery.

PART II

THE ROAD
TO
XANADU

~ 10 ~

CAPTAIN STEVE HOWARD SQUINTED THROUGH a scratched pair of binoculars and scanned the bright aqua blue waters of the Persian Gulf that glistened before him. The waterway was often a bustling hive of freighters, tankers, and warships jockeying for position, particularly around the narrow channel of the Strait of Hormuz. In the late afternoon off Qatar, however, he was glad to see that the shipping traffic had almost vanished. Ahead off his port bow, a large tanker approached, riding low in the water with a fresh load of crude oil in its belly. Off his stern, he noted a small black drill ship trailing a mile or two behind. Tanker traffic was all he was hoping to see and with a slight relief, he lowered the glasses down to the bow of his own ship.

He needed the binoculars to obtain a clear view of his own ship's prow, for the stodgy forepeak stood nearly eight hundred feet away. Looking forward, he noted rippling waves of heat shimmering off the white topside deck of the *Marjan*. The massive supertanker, known as a "Very Large Crude Carrier," was built to transport over two million barrels of oil. Larger than the Chrysler Building, and about as easy to maneuver, the big ship was en route to fill its cavernous holds with Saudi light crude oil pumped from the teeming oil fields of Ghawar.

Passing the Strait of Hormuz had flicked on an unconscious alarm in Howard. Though the American Navy had a visible presence in the gulf, they couldn't blanket every commercial ship that entered the busy waterway. With Iran sitting across the gulf and potential terrorists lurking in a half dozen countries along the Saudi Arabian Peninsula, there was reason to be concerned. Pacing the bridge and scanning the horizon, Howard knew he wouldn't relax until they had taken on their load of crude and reached the deep waters of the Arabian Sea.

Howard's eyes were drawn to a sudden movement on the deck and he adjusted the binoculars until they focused on a wiry man with shaggy blond hair who tore across the deck on a yellow moped. Ducking and weaving around the surface deck's assorted pipes and valves, the daredevil whizzed along at the moped's top speed. Howard tracked him as he rounded a bend and sprinted past a shirtless man stretched out on a lounge chair holding a stopwatch in one hand.

"I see the first mate is still trying to top the track record," Howard said with a grin.

The tanker's executive officer, hunched over a colored navigation chart of the gulf, nodded without looking up.

"I'm sure your record will remain safe for another day, sir," he replied.

Howard laughed to himself. The thirty-man crew of the supertanker was constantly creating ways to stave off boredom during the long transatlantic voyages or the slack periods when oil was being pumped on or off the ship. A rickety moped, used to traverse the enormous deck during inspections, was suddenly seized upon as a competitive instrument of battle. A makeshift oval course was laid out on the deck, complete with jumps and a hairpin turn. One by one, the crew took turns at the course like qualifying drivers for the Indy 500. To the crew's chagrin, the ship's amiable captain had ended up clocking the best time. None had any idea that Howard had raced motocross while growing up in South Carolina.

"Coming up on Dhahran, sir," said the exec, a soft-spoken African American from Houston named Jensen. "Ras Tanura is twenty-five miles ahead. Shall I disengage the auto pilot?"

"Yes, let's go to manual controls and reduce speed at the ten-mile mark. Notify the berthing master that we'll be ready to take tugs in approximately two hours."

Everything about sailing the supertanker had to be done with foresight, especially when it came to stopping the mammoth vessel. With its oil tanks empty and riding high on the water, the tanker was somewhat more nimble, but, to the men on the bridge, it was still like moving a mountain.

Along the western shoreline, the dusty brown desert gave way to the city of Dhahran, a company town, home to the oil conglomerate Saudi Aramco. Steering past the city and its neighboring port of Dammam, the tanker edged toward a thin peninsula that stretched into the gulf from the north. Sprawled across the peninsula was the huge oil facility of Ras Tanura.

Ras Tanura is the Grand Central Station of the Saudi oil industry. More than half of Saudi Arabia's total crude oil exports flow through the government-owned complex, which is linked by a maze of pipelines to the rich oil fields of the interior desert. At the tip of the peninsula, dozens of huge storage tanks stockpile the valuable black liquid next to liquid natural gas tanks and other refined petroleum products awaiting shipment to Asia and the West. Farther up the coast, the largest refinery in the world processes the raw crude oil into a slew of petroleum offshoots. But perhaps the most impressive feature of Ras Tanura is barely visible at all.

On the bridge of the *Marjan*, Howard ignored the tanks and pipelines ashore and focused on a half dozen supertankers lined up in pairs off the peninsula. The ships were moored to a fixed terminal called Sea Island, which stretched beamlike across the water for more than a mile. Like an oasis nourishing a heard of thirsty camels, the Sea Island terminal quenched the empty supertankers with a high-powered flow of crude oil pumped from the storage tanks ashore. Unseen beneath the waves, a network of thirty-inch supply pipes fed the black liquid two miles across the floor of the gulf to the deepwater filling station.

As the *Marjan* crept closer, Howard watched a trio of tugboats align a Greek tanker against the Sea Island before turning toward his own vessel. The *Marjan*'s pilot took control of the supertanker and eased the vessel broadside to an empty berth at the end of the loading terminal, just opposite of the Greek tanker. As they waited for the tugs to push them in, Howard admired the sight of the other seven supertankers parked nearby. All over a thousand feet long, easily exceeding the length of the *Titanic*, they were truly marvels of ship construction. Though he had seen hundreds of tankers in his day and served on several supertankers before the *Marjan*, the sight of a VLCC still filled him with awe.

The dirty white sail of an Arab dhow caught his eye in the distance and he turned toward the peninsula to admire the local sailing vessel. The small boat skirted the coastline, sailing north past the black drill ship that had tailed the *Marjan* earlier and was now positioned near the shoreline.

"Tugs are in position portside, sir," interrupted the voice of the pilot.

Howard simply nodded, and soon the massive ship was pushed into its slot on the Sea Island terminal. A series of large transfer lines began pumping black crude into the ship's empty storage tanks, little by little settling the tanker lower in the water. Secured at the terminal, Howard allowed himself to relax slightly, knowing that his responsibilities were through for at least the next several hours.

IT WAS nearly midnight when Howard awoke from a short nap and stretched his legs with a stroll about the forward deck of the tanker. The crude oil loading was nearly complete, and the *Marjan* would easily meet its three A.M. departure schedule, allowing the next empty supertanker in line to take its turn at the filling depot. The distant blast from a tug's horn told him that a tanker further down the quay had completed its fill-up and was preparing to be pulled away from Sea Island.

Gazing at the lights twinkling along the Saudi Arabian shoreline, Howard was jolted by a sudden banging of the "dolphins" against the tanker's hull. Large cushioned supports mounted along the Sea Island berths, the breasting dolphins supported the lateral force of the ships while being loaded at the terminal. The clanging blows from the dolphins weren't just coming from below, he realized, but echoed all along the terminal. Stepping to the side rail, he leaned his head over and looked down along the loading quay.

Sea Island at night, like the supertankers themselves, was lit up like a Christmas tree. Under the battery of overhead lights, Howard could see that it was the terminal itself that was pulsing back and forth against the sides of the tankers. It didn't make sense, he thought.

The terminal was grounded into the seabed. Any movement ought to come from the ships drifting against the berths. Yet peering down the distant length of the terminal, he could see it waver like a serpent, striking one side of tankers and then the other.

The banging of the bumpers grew louder and louder until they hammered against the ships like thunder. Howard gripped the rail until his knuckles turned white, not comprehending what was happening. Staring in shock, he watched as one after another of the four twenty-four-inch loading arms broke free of the ship, spewing a river of crude oil in all directions. A nearby shout creased the air as Howard spotted a platform engineer clinging for life aboard the swaying terminal.

As far as the eye could see, the steel terminal rocked and swayed like a giant snake, battering itself against the huge ships. Alarm bells rang out as the oil transfer lines were torn away from the other tankers by the rippling force, bathing the sides of the ships in a flowing sea of black. Farther down the quay, a chorus of unseen voices cried for help. Howard peered down to see a pair of men in yellow hard hats sprinting down the terminal, shouting as they ran. Behind them, the lights of the terminal began disappearing in a slow succession. Howard stood unblinking for a second before realizing with horror that the entire Sea Island terminal was sinking beneath their feet.

The clanging of the terminal against the *Marjan* intensified, the mooring dolphins physically mashing the side of the tanker. For the first time, Howard noticed a deep rumble that seemed to emanate from far beneath his feet. The rumble grew in intensity, roaring for several seconds before silencing just as quickly. In its place came the desperate cries of men, running along the terminal.

A tumbling house of cards came to Howard's mind as the footings of the terminal gave way in succession and the mile-long island vanished under the waves in an orderly progression. When he heard the cries of the men in the water, his horror was replaced by a new-found fear for the safety of his ship. Tearing off across the deck, he pulled a handheld radio from his belt and shouted orders to the bridge as he ran.

"Cut the mooring lines! For God's sake, cut the mooring lines," he gasped. A rush of adrenaline surged through his body, the fear pushing him to race across the deck at breakneck speed. He was still a hundred meters from the bridge house when his legs began to throb, but his pace never slowed, even as he hurtled past a river of slippery crude oil that had splashed across the deck.

"Tell . . . the chief . . . engineer . . . we need . . . full power . . . immediately," he rasped over the radio, his lungs burning for oxygen.

Reaching the tanker's stern superstructure, he headed for the nearest stairwell, bypassing an elevator located a few corridors away. Clambering up the eight levels to the bridge, he was heartened to feel the throb of the ship's engines suddenly vibrate beneath his feet.

As he staggered onto the bridge and rushed to the forward window, his worst fears were realized.

In front of the *Marjan*, eight other supertankers lay in paired tandems, divided minutes before by the Sea Island terminal. But now the terminal was gone, plunging toward the Gulf floor ninety feet beneath the surface. The supertankers' mooring lines were still attached, and the force of the sinking terminal was drawing the paired tankers toward one another. In the midnight darkness, Howard could see the lights on the two tankers in front of him meld together, followed by the screeching cry of metal on metal as the sides of the ships scraped together.

"Emergency full astern," Howard barked at his executive officer. "What's the status of the mooring lines?"

"The stern lines are clear," replied Jensen, looking gaunt. "I'm still awaiting word on the bowlines, but it appears that at least two lines are still secure," he added, gazing through binoculars at a pair of taut ropes that stretched from the starboard bow.

"The *Ascona* is drawing onto us," the helmsman said, jerking his head to the right.

Howard followed the motion, eyeing the Greek-flagged ship berthed alongside, a black-and-red supertanker that matched the *Marjan*'s length of three hundred thirty-three meters. Originally moored sixty feet apart, the two ships were slowly moving laterally together as if drawn by a magnet.

The men on the *Marjan*'s bridge stood and stared helplessly, Howard's labored breathing matched by the quickened heartbeats of the others. Beneath their feet, the huge propellers finally began clawing the water in a desperate fury as the tanker's engines were rapidly brought up to high revs by the frantic engineer.

The initial movement astern was imperceptible, then, slowly, the huge ship began to creep backward at a sluggish clip. The momentum slowed for a second as the bow mooring line drew taut, then suddenly the line broke free and the ship resumed its rearward crawl. Along her starboard side, the *Ascona* drew closer. The Korean-built tanker had nearly a full load of crude and rode a dozen feet lower in the water than the *Marjan*. From Howard's perspective, it looked as if he could step right off the side of his ship and onto the deck of the neighboring tanker.

"Starboard twenty," he ordered the helmsman, trying to angle the bow away from the drifting tanker. Howard had managed to back the *Marjan* three hundred feet away from the sunken terminal, but it was not enough to escape the adjacent ship.

The impact was gentler than Howard had expected, not even felt in the wheelhouse. Just an extended low-pitched screech of metal signaled the collision. The *Marjan*'s bow was almost amidships of the *Ascona* when the two ships met, but the rearward motion of Howard's ship had deflected much of the force at impact. For half a minute, the *Marjan*'s bow scraped along the other tanker's port rail, and then suddenly the two ships were clear.

Howard immediately cut his engines and lowered a

pair of lifeboats over the side to search for any dock-workers in the water. Then he gingerly backed his ship another thousand feet away from the melee and watched the carnage.

All ten of the supertankers were damaged. Two of the big ships had locked decks and were so intertwined that it took two days before an army of welders could cut them free. Three of the ships had their double-hulled plates bashed though, leaking thousands of gallons of crude oil freely into the gulf as the ships listed to one side. But the *Marjan* had escaped with minimal damage, none of her tanks compromised in the collision thanks to Howard's fast action. His relief at saving his ship was short-lived, however, when a series of muffled explosions echoed across the gulf waters.

"Sir, it's the refinery," the helmsman noted, pointing toward the western shoreline. An orange glow appeared on the horizon, which grew like the rising sun as a series of additional explosions rocked across the water. Howard and his crew watched the spectacle for hours as the pyre marched along the shoreline. It wasn't long before thick plumes of black smoke mixed with the odor of burned petroleum wafted over the ship.

"How could they do it?" the executive officer blurted. "How could terrorists have gotten in there with explosives? It's one of the most secure facilities in the world."

Howard shook his head in silence. Jensen was right. A private army guarded the whole complex in a tight web of security. It must have been a masterful infiltration to take out the Sea Island terminal as well, he thought, though there were no apparent offshore explosions. Thankfully, his ship and crew were safe, and he intended to keep it that way. Once the search for survivors in the water was completed, Howard moved the tanker several miles out into the gulf, where he circled the big ship slowly until dawn.

By daylight, the full extent of the damage became apparent as emergency response teams from around the region converged on the scene. The Ras Tanura refinery, one of the largest in the world, was a smoldering ruin, nearly completely destroyed by the raging fires. The Sea Island offshore terminal, capable of feeding eighteen supertankers at a time with raw crude oil, had completely vanished beneath the gulf. The nearby tank farm, providing storage for nearly thirty million barrels of petroleum products, was mired in a waist-deep sea of black ooze from dozens of cracked and fractured tanks. Farther into the desert, countless oil supply pipelines were broken in two like twigs, soaking the surrounding sands black with thick pools of crude oil.

Overnight, nearly a third of Saudi Arabia's oil exporting capability was destroyed. Yet a raft of terrorist suicide bombers was not to blame. Around the world, seismologists had already fingered the cause of the destruction. A massive earthquake, measuring 7.3 on the Richter scale, had rattled the east coast of Saudi Arabia. Analysts and pundits alike would lament the happenstance of Mother Nature when the quake's epicenter was computed to be just two miles from Ras Tanura. The shock waves caused by striking at such a critical locale would ultimately ripple far beyond the Persian Gulf, shaking the globe for many months to come.

~ 11 ~

HANG ZHOU DREW A LAST puff from his cheap unfiltered cigarette, then flicked the butt over the rail. He watched in lazy curiosity as the glowing ember flittered to the dirty water below, half expecting the murky surface to ignite in a wall of flames. Heaven knows, there's enough spilled petroleum in the black water to power a small city, he thought as the cigarette fizzled to a harmless demise alongside a belly-up mackerel.

As the dead fish could attest, the dank waters around the Chinese port of Ningbo were anything but hospitable. A flurry of construction activity along the commercial waterfront had helped stir up the polluted waters, already contaminated by the steady stream of leaky containerships, tankers, and tramp freighters that frequented the port. Located in the Yangtze River Delta, not far from Shanghai, Ningbo was rapidly growing into one of China's largest seaports, in part due to its deepwater channel that allowed dockage for giant three-hundred-thousand-ton supertankers.

"Zhou!" barked a Doberman-like voice, whose owner more resembled an overweight bulldog. Zhou turned to see his supervisor, the operations director for Ningbo Container Terminal No. 3, high-stepping down the dock toward him. An unlikable tyrant by the name of Qinglin, he wore a permanent scowl painted on his pudgy face.

"Zhou," he repeated, approaching the longshoreman. "We've had a change in schedule. The *Akagisan Maru*, bound from Singapore, has been delayed due to engine problems. So we're going to allow the *Jasmine Star* to take her berth at dock 3-A. She's due in at seven-thirty. Make sure your crew is standing by to receive her."

"I'll pass the word," Zhou said and nodded.

The containership terminal where they worked operated around the clock. In the nearby waters of the East China Sea, a steady stream of transport ships milled about, waiting their turn at the docks. China's abundant labor pool ground out an endless supply of cheap electronics, children's toys, and clothing that were immediately gobbled up by the consumer markets of the industrialized nations. But it was the lumbering containership, the unsung workhorse of commercial trade, which empowered global commerce and allowed the Chinese economy to skyrocket.

"See to it. And keep after the loading crew. I'm getting complaints again about slow turnarounds," Qinglin grumbled. He lowered his clipboard and slid a yellow pencil over his right ear, then turned and walked away. But he stopped after two steps and slowly wheeled back around, his eyes widening as he stared at Zhou. Or at least Zhou thought he was staring at him.

"She's on fire," Qinglin muttered.

Zhou realized his supervisor was looking past him and turned to see what he meant.

In the harbor surrounding the terminal, a dozen ships milled about the area, an assorted mix of huge containerships and jumbo supertankers overshadowing a handful of small cargo ships. It was one of the cargo ships that distinguished itself, trailing a heavy plume of black smoke.

Through Zhou's eyes, the ship looked to be a derelict, well overdue for an appointment with the scrapyard. She was at least forty years old, he guessed, with a tired blue hull that in most places had turned scaly brown from the onslaught of rust. Black smoke, growing thicker by the second, billowed from the forward hold like an inverse waterfall, obscuring most of the ship's superstructure. Yellow flames danced out of the hold in random leaps, occasionally bursting twenty feet into the air. Zhou turned his gaze toward the ship's prow, which cut a frothy white wake through the water.

"She's running fast . . . and heading toward the commercial terminals," he gasped.

"The fools!" Qinglin cursed. "There's no place to run ashore in this direction." Dropping his clipboard, he took off sprinting down the terminal toward the dock office in hopes of radioing the impaired ship.

Other ships and shore facilities had already witnessed the fire and were filling the airwaves with offers of assistance. But all of the radio calls to the smoking vessel went unanswered.

Zhou stayed perched at the end of the container dock, watching as the burning ship steamed closer to shore. The derelict narrowly skirted between a moored barge and a loaded containership in a deft move that Zhou considered miraculous, given the blanket of smoke engulfing the ship's bridge. For a moment the ship appeared headed for the container terminal adjacent to Zhou's, but then the ship made a sweeping turn to port. As the vessel's path seemed to straighten out, Zhou could see that the ship was now headed toward Ningbo's main crude oil loading facility on Cezi Island.

Oddly, he noted that there were no men on deck fighting the flames. Zhou scanned the length of the ship and even got a glimpse of the bridge through the smoke as the ship turned away from him, but he couldn't catch sight of any crew members aboard. A shiver went down his spine as he silently wondered if it was an unmanned ghost ship.

A pair of deepwater tankers straddled Ningbo's main crude off-loading terminal, which had recently been expanded to accommodate four supertankers. The burning derelict took a bead on the leeward tanker, a black-and-white behemoth owned by the Saudi Arabian government. Alerted by the frantic radio traffic, the tanker's executive officer let loose a blast from the ship's deafening air horn. But the burning freighter held steady. The disbelieving exec stood peering at the flaming vessel from his outside bridge wing, powerless to do anything more.

Alerted by the warning blast, the tanker's crewmen scrambled like ants to flee the floating incendiary tank, converging onto the lone gangplank. The exec stood and watched unblinking, now joined by the harried captain, who stared waiting for the rusty ship to slice into them.

But the impact never came. At the last second, the flaming ship wheeled again, its bow swinging sharply to port and just missing the flanks of the supertanker by a few feet. The freighter seemed to straighten, running parallel with the tanker and taking a bead on the adjacent docking terminal. A semifloating ramp built on sectional pylons that ran six hundred feet into the harbor, the terminal carried the pipelines and pumps used to off-load the tanker's supply of crude oil.

The rusty derelict now ran as straight as an arrow, the flames from its hold engulfing the entire forward deck. No attempt had been made to slow the vessel, and she, in fact, appeared to have actually gained speed. Striking the end of the terminal, the rusty ship's bow tore through the wooden platform like it was a box of matches, sending splintered pieces of the dock flying in all directions. Pylon after pylon disintegrated under the onslaught, barely slowing the vessel as it plowed forward. A hundred yards ahead, several crewmen who had been fleeing the big tanker froze on the gangplank, unsure of which direction to find safety. The answer was presented a few seconds later when the ship drove through the base of the plank. Hidden by smoke and flames, a jumble of steel, wood, and humanity that was the gangplank surged underwater and was quickly lost beneath the churning propellers of the ship.

The ship continued to drive forward, but, at last, began to stagger as a tangled mass of debris piled up before the bow. Yet the old ship had legs and plowed ahead in the last gasp of its life, fighting to reach shore. Mashing through the final pylon, the spent ship made a final surge onto the shorefront off-loading and storage facility. A thunderous crash, accompanied by waves of black smoke, echoed across the island as the mystery ship finally ground to a halt. Those who witnessed the carnage let out a sigh of relief that the worst was apparently over. But then a muffled blast erupted deep in the bowels of the ship, which blew the bow off in a wall of orange fire. In seconds, flames were everywhere, devouring the spilled crude oil that flooded around the ship. The fire raced across the layer of floating oil that reached into the harbor and climbed up to engulf the moored tanker. The entire island was quickly clouded in thick black smoke, which hid the inferno below.

Across the bay, Zhou stood in astonishment as he watched the flames spread across the terminal complex. Staring at the decrepit freighter as it wallowed and rolled onto its side after the fire inside melted its innards, he grasped to comprehend what kind of suicidal maniac would destroy himself in such a rage.

· · ·

A MILE away from Zhou's dock, a faded white runabout motored slowly off Cezi Island. Concealed beneath a low-slung canvas tarp, a coffee-skinned man lay on the bow, surveying the burning holocaust ashore through the lens of a small telescope affixed to a laser sight. Appraising the damage with an upturned grin of satisfaction, he disassembled the laser device and accompanying wireless transmitter that minutes before had relayed course directions to the rusty derelict's automatic navigation system. As smoke drifted over the water, the man hoisted a stainless steel suitcase over the gunnel and gently let it slip from his fingers. A few seconds later, the suitcase and its high-tech components found a permanent home under three inches of soft mud in the murky depths of Ningbo Harbor.

The man turned to the boat's pilot, exposing a long scar that ran across the left side of his face.

"To the city marina," he directed in a low voice. "I have a plane to catch."

THE FIRES raged for a day and a half before the port fire control authorities extinguished the blaze. A fast acting trio of tugboats saved the oil tanker from destruction, converging on the big ship through flaming waters and shoving the mammoth vessel into the bay, where the shipboard fires were quickly controlled.

The onshore facilities were less fortunate. The Cezi Island terminal was completely destroyed, taking the lives of ten oil workers. An additional half-dozen crewmen from the supertanker were still missing and presumed dead.

When investigators were finally able to board the mystery derelict, they were stumped to find no bodies aboard. The eyewitness accounts were beginning to sound correct. It was a deserted ship that had seemingly sailed itself. Unknown in the local waters, the ship was traced by insurance agents back to a Malaysian ship broker who had sold it at auction to a scrap dealer. The scrap dealer had vanished, and his business turned out to be a shell company with a phony address and no traceable links.

Investigators speculated a disgruntled former crew was to blame, angered with the ship's captain and setting the vessel ablaze in revenge. The "Mystery Fire Ship of Ningbo," as it came to be known locally, had sailed to a fiery demise at the Cezi Island terminal by sheer luck. Hang Zhou suspected otherwise, however, and forever believed that somebody had guided the ship of death to shore.

~ 12 ~

JAN, WE'RE ON IN TEN minutes in the Gold Conference Room. Can I get you a coffee before we start?"

Jan Montague Clayton stared at the coworker standing in her doorway like he'd just landed from Mars.

"Harvey, my urine has turned the color of cappuccino, and there's enough caffeine in my bloodstream to fuel the space shuttle. But thanks anyway. I'll be along in a moment."

"I'll make sure the projection system is set up," Harvey replied sheepishly, then disappeared down the corridor.

Clayton couldn't count the number of coffees she had consumed in the last two days, but knew it had been her primary sustenance. Since the news of the earthquake at Ras Tanura had broken the day before, she had been glued to her desk, developing economic impact assessments while quietly gathering oil company reactions from the slate of industry insiders that filled her Rolodex. Only a brief foray to her stylish apartment in the East Village at two in the morning for a catnap and change of clothes had offered a respite from the state of chaos that surrounded her.

As a senior commodities research analyst for the investment banking firm of Goldman Sachs, Clayton was used to working twelve-hour days. But as a specialist in oil and natural gas futures, she was unprepared for the fallout from Ras Tanura. Every sales associate and fund manager in the firm seemed to be calling her, crying for advice on how to handle their clients' accounts. She finally had to unplug her phone in order to concentrate, while steering well clear of her e-mail account. Taking a last look at some oil export figures, she stood and patted down her beige Kay Unger suit, then picked up a laptop computer and headed for the door. Against her better judgment, she stopped suddenly and wheeled back toward the desk, where she scooped up a ceramic cup half full of coffee.

The conference room was a packed house, the mostly male crowd waiting anxiously for her report. As Harvey opened the meeting with a brief economic overview, Clayton studied the audience. The sprinkling of partners and senior managers was easy to spot, their premature-gray hair and paunch bellies signaling the lifetime of hours spent inside the building's walls. At the other spectrum were the younger sales associates, cutthroat and aggressive in their desire to climb the firm's ladder to the holy land of seniority, where seven-figure year-end bonuses were regularly pocketed. Half of the overpaid and overworked investment professionals didn't care whether Clayton's predictions would be accurate or not so long as they had someone to blame for their trades. Yet those who paid attention quickly learned that Clayton knew her stuff. In the short time she had been with the firm, she had already acquired the reputation as a savvy analyst with an uncanny ability to predict trends in the market.

"And Jan will now discuss the current state of the oil markets," Harvey concluded, passing the stage to Clayton. Plugging her laptop into the projection system, she waited a moment for her PowerPoint presentation to appear on the screen. Harvey walked to the side of the conference room and closed the blinds of a large picture window that offered an impressive view of lower Manhattan from the Broad Street high-rise.

"Ladies and gentlemen, this is Ras Tanura," she

began, speaking in a soft but confident voice. A map of Saudi Arabia jumped to the screen, followed by photos of an oil refinery and storage tanks.

"Ras Tanura is Saudi Arabia's largest oil and liquid natural gas export terminal. Or was, rather, until yesterday's massive earthquake. Damage assessments are still under way, but it appears that nearly sixty percent of the refinery was destroyed by fire and that at least half of the storage facilities suffered major structural damage."

"How does that impact oil exports?" interrupted a jug-eared man named Eli, munching on a doughnut as he spoke.

"Hardly at all," Clayton replied, pausing to let Eli take the bait.

"Then why the big oil shock?" he asked, crumbs spraying off his lips.

"Most of the refinery's output is utilized by the Saudis themselves. What will impact oil exports is the damage incurred to the pipelines and shipping terminals." Another image appeared on the screen, showing a dozen supertankers docked at the Sea Island loading terminal.

"Those floating terminals should have been safe from the earthquake at sea," someone commented from the rear of the room.

"Not when the epicenter of the earthquake was less than two miles away," Clayton countered. "And those aren't floating terminals, they are fixed in the seabed. Shifting sediments from the earthquake caused a complete collapse of this offshore terminal, which is known as Sea Island. The Sea Island terminal handles the largest of the supertankers and that capacity has been completely wiped out. Several additional shore-based loading piers were destroyed as well. It appears that over ninety percent of Ras Tanura's export infrastructure has been damaged or destroyed. That is why there has been a 'big oil shock,'" she said, staring at Eli.

A hushed gloom fell over the room. Finally finishing his doughnut, Eli broke the silence.

"Jan, what kind of volume does that translate to?"

"Nearly six million barrels a day of Saudi export oil will immediately be removed from the supply chain."

"Isn't that nearly ten percent of the daily world demand?" a senior associate asked.

"It's closer to seven percent, but you get the picture."

Clayton brought up the next slide, which showed the recent spike in price of a barrel of West Texas intermediate crude oil, as traded on the New York Mercantile Exchange.

"As you know, the markets have reacted with their usual rabid hysteria, blasting the spot price of crude to over one hundred twenty-five dollars a barrel in the last twenty-four hours. Those of you in equities have already seen the resulting collapse on the Dow," she added, to a chorus of groans and nodding heads.

"But where do we go from here?" Eli asked.

"That's the sixty-four-dollar question, or one-hundred-twenty-five-dollar, rather, in our case. We're dealing in fear at the moment, driven by uncertainty. And fear has a habit of producing irrational behavior that isn't easy to predict." Clayton stopped and took a sip from her coffee. She had her audience hanging on every word. Though her attractive looks always drew attention, it was her knowledge that had the crowd enraptured now. She savored the taste of power for a moment, then continued.

"Make no mistake. The destruction at Ras Tanura is going to leave a devastating mark around the world. On the home front, there's going to be an immediate whack to the domestic economy that will rival the post 9/11 downturn. When that one-hundred-twenty-five-dollar barrel of oil trickles down to seven dollars for a gallon of gas next week, Joe Consumer is going to park his Hummer and start riding the bus. Higher prices for everything from diapers to airline tickets will ripple through the economy. No one is prepared for that degree of run-up in price, which will throw a roadblock to consumer purchasing in short order."

"Is there anything the president can do to help?" Eli asked.

"Not much, though there are two things that might soften the blow. Our country's Strategic Petroleum Reserve is now sitting at full capacity. If the president so elects, he could draw down on the reserves to replace some of the shortages from Saudi Arabia. In addition, the drilling in the Arctic National Wildlife Refuge approved by the prior administration has now come on line, so the Alaska Pipeline is now running at full capacity again. That will provide a slight boost to domestic production numbers. Neither item will be sufficient to prevent fuel shortages in some regions of the country, however."

"What can we expect in the long term?" he inquired.

"While we can't forecast the impact that fear will have on the markets, we can predict the dynamics of supply and demand that will ultimately prevail. The spike in price should soften current levels of demand over the next few months, easing the pressure on oil prices. In addition, the other ten OPEC countries will clamor to make up Saudi Arabia's lost exports, though it is unclear whether they have the infrastructure to cover the shortfall."

"But wouldn't OPEC want to keep the price of oil over one hundred dollars?" Eli pestered.

"Sure, if demand stayed constant. But we're going to face a sharp economic contraction as it is. If the price was maintained at one hundred twenty-five dollars arbitrarily, you would see a global economic collapse rivaling the Great Depression."

"You don't think that's in the cards?"

"It's possible. But OPEC doesn't want to see a worldwide economic collapse any more than the industrialized nations do, as that will reduce their revenues. The main concern today is still one of supply. We witness another supply disruption, then all bets are off."

"So what's the investment play?" Eli asked pointedly.

"Initial estimates from Ras Tanura suggest that the shipping terminals can be repaired or replaced within six to nine months. My trading recommendation would be to short oil positions at the current price, with the expectation that pricing will retreat to more moderate levels within nine to twelve months."

"You're sure of that?" asked Eli with a hint of skepticism.

"Absolutely not," Clayton fired back. "Venezuela could be hit by a meteorite tomorrow. Nigeria could be taken over by a fascist dictator next week. There are a thousand and one political or environmental forces that could disrupt the oil markets in a heartbeat. And that's the unnerving point. Any bit of further bad news may drive us past a recession and into a depression that will take years to recover from. But it seems a bit tenuous to me to assume that another natural disaster will strike soon with the impact of Ras Tanura. Are there any more questions?" Clayton asked, reaching her final slide.

Harvey opened the window shades, letting in a blast of sunlight that made everyone in the room squint for a moment.

"Jan, my desk trades in global equities," stated a short blond woman in a garnet-colored blouse. "Can you tell me which countries are most vulnerable to the reduced Saudi oil exports?"

"Sandra, I can only tell you where the Saudi oil exports are currently going. The U.S., as you know, has been a prime customer of Saudi oil since the 1930s.

Washington has long pursued a goal of reducing our reliance on Middle East crude, but Saudi oil still accounts for nearly fifteen percent of our total imported oil. "

"How about the European Union?"

"Western Europe obtains most of their oil from the North Sea, but Saudi imports do play a factor. Their proximity to other suppliers should mitigate severe shortages, I believe. No, the hardest-hit countries will be in Asia."

Clayton drained the last of her coffee while she pulled up a file on her computer. She curiously noted that the occupants of the entire room remained seated and listening to her every word.

"Japan will feel a major jolt," she said, scanning the report. "The Japanese import one hundred percent of their oil requirements and were already stung by the recent earthquake in Siberia that took out a section of the Taishet–Nakhodka pipeline. Though not widely publicized, that accident had already pushed the price of oil up three to four dollars a barrel," she noted. "I can tell you that Japan imports twenty-two percent of its oil from Saudi Arabia, so they will feel a significant contraction. However, a temporary boost in Russian oil exports could take away something of the strain once the Siberian pipeline is repaired."

"And China?" an anonymous voice asked. "What about that fire near Shanghai?"

Scanning down the page, Clayton furrowed her brow.

"The Chinese will be facing a similar shock. Nearly twenty percent of China's oil imports come from Saudi Arabia," she said, "all of which arrives by tanker ship. I haven't assessed the impact of the fire at the Ningpo oil terminal, but I can only speculate that combined with the Ras Tanura disaster, the Chinese will be facing a major hurdle in the near term."

"Are alternative sources available to the Chinese?" a voice in the back asked.

"Not readily. Russia would be the obvious source, but they are more inclined to sell their oil to the West and Japan. Kazakhstan might provide some relief, but their pipeline to China is already at capacity. I think there could be a dramatic impact to the Chinese economy, which is already suffering a shortage of energy resources." Clayton made a mental note to review the Chinese situation in more depth when she returned to her office.

"You mentioned domestic fuel shortages earlier," a pasty-faced man in a purple tie asked. "How severe will that be?"

"I would expect only temporary shortages in limited areas, assuming no other market impacts. Again, the main problem we are facing is fear. Fear of another supply disruption, either real or imagined, is the real culprit that could drive us to a complete meltdown."

The meeting wound down as the crowd of financiers glumly scurried back to their gray work cubicles. Clayton gathered her laptop and headed for the door as a figure drew up alongside her. Turning her head, she gazed with apprehension at the slovenly figure of Eli, a doughnut crumb on his tie.

"Great meeting, Jan." Eli grinned. "Can I buy you a cup of coffee?"

Gritting her teeth, all she could do was smile and nod.

~ 13 ~

IT WAS A STIFLING DAY in Beijing. A suffocating conflux of hcat, smog, and humidity doused the congested city in a thick soup of misery. Tempers flared on the streets as cars and bicycles jostled for position in the jammed boulevards. Mothers grabbed their children and flocked to the city's numerous lakes in an attempt to seek a reprieve from the heat. Teenage street vendors hawking chilled Coca-Colas made stellar profits quenching the thirst of sweaty tourists and businessmen.

The temperature was little cooler in the large meeting room of the Chinese Communist Party headquarters, situated in a secure compound just west of Beijing's historic Forbidden City. Buried in the basement of an ancient edifice inaptly named the Palace Steeped in Compassion, the windowless conference room was an odd conglomeration of fine carpets and antique tapestries mixed with cheap 1960s office furniture. A half dozen humorless men, comprising the elite Standing Committee of the Political Bureau, the most influential body in China's government, sat at a scarred round table with the general secretary and president of China, Qian Fei.

The stuffy room felt much hotter to the minister of commerce, a balding man with beady eyes named Shinzhe, who stood before the party chiefs with a young female assistant at his side.

"Shinzhe, the State just approved the five-year plan for economic progress last November," President Fei lectured in a belittling tone. "You mean to tell me that a few 'accidents' have rendered our national objectives unfeasible?"

Shinzhe cleared his throat while wiping a damp palm on his pant leg.

"Mr. General Secretary, politburo members," he replied, nodding to the other assembled bureaucrats. "The energy needs of China have changed tremendously in the last few years. Our rapid and dynamic economic growth has driven a high thirst for energy resources. Just a few short years ago, our country was a net exporter of crude oil. Today, more than half of our consumption is supplied by crude oil imports. It is a regrettable fact due to the size of our economy. Whether we like it or not, we are captive to the economic and political forces surrounding the foreign petroleum market, just as the Americans have been for the last four decades."

"Yes, we are well aware of our growing energy appetite," stated Fei. The recently elected party head was a youthful fifty-year-old who catered to the traditionalists in the bureaucratic system with equal parts charm and wile. He had a reputation for being hot-tempered, Shinzhe knew, but respected the truth.

"How severe is the shock?" another party member asked.

"It is like having two of our limbs cut off. The earthquake in Saudi Arabia will drastically restrict their ability to ship us oil for months to come, though we can develop alternate suppliers over time. The fire at Ningbo Harbor is perhaps more damaging. Nearly a third of our imported oil flows through the port facility there. The infrastructure necessary to receive oil imports by ship is not something that can be quickly replaced. I am afraid to report that we are facing immediate and drastic shortages that cannot be easily remedied."

"I have been told the damage repairs may take as long as a year before the current level of imports can be restored," a white-haired politburo member said.

"I cannot dispute the estimate," Shinzhe said, bowing his head.

Overhead, the room's fluorescent lights suddenly flashed off, while the noisy and mostly ineffective air-conditioning system fell silent. A stillness settled over the darkened room before the lights flickered back on and the cooling system slowly clanged back to life. Along with it came the temper of the president.

"These blackouts must stop!" he cursed. "Half of Shanghai was without power for five days. Our factories are operating limited hours to conserve electricity, while the workers have no power to cook their dinner at night. And now you tell us that we will be short of fuel oil from abroad and our five-year plan is rubbish? I demand to know what is being done to solve these problems," he hissed.

Shinzhe visibly shrunk before the tirade. Glancing around the table, he saw that none of the other committee members were brave enough to reply, so he took a deep breath and began speaking in a quiet tone.

"As you know, additional generators will go on line shortly at the Three Gorges Dam hydroelectric development, while a half dozen new coal- and gas-fired power plants are in various stages of construction. But obtaining sufficient natural gas and fuel oil supplies to operate the non-hydro power plants has been a problem, and is more so now. Our state-sponsored oil companies have stepped up exploration in the South China Sea, despite protests from the Vietnamese government. Furthermore, we continue to broaden supply relationships abroad. The foreign ministry has recently completed successful negotiations to purchase significant quantities of fuel oil from Iran, I might remind the committee. And we are continuing efforts to acquire Western oil companies that own rich stocks of reserves."

"Minister Shinzhe is correct." The gray-haired foreign minister, who sat quietly to the side, coughed. "These activities address long-term sources of energy, however, and will do nothing to solve the immediate problem."

"Again, I ask, what is being done to address the shortfall?" Fei nearly shrieked, his voice rising an octave.

"In addition to Iran, we have spoken with several Middle Eastern countries about boosting their exports. We must of course compete with the Western countries on price," Shinzhe said softly. "But the Ningbo Harbor damage physically limits the amount of oil we are able to bring in by sea."

"What about the Russians?"

"They are in love with the Japanese," the foreign minister spat. "Our attempt to jointly develop a pipeline from the western Siberian oil fields was rejected by the Russians in favor of a line to the Pacific that will supply Japan. We can only boost rail shipments of oil from Russia in the short term, which, of course, is not a feasible means to transport any sizeable quantities."

"So there is no real solution," Fei grumbled, his anger still simmering. "Our economic growth will terminate, our gains against the West will cease, and we can all just return to our cooperative farms in the provinces, where we will enjoy continuing blackouts."

The room fell silent again as no one dared even breathe in the face of the general secretary's ire. Only the tinny rattle of the air-conditioning rumbling in the background stirred the heavy morose in the air. Then Shinzhe's assistant, a petite woman named Yee, cleared her throat.

"Excuse me, General Secretary, Minister Shinzhe,"

she said, nodding to the two men. "The State has just today received a peculiar offer of energy assistance through our ministry. I am sorry I didn't have the opportunity to brief you, Minister," she said to Shinzhe. "I didn't recognize the importance at the time."

"What is the proposal?" Fei asked.

"It is an offer from an entity in Mongolia to supply high-quality crude oil . . ."

"Mongolia?" Fei interrupted. "There's no oil in Mongolia."

"The offer is to supply one million barrels a day," Yee continued. "Delivery commencing within ninety days."

"That's preposterous," Shinzhe exclaimed, glaring at Yee with irritation for publicly sharing the communiqué.

"Perhaps," Fei replied, a look of intrigue suddenly warming his face. "It is worth investigating. What else does the proposal say?"

"Just the terms they demand in return," Yee replied, suddenly looking nervous. Pausing in hopes the discussion would end there, she sheepishly continued when she saw all eyes were fixed on her. "The price of the oil shall be set at the current market price and locked for a period of three years. In addition, exclusive use of the northeast oil pipeline terminating at the port of Qinhuangdao shall be granted, and, further, the Chinese-controlled lands denoted Inner Mongolia shall be formally ceded back to the ruling government of Mongolia."

The staid audience erupted in an uproar. Cries of out-rage rocked through the room at the shocking demand. After minutes of boisterous dissent, Fei pounded an ashtray on the table to regain silence.

"Silence!" the president shouted, immediately qui-eting the crowd. A pained look crossed his face, then he spoke calmly and quietly. "Find out if the offer is real, if the oil does, in fact, exist. Then we shall worry about negotiating an appropriate price."

"As you wish, General Secretary," Shinzhe bowed.

"Tell me first, though. Who is it that is making this contemptuous demand?"

Shinzhe looked helplessly at Yee. "It is a small entity that is unknown to our ministry," she answered, addressing the president. "They are called the Avarga Oil Consortium."

～ 14 ～

THEY WERE HOPELESSLY LOST. Two weeks after departing Ulan-Ude with instructions to explore the upper Selenga River valley, the five-man seismic exploration team had lost its way. None of the men from the Russian oil company LUKOIL were from the region, which added to their misfortune. The trouble began when someone spilled a hot coffee on the GPS unit, drowning it in a quick death. It was not enough to halt their progression south, even when they stumbled across the Mongolian border and off the edge of the

Siberian maps they carried for insurance. What kept them going was a series of subsurface folds detected from the pounding of the "thumper" truck that indicated possible structural traps. Structural traps in the sediment are natural collection basins where pockets of oil and gas can accumulate. The survey team had meandered southeast while tracking the deep traps that meant possible oil and completely lost track of the river.

"All we have to do is head north and follow our tracks where they're visible," said a short, balding man named Dimitri. The team leader stood peering west, watching the long shadows cast by the trees as sunset approached.

"I knew we should have left a trail of bread crumbs," grinned a young assistant engineer named Vlad.

"I don't think we have enough fuel to reach Kyakhta," replied the thumper's driver. Like the vehicle itself, he was a big, burly man with thick limbs. He climbed into the open driver's door and stretched out on the bench seat for a catnap with his meaty hands tucked behind his head. The big thirty-ton rig carried a steel slab under its belly, which pounded the ground, sending seismic shocks deep into the earth. Small transceivers were placed various distances from the truck, which received the signals as they bounced off the subsurface sediment layers. Computerized processing converted the signals into visual maps and images of the ground below.

A dirty red four-wheel-drive truck pulled alongside

and stopped, its two occupants jumping out to join the debate.

"We had no authorization to cross the border, and now we don't even know where the border is," complained the support truck's driver.

"The seismic readings justify our continued tracking," Dimitri replied. "Besides, we were ordered to take to the field for two weeks. We'll let the company bureaucrats worry about obtaining permission to drill. As for the border, we know it is somewhere north of us. Our immediate concern will be to acquire fuel in order to reach the border."

The driver was about to complain when a muffled boom in the distance diverted his attention.

"Up there, on the hill," Vlad said.

Above the rocky hill they stood on rose a small mountain range, which glimmered green from its pine-covered crags. A few miles distant, a puff of gray smoke drifted into the cloudless sky from a thick-wooded ridge. After the blast's echo receded from the hilltops, the sound of heavy machinery rumbled faintly down the slopes.

"What in the name of Mother Russia was that?" grumbled the truck's driver, awakened by the blast.

"An explosion up on the mountain," Dimitri replied. "Probably a mining operation."

"Nice to know we're not the only people in this wilderness," the driver muttered, then returned to his nap.

"Perhaps someone up there can tell us the way home," Vlad ventured.

An answer was short in the waiting. The hum of an engine drew closer until a late-model four-wheel drive appeared in the distance. The vehicle rounded a hill, then barreled across the open flats toward the surveyors. The car hardly slowed until it was nearly upon them, then stopped abruptly in a cloud of dust. The two occupants sat motionless for a moment, then exited the vehicle cautiously.

The Russians could tell immediately that the men were Mongolian, with their flat noses and high cheekbones. The shorter of the two stepped forward and barked harshly, "What are you doing here?"

"We're a bit off track," replied the unflappable Dimitri. "We somehow lost the road while surveying the valley. We need to get back across the border to Kyakhta, but we're not sure if we have enough fuel. Can you help us out?"

The Mongol's eyes grew larger at hearing the word "survey," and for the first time he carefully studied the thumper truck parked behind the men.

"You are conducting oil exploration?" he asked in a calmer tone.

The engineer nodded yes.

"There is no oil here," the Mongol barked. Waving his arm around, he said, "You will bivouac here for the night. Stay in this spot. I will bring fuel for your truck in the morning and direct you toward Kyakhta."

Without a farewell or pleasantry, he turned and climbed into the car with his driver and roared back up the mountain.

"Our problems are solved," Dimitri said with satisfaction. "We'll set up camp here and get an early start in the morning. I only hope you have left us some vodka," he said, patting the shoulder of his sleepy truck driver.

DARKNESS FELL rapidly once the sun set over the hills, bringing with it a ripe chill to the night air. A fire was built in front of a large canvas tent, which the men crowded around while downing a tasteless dinner of canned stew and rice. It didn't take long for the nightly entertainment of cards and vodka to emerge, with cigarettes and pocket change ruling the pots.

"Three hands straight." Dimitri laughed as he raked in the winnings from a hand of preference, a Russian card game similar to gin rummy. His eyes glistened under heavy lids, and a trickle of vodka dripped from his chin as he gloated to his equally inebriated co-workers.

"Keep it up and you'll have enough for a dacha on the Black Sea," one countered.

"Or a black dachshund on the Caspian Sea," said another and laughed.

"This game is too rich for my blood, I'm afraid," griped Vlad, noting he was down a hundred rubles for the night. "I'm off to my sleeping bag to forget about Dimitri's cheating ways."

The young engineer ignored a slew of derisive remarks from the others as he staggered to his feet. Eyeing the canvas tent, he instead walked toward the rear of the thumper truck to relieve himself before turning in. In his inebriated state, he tripped and tumbled into a small gully beside the truck, sliding several feet downhill before colliding with a large rock. He lay there for a minute, clutching a wrenched knee and cursing his clumsiness, when he heard the clip-clop sound of horse hooves approaching the camp. Rolling to his hands and knees, he sluggishly crawled to the top of the ravine, where he could peer beneath the thumper truck and see the campfire on the opposite side.

The voices of his comrades fell silent as a small group of horses approached the camp. Vlad rubbed his eyes in disbelief when they came close enough to be illuminated by the fire's light. Six fierce-looking horsemen sat tall in the saddle, looking as if they had just ridden off a medieval tapestry. Each wore a long orange silk tunic, which ran to the knees and covered baggy white pants that were tucked into heavy leather boots. A bright blue sash around their waists held a sword in a scabbard, while over their shoulders they carried a compound bow and a quiver of feathered arrows. Their heads were covered by bowl-shaped metal helmets, which sprouted a tuft of horsehair from a center spike. Adding to their menacing appearance, the men all wore long thin mustaches that draped beneath their chins.

Dimitri raised himself from the fireside with a nearly full bottle of vodka and welcomed the horsemen to join them.

"A drink to your fine mounts, comrades," he slurred, hoisting the bottle into the air.

The offer was met by silence, all six riders staring coldly at the engineer. Then one of the horsemen reached to his side. In a lightning-quick move that Vlad would later replay in his mind a thousand times over, the horseman slammed a bow to his chest, yanked back the bowstring, and let fly a wooden arrow. Vlad never saw the arrow in flight, only watched as the bottle of vodka suddenly lurched from Dimitri's hand and shattered to the ground in a hundred pieces. A few paces away, Dimitri stood clutching his throat with his other hand, the feathered shaft of an arrow protruding through his fingers. The engineer sank to his knees with a gurgling cry for help, then fell to the ground as a torrent of blood surged down his chest.

The three men around the campfire jumped to their feet in shock, but that was to be the last move they would make. In an instant, a hail of arrows rained down on them like a tempest. The horsemen were killing machines, wielding their bows and firing a half dozen arrows apiece in mere seconds. The drunken surveyors had no chance, the archers finding their targets with ease at such close range. A brief sprinkling of cries echoed through the night and then it was over, each man lying dead with a tombstone of arrows protruding from his lifeless body.

Vlad watched the massacre in wide-eyed terror, nearly crying out in shock when the first arrows took flight. His heart felt like it would beat out of his chest, and then the adrenaline hit, urging his body to get up and flee like the wind. Scrambling down the gully, he started to run, faster than he had ever run in his life before. The pain in his knee, the alcohol in his blood, it all vanished, replaced by the singular sensation of fear. He ran down the sloping foothills, oblivious to any unseen nighttime obstructions, pushed on by sheer panic. Several times he fell, cutting nasty gashes on his legs and arms, but immediately he staggered to his feet and resumed the pace. Over the pounding of his heart and the gasping from his lungs, he listened for the sound of pursuing hoofbeats. But they never came.

For two hours, he ran, staggered, and stumbled until he came to the rushing waters of the Selenga River. Moving along the riverbank, he came upon two large boulders that offered both shelter and concealment. Crawling into the crevice beneath the rocks, he quickly fell asleep, not wanting to awake from the living nightmare he had just witnessed.

~ 15 ~

THE RIDE, THERESA DECIDED, REPLICATED the jarring discomfort of a Butterfield stagecoach passage across the American Southwest in 1860. Every bump and rut seemed to vibrate directly from the wheels to the bed of the two-ton panel truck, where the energy was transferred up her backside in a force that made her bones rattle. Bound, gagged, and seated on a hard-wood bench across from two armed guards did not improve the comfort factor. Only the presence of Roy and Wofford shackled beside her offered a small degree of mental consolation.

Sore, tired, and hungry, she struggled to make sense of the events at Lake Baikal. Tatiana had said very little after waking her in their shared cabin with a cold pistol pressed against her chin. Marched at gunpoint off the *Vereshchagin* and onto a dinghy, she and the others had been transferred to the black freighter briefly, then pushed ashore and bound into the back of the panel truck. They waited on the dock nearly two hours, hearing gunshots and a commotion on the ship before the truck was started and they were driven away.

She wondered grimly what had become of the Russian scientist Sarghov. He had been roughly pulled away from the group when they first boarded the freighter and herded off to another part of the ship. It hadn't looked good, and she feared for the safety of the jolly scientist. And what of the *Vereshchagin*? It appeared to be sitting low in the water when they were forced off. Were Al, Dirk, and the rest of the crew in danger as well?

The larger question was why had they been abducted? She feared for her life, but her self-pity quickly vanished when she gazed at Roy and Wofford. The two men were suffering far worse pain. Wofford was nursing a badly injured leg, likely fractured when he was shoved off balance from the black freighter. He held the leg stiffly in front of him, wincing in pain every time the truck lurched.

Gazing at Roy, she saw that he had fallen asleep with a small accretion of dried blood caked to his shirt. Stopping to help Wofford up from his fall, a spiteful guard had swung his carbine at Roy, cutting a wide gash across his scalp. He was unconscious for several minutes, his limp body having been roughly tossed into the back of the truck.

Theresa's dread was temporarily displaced by another jolt from the truck, and she tried to close her eyes and sleep away the nightmare. The truck bounced along for another five hours, at one point passing through a sizeable city, as judged by its stop-and-go progress and the sounds of other vehicles. The traffic noise soon vanished and the truck again picked up speed, swaying across a winding dirt road for another four hours. Finally, the truck slowed, and from the sudden alertness exhibited by the two guards Theresa knew they were arriving at their destination.

"We might as well have flown, given the amount of time we've been airborne," Wofford grimaced as they all flew off the bench seat from another encounter with a pothole.

Theresa smiled at the brave humor but offered no reply as the truck ground to a halt. The clattery diesel motor was turned off and the back doors of the truck flung open, bathing the bay in a shock of bright sunlight. At the guards' nodding, Theresa and Roy helped

Wofford from the truck, then stood absorbing their surroundings.

They stood in the center of a walled compound that
encompassed two freestanding buildings. Under a
bright blue sky, the temperature was much warmer
than at Lake Baikal, despite a light breeze blowing
across their faces. Theresa sniffed the air, noting a dry
and dusty flavor. A rolling grass valley appeared far
below in the distance, while a gray-green mountain
peak rose adjacent to the complex. The compound
appeared to be dug into the side of the mountain,
which she noticed was covered by low shrubs and
thick clusters of tall pines.

To their left, half hidden behind a long row of
hedges, stood a low-rise brick building, similar to
those found in a modern industrial park. Seemingly out
of place, there was a horse stable attached to one end
of the building. A half dozen stodgy horses milled
about a large corral, nibbling remnants of grass that
poked through the dust. At the other end of the
building was a large steel garage, which housed a fleet
of trucks and mechanical equipment. Inside, a handful
of workers in black jumpsuits were working on a dusty
fleet of earthmoving equipment.

"I thought the Taj Mahal was in India," Roy said.

"Well, maybe we are in India," Wofford replied with
a pained smirk.

Theresa turned and studied the other building in the
compound. She had to agree with Roy, it did bear a
slight resemblance to the Indian landmark, albeit a

much smaller version. In contrast to the functional efficiency of the brick industrial building, the structure before her was built with ornate flair and drama. Thick columns fronted a gleaming white marble edifice that was built low to the ground. At its center, a circular portico enveloped the main entrance. A bulbous white roof capped the entry hall, topped by a golden spire protruding from its peak. The design was, in fact, little removed from the dome of the Taj Mahal. Though elegant, the image looked to Theresa as if a giant scoop of vanilla ice cream had fallen from the heavens.

The landscape in front of the structure was equally palatial. A pair of canals flowed across the compound, feeding a large reflecting pool before disappearing under the front of the building. Theresa could hear the rushing waters of a nearby river, which fed the canals some distance from the compound. Around the canals and pool stretched a lush green ornamental garden, manicured to a detail that would shame an English nobleman.

Across the lawn, Theresa spied Tatiana and Anatoly conversing with a man who wore a holster on his side. The man nodded, then approached the back of the truck and said, "This way," in a thick accent. The two guards bunched up behind Roy and Wofford to emphasize the command.

Theresa and Roy each lent an arm to Wofford and followed the squat man as he marched down a walkway toward the opulent building. They approached the portico, where a large carved wooden door led into the premises. Flanked on either side, like doormen at the Savoy Hotel, was a pair of guards dressed in ornately embroidered long silk coats colored orange. Theresa knew they were guards, as they made no move to open the door, instead standing perfectly still, firmly grasping sharp-pointed lances in one hand.

The door opened and they entered the domed foyer, which was filled with aged pastoral paintings of horses in the field. A short housekeeper with a crooked grin slipped from behind the door and nodded for the group to follow. Padding across the polished marble floor, he led them down a side hallway to three interior guest rooms. One by one, Theresa, Roy, and Wofford were escorted into comfortably decorated rooms, then were left facing a closed door that the housekeeper locked and bolted behind him.

Theresa found a side table next to the bed that was set with a bowl of steaming soup and a loaf of bread. Quickly washing the road grime from her face and hands, she sat down and devoured the food in hunger. Exhaustion finally overcoming her fears, she lay on the soft bed and promptly fell asleep.

Three hours later, a hard knock at the door jolted her from a deep sleep.

"This way, please," the little housekeeper said, eyeing Theresa with a hint of lasciviousness.

Roy and Wofford were already waiting in the hallway. Theresa was surprised to see that Wofford's leg had been wrapped and he now sported a wooden cane. Roy's head gash was also bandaged, and he wore a loose cotton pullover in place of his bloodstained shirt.

"Don't you two look the model of health?" she said.

"Sure. Assuming the model is a crash test dummy," Roy replied.

"The hospitality has taken a slight turn for the better," Wofford said, tapping his cane on the floor.

The three were led back to the foyer and down the main hallway to an expansive sitting room. Shelves of leather-bound books lined the walls, punctuated by a fireplace at the far end and a bar along one side. Theresa looked up nervously at the torso of a black bear that lunged from the wall above her head, its sharpened claws and bared teeth frozen in a permanent display of aggression. Panning the room, she saw it was a taxidermist's heaven. A variety of stuffed deer, bighorn sheep, wolves, and foxes guarded the enclave, all leering viciously at the visitors. Tatiana stood in the middle of the room, next to a man who looked like he could have been mounted on the wall as well.

It was the grin, she decided. When he smiled, a row of sharp pointy teeth flashed like a shark's, seemingly eager to devour some raw flesh. Yet the rest of his appearance was less imposing. He had a slight though muscular build, and wore his jet-black hair brushed back loosely. He was handsome in the classic Mongol sense, with high cheekbones and almond-shaped eyes that had an odd golden-brown tint. A sprinkling of wind- and sun-borne wrinkles suggested he had spent his earlier years working outdoors. However, the mannerisms of the man dressed in the fashionable gray suit suggested that those days were long over.

"It is good of you to join us," Tatiana said in an emotionless tone. "May I present Tolgoi Borjin, president of the Avarga Oil Consortium."

"Pleased to meet you." Wofford hobbled over, and shook the man's hand as if he were an old friend. "Now, would you mind telling us where we are and why the hell we're here?" he asked, applying a vise grip to his handshake.

Wofford's sudden demand seemed to catch the Mongol off guard and he hesitated before answering, quickly letting go of Wofford's hand.

"You are at my home and enterprise headquarters."

"Mongolia?" Roy asked.

"My regrets for your hasty exit from Siberia," Borjin replied, ignoring Roy's remark. "Tatiana tells me that your lives were in peril."

"Indeed?" Theresa said, casting a wary eye toward her former cabinmate.

"The forced departure at gunpoint was most necessary for your security," she explained. "The environmental radicals of Baikal are very dangerous. They had apparently infiltrated the institute's survey ship and tried to sink it with all hands. I was fortunately able to contact a leased vessel nearby that assisted in our evacuation. It was best that we departed secretly, so as not to call attention to ourselves and risk further attacks."

"I have never heard of the Lake Baikal environmentalist groups acting in such a violent manner," Theresa replied.

"It is a new breed of youthful radicals. With the reduction in state administrative controls in recent years, I am afraid that the rebellious youths have become much more brazen and forceful."

"And what about the scientist, Dr. Sarghov, who was taken off the ship with us?"

"He was insistent on returning to the ship to alert the other institute members. I'm afraid we could no longer vouch for his safety."

"Is he dead? What about the others on the ship?"

"We were forced to evacuate the area for everyone's safety. I have no information on the research ship or Dr. Sarghov."

The color drained from Theresa's face as she contemplated the words.

"So why haul us here?" Roy asked.

"We have abandoned the Lake Baikal project for the time being. Your assistance in evaluating potential oil field sites is still of value to us. You were contracted to work for us for six weeks, so we will honor the contract through another project."

"Has the company been notified?" Theresa asked, realizing her cell phone had been left behind on the *Vereshchagin*. "I shall need to contact my supervisor to discuss this."

"Regrettably, our microwave phone line is down at the moment. A common problem in remote regions, as you can surely understand. Once the service is restored, you will of course be free to make any calls you like."

"Why are you locking us in our rooms like animals?"

"We have a number of sensitive research projects in development. I'm afraid we can't let outsiders go wandering around the facilities. We can give you a limited tour at the appropriate time."

"And if we wish to leave right now instead?" Theresa probed.

"A driver will take you to Ulaanbaatar, where you can catch a flight to your home." Borjin smiled, his sharp teeth glistening.

Still weary from the trip, Theresa didn't know what to think. Perhaps it was best not to test the waters just yet, she decided. "What is it that you would like us to do?"

Reams of folders were wheeled into the study along with several laptop computers, all chock-full of geological assessments and subsurface seismic profiles. Borjin's request was simple.

"We wish to expand drilling operations into a new geographical region. The ground studies are at your fingertips. Tell us where the optimal drilling locations would be." Saying nothing more, he turned his back and left the room, Tatiana tailing close behind.

"This is a load of bunk," Roy muttered, standing up.

"Actually, this looks like professionally gathered data," Wofford replied, holding up a subsurface isopach map, which portrayed the thickness of various underground sedimentary layers.

"I don't mean the data," Roy said, slamming a file down on the table.

"Easy, big fella," Wofford whispered, tilting his head toward the corner ceiling. "We're on *Candid Camera.*"

Roy looked up and noticed a tiny video camera mounted beside the smiling stuffed head of a reindeer.

"Best we at least pretend to study the files," Wofford continued in a low voice, holding the map in front of his mouth as he spoke.

Roy sat down and pulled one of the laptops close, then slunk down in the chair so that the opened screen blocked his face.

"I don't like the looks of this. These people are warped. And let's not forget we were brought here at gunpoint."

"I agree," Theresa whispered. "The whole story about trying to protect us at Lake Baikal is ludicrous."

"As I recall, Tatiana threatened to blow my left ear off if I didn't leave the *Vereshchagin* with her," Wofford mused, tugging his earlobe. "Not the words of someone who cares about my well-being, I should think."

Theresa unfolded a topographical map of a mountain range and pointed out meaningless features to Wofford as she spoke.

"And what about Dr. Sarghov? He was taken captive with us by accident. I think they may have killed him."

"We don't know that, but it may be true," Roy said. "We have to assume the same outcome awaits us, after we have provided them the information they are looking for."

"It's all so crazy," Theresa said with a slight shake of her head. "But we've got to find a way out of here."

"The garage, next to the industrial building across the lawn. It was full of vehicles," Wofford said. "If we could steal a truck and drive out of here, I'm sure we could find our way to Ulaanbaatar."

"They've got us either locked in our rooms or under surveillance. We'll have to be prepared to make a break for it on short notice."

"Afraid I'm not up for any wind sprints or pole vaults," Wofford said, adjusting his injured leg. "You two will need to try without me."

"I've got an idea," Roy said, eyeing a desk across the room. Making a show of looking for a lost pen among the maps, he stood and walked to the desk, where he grabbed a pencil from a round leather holder. Turning his back to the video camera, he scooped out a silver metal letter opener that was mixed in with the pencils and slid it up his sleeve. Returning to the table, he pretended to write some notes while whispering to Theresa and Wofford.

"Tonight we'll check things out. I'll get Theresa and we'll reconnoiter the area and figure out an escape route. Then tomorrow night, we'll make our break. With the invalid in tow," he added, grinning at Wofford.

"I'd be much obliged," Wofford nodded. "Much obliged indeed."

ROY AWOKE PROMPTLY AT TWO A.M. and dressed quickly. Removing the letter opener from its hiding place under his mattress, he groped his way across the darkened bedroom to the locked door. He felt along the doorframe, finding the raised edges of three metal hinges that protruded on the interior side. Sliding the letter opener into the top hinge, he carefully pried out a long metal pin that held the interlocking hinge together. Removing the pins from the other two hinges, he gently lifted the door and pulled it into the room laterally as the exterior dead bolt popped out of the opposite doorframe. Roy then crept into the hallway and pulled the door back against the frame, so that upon a casual glance it still appeared closed and locked.

Finding the hallway empty, he tiptoed to Theresa's room next door. Unlocking the latch, he opened the door to find her sitting on the bed, waiting.

"You did it," she whispered, seeing his figure in the light from the hallway.

Roy flashed a thin smile, then nodded for her to follow. They crept into the corridor and moved slowly toward the main foyer. A row of low-wattage footlights provided muted lighting along the hallway, which by all sight and sound appeared completely deserted. Theresa's rubber-soled shoes began squeaking on the polished marble floor, so she stopped and removed them, continuing on in her stocking feet.

The foyer was brightly illuminated by a large crystal chandelier, which prompted Roy and Theresa to hug the walls and approach cautiously. Roy knelt down and scurried over to a narrow window, which fronted the main doorway. Peering outside, he turned to Theresa and shook his head. Despite the late hour, there was still a pair of guards stationed outside the front door. They would have to find another way out.

Standing in the foyer, they found themselves at the base of an inverted T. The guest rooms had been to the left and the occupant's private rooms were presumably to the right. So they crept instead down the wide main corridor that led to the study.

The house remained still but for an old grandfather clock ticking loudly in the hallway. They reached the study and kept moving, tiptoeing past the main dining hall and a pair of small conference rooms, all decorated with an impressive collection of Song and Jin dynasty antiques. Theresa scanned the ceilings searching for additional video camera monitors but saw nothing. A whispering sound played on her ears, and she instinctively clutched at Roy's arm until he winced in pain from her sharp fingernails. They both relaxed when they realized the sound was only the wind blowing outside.

The corridor ended in a large open sitting room with floor-to-ceiling windows on three sides. Though there was little to be seen at night, Theresa and Roy could still sense the dramatic view offered from the mountain perch, which overlooked the rolling steppes of the valley below. Near the entrance to the room, Roy spied a carpeted stairwell that ran to a lower level. He motioned toward the stairs and Theresa nodded, following him quietly. The thick carpet was a welcome relief to her feet, which were beginning to tire of the hard marble floor. As she reached a turn in the stairwell, she looked up to face a huge portrait of an ancient warrior. The man in the image sat tall on a horse wearing a fur-trimmed coat, orange sash, and the classic Mongol bowl helmet. He stared at her triumphantly through gold-black eyes. His mouth showed a wisp of a grin, exposing sharpened teeth that reminded her of Borjin. The intensity of the image made her shudder and she quickly turned her back on the painting and moved down the next set of steps.

The landing opened onto a single corridor, which ran away from the house a short distance. One side of the corridor was windowed, which looked out upon a large courtyard. Theresa and Roy peered out the nearest window, faintly observing a freestanding structure across the way.

"There must be a door to the courtyard along here," Roy whispered. "If we can get out here, we ought to be able to move around the end of the guest wing and sneak toward the garage."

"It's going to be a long way for Jim to hobble, but at least there don't seem to be any guards around here. Let's find that door."

They moved rapidly to the end of the corridor where they at last found an exit door. Theresa tested the unlocked door, half expecting an alarm to sound when the latch released, but all remained silent. Together they crept into the open courtyard, which was partially illuminated by a few scattered pathway lamps. Theresa slipped her shoes back on soon after her feet touched the cold ground. The night air was brisk, and she shivered as a chill breeze blew through her light clothes.

They followed a slate pathway that angled across the courtyard toward a stone structure at the rear of the property. It appeared to be a small chapel, though it was circular in shape with a domed roof. Its stone composition differed from the marble used in the main house, and it had a decidedly ancient look to it. As they drew close, Roy bypassed the tunneled entrance and followed its curved walls toward the rear.

"I think I saw a vehicle in back," he whispered to Theresa, who hung tight on his heels.

Reaching the back of the stone building, they found a covered bay enclosed by a low split-rail fence. Once a corral, the interior was crammed with a half dozen old horse-drawn wagons, their wooden beds stacked with shovels, picks, and empty crates. From beneath a canvas tarp poked the front wheel of a dust-covered motorcycle, while, in the back of the bay, Roy studied the car he had seen across the courtyard. It was a huge old antique, layered with decades of dust and sitting on at least two flat tires.

"Nothing here that's going to get us to Ulaanbaatar,"

Theresa remarked with disappointment.

Roy nodded. "The garage on the other side of the mansion will have to be our ticket." He froze suddenly as a shrill whine carried near on the breeze.

It was the neighing of a horse, he recognized, not far from the courtyard.

"Behind the wagon," he whispered, pointing to the corral.

Dropping to the ground, they silently crawled through the rail fence and slithered beneath the nearest wagon. Lying behind one of the wagon's old-fashioned wooden wheels, they cautiously peeked through the spokes.

Two men soon appeared on horseback, preceded by the clopping sound of horse hooves on the slate walkway. The horsemen curled around the stone building, then paced alongside the corral and stopped. Theresa's heart nearly stopped when she caught sight of the men. They were dressed in nearly the same garb as the warrior in the hall painting. Their orange silk tunics reflected gold under the courtyard lights. Baggy pants, thick-soled boots, and a round metal helmet with horsehair spike completed their warrior appearance. The two men milled about for several minutes, just a few feet from where Theresa and Roy lay hidden. They were so close Theresa could taste the dust kicked up by the horses as they pawed at the ground.

One of the men barked something unintelligible, and then the horses suddenly bolted. In an instant, both horsemen disappeared into the darkness amid a small thunder of hoofbeats.

"The night watchmen," Roy declared as the sound of the horses vanished.

"A little too close for comfort," Theresa said, standing and shaking the dust from her clothes.

"We probably don't have much time before they make another pass. Let's see if we can skirt around the other end of the main house and try for the garage."

"Okay. Let's hurry. I don't want to meet up with those guys again."

They scrambled through the rail fence and headed toward the guest wing of the complex. But midway across the courtyard, they heard a sharp cry and the sudden gallop of horses. Looking back in horror, they saw the horses charging them from just yards away. The two horsemen had quietly backtracked to the stone building and broke when they saw Theresa and Roy sprinting across the courtyard.

They both froze in their tracks, unsure whether to run back to the main house or flee the courtyard. It made no difference, as the horsemen were already at the edge of the courtyard and had them plainly in view. Theresa watched one of the horses rear up in the air as the rider suddenly yanked on the reins, pulling the horse to a standstill. The other rider continued on at a gallop, directing his mount to where Theresa and Roy stood.

Roy saw immediately that the horseman was going to try to bowl them over. A quick glance to Theresa revealed fear and confusion in her eyes, as she stood frozen in place.

"Move!" Roy shouted, grabbing Theresa's arm by the elbow and flinging her out of harm's way. The horseman was nearly upon them, and Roy barely managed to sidestep the charging mount, the rider's stirrup grazing his side. Regaining his balance, Roy did the unthinkable. Rather than looking for cover, he turned and sprinted after the charging horse.

The unsuspecting horseman galloped a few more yards, then slowed the horse and pivoted it to his right, intending to make another charge. As the horse wheeled around, the horseman was shocked to find Roy standing in his path. The seismic engineer reached up and grabbed the loose reins dangling beneath the horse's chin and jerked them sharply downward.

"That's enough horseplay," Roy muttered.

The rider had a blank look on his face as Roy fought to restrain the trained horse, the animal heaving clouds of vapor from its nostrils.

"Nooooo!" The piercing cry came from Theresa's lips, in a volume that could have been heard in Tibet.

Roy glanced at Theresa, who lay sprawled on the ground but appeared in no imminent danger. Then he detected a faint object whisking toward him. A viselike grip suddenly squeezed his chest, while a fiery sensation started to burn from within. He dropped to his knees in a wave of light-headedness as Theresa immediately appeared and cradled his shoulders.

The razor-tipped arrow fired by the second horseman

had missed Roy's heart, but just barely. Instead, the projectile penetrated his chest just outside his heart, puncturing the pulmonary artery. The effect was nearly the same, with massive internal bleeding leading to imminent heart failure.

Theresa desperately tried to stem the flow of blood from the arrow's entry point, but there was nothing she could do about the internal damage. She held him tight as the color slowly drained from his face. He gasped for air before his body began to sag. For a moment, his eyes turned bright, and Theresa thought he might hang on. He looked at Theresa and painfully gasped the words, "Save yourself." And then his eyes closed and he was gone.

— 17 —

THE AEROFLOT TU-154 PASSENGER JET banked slowly over the city of Ulaanbaatar before turning into the wind and lining up on the main runway of Buyant Ukhaa Airport for its final approach. Under a cloudless sky, Pitt enjoyed an expansive vista of the city and outlying landscape from his cramped passenger's seat window. A large sprinkling of cranes and bulldozers indicated that the capital of Mongolia was a city on the move.

A first impression of Ulaanbaatar is that of an Eastern Bloc metropolis mired in the 1950s. Home to 1.2 million people, the city is mostly built with Soviet-style design, featuring Soviet-style blandness and conformity. Drab gray apartment buildings dot the city by the dozen, offering all the warmth of a prison dormitory. Architectural consciousness was an afterthought for many of the large block government buildings surrounding the city center. Yet recent autonomy, a taste of democratic governing, and a dose of economic growth has added a vibrancy to the city that openly seeks to modernize itself. Colorful shops, upscale restaurants, and booming nightclubs are creeping into the scene of the once-staid city.

At its heart, there is a comfortable blend of old and new. Outlying suburbs are still filled with *ger*s, muffin-shaped tents made of felt that are the traditional homes of the nomadic Mongolian herdsmen and their families. Hundreds of the gray or white tents jam the empty fields around the capital city that comprises the only true metropolis in the country.

In the West, little is known of Mongolia save for Genghis Khan and Mongolian beef. The sparsely populated country wedged between Russia and China occupies an expansive territory just slightly smaller than the state of Alaska. Rugged mountains dot the northern and western fringes of the landscape, while the Gobi Desert claims the south. Across the belt of the country run the venerable steppes, rolling grasslands that produced perhaps the finest horsemen the world has ever known. The glory days of the Mongol Horde are a distant memory, however. Years of Soviet dominion, during which Mongolia became one of the largest communist nations, stifled the country's identity and development. Only in recent years have the Mongolian people begun to find their own voice again.

As Pitt stared down at the mountains ringing Ulaanbaatar, he wondered whether chasing to Mongolia was such a good idea. It was after all a Russian vessel that had nearly been sunk at Lake Baikal, not a NUMA ship. And none of his crew had been harmed. The oil survey team was certainly not his responsibility either, though he was confident they were an innocent party. Still, there was some connection with their survey on the lake that had contributed to the foul play and abductions. Somebody was up to no good and he wanted to know why.

As the jet's tires screeched onto the runway, Pitt jabbed his elbow toward the passenger's seat next to him. Al Giordino had fallen asleep seconds after the plane lifted off from Irkutsk, and he continued to snooze even as the flight attendant spilled coffee on his foot. Prying a heavy eyelid open, he glanced toward the window. Spotting the concrete tarmac, he popped upright in his seat, instantly awake.

"Did I miss anything on the flight down?" he asked, suppressing a yawn.

"The usual. Wide-open landscapes. Some sheep and horses. A couple of nude communes."

"Just my luck," he replied, eyeing a brown stain on his shoe with suspicion.

"Welcome to Mongolia and 'Red Hero,' as Ulaanbaatar is known," Sarghov's jolly voice boomed from

241

across the aisle. He was wedged into a tiny seat, his face wallpapered with bandages, and Giordino wondered how the Russian could be so merry. Eyeing the fat scientist slip a flask of vodka into a valise, he quickly determined the answer.

The trio made their way through immigration, Pitt and Giordino garnering extraordinary scrutiny, before collecting their bags. The airport was small by international standards, and while waiting for a curbside cab Pitt noticed a wiry man in a red shirt studying him from across the concourse. Scanning the terminal, he observed that many of the locals gawked at him, not used to seeing a six-foot-three Westerner every day.

A weathered cab was flagged down, and they quickly motored the short distance into the city.

"Ulaanbaatar—and all of Mongolia, really—has changed a good deal in the past few years," Sarghov said.

"Looks to me like it hasn't changed much in the past few centuries," Giordino said, noting a large neighborhood of felt *gers*.

"Mongolia somewhat missed the station on the twentieth century," Sarghov nodded, "but they're catching up in the twenty-first. As in Russia, the police state no longer controls daily life and the people are learning to embrace freedom. The city may look grim to you, but it is a much livelier place than a decade ago."

"You have visited often?" Pitt asked.

"I have worked on several projects with the Mongolian Academy of Sciences at Lake Khovsgol."

The taxi careened around a crater-sized pothole then screeched to a stop in front of the Continental Hotel. As Sarghov checked them in, Pitt admired a collection of reproduced medieval artwork that decorated the large lobby. Glancing out the front window, he noticed a car pull up to the entrance and a man in a red shirt climb out. The same man he had seen at the airport.

Pitt studied the man as he lingered by the car. His features were Caucasian, which suggested he wasn't with the Mongolian police or immigration authorities. Yet he looked comfortable in his surroundings, earmarked by a toothy grin that habitually flashed from his friendly face. Pitt noticed that he moved with a measured balance, like a cat walking atop a fence. He was no tap dancer, though. In the pit of his back just above the waistline, Pitt saw a slight bulge that could only be a gun holster.

"All set," Sarghov said, handing room keys to Pitt and Giordino. "We're in neighboring rooms on the fourth floor. The bellboys are taking our bags up now. Why don't we grab lunch in the hotel café and strategize our plan of inquiry?"

"If there's a prospect of a cold beer in this joint, then I'm already there," Giordino replied.

"I'm still stiff from the plane ride," Pitt said. "Think I'll stretch my legs a bit with a walk around the block first. Order me a tuna sandwich, and I'll join you in a few minutes."

As Pitt exited the hotel, the man in red quickly turned his back and leaned on the car, casually checking his watch. Pitt turned and walked in the other direction, dodging a small group of Japanese tourists checking into the hotel. Walking briskly, he set a fast pace with his long legs and quickly covered two blocks. Turning a corner, he shot a quick glance to his side. As he suspected, the man in the red shirt was tailing him a half block behind.

Pitt had turned down a small side street lined with tiny shops that sold their goods along the sidewalk. Temporarily out of sight of his pursuer, Pitt started running down the street, sprinting past the first half-dozen shops. Ducking past a newsstand, he slowed in front of an open-air clothing shop. A rack of heavy winter coats jutted from the shop's side wall, offering a perfect concealment spot from someone rushing down the street. Pitt stepped into the shop and around the coatrack, then stood with his back to the wall.

A wrinkled old woman wearing an apron appeared from behind a counter piled with shoes and looked up at Pitt.

"Shhh," Pitt smiled, holding a finger to his lips. The old woman gave him an odd look, then returned to the back of the shop shaking her head.

Pitt had only to wait a few seconds before the man in the red shirt came hurrying along, nervously scanning each shop he came to. The sound of the man's footsteps announced his arrival as he approached and stopped in front of the shop. Pitt stood perfectly still, listening for the sound of heavy leather soles on concrete. When the patter resumed, Pitt sprang from the rack like a coiled spring.

The man in the red shirt had started to jog to the next shop when he detected a movement behind him. He glanced over his shoulder to find Pitt, towering nearly a foot taller, only a step behind him. Before he could react, he felt Pitt's large hands grasp his shoulders.

Pitt could have tackled the man, or spun him around, or thrown him to the ground. But he wasn't one to fight physics and instead simply used their forward momentum and pushed the smaller man ahead toward a round metal hat rack. The assailant smacked face-first into the rack and fell forward onto his stomach amid a clutter of baseball caps. The fall would have incapacitated most, but Pitt was hardly surprised when the wiry man bounced up immediately and crouched to strike Pitt with his left hand while his right hand reached behind his back.

Pitt took a step back and grinned at the man.

"Looking for this?" he asked. With a slight flick of his wrist, he flashed a Serdyukov SPS automatic pistol, which he leveled at the man's chest. A blank look crossed the man's face as his right hand came up behind his back empty. He coolly looked Pitt in the eye, then smiled broadly.

"Mr. Pitt. You seem to have taken advantage of me," he said in English only slightly tinged with a Russian accent.

"I don't like people crowding my space," Pitt replied, holding the gun steady.

The other man looked up and down the street nervously, then spoke quietly to Pitt. "You need not fear me. I am a friend looking out for you."

"Good. Then you can join me for lunch with some of my friends, who will be interested to meet you."

"To the Continental Hotel." The man smiled, removing a child's hat with the image of a running camel on its crest that had somehow stuck to his head during the scuffle. He slowly sidestepped Pitt and began walking in the direction of the hotel. Pitt followed a few steps behind, concealing the gun in his pocket and wondering what sort of eccentric this was who had been following him.

The Russian made no move to escape, instead marching boldly into the hotel and across the lobby to the main restaurant. To Pitt's surprise, he walked directly up to a large booth where Giordino and Sarghov were sitting, enjoying a drink.

"Alexander, you old goat!" he greeted Sarghov with a laugh.

"Corsov! They haven't run you out of the country yet?" Sarghov replied, standing and giving the smaller man a hug.

"I am an invaluable presence to the state mission," Corsov replied with mock seriousness. Eyeing Sarghov's bruised face, he frowned and said, "You look as if you just escaped from the gulag."

"No, just the inhospitable mongrels I told you about. Forgive me, I have not properly introduced you to my American friends. Dirk, Al, this is Ivan Corsov, special attaché to the Russian embassy here in Ulaanbaatar.

Ivan and I worked together years ago. He's agreed to help us with the investigation of Avarga Oil."

"He followed us from the airport," Pitt said to Sarghov with lingering doubt.

"Alexander told me you were coming. I was just making sure that no one else was following you."

"It seems I owe you an apology," Pitt smiled, covertly handing the pistol back to Corsov, and then shaking hands.

"Quite all right," he replied. "Though my wife may not like the looks of my new nose," he added, rubbing a purple welt administered by the hat rack.

"How your wife liked the looks of your old one is a mystery to me," Sarghov laughed.

The four men sat down and ordered lunch, the conversation turning serious.

"Alexander, you told me of the attempted sinking of the *Vereshchagin* and the abduction of the oil workers, but I didn't know you were seriously injured in the ordeal," Corsov said, nodding at a thick bandage around Sarghov's wrist.

"My injuries would have been a lot worse had my friends not intervened," he replied, tilting a glass of beer toward Pitt and Giordino.

"We weren't too happy about getting our feet wet in the middle of the night, either," Giordino added.

"What makes you think that the captives were brought to Mongolia?"

"We know that the freighter was leased by Avarga Oil, and the survey team was working under contract for them as well. The regional police authorities could find no permanent holdings in all of Siberia for the company, so we naturally assumed they would return to Mongolia. Border security confirmed that a truck caravan matching the description of those seen at Listvyanka had crossed into Mongolia at Naushki."

"Have the appropriate appeals for law enforcement assistance been made?"

"Yes, a formal request was sent to the Mongolian national police, and cooperation is taking place at the lower levels as well. An Irkutsk police official cautioned me that assistance would likely be forthcoming very slowly here."

"It is true. Russian influence in Mongolia is not what it used to be," Corsov said, shaking his head. "And the level of security here is much reduced from the past. These democratic reforms and economic issues have loosened the state's control over its own people," he said, raising his eyebrows at Pitt and Giordino.

"Freedom has its costs, pal, but I wouldn't take it any other way," Giordino replied.

"Comrade Al, believe me, we all relish the reforms that have expanded the freedom of individuals. It just occasionally makes my job a little more demanding."

"And what exactly is your job with the embassy?" Pitt asked.

"Special attaché and assistant director of information, at your service. I help ensure that the embassy is well informed about events and activities within the host country."

Pitt and Giordino gave each other a knowing look, but said nothing.

"Gloating again, Ivan?" Sarghov smiled. "Enough about you. What can you tell us about Avarga Oil?"

Corsov tilted back in his seat and waited for the waitress to lay a round of drinks on the table, then spoke in a low voice.

"The Avarga Oil Consortium. A strange animal."

"In what manner?" asked Sarghov.

"Well, the corporate entity is a relatively new concept in Mongolia. Obviously, there was no private ownership under communist rule, so the appearance of autonomous Mongolian companies has only occurred in the last fifteen years. Aside from the explosion of individual or publicly owned companies in the past five years, the earlier entities were all created in partnership with the state or foreign corporations. This is especially true of the mining companies, as the locals had no capital to start with and the state owned the land. Yet this wasn't the case with Avarga."

"They are not partnered with the Mongolian government?" Pitt asked.

"No, their registry confirms that they are fully privately owned. The point is more interesting, as they were one of the first companies licensed under the newly autonomous Mongolian government in the early 1990s. The company name, by the way, comes from an ancient city believed to be the first capital of Mongolia."

"It doesn't take much more than a land lease to start

an oil company," Giordino said. "Maybe they only started with a piece of paper and a pickup truck."

"Perhaps. I can't say what resources they began with, but their current assets are certainly more substantial than a pickup truck."

"What have you been able to verify?" asked Sarghov.

"They are known to have a minimally producing oil field in the north near the Siberian border, as well as a few exploratory wells in the Gobi. They also own exploration rights to some sizeable lands around Lake Baikal. Their only real physical asset is an oil field services yard in south Ulaanbaatar near the rail depot that's been around for years. And they recently announced commencement of mining operations at a small copper mine near Kharakhorum."

"Nothing outlandish in any of that," Pitt said.

"Yes, but those are only the publicly acknowledged holdings. A listing of their more intriguing assets I was able to acquire from the Ministry of Agriculture and Industry." Corsov's eyes shifted back and forth, indicating that the minister of agriculture and industry did not actually know that Corsov had acquired the information.

"Avarga Oil Consortium has acquired oil and mineral rights to vast tracts of land throughout the country. And more amazingly, they have acquired outright ownership of thousands of acres of former state land spreading all across the country. That is an unusual privilege in Mongolia. My sources tell me that the company paid a considerable sum to the Mongolian government for these land rights. Yet it does not appear to the eye that the company would have the resources to do so."

"There's always a bank somewhere that's willing to loan money," Pitt said. "Perhaps funds were fronted by outside mining interests."

"Yes, it is possible, though I found no evidence to that end. The funny thing is, much of the land is in regions with no known oil or mining geology. A large section courses through the Gobi Desert, for example."

The waitress appeared and slid a plate of roast lamb in front of Corsov. The Russian stuffed a large piece of meat in his mouth, then continued talking.

"I found it interesting that the company head does not appear to have any political clout or connections, and is actually unknown to most Mongolian government officials. The deals the company made were apparently conjured up with cash, the source of which is a mystery to me. No, the company head keeps a low profile in Xanadu."

"Xanadu?" asked Pitt.

"It's the name given to the residence, and headquarters, such as it is, of the company's chairman. Located about two hundred fifty kilometers southeast of here. I've never seen it, but was told about it by a Yukos oil executive who was invited there for a business deal some years ago. It is supposed to be a small but opulent palace built on the design of the original summer home of the thirteenth-century Mongol emperor. Filled with antiques. There is supposedly nothing else like it in Mongolia. Oddly, I've never known any Mongolians who have been inside the place."

"More evidence of unaccountable wealth," Sarghov said. "So what of our captives? Would they have been taken to the industrial site in town or to this Xanadu?"

"It is difficult to say. The trucks would easily pass unnoticed in and out of the facility here, so that would be a good starting point. Tell me, though, why were these oil workers abducted?"

"That is a good question, and one we would like to find out," Pitt replied. "Let's start with the industrial site. Can you get us inside for a look?"

"Of course," Corsov replied as if insulted by the question. "I have already surveyed the facility. It is protected by security guards; however, access should be attainable near the rail line."

"A quick nighttime look-see around shouldn't bother anyone," Giordino said.

"Yes, I suspected that would be your wish. You only need verify the presence of the survey team. Once we establish they are here, then we can push the Mongolian police authorities to act. Otherwise, we will be old men before anything gets done. Believe me, comrades, time can indeed stand still in Mongolia."

"What about the woman, Tatiana. Have you any information on her?"

"Unfortunately, no. She may have traveled to Siberia under an assumed name, if the immigration authorities are to be believed. But if she is part of Avarga Oil and here in Mongolia, then we will find her."

Corsov finished devouring his lamb and knocked back a second Chinese-brewed beer.

"Midnight tonight. Meet me at the back of the hotel and I will take you to the facility. Of course in my capacity, it is too dangerous for me to join you." He smiled, his large teeth glistening.

"I'm afraid I must be sidelined from the cloak-and-dagger business as well," Sarghov said, waving a bandaged wrist. "I'll do my best to assist in any other way," he added with disappointment.

"Not a problem, comrades," Pitt replied. "No sense in creating an international incident with both our countries. We'll just play the lost tourists if anything happens."

"There should be little danger in some harmless trespassing," Sarghov agreed.

Corsov's cheerful face suddenly turned solemn.

"There is some tragic news I must warn you about. A LUKOIL Russian oil survey team was ambushed and killed by men on horseback in the mountains north of here two days ago. Four men were brutally murdered for no apparent reason. A fifth man witnessed the murders but managed to escape undetected. A sheepherder found him exhausted and terrified not far from the village of Erõõ. When the man returned to the scene with the local police, everything was gone—bodies, trucks, survey gear—it had all vanished. An embassy representative met him and escorted him back to Siberia, while LUKOIL officials confirmed that the rest of the survey team had gone missing."

"Is there any link with Avarga Oil?" Giordino asked.

"Without any evidence, we just don't know. But it does seem an odd coincidence, you must agree."

The table fell silent for a moment, then Pitt said, "Ivan, you have told us little about the owners of Avarga Oil. Who is the face behind the company?"

"Faces, actually," Corsov corrected. "The company is registered to a man named Tolgoi Borjin. He is known to have a younger sister and brother, but I could not produce their names. The woman, Tatiana, may well in fact be the sister. I will attempt to find further information. Public records being what they are in Mongolia, little is known of the family publicly or even privately. State records indicate that Borjin was raised in a state commune in the Khentii province. His mother died at an early age and his father was a laborer and surveyor. As I mentioned, the family doesn't seem to have any particular political influence and are not known to have a visible presence in Ulaanbaatar's upper society. I can only repeat a rumor that the family are self-proclaimed members of the Golden Clan."

"Deep pockets, eh?" Giordino asked.

Corsov shook his head. "No, the Golden Clan has nothing to do with wealth. It is a reference to lineage."

"With a name like that, there must have been some old money somewhere along the line."

"Yes, I suppose you could say that. Old money and land. Lots of it. Nearly the entire Asian continent, as a matter of fact."

"You're not saying . . . ," Pitt started to ask.

Corsov cut him off with a nod. "Indeed. The history books will tell you that the Golden Clan were direct descendants of Chinggis."

"Chinggis?" Giordino asked.

"Accomplished tactician, conqueror, and perhaps the greatest leader of the medieval age," Pitt injected with regard. "Better known to the world as Genghis Khan."

⁓ 18 ⁓

DRESSED IN DARK CLOTHES, PITT and Giordino left the hotel after a late dinner, making a loud show of asking the front desk where the best neighborhood bars were located. Though foreign tourists were no longer a rarity in Ulaanbaatar, Pitt knew better than to raise suspicions. Casually walking around the block, they settled into a small café across from the hotel's rear entrance. The café was crowded, but they found a corner table and nursed a pair of beers while waiting for the clock to strike twelve. A nearby throng of drunken businessmen warbled ballads in noisy unison with a red-haired barmaid who played a stringed instrument called a "yattak." To Pitt's amusement, it seemed as if the song never changed.

Corsov appeared promptly at midnight driving a gray Toyota sedan. He barely slowed for Pitt and Giordino to climb in, then accelerated down the street. Corsov took a circuitous route around the city, driving past the large open Sukhbaatar Square. The public gathering place in the heart of Ulaanbaatar was named for a revolutionary leader who defeated the Chinese and declared Mongol independence on the site in 1921. He would have probably been disappointed to know that a local rock band surrounded by teens in grunge attire was the main draw as Corsov drove by.

The car turned south and soon left the city center traffic as Corsov drove through darkened side streets.

"I have a present for you on the backseat," Corsov smiled, his buckteeth gleaming in the rearview mirror. Giordino searched and found a couple of weathered brown jackets folded on the seat, topped by a pair of battered yellow hard hats.

"They'll help ward off the evening chill and make you look like a couple of local factory workers."

"Or a couple of skid row hobos," Giordino said, pulling on one of the jackets. The worn coat was moth-eaten in places and Giordino felt like his muscular frame would burst the shoulder seams. He smiled when he saw that the sleeves on Pitt's jacket came up six inches short.

"Any all-night tailors in the neighborhood?" Pitt asked, holding up an arm.

"Ha, very funny," Corsov laughed. He then reached under the seat and handed Pitt a large envelope and a flashlight.

"An aerial photo of the area, courtesy of the Ministry of Construction and Urban Development. Not very detailed, but it gives you a rough layout of the facility."

"You've been a busy boy this evening, Ivan," Pitt said.

"With a wife and five kids, you expect me to go home after work?" he laughed.

They reached the southern fringe of the city where Corsov turned west, following alongside a set of railroad tracks. As they passed Ulaanbaatar's main train station, Corsov slowed the car. Pitt and Giordino quickly studied the photograph under the glow of the flashlight.

The fuzzy black-and-white aerial photograph covered a two-square-mile area, but Corsov had circled the Avarga facility in red. There wasn't much to see. Two large warehouse buildings sat at either end of the rectangular compound, with a few small structures scattered in between. Most of the yard, which was walled on the front street and fenced on the rear and sides, was open-air storage for pipes and equipment. Pitt tracked a rail spur that ran out of the east end of the yard and eventually met up with the city's main rail line.

Corsov turned off the headlights and pulled into a vacant lot. A small, roofless building sat at the edge, streaked with black soot marks. A former bakery, it had long ago caught fire and burned, leaving only singed walls as its skeletal remains.

"The rail spur is just behind this building. Follow the tracks to the yard. There is just a chain-link gate over the rail entry," Corsov said, handing Pitt a small pair of wire cutters. "I'll be waiting at the train depot until three, then I'll make a brief stop here at three-fifteen. Any later and you are on your own."

"Thanks, Ivan. Don't worry, we'll be right back," Pitt replied.

"Okay. And please remember one thing," Corsov grinned. "If anything happens, please call the U.S. embassy, not the Russian embassy."

Pitt and Giordino made their way to the burned-out building and waited in the shadows for Corsov's tail-lights to disappear down the road before moving around back. A few yards away, they found the ele-vated rail spur running through the darkness and began following the tracks toward an illuminated facility in the distance.

"You know, we could be back sampling the local vodka in that cozy café," Giordino noted as a chilled gust of wind blew over them.

"But the barmaid was married," Pitt replied. "You'd be wasting your time."

"I've never yet found drinking in a bar to be a waste of time. As a matter of fact, I have discovered that time often stands still while in a bar."

"Only until the tab arrives. Tell you what, let's find Theresa and her pals, and the first bottle of Stoli is on me."

"Deal."

Walking several feet to the side of the railroad tracks, they moved quickly toward the facility. The gate across the rail spur was as Corsov described, a swinging chain-link fence padlocked to a thick steel pole. Pitt pulled the wire cutters from his pocket and quickly snipped an inverted L shape in the mesh. Giordino reached over and pulled the loose section away from the fence so Pitt could crawl through, then scampered in after him.

The rambling yard was well lit, and, despite the late hour, a steady buzz of activity hummed from within. Keeping to the shadows as best they could, Pitt and Giordino moved alongside the large fabricated building on the east end of the yard. The building's sliding doors opened to the interior of the yard, and the men crept toward the entrance, pausing behind one of the large doors.

From their vantage point, they had a clear view of the facility. To their left, a dozen or so men were working near the rail line, milling over four flatbed railcars. An overhead crane loaded bundled sections of four-foot-diameter pipe onto the first railcar, while a pair of yellow forklifts loaded smaller drill pipe and casings onto the other cars. Pitt was relieved to see that several of the men wore mangy brown jackets and battered yellow hard hats that matched their own.

"Drill pipe for an oil well and pipeline to transfer it to storage," Pitt whispered as he watched the loading. "Nothing unusual there."

"Except they have enough materials to drill to the center of the earth and pipe it to the moon," Giordino mused, gazing across the yard.

Pitt followed his gaze and nodded. Acres of the yard were jam-packed with forty-foot sections of the large-diameter pipe, stacked up in huge pyramids that towered over them. It was like a huge horizontal forest of metal trees, cut and stacked in an orderly sequence. A side section of the yard was filled with an equally impressive inventory of the small-diameter drill pipe and casings.

Turning his attention to the open warehouse, Pitt inched around the corner and peered in. The interior was brightly illuminated, but Pitt saw no signs of movement. Only a portable radio blaring an unrecognizable pop tune from a small side office indicated the presence of any workers. Striding into the warehouse, he walked behind a truck parked near the side wall and took inventory with Giordino beside him.

A half dozen large flatbed trailers occupied the front of the building, wedged between two dump trucks. A handful of Hitachi heavy-construction excavators and bulldozers lined the side wall, while the rear of the building was sectioned off as a manufacturing area. Pitt studied a stack of prefabricated metal arms and rollers that were in various stages of assembly. A nearly complete example stood in the center, resembling a large metal rocking horse.

"Oil well pumps," Pitt said, recalling the bobbing iron pumps he used to see as a kid dotting the undeveloped fields of Southern California. He noted that they appeared shorter and more compact than the type he remembered, which were used to pump oil out of mature wells that were not pressurized enough to blow the black liquid to the surface on their own.

"Looks more like the makings of a merry-go-round for welders," Giordino replied. He suddenly nodded toward a corner office, where they could see a man talking on the telephone.

Pitt and Giordino were creeping behind the cover of one of the flatbed trucks and inching toward the warehouse entrance when two more voices materialized near the door. The two men quickly ducked down and scurried around the back of the flatbed and knelt behind its large rear wheel. Through the wheel well, they watched as two workers strolled by on the opposite side of the truck, engaged in an animated conversation as they walked to the office in back. Pitt and Giordino quickly moved through the line of trucks and exited the building, regrouping behind a stack of empty pallets.

"Any one of those flatbeds could have been at Lake Baikal, but there was nothing that resembled the covered truck we saw at the dock," Giordino whispered.

"There's still the other side of the yard," Pitt replied, nodding toward the warehouse on the opposite side of the facility. The other building sat in a darkened section of the yard and appeared sealed shut. Together, they moved off toward the second building, threading their way through a small collection of storage sheds that dotted the northern side of the yard. Midway across, they approached a cluster of sheds and a small guard office that marked the main entrance to the complex. With Giordino on his heels, Pitt circled well clear of the entrance, then picked his way closer. Stopping at the last shed, which contained a bin full of grease-stained yard tools, they studied the second warehouse.

It was the same dimension as the first warehouse yet devoid of activity. Its front bay door was sealed shut, as was a small doorway to the side. What also made the building different was that an armed guard patrolled the perimeter.

"What's worth guarding at an oil field depot?" Giordino asked.

"Why don't we find out?"

Pitt stepped over to the tool bin and rummaged through its contents. "Might as well look the part," he said, hoisting a sledgehammer off the rack and toting it over his shoulder. Giordino picked up a green metal toolbox and emptied its contents, save for a hacksaw and monkey wrench.

"Let's go fix the plumbing, boss," he muttered, following after Pitt.

The twosome marched into the open and toward the building's façade as if they owned it. The guard initially paid little attention to the two men, who, in their ragged coats and banged-up hard hats, looked like any other workers in the yard. But when they completely ignored his presence on the way to the smaller entry door, he snapped into action.

"Stop," he barked in Mongolian. "Where do you think you're going?"

Giordino did stop, but only to bend down and retie his shoelace. Pitt kept walking toward the door as if the guard did not exist.

"Stop," the guard yelled again, shuffling toward Pitt as his hand reached for his holster.

Pitt kept walking until the guard was only a step away, then he slowly turned and smiled broadly at the man.

"Sorry, *no habla,*" Pitt said, shrugging his shoulders benignly.

The guard contemplated Pitt's Caucasian features and indecipherable phrase with a look of utter confusion. Then the blunt side of a green toolbox arced out of nowhere and struck him in the side of the head, knocking him cold before his body could hit the ground.

"I think he bent my toolbox," Giordino said huffily, rubbing a large dent on the end of the green case.

"Maybe he's got insurance. I think we might want to find a different resting place for Sleeping Beauty," Pitt replied, stepping around the body.

He walked over and tried the handle on the entry door but found it locked. Hoisting the sledgehammer, he swung the iron head against the door handle with a punishing blow. The lock smashed free of the door-jamb and Pitt easily kicked the door open. Giordino already had the guard's torso in his arms, and dragged the unconscious man through the doorway and deposited him to the side as Pitt closed the door behind him.

The interior was dark, but Pitt flicked on the light switches next to the door and flooded the interior with fluorescent light. To his surprise, the building was nearly empty. Just two flatbed haulers sat side by side in the middle of the floor, taking up a fraction of the otherwise deserted warehouse. One of the flatbeds was empty, but the other held a large protruding object covered from view by a canvas tarp. The object under wraps had a streamlined shape resembling a subway car. It was nearly the opposite in dimension of the jaggedly vertical object that they had seen concealed on the truck at Lake Baikal.

"Doesn't look like the present we were looking for," Pitt remarked.

"Might as well unwrap it and find out what the big secret is," Giordino replied, pulling out the hacksaw from his battered toolbox. Jumping onto the flatbed, he attacked a maze of ropes that secured the canvas in a mummy wrap. As the cut ropes fell away, Pitt reached up and yanked at the canvas covering.

As the canvas tarp fell to the floor, they stood staring at a tube-shaped piece of machinery that stretched almost thirty feet long. A tangled maze of pipes and hydraulic lines ran from a large cylinder head at the front end to a frame support at the tail. Pitt walked around and studied the prow of the device, finding a circular plate eight feet in diameter studded with small beveled disks.

"A tunnel-boring machine," he said, rubbing one of the cutterheads that was worn dull from usage.

"Corsov mentioned the company had some mining interests. I've heard there are some rich copper and coal reserves in the country."

"A rather expensive piece of equipment for a hack oil company."

A shrill whistle suddenly sounded from somewhere across the yard. Pitt and Giordino glanced toward the door and immediately saw that the guard had disappeared.

"Somebody woke up and ordered room service without telling us," Pitt said.

"And I don't have any change for a tip."

"We've seen all there is to see. Let's go meld into the woodwork."

They sprinted to the door, which Pitt opened a crack to peer out. Across the yard, a trio of armed guards was headed toward the warehouse in a jeep. Pitt recognized the man in the backseat rubbing his head as the guard Giordino had clobbered.

Pitt didn't hesitate, throwing open the door and bolting out of the building with Giordino on his heels. They turned and ran toward the maze of stacked pipes that paralleled the railroad spur. The pursuing guards shouted across the yard, but Pitt and Giordino quickly disappeared behind the first pallet of pipes.

"I hope they don't have dogs," Giordino said as they paused to catch their breath.

"I don't hear any barking." Pitt had instinctively grabbed the sledgehammer on the way out the door and held it up to show Giordino they weren't completely defenseless. He then surveyed the stacks of pipe around them and forged an exit strategy.

"Let's maze our way through the pipes to the rail

line. If we can skirt around the loading platform undetected, then we ought to be able to make it back to the
gate while they're still sniffing around here."

"I'm right behind you," Giordino replied.

They took off again, skirting in and around the mammoth stacks of pipe that stood twenty feet high. A few
yards behind, they heard the shouts of the guards as
they fanned out in pursuit. Fording through the dozens
of huge pallets was like snaking through a dense
sequoia forest. The pursuers were at a decided disad-
vantage.

Making a beeline as best he could, Pitt steered them
in the direction of the railroad tracks, stopping again as
they approached the last line of pallets. The rail spur
ended just a few feet away, while just beyond was the
southern boundary of the compound, marked by a
twelve-foot brick wall.

"No chance at scaling that," Pitt whispered. "We'll
have to follow the tracks."

They jumped over the railroad tracks and moved
toward the loading ramp at a fast walk so as not to
attract attention. Ahead of them, the loading of the flatcars continued unimpeded. The workers had stopped
briefly when the security alarm sounded, but resumed
their loading when they saw the guards driving to the
warehouse building.

Pitt and Giordino approached the dock, walking
along the backside of the flatcars with their hard hats
pulled low over their eyes. They were nearly past the
first of the three railcars when a foreman jumped off

the flatcar, landing a few steps from Giordino. The workman lost his balance, stumbling into Giordino and bouncing off the stocky Italian like he'd hit a concrete wall.

"Sorry," the man muttered in Mongolian, then looked Giordino in the face. "Who are you?"

Giordino could see the glint of alarm register in the man's face and immediately extinguished it with a right cross to the chin. The man slumped to the ground just as a loud shout erupted in front of them. Standing on the next flatcar, two other workers witnessed Giordino punch out their supervisor and yelled out in bewilderment. The workers turned and yelled across the yard, waving their arms at the security jeep, which was just pulling away from the warehouse.

"So much for a stealthy getaway," Pitt quipped.

"I swear I was just minding my own business," Giordino muttered.

Pitt peered down the rail line toward the gate they had cut through. If they took off at a sprint they had a chance to reach it before the jeep cut them off, but the guards would be right on their tail.

"We need a diversion," Pitt said quickly. "Try to attract the attention of the jeep. I'll work on getting us a lift out of here."

"Attracting attention won't be a problem."

Together they ducked under the railcar and crawled to the other side. Pitt hesitated in the shadows while Giordino jumped into view and started running back toward the stacks of pipes. A second later, several dockworkers came streaking by after him, dust and gravel rising from their feet inches from Pitt's face. He looked out and saw the security jeep make a sudden turn, its headlights capturing Giordino's image in the distance.

It was Pitt's turn to move now and he jumped from beneath the flatbed and ran toward the next railcar in line. One of the forklifts was setting a pallet of pipe casings on the flatbed when Pitt charged toward the driver's compartment. He still carried the sledge-hammer with him and made a flying downward swing as he sprang into the cab. The heavy mallet head struck the foot of the operator before Pitt even landed. The startled driver stared at Pitt with wide eyes before the pain from two broken toes registered in his brain. Pitt raised the hammer as a first cry of agony trickled from the man's lips.

"Sorry, pal, but I need to borrow your rig," Pitt said.

The stunned operator flew out the opposite side of the open cab as if he had wings, disappearing into the darkness before Pitt could wield another blow. Pitt dropped the hammer and slid into the seat, quickly backing the forklift away from the railcar. He had driven a forklift decades before while working at a car parts distributor in high school and the controls quickly came back to mind. He whipped the forklift around on its lone rear wheel and stomped on the accelerator, aiming the twin prongs in the direction of Giordino.

Pitt's partner had streaked toward the maze of

stacked pipes until he saw one of the armed security guards emerge from the nearest piling. The jeep was descending from the center of the yard with the two other guards while a trio of dockworkers was chasing him from behind. Despite the odds, Giordino quickly figured his best chance was against the unarmed workers trailing him. Grinding to a stop in his tracks, he turned and charged directly at the first man in pursuit. The startled worker hesitated in surprise as Giordino suddenly bore into him, driving his shoulder into the man's stomach. It might as well have been a bull charging a rag doll. A gasp of air wheezed from the man's lips, then his face turned blue as he fell limp across Giordino's shoulders. The tough Italian didn't miss a step, bulling forward with the dead weight into the second worker, who was following only a step behind. The three bodies collided with a sickening thud, Giordino using the body over his shoulder to soften the blow from the second man. In a tumble of arms and legs, the three bodies fell to the ground in a heap, Giordino somehow landing on top.

In an instant, he was on his feet, wheeling to face the next pursuer. But the third dockworker, a wiry man with long sideburns, had deftly sidestepped the mass of bodies and whirled behind Giordino. As Giordino rose, sideburns sprang onto his back and cupped an elbow around his throat. A simultaneous fusion of forces converged on him, as the jeep screeched to a halt just inches away while the guard on foot approached yelling with his gun drawn. Realizing he could no longer fight his way out, Giordino relaxed under the grip of the headlock, thinking that this was not quite the end of the diversion that he had in mind.

Staring through the windshield, he noticed the driver of the jeep glare triumphantly as if he had just bagged a trophy caribou. The smug guard, obviously head of the security force, started to climb out of the jeep, then hesitated with a quizzical look on his face. The look turned to horror as he turned toward a bright yellow blur flashing out of the darkness.

Blazing across the yard, Pitt had the forklift floored and aimed for the driver's side of the jeep. A warning cry erupted from the jeep's passenger, who tried to scramble clear, but there was nothing the driver could do. The twin forks sliced into the jeep like it was made of cheese, penetrating just fore and aft of the driver's seat. The nose of the forklift then bashed into the door-sill, mashing the jeep sideways for several feet and sending its occupants airborne out the opposite side. The two guards tumbled to the ground as the jeep skidded to a halt beside them. Pitt quickly jammed the forklift in reverse and backed away from the mangled car.

With the shock of the collision just in front of them, Giordino felt sideburns's grip around his neck loosen a fraction and he reacted immediately. Shoving the man's wrist up, Giordino flung his free elbow into the worker's ribs. It was enough to stun the man and allow Giordino to slip his grasp. Giordino turned and ducked as sideburns threw a roundhouse punch, which he countered with a hard jab below the man's ear. The smaller man quickly dropped to his knees, gazing at Giordino with a dazed look in his eyes.

That still left the security guard on foot. Giordino glanced at the armed man a few feet away and was relieved to see that he was no longer pointing the gun in his direction. The guard had instead turned his attention toward the forklift, which was now racing directly toward him. The guard fired two panicked shots in the general direction of the cab, then leaped out of the path of the charging vehicle. Ducking low in the cab, Pitt heard the shots whistle over his head, then yanked hard on the steering wheel as he passed by the guard. The nimble forklift quickly spun around and in an instant Pitt was back on the heels of the man. The surprised guard stumbled as he now tried to flee the rabid forklift and fell facedown in its oncoming path. Pitt quickly lowered the front prongs and moved in for the kill.

The guard should have rolled to the side but instead tried to stand up and run. As he rose, one of the prongs struck him along the backside and rode up his coat. Pitt jammed the lift lever and elevated the twin prongs above the cab, hauling the guard up into the air with them. Kicking and flailing, the guard dropped his gun as he desperately grabbed at the prong to keep from falling to the ground.

"You know, you could hurt someone with this thing, if you're not careful," Giordino said, jumping into the cab and grabbing an overhead roll bar for support.

"Safety first, I always say. Or is it second?" Pitt replied.

He had already spun the forklift around and was accelerating alongside the railroad tracks toward the gate. As he was passing by the loading dock, several workers stepped forward, then jumped back as the forklift raced by, the security guard dangling from the elevated prong and shouting out for help.

Pitt spied a high stack of oil drums ahead and veered the forklift toward the pile.

"End of the line for our first-class passengers," he muttered.

Driving straight for the drums, he slammed on the brakes when just a few yards away. The forklift screeched and skidded, banging to a jolting stop against the lower wall of drums. Dangling from the elevated prong, the sudden stop jerked the security guard forward, sending him flailing like a bird into the upper stack of oil drums. As he backed the forklift away, Pitt heard mumbled curses from the stack that told him the guard was still alive.

Pitt turned the forklift back toward the railroad tracks and mashed the round accelerator to the floorboard. Shouts could be heard from the scene of the wrecked jeep, and Pitt glanced over his shoulder to see that two of the men were on their feet and chasing after them. The popping sound of gunfire echoed from behind, and a few of the rounds found the body of the forklift with a metallic thud. But the humming electric forklift buzzed quietly along, spreading the distance between itself and the angry pursuers.

Nearing the gate, Pitt inched the forklift closer to the railroad tracks until the right wheel was bouncing over the wooden ties.

"Ramming speed," Giordino said, eyeing Pitt's move and bracing himself for impact.

Pitt steered for the left edge of the gate and gripped the steering wheel tight. The left prong struck the gate support post dead-on, severing through the lower metal hinge, as the right prong sliced through the metal fencing. The nose of the forklift then rammed into the gate with the full force of its momentum. The impact drove the forklift into the air momentarily before it mashed the gate off its hinges and sent it flying off to the side.

Pitt had to fight the controls to keep the forklift from flipping as it burst out of the facility. The battered forklift bounded over the tracks and onto the gravel track that sided the rail line before settling onto its three wheels. Pitt steered down the gravel path, never lifting his foot off the accelerator.

"I hope our taxi driver is early," Pitt yelled.

"He better be. We're not going to outrun anybody much longer." Peering back toward the facility, Giordino spotted the headlights of another vehicle skirting the railroad tracks toward the battered gate.

Pitt muscled the forklift's controls as it bounced wildly over unseen ruts and rocks in the starlit darkness. Not wanting to give any pursuing shooters an exact target, he had flicked off the headlights when they broke clear of the facility. The darkened shadow of the burned-out bakery atop the hill finally appeared ahead and Pitt skidded the forklift to a stop.

"Everybody off," he said, holding the brake down until they came to a complete stop. Jumping down, he searched the ground around him until finding a large flat rock. Turning the steering wheel of the forklift so it aimed down the gravel track, he dropped the rock on the accelerator and jumped back. The yellow forklift sprung down the path, humming quietly as it disappeared into the night.

"A shame. I was starting to get attached to that machine," Giordino muttered as they quickly scrambled up the hill.

"Hopefully, a camel herder in the Gobi Desert will put it to good use."

Cresting the ravine, they ducked behind a crumbling wall of the bakery and peered around the front lot. Corsov's car was nowhere to be seen.

"Remind me to bad-mouth the KGB next time we're in public," Giordino said.

A half mile down the road, they suddenly eyed the red flash of a pair of taillights, illuminated from a tap on the brakes.

"Let's hope that's our boy," Pitt said.

The duo took off from the building and ran down the road at a sprint. Approaching the crunching sound of tires on gravel, they jumped to the side of the road and hesitated as a car with its headlights off crept out of the darkness. It was the gray Toyota.

"Good evening, gentlemen," Corsov grinned as Pitt and Giordino climbed into the car. His breath filled the interior with the odor of vodka. "A successful tour?"

"Yes," Pitt replied, "but our hosts wish to follow us home."

Behind the bakery, they could see the flash of a bouncing headlight beam from down the hill. Without a word, Corsov whipped the car around and sped off down the road. In minutes, he was barreling down a mix of back-road city streets before suddenly appearing at the rear of their hotel.

"Good night, gentlemen," Corsov slurred. "We shall reconvene tomorrow, when you can give me a full report."

"Thanks, Ivan," Pitt said. "Drive safe."

"But of coursc."

As Pitt slammed the door shut, the Toyota burst off down the street, disappearing around a corner with its tires squealing. Walking to the hotel, Giordino suddenly stopped and pointed. Across the street, music and laughter wafted from the little café, still bustling at the late hour.

Giordino turned to Pitt and smiled. "I believe, boss, that you owe me a diversion."

19

T HERESA SAT IN THE STUDY, looking through a seismic report with a thousand-mile stare. A melancholy depression, tinged with anger, had gradually replaced her shock at Roy's brutal killing. He had been like a brother to her and his murder the night before was painful to accept. It had been made worse by the appearance of Tatiana in the courtyard shortly after Roy expired. With glaring eyes that spit fire, she'd hissed at Theresa.

"Do not obey and the same fate will befall you!"

The guard who had killed Roy was summoned to crudely drag Theresa back to her room and keep her under armed guard.

Since that moment, she and Wofford had been under constant surveillance. She gazed across the study to the entryway, where two stone-faced guards stood staring back at her. Their brightly colored silk *del*s, or tunics, softened their appearance, but she knew from the night before that they were highly trained killers.

Alongside her, Wofford sat with his bum leg propped on a chair, deeply engrossed in a geological report. He had been shocked by Roy's death but seemed to have shaken it off quickly. More likely, he was using the task at hand to conceal his emotions, Theresa decided.

"We might as well give them the work they asked

for," he had told her. "It might be the only thing that keeps us alive."

Maybe he was right, she thought, trying to regain focus on the report in her hands. It was a geological assessment of a basin area in an unidentified plain. Sandstone and limestone rifts were identified as being overlaid with clay and shale stretched across the basin. It was just the type of stratigraphy that was conducive to subsurface petroleum reserves.

"The geology seems promising, wherever it is," she said to Wofford.

"Take a look at this," he replied, unrolling a computer printout across the table. Known as a seismic section, the printout showed a computer-enhanced image of several layered levels of sediment for a confined location. The chart was created by a seismic survey team that sent man-made shocks into the ground and recorded the sound reflections. Theresa stood up to get a better look, examining the chart with fresh interest. It was unlike any seismic image she had seen before. Most subsurface profiles were opaque and smudgy, resembling a Rorschach inkblot left out in a rainstorm. The profile before her was a crisp image, with clearly delineated subsurface layers.

"Amazing image," she remarked. "Must be made with some cutting-edge technology. I've never seen anything this precise."

"It definitely beats anything we've ever used in the field. But that's not the amazing aspect," he added. Reaching over, he pointed to a bulbous shape near the bottom of the page that extended off the edge. Theresa leaned over and studied it carefully.

"That looks like a classic, not to mention nicely sized, anticlinal trap," she said, referring to the dome-shaped layer of sediments. The cusp of a sedimentary dome like the one before her was a flashing red light for geophysicists, as it is a prime spot for petroleum deposits to accumulate.

"Nicely sized, indeed," Wofford replied. Pulling over a stack of similar profiles, he spread several on the table. "That particular trap stretches nearly forty kilometers. There's six other smaller ones I've found in the same region."

"It certainly looks like the right conditions for a deposit."

"You never know until the drill gets wet, but from these images, it looks pretty promising."

"And there's six more? That's a tremendous reserve potential."

"At least six more. I haven't digested all the reports yet, but it is mind-boggling. Taking a stone's throw from the image, there might be two billion barrels potentially sitting in that one trap alone. Add in the others and you could have over ten billion barrels. And that's just for one field. No telling how much is in the entire region."

"Incredible. Where is the field located?"

"That's the hitch. Someone has carefully removed all geographic references from the data. I can only tell that it is subterranean, and that the surface topography is flat with a predominant sandstone base."

"You mean we might be looking at the next North Sea oil fields and you don't know where they are located?"

"I haven't a clue."

SARGHOV LAUGHED between sips from a cup of tea, his big belly jiggling with each guffaw.

"Charging through the night on a forklift, toting an Avarga security guard through the air," he chuckled. "You Americans always have such a flair for dramatics."

"It wasn't the understated exit I would have preferred," Pitt replied from across the café table, "but Al insisted we ride, not walk."

"And we still nearly missed last call." Giordino smirked before sipping his morning coffee.

"I'm sure management is scratching their heads, wondering why a pair of Westerners were waltzing around their facility. A shame you didn't find any evidence that our oil survey friends had been there."

"No, the only item of interest was the tunnel-boring machine. And it was concealed under a canvas tarp similar to the object that was removed from the freighter at Baikal."

"It is possible the machine was stolen and brought into the country surreptitiously. Mongolia does not have easy access to high technology. Perhaps the company does not want the government to be aware of its technological equipment."

"Yes, that could be true," Pitt replied. "I would still like to know what it was that they hauled away from Baikal under wraps."

"Alexander, have there been any developments in the abduction investigation?" Giordino asked before biting into a buttered roll.

Sarghov looked up to see Corsov enter the busy café situated across from Sukhbaatar Square. "I shall let our local expert address that question," he said, standing and greeting his embassy friend. Corsov smiled his toothy grin and pulled a chair up to the table.

"I trust everyone had a comfortable night?" he said to Pitt and Giordino.

"Just until the vodka wore off," Pitt grinned, cognizant that Giordino was nursing a mild hangover.

"Ivan, we were just discussing the investigation. Has there been any news on the official front?" Sarghov asked.

"*Nyet,*" Corsov said, his jovial face turning solemn. "The National Police have still not been assigned the case. The investigative request is being held up in the Justice Ministry. My apologies, I misspoke when I said that Avarga Oil has no influence within the government. It is clear that a bribe is in effect at some level."

"Every hour might count for Theresa and the others," Giordino said.

"Our embassy is doing everything they can through official channels. And I am, of course, pursuing leads through unofficial means. Do not worry, my friend, we will find them."

Sarghov drained the rest of his tea and set down the empty cup. "I'm afraid there is little more that we can ask of Ivan. The Mongol authorities often work on their own time frame. They will ultimately respond to the continued inquisitions from our embassy, despite whatever bribes are impeding the investigation. It may be best if we step back and wait for the bureaucratic hurdles to be cleared before any further action. As it is, I must return to Irkutsk to file a report on the damage to the *Vereshchagin*. I have gone ahead and booked airline tickets for the three of us this afternoon."

Pitt and Giordino looked knowingly at Corsov, then turned to Sarghov.

"Actually, we have already made alternate travel plans, Alexander," Pitt said.

"You are returning directly to the United States? I thought perhaps you would return to Siberia and collect your comrade Rudi first."

"No, we're not going to the United States, or Siberia, just yet."

"I don't understand. Where is your intended destination?"

Pitt's green eyes glimmered as he said, "A mystical place called Xanadu."

20

CORSOV'S INTELLIGENCE NETWORK PAID off again. Though the central government in Ulaanbaatar had taken a hard turn toward democracy after the fall of the Soviet Union, there was a sizeable communist minority opposition in the government ranks, many of whom still harbored pro-Moscow sentiments. It was a low-level analyst in the Ministry of Foreign Affairs that had notified Corsov about the pending Chinese state visit. But it was Corsov who had recognized it as a golden opportunity for Pitt and Giordino.

The Chinese minister of commerce was arriving on short notice, ostensibly to tour a new solar energy plant recently opened at the edge of the capital city. Yet the bulk of the minister's time was scheduled for a private visit with the head of the Avarga Oil Consortium, at his secluded residence southeast of Ulaanbaatar.

"I can put you in the motorcade, which will get you past Borjin's front door. The rest will be up to you," Corsov had told Pitt and Giordino.

"No offense, but I don't see how anyone is going to buy us being part of the Chinese delegation," Giordino said.

"They won't have to, because you'll be part of the Mongolian state escort."

Giordino wrinkled his brow at what seemed to be a small difference.

Corsov explained that a formal reception was planned for the minister's arrival later in the day. A large welcoming escort from the Foreign Affairs Ministry would accompany the Chinese delegation for the evening. But tomorrow, when the delegation toured the solar energy plant and traveled to Avarga headquarters, only a small Mongolian security force had been requested to accompany the minister.

"So we are joining the Mongolian Secret Service?" Pitt asked.

Corsov nodded. "Ordinary officers of the National Police actually fill the roles. It took only a modest enticement to have you inserted as replacement security escorts. You will swap places with the real guards at the solar energy plant and follow the procession to Xanadu. As I told you, I would gladly use my own operatives for the assignment."

"No," Pitt replied, "we'll take the risk from here. You have gone out on a limb for us as it is."

"It is all deniable by me. And I trust you not to reveal your sources," he added with a grin.

"Cross my heart."

"Good. Now just remember to keep a low profile and see if you can prove that your abducted friends are on the premises. We can prompt the Mongolian authorities to action if we have some evidence."

"Will do. What do we owe you for the bribes?"

"That is such an ugly word," Corsov replied, a pained look crossing his face. "I am in the information business. Anything you can share with me about

Avarga Oil, Mr. Borjin, and his aspirations will more than repay the pittance spent on the police escort. Which means I expect you back here for borscht tomorrow night."

"Now, there's an enticement," Giordino groaned.

"And just one more thing," Corsov added with a smile. "Try not to forget to keep the Chinese minister alive."

PITT AND Giordino took a cab to the solar energy facility, arriving an hour ahead of the Chinese minister's scheduled appearance. Smiling at a sleepy-eyed guard at the gate, they flashed a pair of dummy press credentials provided by Corsov and waltzed right into the facility. It was little more than a ten-acre lot peppered with dozens of flat black solar panels that supplemented the electricity produced by a large adjacent coal-burning power plant. Built by the power company as an experimental test station, it barely provided the power to light a football stadium. With more than two hundred sixty days of sunshine a year, Mongolia was rich in the essential resource needed to generate solar power, though the technology was well beyond affordability at the consumer level.

Steering clear of a hastily assembled greeting platform where a handful of state officials and power plant executives waited nervously, Pitt and Giordino concealed themselves behind a large solar panel near the entrance. Dressed in dark Chinese-tailored sport coats and sunglasses, with black woolen beret-type hats on their heads, they easily passed for local security types to those observing from a distance. They didn't have to wait long before the motorcade rolled through the gates a few minutes early and pulled up to the greeting platform.

Pitt smiled to himself at the unceremonious vehicles that made up the motorcade, a far cry from the ubiquitous black limousines found in Washington. A trio of clean but high-mileage Toyota Land Cruisers chauffeured the Chinese minister and his small cadre of assistants and security guards. The contingent was led by a Mongol security escort driving a yellow UAZ four-door jeep. Another UAZ jeep tailed the delegation, its left front fender battered by a prior traffic accident. The Russian-built UAZs, an offshoot of a military jeep, reminded Pitt of the boxy International Harvester four-wheel drives built in the U.S. back in the late 1960s.

"That's our ride," Pitt said, referring to the battered UAZ at the rear.

"I hope it's got a satellite radio and a nav system," Giordino replied.

"I just hope it's got tires that were manufactured in this century," Pitt muttered.

Pitt watched as the two men in the car casually got out and disappeared into the field of solar panels as the welcoming committee greeted the Chinese minister. With the delegation preoccupied, Pitt and Giordino moved undetected to the car and took the guards' place in the front seats.

"Here's your nav system," Pitt said, grabbing a map from the dashboard and tossing it on Giordino's lap. He smiled when he noticed that the car didn't even have a radio.

A few yards in front of them, Commerce Minister Shinzhe was making quick order of the welcoming committee. He briskly shook hands with the plant officials, then walked off toward some solar panels to hasten the tour. In less than ten minutes, he was thanking the officials and climbing back into his car.

"He's sure got ants in his pants," Giordino said, surprised at the brevity of the tour.

"Guess he's anxious to get to Xanadu. The tour of the solar energy facility is apparently not the highlight of his visit."

Pitt and Giordino scrunched down in their seats as the motorcade looped around the facility and passed right by them on the way to the gate. Pitt then started the car and quickly caught up to the third Toyota in line.

The caravan rumbled east out of Ulaanbaatar, curving past the Bayanzurkh Nuruu Mountains. Mount Bayanzurkh, one of four holy peaks that surround Ulaanbaatar like points on a compass, capped the range. The scenic mountain peaks gradually gave way to rolling empty grasslands that stretched treeless as far as the eye could see. This was the famous Asian Steppe of historical lore, a swath of rich pasturelands that spanned central Mongolia like a wide, green belt. Stands of the thick summer grass rippled like waves on the ocean under a stiff breeze that blew across the open range.

The lead vehicle followed an uneven paved road, which eventually turned to dirt, then transgressed into little more than a pair of ruts through the grassland. Driving at the back of the pack, Pitt was forced to navigate through a dirty haze kicked up by the other vehicles and magnified by the dust-laden winds.

The caravan traveled to the southeast, bounding across the grass-covered hills for another three hours before ascending a small cluster of mountains. At a nondescript iron gate, the delegation turned onto another road, which Pitt noted was professionally groomed. The road climbed several miles up the mountain before skirting a ridge and approaching a fast-moving river. An aqueduct had been built off the river and the caravan followed the cement-lined waterway as it twisted around a tight bend and approached a high-walled compound. The aqueduct continued up to the compound, running underneath its facing stone wall near a single-arched entryway. Two guards wearing bright silk *del*s stood on either side of a massive iron gate blocking the entrance. As the vehicles slowed to a stop in front of the gate, Pitt contemplated their next move.

"You know, we probably don't want to join the party for the grand entrance," he said.

"You never were one to fit in with the crowd," Giordino remarked. "Do you know if the other Mongol escorts are aware that we replaced their pals for the afternoon?

"I don't know. And I guess there is no sense in finding out."

Giordino gazed toward the entrance, then squinted. "Car problems?" he asked.

"I was thinking a flat tire."

"Consider it done."

Slipping out the passenger's door, Giordino crawled beside the front tire and removed the valve stem cap. Jamming a matchstick into the stem, he waited patiently as a rush of air whistled out of the valve. In a few seconds, the tire deflated to the ground and he screwed the cap back on. Just as he climbed back into the jeep, the iron gate was shoved open at the front of the line.

Pitt followed the line of cars as they entered the compound but stopped at the gate as one of the guards gave him a cross look. Pitt pointed toward the flat tire and the guard looked, then nodded. Barking something in Mongolian, he motioned for Pitt to turn right after he entered the compound.

Pitt made a show of limping slowly behind the other cars as he quickly surveyed the complex. The ornate marble residence was directly ahead, fronted by the manicured garden. Pitt had no idea what the real Xanadu looked like centuries ago, but the structure before him was spectacular in its own right. Plenty of pageantry was on display for the minister as a pair of escorts riding snow white horses led the procession to the front portico. A Chinese flag blew stiffly on a mast adjacent to an arrangement of nine tall wooden poles.

Pitt noticed that a chunk of white fur resembling a fox-tail dangled from each pole top. As the procession approached the residence, Pitt strained to identify Borjin among the greeting party on the porch but he was too far away to see any faces.

"Any sign of Tatiana in the welcoming committee?" he asked as he began wheeling the car out of line and toward the building on the right.

"There's at least one woman standing on the porch, but I can't make out if it is her," Giordino said, squinting through the windshield.

Pitt guided the car toward the garage and drove through its open bay doors. The flat tire flopped loudly on the concrete floor as he brought the car to a stop beside a segregated bay flanked with tool chests. A grease-stained mechanic in a red baseball cap came running over, yelling and waving his arms at the jeep's occupants. Pitt ignored the man's ravings and flashed a friendly smile.

"Pfffft," he said, pointing toward the flat tire.

The mechanic walked around the front of the car and examined Giordino's handiwork, then looked through the windshield and nodded. He turned and walked to the end of the bay, returning a moment later with a floor jack.

"Might be a good time to take a walk," Pitt said, climbing out of the car.

Giordino followed him as they walked toward the open garage door, then stopped as if to mill about while waiting for the tire to be repaired. But rather than watch the mechanic, they carefully scrutinized the interior of the garage. Several late-model four-wheel drives were parked in front, while the rest of the building was filled with large trucks and some excavating equipment. Giordino rested his foot on a maintenance cart parked by the door and studied a dusty brown panel truck.

"The enclosed truck," he said quietly. "Looks a lot like the one at Baikal."

"Indeed, it does. How about the flatbed over there?" Pitt said, motioning to a cab and flatbed sitting nearby.

Giordino glanced at the truck and flatbed, which were empty save for some canvas and ropes strewn over one side.

"Our mystery prize?"

"Perhaps," Pitt replied. He peered across the grounds and then at the building next to the garage.

"We probably have some temporary immunity around here," he said, nodding toward the building. "Let's take a walk next door."

Proceeding as if they knew where they were going, they strolled to the brick building next door. They passed a large loading dock and walked through an adjacent glass entry door. Pitt expected to find a reception area, but the entrance led instead into the middle of a large work bay that opened onto the empty dock. Test equipment machines and electronic circuit boards were scattered around several workbenches, being tinkered with by a pair of men in white antistatic lab coats. One of the men, who had small birdlike eyes set behind wire-rimmed glasses, stood and looked at Pitt and Giordino suspiciously.

"Stualét?" Pitt asked, recalling the Russian word for "toilet" that he picked up in Siberia.

The man studied Pitt for a moment, then nodded and pointed down a corridor that ran from the center of the room. "On the right," he said in Russian, then sat down and resumed his tinkering.

Pitt and Giordino walked past the two men and turned down the corridor.

"Impressive language skills," Giordino said quietly.

"Just one of the nearly five words I know in Russian," Pitt boasted. "I just recalled Corsov saying that most Mongolians know a smidgen of Russian."

They moved slowly down the wide tiled corridor, which stretched twenty feet across, and whose ceiling was nearly as high. Skid marks on the floor indicated the movement of large equipment up and down the corridor. The hallway was lined with large plate-glass windows that revealed the interior of the rooms on either side. Small labs, stockpiled with various electronic test and assembly equipment, occupied most of the building space. Only an occasional office and desk, decorated in Spartan blandness, broke up the technical areas. The entire building was strangely cold and silent, in part because only a handful of technicians appeared to work there.

"Looks more like the back of a Radio Shack than an Exxon gas station to me," Giordino said.

"It does give the appearance they are interested in

something other than pumping oil out of the ground. Unfortunately, that may mean that Theresa and the others weren't brought here."

Passing by the restroom, they continued down the corridor until it ended at a thick metal door that closed over a high floor sill. Glancing around the empty hallway, Pitt grabbed the handle and pushed on the heavy door, which opened inward. The thick door swung back slowly, revealing a vast chamber. The room occupied the entire end of the building, with a high ceiling that rose over thirty feet. Row after row of cone-shaped spikes protruded from the walls, ceiling, and even the floor, which lent the appearance of some sort of medieval torture chamber. But there was no danger from the spikes, as Pitt confirmed when he squeezed one of the foam-rubber cone tips between his fingers.

"An anechoic chamber," he said.

"Built to absorb radio-frequency electromagnetic waves," Giordino added. "These babies are usually the property of defense contractors, used for testing sophisticated electronics."

"There's your sophisticated electronics," Pitt said.

He pointed to the center of the room, where a large platform stood on stilts above the foam floor. A dozen large metal cabinets were jammed onto the platform next to several racks of computer equipment. In the middle of the platform was an open center section, where a torpedo-shaped device hung from a gantry. Pitt and Giordino climbed across a catwalk that led from the door to the platform.

"This ain't the stuff of roughnecks," Pitt said, eyeing the equipment.

The cabinets and racks contained over forty computer-sized modules linked together with several yards of thick black cable. Each rack had a small LED display and several power meters. A large box with dials marked ERWEITERUNG and FREQUENZ sat at the end, next to a monitor and keyboard.

Pitt studied the markings on the equipment and raised a brow in curiosity.

"My high school foreign language skills may be a little rusty, but those dials are marked in German. I believe that last dial translates to 'Frequency.'"

"German? I would have thought Chinese or Russian would be more in vogue."

"Most of the electronics equipment looks to be of German manufacture as well."

"There's some serious horsepower involved," Giordino said, counting the array of transmitter cabinets cabled in sequence. "What do you make of it?"

"I can only guess. The large cabinets look like commercial-grade radio transmitters. The racks of computers must be used for performing data processing. Then there's the hanging tripod."

He turned and examined the device dangling from the center of the platform. It consisted of three long tubes fashioned together and standing nearly ten feet high. The lower ends flared near the floor, bound with a thickly matted material. The opposite ends, standing well above Pitt's head, sprouted a thick bundle of cables, which trailed to the computer racks.

"They resemble some sort of amplified transducers, though bigger than I've ever seen. It could be a beefed-up seismic-imaging system, used for oil exploration," he said, studying the tripod-shaped device that hung vertically.

"Looks more advanced than any drill operation I've ever seen."

Pitt glanced at several manuals and notebooks lying beside the equipment. He flipped through them casually, noting that they were all written in German. He opened what appeared to be the key operating manual and tore the first few pages out, stuffing them in his pocket.

"A little light reading material for the ride home?" Giordino said.

"Some practice for my German verb conjugations."

Pitt closed the manual, then they both made their way back across the catwalk and exited the chamber. Walking down the hallway, they heard a sudden commotion coming from the lab at the far end.

"The rat fink may have called the heat on us," Giordino said.

"A good bet," Pitt said, scanning the hallway. He took a few steps back and opened the chamber door, then returned to Giordino. "Maybe we can try to sneak past them."

They quickly moved up the hallway, then Pitt opened the door to one of the windowed labs and slipped in.

Giordino followed behind, then closed the door and turned off the lights. As they stood out of sight from the hall window, they noticed an odd chemical smell permeating the room. Peering across the darkened room, Pitt made out a number of stainless steel vats, along with a table full of small brushes and dental picks.

"I think they're taking the bait," Giordino whispered.

The sound of footsteps echoed down the hallway, drawing close and then passing by. Peeking through the glass, Giordino could see two men in silk uniforms marching toward the chamber door.

"Find me a broom," he whispered to Pitt, then flung the door open.

In a flash, he was running down the hall. But instead of heading for the exit, he ran barreling toward the two men. Like a charging linebacker delivering a blindside hit, he plowed into the backs of both men as they were peeking through the chamber door. The collision reminded Pitt of a bowling ball striking a pair of pins to pick up a spare. The two men went sprawling into the chamber, flying face-first onto the padded floor. Before they knew what hit them, Giordino had popped up from the ground and yanked the chamber door shut behind them. Pitt arrived a second later with a mop he found by the bathroom and broke off a four-foot section of the handle. Giordino rammed the stick through the door handle and wedged it tightly against the side frames.

"That should give us a head start," Giordino said,

rubbing his shoulder in pain.

Pitt smiled at hearing shouts from the men, their voices muffled to a whisper by the sound-deadening materials inside the chamber. They began moving down the corridor when Pitt suddenly stopped by the room in which they had hidden.

"Just curious," he said, flicking the lights on and reentering the lab.

"Remember the cat."

Pitt circled the room surveying the steel vats, which were filled with a clear fluid that smelled of formaldehyde. He stopped in front of one of the vats, gazing at a shiny object that lay in a tray at the bottom. Finding a pair of tongs, he pulled out the item and dried it off on a towel.

It was a pendant, made of silver formed in an ornate diamond shape. A falcon or eagle with two heads was engraved on the top edge, above a lustrous red stone that sparkled from the center. A finely detailed inscription in Arabic lettering circled the bottom. It had an ancient and imperial look about it, as if it was commissioned for a woman of high royalty.

"An artifact conservation lab mixed in with an electrical engineering facility?" Pitt asked. "An odd combination."

"Maybe he just likes to collect coins. How about we get out of here before our friends remember they are carrying guns?"

Pitt slipped the pendant into his pocket, then shut off the light and followed Giordino down the corridor at a fast clip. Reaching the large bay at the end, they zipped through the exit door as the white-coated engineer stared at them in surprise.

"Thanks for the pit stop." Pitt smiled, then disappeared out the door.

Outside, the winds had gradually increased, buffeting the compound with gusting swirls of thick dust. Pitt and Giordino stepped back into the garage, finding the mechanic wrestling some frozen lug nuts to get the front wheel off. Pitt moved to the doorway and looked across the lawn toward the main residence. He could just barely make out the two Mongolian escorts talking casually on the porch. Two other men stood on either side of the doorway that led into the residence.

"If they didn't let our Mongol cohorts in the front door, then I don't think they are going to let us stroll right in," he said.

"We'll have to find another entrance. If Theresa and the others are here, they would have to be somewhere in that building." Giordino said, scanning the grounds around the residence. "We won't have a lot of time to walk around the complex before our chamber maids get loose."

"Who said anything about walking?" Pitt asked.

Returning to the garage, he nodded toward the grounds maintenance cart parked near the doorway and checked to see that the key was in the ignition. When nobody in the garage was looking, he grabbed the steering wheel and pushed the cart toward the open door. Giordino stepped over and helped, practically lifting the cart out the door and around the side wall. Out of view of the garage occupants, Pitt hopped in and started up the gas engine.

Normally utilized by golf course maintenance crews, the green cart had a small flat bed built behind the two front seats. Pitt jammed the accelerator down and the cart burst off across the grounds as the rear tires spit gravel. Glancing to his right, he noticed two men on horseback exiting the stable at the far end of the laboratory building, their shapes temporarily disappearing in a blowing swirl of dust. He quickly spun the steering wheel to the left and drove toward the opposite side of the compound.

The cart zipped past the main entrance as Pitt followed a path around the perimeter wall, the guards outside paying no attention to the green maintenance vehicle whizzing by. Pitt slowed as the gravel path led to a small decorative bridge. Beneath it, the deep aqueduct waters from the nearby river flowed into the numerous canals that crisscrossed the landscaped grounds.

"Nice irrigation system," Giordino remarked as Pitt stopped the cart on top of the bridge. To their left, they could see the top halves of a pair of large pipes that carried the water under the compound wall before being dispersed into the canals. Pitt continued on, following the wall around toward the left edge of the residence. There still appeared to be no access to the building, other than through the main portico where the Mongol escorts and entry guards still stood.

Ahead, the compound wall ended abruptly at a sharp, rocky precipice. On the other side of the wall, an underground pipe spewed the outgoing canal water in a man-made waterfall that tumbled down the mountainside before rejoining the river below. Pitt parked the cart behind a tree and walked to the edge. An open gap stretched between the wall and the residence, too steep to drive the cart down but not as harrowing as the waterfall drop-off. A small footpath zigzagged down to a narrow plateau that formed the foundation for the hillside residence. Beyond the narrow strip of level ground, the terrain sloped steeply down the mountain for nearly half a mile, eliminating the need for a rear security wall.

"Try the back door?" Giordino asked.

"It's either that, or drive the golf cart through the front door. Let's just hope there is a back door."

They proceeded to hike down the short but steep trail, which they found heavily trodden with hoofprints. Mist from the adjacent waterfall blew onto them from the strong breeze, sending a damp chill through to their bones. Making their way to the back side of the residence, they found it was built up on a slight berm that rose above them, sided by a rock wall.

"Not a lot of easy ways in and out of this joint, are there?" Giordino asked, eyeing the rock wall that appeared to stretch for the length of the building.

"I guess the fire marshal hasn't paid them a visit yet."

They moved toward the center of the house, hugging the stone wall so as to stay out of view of any windowed rooms above them. The wind was gusting fiercely now, and they shielded their faces with their hats to keep the blowing dust from stinging their eyes.

Reaching the edge of the courtyard, they crept behind a low hedge and surveyed the grounds. They immediately spotted the entry door off the courtyard, which was advertised by the presence of two silk-clad guards standing at either side.

"Do you want to try your language skills with these two?" Giordino asked in seriousness.

Pitt really didn't want to fight his way into the residence, as there was no real proof that Theresa and the others were even there. But they were already facing a tenuous departure after the encounter at the lab, so there was little more to risk anyway. They needed to know one way or the other.

"There's a line of bushes across the interior that runs close to the door," he noted. "If we can get over to that stone building and work our way around the back side, we might be able to creep up and surprise them."

Giordino nodded, looking at the odd stone building across the courtyard. They waited until a thick swirl of dust kicked up, then sprinted toward the round stone structure. Skirting around its back side, they moved toward its entryway. Ducking into the tunnel-like opening, they crouched down and peered at the two guards across the yard. The security men were still standing beside the residence door, cowering slightly in the alcove to escape the bite of the wind. Pitt and Giordino had made it across the courtyard unseen.

Or so they thought.

~ 21 ~

AFTER A BOUNCY FOUR-HOUR ride across the mountains and steppes of Central Mongolia, traversing a road that barely qualified as a pair of ruts, Commerce Minister Shinzhe was convinced his trek was a wild-goose chase. There was no magic supply of oil hiding in Mongolia. He had seen not a single oil well during the entire trip. It was President Fei's fault, foolishly charging at windmills rather than accepting reality. Only Shinzhe had inherited the Don Quixote outfit.

The commerce minister waited angrily for his driver to pull up to the next *ger,* half expecting the president of Avarga Oil to welcome him on a broken-down pony. His anger and disgust softened rapidly when the dusty caravan rolled through the iron gates and into the stately compound of Tolgoi Borjin. Arriving at such an outpost in the middle of nowhere suddenly gave a jolt of credence to their journey. And pulling up to the front of the elegant residence, Shinzhe could see that Borjin was no sheepherder.

The host was dressed in a finely cut European suit and bowed deeply as Shinzhe exited the vehicle. A translator at his side relayed his greetings in Mandarin.

"Welcome, Minister Shinzhe. I trust your journey was pleasant?"

"A delight to see the beautiful Mongolian country-side," Shinzhe replied, maintaining his diplomatic form as he rubbed dust from his eyes.

"May I present my sister Tatiana, who is our director of field operations?"

Tatiana bowed gracefully to Shinzhe, who noted she wore the same look of conceit that Borjin carried. Shinzhe smiled warmly, then dutifully introduced his entourage. He turned and admired a contingent of horsemen in warrior attire that ringed the driveway.

"I have heard much about the Mongol horse," Shinzhe said. "Do you breed horses, Mr. Borjin?"

"Just a small stock for my security detail. I require that all my security employees be proficient in horse-manship and expert marksmen with the bow."

"An interesting testament to the past," Shinzhe said.

"A practical one as well. In these parts, a Mongol horse can go where no vehicle can. And some skills of warfare never lose their value. Modern technology is well and fine, but my ancestors conquered half the world with the horse and bow. I find they are still per-fectly useful skills today. Please, let us escape this infernal wind and relax indoors," Borjin said, leading the group through the front door. He then led the group down the main hallway toward the large room at the end. Admiring the array of antiques decorating the cor-ridor, Shinzhe stopped in front of a bronze sculpture of a prancing horse. The patinated green stallion was reflected off a colorful, framed mosaic mounted on the wall.

"A lovely sculpture," Shinzhe said, recognizing the design as Chinese. "Yuan Dynasty?"

"No, the Song Dynasty of slightly earlier," Borjin replied, impressed with the minister's eye. "Most of the antiques in the house date from the early thirteenth century, a time of the greatest conquests in Mongol history. The tile mosaic on the wall is an ancient work from Samarkand, and the carved pedestal on which the sculpture sits is from India, circa 1200 A.D. Are you a collector?"

"Not officially," the minister smiled. "I possess a few modest pieces of porcelain from the Yuan and Ming dynasties, but that is all. I am very impressed with your collection. Objects from that era are not readily marketed."

"I have an antiquities dealer in Hong Kong," Borjin explained with a flat look.

The entourage reached the conference room at the end of the corridor. Its huge floor-to-ceiling windows normally offered an expansive view from the hilltop, but little could be seen beyond the courtyard and sanctuary just below. The strong winds obscured most of the vista with swirling dust, the distant steppes peeking through the haze at only random intervals. Borjin strolled past a sitting area with couches and a bar, leading the group to a formal mahogany table where everyone was seated.

Borjin took a seat at one end, with his back to the wall. Behind him was a wide set of shelves that displayed a medieval arsenal. A collection of ancient spears, lances, and swords lined half the wall, while several handmade composite bows and metal-tipped arrows were hung opposite. Round metal helmets spiked with horsehair plumes lined the top shelf, fronted by several round clay objects that resembled primitive hand grenades. Guarding the entire collection was a huge stuffed falcon, its wings spread ominously at full breadth. The bird's head was tilted upward and its sharp beak pried open, as if it were shrieking a final cry of death.

Shinzhe looked from the weapons to the falcon and then to the man who owned them and felt an involuntary shiver. There was something about the oil executive that was savage like the falcon. The cold eyes seemed to hint at a hidden brutality. Shinzhe imagined that his host could pull one of the spears from the wall and thrust it through a man without a second thought. As a cup of hot tea was placed before him, the commerce minister tried to dispel his feelings and focus on the purpose of his visit.

"My government has received your proposal to supply a significant quantity of crude oil to our country. The party leadership is grateful for your offer and most intrigued by the bountiful nature of the proposal. On behalf of the party, I have been asked to confirm the validity of the proposal and discuss the remuneration necessary to conclude an agreement."

Borjin leaned back in his chair and laughed.

"Yes, of course. Why does Mongolia, nemesis to Cathay for a thousand years, suddenly desire to assist our uneasy neighbor to the south? How can a dust-laden receptacle of sand and grass, inhabited by ragtag peasants and sheepherders, suddenly materialize as a major source of natural resources? I will tell you why. It is because you made us prisoners in our own land. You and the Russians have barricaded us from the rest of the world for decades. We have become an isolated wasteland, a landlocked island of a forgotten time and place. Well, I'm afraid those days are over, Minister Shinzhe. You see, Mongolia is a rich land in more ways than one, and you didn't take the time or effort to appreciate that when you had the chance. Only now, Western companies are clamoring to come in and develop our mines and cut timber from our forests. But they are too late for the oil. For when nobody was even interested in prospecting our grounds we made the effort ourselves, and now we shall reap the rewards."

He nodded at Tatiana, who retrieved a map from a side bureau and unrolled it in front of the Chinese minister. She plucked a pair of jade carvings from the center of the table and used them to hold open the scrolled chart.

It was a country map of Mongolia. An irregular red oval was overlaid on a section near the southeastern border, appearing like an amoeba that had drowned in a cheap Merlot. The spot stretched for nearly fifty miles, its lower end rounding alongside the border of Chinese Inner Mongolia.

"The Temujin field. A natural basin that makes your aging Daqing field look like a bowl of spit," Borjin said, referring to China's largest oil field, which was in a state of decline. "Our test wells indicate potential reserves of forty billion barrels of crude oil and fifty trillion cubic feet of natural gas. The million barrels a day we will sell to you will be a pittance."

"Why has such a discovery not been publicized?" Shinzhe asked with a hint of skepticism. "I have heard nothing of such a find so close to our borders."

Borjin smiled, his teeth bared in a sharklike grin. "Few living people outside of this room are aware of the find," he said cryptically. "My own government knows nothing of these reserves. How else do you think I was able to acquire the entire land rights to the region? There have been minor exploratory forays into Mongolia that have touched upon the oil potential, but they have all missed the primary bonanza, if you will. A proprietary technology of ours helped pinpoint the windfall somewhat by accident," he said with a smile. "These are deep reserves, which explains in part why they were overlooked by previous exploration teams. But I need not bore you with the details. Suffice it to say that a number of test wells have provided initial confirmation of the reserve estimates."

Shinzhe sat quietly, the color draining from his face. He had little choice but to acknowledge the reality of the vast oil field. The fact that an arrogant charlatan of questionable morality controlled it made him sick to his stomach. Shinzhe was playing a weak hand and he knew that Borjin controlled the deck.

"Having oil in the ground is one thing, but delivering it within ninety days is quite another," the minister said soberly. "Your offer suggests we could see crude oil flowing within that time frame. I don't see how that is possible."

"It will take some doing on your part, but it is quite feasible," Borjin replied. Turning to Tatiana, he asked for another map from the bureau. She unrolled a second chart, which showed a map of Mongolia and northern China. A spiderweb of red lines crisscrossed the Chinese section of the map.

"The existing oil pipelines of China," Borjin explained. "Take a look at your recently completed northeast pipeline from Daqing to Beijing, with a spur from the port terminal at Qinhuangdao."

Shinzhe studied the map, noting a small X along a barren stretch of pipeline that ran through Inner Mongolia.

"The X is thirty kilometers from the Mongolian border and forty kilometers from a nearly completed pipeline span I am building to the border. You need only extend the pipeline from my termination to that spot on your Daqing line and the oil will begin to flow."

"Forty kilometers of pipeline? That can't be completed in ninety days."

Borjin stood up and paced around the table. "Come now, the Americans laid ten miles of rail track in a day constructing their transcontinental railroad in the 1860s. I have taken the liberty of already surveying the route and have the necessary pipe committed from a supplier. For additional consideration, I can also provide temporary excavation equipment. Surely for the country that has built the Three Gorges Dam, this should be child's play."

"You seem to have considered our needs well," Shinzhe said with veiled contempt.

"As a good business partner should." Borjin smiled. "And, in return, my demands are simple. You will pay a per barrel rate of one hundred forty-six thousand *togrog,* or one hundred twenty-five dollars U.S. You will accede the lands of southern Mongolia, or the Inner Mongolia Autonomous Region, as you inanely refer to the territory. And you will provide me a direct and exclusive pipeline to the port of Qinhuangdao, where you will provide me an off-loading port facility where I may export my excess supply of oil."

As Shinzhe gasped at the demand, the Mongol turned and gazed out the window, watching the winds swirl like tongues of fire. A movement caught his eye and he peered down at the courtyard. Two men dressed in dark suits were sprinting across it toward the sanctuary. Borjin watched as the two figures looped around the back side of the structure, then reappeared by the entrance and ducked inside. A tightness gripped his throat as he turned to the minister.

"If you will excuse me for a moment, I must attend to an urgent matter."

Turning his back before the minister could say another word, Borjin strode briskly from the room.

～ 22 ～

THE WINDS HAD DIED DOWN TEMPORARILY, forcing Pitt and Giordino to remain under cover in the stone entryway. Pitt looked up and admired the high archway that led to the main chamber of the stone edifice. Though the construction appeared ancient, it had obviously been rebuilt or refurbished, as evidenced by the smooth and unbroken layer of mortar between the stones. Situated in the center of the courtyard, Pitt realized that the main residence was probably built around the little stone building.

"A Buddhist temple?" Giordino asked, noting the flicker of candlelight down the corridor.

"Most likely," Pitt replied, aware that Buddhism was the predominant religion in Mongolia. Their curiosity piqued while waiting for the winds to resume, the two men moved quietly down the wide corridor and stepped into the main chamber.

Under the glow of a dozen burning torches and candles, Pitt and Giordino were surprised to find the chamber was a mausoleum rather than a temple. Though a small wooden altar was built at the far end, a pair of large marble sarcophaguses occupied either side. The tombs were made of white marble and had a modern look, suggesting the occupants had been interred within the last twenty or thirty years. Though Pitt couldn't read the Cyrillic script carved on the top slabs, he guessed they were the tombs of Borjin's mother and father, based upon Corsov's biography of the oilman.

He could not wager a guess about who lay in the centerpiece of the crypt, however. Standing on a polished marble pedestal was a carved granite sarcophagus that appeared much older. Although not massive in size, the tomb was illustrated with horses and wild animals carved across the top and sides, overlaid with paint. Though the images were clear, the paint had worn thin from aging. At the head of the tomb, nine posts rose into the air, each dangling a shock of white fur, as they had seen at the entrance to the residence.

"Somebody got a nice sendoff to the afterlife," Giordino said, eyeing the tomb.

"The illustrious Mr. Borjin must be something of a blueblood," Pitt replied.

Giordino looked past the sarcophagus and noted an object lying beneath the altar.

"Looks like they're going to need another coffin in here," he said, nodding toward the object.

Overlooked as they entered the chamber, the body both men now saw was stretched out on a bench beneath the altar. Pitt and Giordino walked over and were shocked to recognize the corpse. It was Roy, half covered in a thin blanket, but with the shaft of the arrow still protruding from his chest.

"Theresa and Wofford are here," Giordino said, his voice trailing off.

"Let's hope they haven't suffered the same fate," Pitt said quietly, pulling the blanket up so that it covered Roy's face. As he wondered whether they might be too late, the stillness of the chamber was suddenly broken by the approaching clatter of boots on the stone floor. A second later, the two guards Pitt had spied across the courtyard burst into the mausoleum. Dressed like the guards at the front gate, they didn't appear to be carrying traditional firearms. Instead, each man clutched a wooden spear capped by a razor-sharp metal tip. A short knife in a scarab hung from their waists, while on their backs they carried a small quiver and bow. They were the weapons of war used by the ancient Mongol horse soldiers and were every bit as deadly at short range as a modern handgun or rifle.

The guards slowed as they entered the chamber until spotting Pitt and Giordino at the altar. Regaining their speed, they charged around the central crypt with their spears thrust in front of them. It was a small stroke of luck that the guards did not stop and hurl their pikes at Pitt and Giordino but instead tried to impale them at close range.

Giordino reacted first, grabbing a small wooden bench by the altar and pitching it toward the legs of the charging guards. His aim was true and the wooden seat struck the nearer man's legs hard in the shin, taking his feet out from under him. He stumbled face-first to the

, his wooden spear rolling harmlessly to the side.

The second guard leaped over the bench like a high hurdler and continued the charge, heading straight for Pitt at full speed. Pitt stood lightly on the balls of his feet, his legs coiled and his eyes glued to the tip of the spear as he waited for the attacker to lunge. Seeming to defy reason, he stood perfectly still, providing a stable target to aim for. The guard assumed Pitt was frozen with fear and would soon be an easy kill. But Pitt waited and watched until the guard was just a step away, drawing back the spear for a lethal forward jab. With a quick thrust of his legs, he sprang to one side while reaching out with his left hand and shoving the shaft of the spear in the other direction. The guard charged past, realizing with a sudden blank look on his face that he was stabbing air. He attempted to twist the spear to the side, but he had already run the spear tip past Pitt's body. Pitt tried unsuccessfully to grab the shaft but lost his grip as the guard barreled by and swung it toward him. The side of the shaft whipped around and jammed Pitt on the shoulder as it slipped through his fingers.

Both men were thrown off balance and staggered in different directions, the guard falling across the altar while Pitt was knocked toward the crypt. Pitt quickly rolled to his feet to face his attacker, then backed up toward the stone tomb that loomed a few inches behind him. The guard was leery of Pitt now, eyeing him for a moment as he regained his balance. Tightening his grip on the spear, he took a deep breath then charged again at Pitt, his eyes locked on his prey to ensure the kill.

Pitt stood unarmed with his back to the crypt, his eyes darting about in search of a weapon. Off to the side, he saw Giordino lunge at the fallen man on the ground. Preoccupied with subduing the first guard, Giordino was in no position to offer immediate help. Then Pitt remembered the fur-tailed poles.

The nine tall wooden poles stood in individual marble base plates at the head of the tomb. Pitt quickly backed over to the poles and reached around with his right hand, covertly gripping one of the poles behind his back. The guard thought nothing of the movement, simply adjusting his angle toward Pitt as he accelerated his charge. Pitt hesitated until the guard was a dozen steps away, then quickly yanked the upright pole toward the ground in front of him. At eight feet in length, the pole easily outstretched the guard's spear. With a stunned look, the guard helplessly tried to slow his charge as he realized Pitt was lunging at him with the huge rod. Too late, the blunt end of the pole struck in his stomach, driven forward by Pitt with all his might. The shocked guard was driven off his feet before falling to one knee, gasping for air as the wind was knocked out of him. The blow pried the spear from his clawlike grip, the lance rattling across the polished floor. Ignoring Pitt, he desperately crawled toward the weapon before looking up in horror. The wooden pole had been flipped around and now the marble base was hurtling toward him like a wrecking ball. Attempting to duck, the guard was struck on the top of his skull, dropping him flat to the floor in total unconsciousness.

"No respect for a man's furnishings," Giordino's voice grumbled as the pole and marble base crashed to the floor. Pitt looked over and saw Giordino rubbing the back of his fist as he stood over the unconscious body of the first guard.

"You okay?"

"Much better than my friend here. What do you say we get out of this box before any more Royal Lancers show up?"

"Agreed."

The two men hustled out of the chamber, Pitt scooping up one of the loose spears on their way out. The wind whistled through the archway as they reached the entryway and peeked cautiously into the compound. The sight was not encouraging.

Two horsemen, clad in bright silk tunics and round metal helmets, sat on their mounts near the residence door, replacing the foot guards. Nearby, another guard on horseback was combing the courtyard for signs of Pitt and Giordino. Knowing nothing good would come by hanging around, the two men ducked out the opposite side of the archway under a dirty gust of wind and crept around the back side of the stone mausoleum. As they moved toward the rear of the stone structure, they could see down the right wing of the residence. Curling around the far edge of the building, they spotted a half dozen horsemen in brightly colored garb riding in their direction. Unlike the guards they had encountered so far, these men appeared to have rifles slung over their shoulders.

"Fine time for the cavalry to appear," Giordino said.

"Just makes our exit route a little clearer," Pitt replied, knowing they would have to quickly cross the courtyard and backtrack the way they came in order to avoid the patrol.

Reaching the covered corral at the rear of the crypt, they ducked in to cut to the other side. Winding through a maze of crates and equipment, Pitt briefly eyed the large dust-covered antique car parked in back, surprised to identify it as an early 1920s Rolls-Royce. He started to take a step over the opposite rail when a whistling sound ripped past his ear, followed by a sharp twang. He glanced to his side to see an arrow fluttering out the side of a wooden crate just inches from Giordino's head.

"Incoming," he yelled, ducking as another arrow whistled by.

Giordino was already crouching behind a wooden barrel when the arrow slammed into a support post. "A fourth horseman," Giordino said, peering over the top of the barrel.

Pitt looked into the courtyard and saw the horseman beside a hedge, pulling on a bowstring to fire a third arrow. Pitt was the intended target this time and he just barely slipped behind a cart before the arrow zinged by. It no sooner struck the cart then Pitt jumped to his feet and turned toward the guard. It was his turn to retaliate now. As the horseman reached over his back to draw an arrow, Pitt let fly the spear he'd carried from the crypt.

The horseman was nearly fifty feet away, but Pitt's throw held true as the lance soared toward the man in the saddle. Only a quick turn saved the guard from being impaled, but the sharpened spear still pierced flesh, striking the man's right arm above the elbow. His bow fell to the ground as he clasped the wound with his left hand to stop the flow of blood.

Pitt and Giordino's respite from attack was short-lived, however. The other three horsemen quickly closed ranks with their wounded partner and resumed the aerial barrage. On the opposite side of the corral, the galloping hoofbeats of the other patrol echoed above the shrieking wind as they too raced to the scene. Within minutes, the air in the corral was filled with a flying maelstrom of razor-tipped arrows, bursting into the wooden crates and carts with deadly force. The archers were highly skilled at their lethal talent, their arrows following Pitt and Giordino's every movement like a magnet. If not for the gusting winds, the two men would have been killed quickly. But the swirling gusts hampered the horsemen's vision, as well as deflected the flight of their arrows. For their part, Pitt and Giordino kept the attackers from approaching too closely.

Though weaponless, the two men improvised a defense as best they could. They found the wagons to be full of tools and field implements, which they turned into makeshift projectiles. Giordino was particularly proficient at heaving double-pronged picks, managing to impale one guard in the thigh with a throw while knocking another from his horse with a swirling toss. The flying picks and shovels temporarily kept the riders at bay, but the horsemen knew that they had the men trapped.

Amid the battle, the dusty winds had served as an ally to Pitt and Giordino, providing intermittent clouds of cover while distorting the archers' fire. But as if the atmospheric gods decided to take a respite to inhale, the blowing winds suddenly fell for a moment. As the dust settled and the howling ceased, the sudden calm spelled doom for the two trapped men. Readily visible in the middle of the corral, the men now had arrows flying at them in a relentless fury. Standing to fight would mean instant death and the two men dropped their tools and dove for cover. They both rolled under a large wagon, finding minimal protection behind the large-spoked wheels. A half dozen arrows buried their razor tips into the sides of the wagon just inches above their heads. From the opposite side of the corral, gunfire now erupted, as the second patrol abandoned their bows and sought to end the siege with rifle fire.

"I can do without the Custer scene," Giordino muttered, a trickle of blood running down his cheek where a splintered arrow shaft had ricocheted. "You don't suppose they would bite at a white handkerchief?"

"Not likely," Pitt replied, thinking of Roy. An arrow smashed into the wagon wheel beside him and he instinctively rolled away from the impact. A thin knobby protrusion struck him in the back, halting his turn. He twisted his head to find an object covered in a dirty canvas tarp sitting next to the wagon. Another wave of arrows came flying in, forcing him to crouch to the ground alongside Giordino.

"The next cloud of dust, what do you say we rush one of the horsemen on the fringe?" Giordino asked. "You grab the reins, I'll grab the rider, and we've got ourselves a mount. Only way I can see us getting out of here is to make a play for one of the horses."

"Risky," Pitt replied, "but likely our best chance." Rolling onto his side to survey the perimeter, he accidentally kicked off a section of the tarp covering the object by the wagon. Giordino noticed a sudden glint sparkle in Pitt's eyes as he peeked under the tarp.

"A change of plans?" he asked.

"No," Pitt replied. "We'll just try riding out of here on a horse of a different color."

~ 23 ~

THE WALL-MOUNTED RADIO POPPED with the receipt of a signal, followed by the caller's voice. The blowing wind created a background static that muffled the gravelly voice, though the proximity of the transmission made for a strong signal.

"We have them surrounded behind the sanctuary. They arrived with the Chinese delegation as Mongolian state security escorts, but are apparently imposters.

My guards who were locked in the test chamber claim they are not Chinese but appear Russian."

"I see," Borjin replied, speaking into the handset in an irritated voice. "Government agents or, more likely, spies from a Russian oil company. See that they don't leave the compound alive, but hold the gunfire until the delegation has departed. I will expect a full report from security as to why they were not monitored at their arrival."

Borjin replaced the handset, then closed a cherry-wood cabinet that concealed the two-way radio transmitter. Exiting the small anteroom, he walked down the hall and returned to the formal conference room. The Chinese minister stood at the window staring into the dust storm outside with his own sense of swirling obfuscation.

"Excuse the interruption," Borjin said, taking a seat with a grim smile. "A slight mishap has occurred with two of your state escorts. I'm afraid they won't be able to join you on your return trip. I will, of course, provide replacement escorts, if you desire."

Shinzhe nodded vaguely. "The gunshots we are hearing from the outside?" he asked.

"A training exercise by my security guards. No reason to be alarmed."

The minister stared blankly out the window, his mind clearly elsewhere. As if slowed by age, he sluggishly turned and sat down across from Borjin. "Your offer is akin to blackmail and your demands are preposterous," he said, his anger finally surfacing.

"My demands are nonnegotiable. And perhaps they are not so preposterous for a country facing an economic meltdown," Borjin hissed.

Shinzhe stared at his host with contempt. He had disliked the arrogant and demanding magnate from the moment they met. Though perfunctorily gracious, he obviously had no respect at all for China or its leadership position in the world. It pained Shinzhe even to attempt to negotiate, but he knew the state leaders, and the president in particular, were expecting a deal for the oil. With reason, he feared his country's leadership would accept the abominable proposal out of desperation. If only there was another way.

"Minister Shinzhe, you must view it as a mutually beneficial transaction," Borjin continued, regaining his composure. "China gets the oil it needs to keep its economy running, I get a long-term commitment as a major supplier, and the Mongolian Autonomous Republic rejoins its rightful place as part of greater Mongolia."

"Acceding sovereign territory is not an act taken lightly."

"There is nothing of significance that China must accede. We both know the region is little more than a rural dust bowl that is largely occupied by Mongol herders. My interest in reunifying the region is born of a cultural desire to restore the lands that once belonged to our nation."

"You may be correct that the region represents little of value. Still, it is most unusual for a private entity to be interfering in territorial exchanges."

"This is true. In fact, my government knows nothing of our accord. They will find it a quite pleasing political gift, one that will be most favored by the masses."

"And you will benefit handsomely, no doubt?"

"As broker, I have assigned a portion of the land rights to my company, but it represents only a small percentage of the total," he smiled devilishly. He handed a thick leather binder to Shinzhe. "I have already worked up the necessary agreements for state representatives of both countries to sign. It would please me to receive acknowledgment of your country's acceptance at the earliest opportunity."

"I will be reporting to the general secretary's council tomorrow afternoon. A decision will be forthcoming. Your fixed position on the terms may negate an agreement, I must warn."

"So be it. Those are my terms." Borjin rose to his feet. "I look forward to a long and fruitful relationship, Minister Shinzhe." Borjin bowed graciously, if insincerely.

Shinzhe rose and bowed stiffly in return, then left the room with his entourage. Borjin and Tatiana followed the Chinese delegation to the door and watched as they staggered through the howling dust storm to their cars. As the taillights blinked past the guard gate, Borjin closed the door and turned to Tatiana.

"The plum is ours for the taking," he said, walking back down the corridor.

"Yes, but the risks are many. They will not find it

easy to give up the lands of Inner Mongolia. Perhaps they will begin to suspect something."

"Nonsense. The Chinese can appreciate the cultural desire of Mongolia to seek unification with its prior territory. A perfect cover story. And a rich irony, that they will give us the lands that we will in turn exploit to sell them oil."

"They will not be happy once they learn the truth. They might nullify the agreement, or worse. And they won't want to pay prices above the market rate."

"The latter point is a simple matter. With our new-found technology, we can keep the entire market unstable for years and profit richly. We have already proven that in the Persian Gulf, and will do so again."

They reached the conference room and stepped inside, moving to the small bar that was surrounded by dozens of shelved liquor bottles. Borjin reached for a bottle of cognac and poured two glasses.

"My dear sister, we have already won. Once the oil starts flowing, we will have the Chinese by the throat and they dare not renege. Should they have a change of heart, we simply accelerate the pipeline to Siberia and link up with the connection to Nakhodka. Then we will be able to sell our oil to Japan and the rest of the world and laugh in their face."

"Yes, thanks to our brother's fire ship incident at Ningbo the Chinese are in a desperate bind."

"Temuge has been working miracles, hasn't he?"

"I need not remind you that he nearly caused my death in Baikal," she said irritably.

"An unforeseen side effect, the large wave. But no matter, you are here safe now," he said with a slightly patronizing tone. "You must admit, he has been most effective. Coordinating the pipeline destruction in Siberia, then setting fire to the Chinese port when a suitable fault line could not be found. And the Persian Gulf team he assembled has been most effective. After the next demonstration in the Middle East, the Chinese will be crawling to us on their knees."

"And Temuge is proceeding across the Pacific to North America for the final strike?"

"They are already at sea. The Baikal equipment arrived in Seoul two days ago, and they departed shortly thereafter. I sent the Khentii excavation team with Temuge, since we had to cease operations after the incident with the Russian survey team."

"Their search efforts have produced nothing anyway. It is apparent from the empty crypt we found near Genghis that the other tomb was ransacked or else never interred. It is a mystery why the associated riches have never come to light."

"No matter, as the Chinese will soon provide us a healthy cash flow. We'll have to wait a week or two for the next oil shock," he said and smiled, "then they will be agreeably inclined."

Stepping out of the conference room, he walked to the adjacent staircase, his sister following close behind. Stopping at the head of the stairs, he raised his glass to the huge portrait of the ancient Mongol warrior that hung on the facing wall.

"The first step is complete. We are well on our way now to restoring the riches and glory of the Golden Clan."

"Our father would be proud," Tatiana said. "He has made it possible."

"To father and to our lord, Chinggis," he said, swallowing a gulp of the cognac. "May the conquests begin again."

~ 24 ~

BEHIND THE RESIDENCE, THE HEAD of security refastened a handheld radio to his belt. A bear-sized man by the name of Batbold, he had just received word that the Chinese delegation had left the compound. If the two marauders were still alive in the corral, they could be finished off with the rifles now.

The swirling dust obscured the interior of the corral, but the earlier rain of lead and arrows must have taken the two spies down. There was no longer the futile attempt to fling field implements at the surrounding forces. And, in fact, there had been no sight of either man for several minutes. They were surely dead by now, he surmised. Just to be sure, he ordered three more volleys of rifle fire into the center of the corral, then halted the shooting.

Removing a short sword he carried at his waist, Batbold dismounted and led three other men on foot toward the corral to examine the bodies. They marched to within ten feet of the wooden fence when they heard the sound of a wooden crate being smashed inside. As Batbold and his men froze in their steps, a new sound emerged, that of a metallic whirring that slowly died away. The security head took a tentative step forward, finally seeing movement behind one of the wagons as the whirring noise repeated itself again and again.

"There!" he shouted, pointing toward the wagon. "Aim and fire."

The three guards raised their carbines to their shoulders as a loud pop reverberated from inside. As the gunmen tried to take aim, a wall of boxes suddenly erupted from the side of the corral, knocking out a section of the wooden fence. An instant later, a low-slung object came bursting toward them accompanied by a screeching din.

Batbold stared wide-eyed as he watched a faded red motorcycle with attached sidecar racing straight toward him. The motorcycle appeared riderless, with a wooden crate propped on the seat, next to another crate atop the sidecar. Sidestepping its path, Batbold realized his eyes were deceiving him and quickly hoisted his sword in defense of the approaching machine. But it was too late.

As the motorcycle brushed by, Al Giordino popped through the crate on the sidecar like a crazed jack-in-the-box. In his hands he gripped a square-bladed shovel, which he swung at Batbold. The blunt face of the blade struck the security chief on the side of his jaw with a hard smacking sound. Batbold quickly melted to the ground, a look of stunned confusion frozen on his face.

The motorcycle charged toward the three guards behind Batbold, who scattered in panic without firing a shot. One man slipped and fell, his legs run over by the sidecar's wheels. The second man dove to safety, while the third got whacked in the back of the head by Giordino's shovel, sending him sprawling.

Peeking through a slot in the wooden crate draped over his shoulders, Pitt gunned the motorcycle away from the mounted riflemen and steered toward the group of archers. Picking a gap in the horses, he blasted toward the hole to break through the siege line.

"Keep down, the heat's about to turn up," he shouted to Giordino.

An instant later, a flurry of arrows began pinging into the sidecar and ripping into their makeshift wooden armor. Pitt felt a stinging in his left thigh from an arrow nick, and would have noticed a trickle of warm blood running down his leg had his senses not been focused elsewhere.

The aged motorcycle ripped toward the line of horsemen, trailing a cloud of black smoke from its overrich carburation. As Pitt had hoped, the riflemen behind him had held their fire for fear of shooting the archers. But the archers themselves had no such qualms and let loose with a flurry of flying arrows.

Pitt decided to lessen the fire and drove directly toward one of the horses. The startled beast reared on its hind legs and spun to the side to let the noisy contraption pass, leaving its rider hanging on for dear life. Pitt saw the flash of a lance go soaring by inches in front of his face, piercing the ground nearby. Then he was past the rearing horse and the line of archers, speeding away from the courtyard.

Giordino spun backward in the sidecar and peeked over the edge of his protective crate. The horsemen had quickly regrouped and began chasing after the motorcycle.

"Still on our heels," he shouted. "I'm going to play toss with these guys. Let me know when we get to the ski jump."

"Coming up," Pitt replied.

Before climbing aboard the motorcycle, Giordino had noticed a gunnysack full of horseshoes hanging from the wagon. He had judiciously tossed the bag into the sidecar and now used the metal shoes as projectiles. Popping out of the crate, he began hurling horseshoes at the nearest rider's head. The loopy hunks of metal were awkward to throw, but Giordino quickly took note of their aerodynamic qualities and began zeroing in on his targets. He quickly dazed two of the riders and disrupted the bow fire of several others, forcing the pursuers to keep their distance.

In the driver's seat, Pitt raced the motorcycle across the edge of the courtyard while holding the throttle at full. When he rolled against the Czechoslovakian motorcycle in the corral, he figured the 1950s-era bike was a metal corpse. But the 1953 Czech JAWA 500 OHC still had air in its tires, a couple of gallons of stale gas in its tank, and its engine turned over freely. On the seventh kick of its manual starter, the old twin-cylinder motor coughed to life, giving Pitt and Giordino a slim chance at freedom.

With the help of Giordino's horseshoe toss, they had opened up a comfortable lead over the pursuing horsemen. Pitt suddenly swung the handlebars to one side and aimed for the rear edge of the property.

"Fasten your seat belt, we're ready for takeoff," he yelled to Giordino.

Giordino ducked back into the sidecar and grabbed a handrail that ran across the front of the compartment. In his other hand, he gripped the last of the horseshoes he was preparing to toss.

"For luck," he muttered, and wedged the horseshoe into the cowling of the sidecar.

There was no wall at the back of the estate, as the edge of the yard dropped down a steep precipice. Pitt knew it might be suicidal to make the attempt, but there was no other avenue for escape. Blasting toward the edge of the yard, he braked slightly then guided the motorcycle over the brink.

Pitt could feel his stomach drop as the ground disappeared from beneath their wheels and the motorcycle thrust forward. The first thirty feet were nearly a vertical drop and they plunged through the air before the front wheel kissed the ground. The rest of the motorcycle struck hard, jarring the wooden crates off the driver and passenger. The wooden shields, stitched with arrows, crashed to the ground beside them. Pitt was thankful to be free of the clumsy obstacle, though he knew the boxes had probably saved their lives. His focus quickly diverted to keeping the motorcycle balanced.

With the uneven weight of the sidecar, the motorcycle by all rights should have flipped when they struck the ground. But Pitt kept a firm hand on the handlebars and deftly adjusted the front wheel to compensate for the uneven landing. Fighting the natural instinct to pull away, he kept the motorcycle aimed straight down the mountain. The forward momentum stabilized the bike and sidecar, though they now tore down the slope at breakneck speed. Giordino's horseshoe seemed to bring them luck, as they faced no large rocks or major obstacles in their path down the steep face. Flecks of gravel occasionally spewed off the ground in front of them and Pitt realized they were being shot at from the ledge above. The roar of the motorcycle and the howl of the wind easily obscured the sound of the gunshots. A swirl of dust blew over them, providing temporary cover from the peppering gunfire. But the winds also blinded Pitt. He held the handlebars rigid and just hoped they wouldn't fatally collide with a rock or tree.

Up on the ledge, several guards stood and fired at the fleeing motorcycle with their carbines, cursing as it disappeared into a blowing cloud of dust. A half dozen other horsemen continued the chase, leading their mounts down the steep incline. It was a slow decent for the horses, but once past the initial drop, the guards continued the pursuit with speed.

On the motorcycle, Pitt and Giordino hung on for dear life as the machine barreled down the mountain at nearly eighty miles per hour. Pitt finally released the rear brake, which he had instinctively held locked up since they went over the edge, realizing it was doing little to slow their decent.

After several seconds of a near-vertical plunge, the incline gradually eased. The slope still fell away sharply, but they no longer had the feeling of free falling. Pitt began to twist the handlebars slightly to avoid shrubs and rocks that dotted the hillside, regaining a minor control over the bike. Bounding over a sharp rut, both men flew out of their seats but were able to recover before the next dip. Pitt felt like his kidneys were being crushed with each bump, the stiff springs and hard leather seat offering little in the way of comfort.

Several times the motorcycle careened to one side or another, teetering on the brink of flipping over. Each time, Pitt nudged the front wheel just enough to keep them upright, while Giordino would shift to aid balance. Pitt couldn't avoid every obstacle and several times the sidecar crashed over small boulders. The streamlined nose of the sidecar soon looked like it had been battered with a sledgehammer.

Gradually the steep incline abated and the rocks, shrubs, and scattered trees gave way to dry grass. Pitt soon found himself feathering the throttle to maintain speed as the terrain softened. The wind was as harsh as ever and seemed to blow directly into Pitt's face. The swirling dust was thick and constant, limiting visibility to a few dozen feet.

"We still have a tail?" Pitt shouted.

Giordino nodded yes. He had stolen glances behind them every few seconds and had observed the initial contingent of horsemen start their ascent down the mountain. Though the pursuers were well behind now and long since obscured by the blowing blankets of dust, Giordino knew the chase was just beginning.

Pitt knew it as well. As long as the old motorcycle surged on, they would remain well ahead of the pursuing horses. But it might be a contest of elusion, and Pitt could only hope that their tracks would be obscured by the windstorm. The fact remained that their lives were pinned on an aged motorcycle with limited gas.

Pitt inquisitively reflected on the Czech motorcycle. The JAWA originated before the war, growing out of a factory that produced hand grenades and other armaments. Known for their lightweight but powerful engines, the postwar JAWAs were fast and technically innovative bikes with a reputation for durability, at least until the factory was nationalized. Despite gulping on a tank of flat gas, the old motorcycle purred along with barely a sputter. I'll take what you give me, Pitt thought, realizing that the more distance he put between himself and the horsemen, the better. Gritting his teeth, his squinted into the blowing dust and squeezed the throttle harder, holding tight as the old motorcycle roared into the swirling gloom.

D ARKNESS SETTLED QUICKLY OVER THE broad, rolling steppes. High clouds floating above the blowing dust blotted out the moon and stars, pitching the grasslands into an inky black. Only a tiny pinprick of light poked sporadically through the dry ground storm. Then the shaft of light would disappear, devoured by a blowing blanket of dust. In its wake was left the accompanying roar from a two-cylinder, four-stroke motor, whose constant rumble throbbed on without missing a beat.

The Czech motorcycle and sidecar bounded over the sea of grass like a Jet Ski hopping the waves. The aged bike groaned over every bump and rut but charged steadily across the hills. Pitt's hand ached from holding the throttle at full, but he was driven to coax every ounce of horsepower out of the old motorcycle. Despite the lack of a road and the wallowing sidecar, the old cycle charged across the empty grasslands at almost fifty miles per hour. At their sustained speed, they were widening the gap between their pursuers with every mile. But at the moment, it was an inconsequential point. The motorcycle's tires left an indelible track in the summer grass, which offered a conspicuous trail to their whereabouts.

Pitt had hoped to discover a crossroad that he could use to obscure their tracks, but all he found was an occasional horse path, too narrow to hide their tire marks. Once, he saw a light in the distance and attempted to steer toward it. But the brief ray vanished under a dust cloud, and they were left running across the darkened void. Though no roads appeared under the dim glow of the headlamp, Pitt could see that the landscape was gradually changing. The rolling hills had softened, while the grassland underfoot had thinned. The terrain must have moderated, Pitt noted wryly, as it had been awhile since he had heard Giordino curse from the jolts. Soon the hills disappeared altogether and the thick grassland turned to short turf, which eventually gave way to a hard gravel surface dotted with scrub brush.

They had entered the northern edge of the Gobi Desert, a vast former inland sea that covers the lower third of Mongolia. More stony plain than billowy sand dune, the arid landscape supports a rich population of gazelles, hawks, and other wildlife, which thrive in a region once swarming with dinosaurs. None of that was visible to Pitt and Giordino, who could just barely make out rising granite uplifts among the sand and gravel washes. Pitt leaned hard on the handlebars, steering around a jagged stone outcropping before following a seam through giant boulders that eventually opened into a wide flat valley.

The motorcycle picked up a burst of speed as its tires met firmer ground. Pitt was blasted by thicker swirls of dust, though, which made the visibility worse than before. The three-wheeled machine charged across the desert for another hour, smacking shrubs and small rocks with a regular battering. At last the engine began to hiccup, then gradually stuttered and coughed. Pitt coaxed the bike another mile before the fuel tank finally ran as dry as the surrounding desert and the engine wheezed to a final stop.

They coasted to a stop along a flat sandy wash, the silence of the desert enveloping them. Only the gusting winds whistling through the low brush and the blowing sand skittering over the ground tested their hearing, blown raw by the motorcycle's loud exhaust. The skies above them began to clear and the winds settled down to just sporadic bursts. A sprinkling of stars peeked through the dusty curtain overhead, offering a snippet of light across the empty desert.

Pitt turned to the sidecar and found Giordino sitting there caked in grit. Under the twilight, Pitt could see his friend's hair, face, and clothes saturated with a fine layer of khaki dust. To his utter disbelief, Giordino had actually fallen asleep in the sidecar, his hands still tightly gripping the handrail. The cessation of the engine's blare and the nonstop swaying eventually stirred Giordino. Blinking open his eyes, he peered at the dark, empty wasteland surrounding them.

"I hope you didn't bring me here to watch the submarine races," he said.

"No," Pitt replied. "I think it's a horse race that is on tonight's billing."

Giordino hopped out of the sidecar and stretched while Pitt examined the wound to his shin. The arrow had just nicked the front of his shin before embedding itself in a cooling fin on the motor. The wound had stopped bleeding some time ago, but a splatter of red-based dust ran down to his foot like a layer of cherry frosting.

"Leg okay?" Giordino asked, noticing the wound.

"A near miss. Almost nailed me to the bike," Pitt said, pulling the broken arrow shaft from the engine.

Giordino turned and gazed in the direction they had traveled. "How far behind do you suppose they are?"

Pitt mentally computed the time and approximate speed they traveled since leaving Xanadu. "Depends on their pace. I'd guess we have at least a twenty-mile buffer. They couldn't run the horses faster than a trot for any sustained amount of time."

"Guess there wasn't a short road down the back of that mountain or they would have sent some vehicles after us."

"I was worried about a helicopter, but they couldn't have flown in that dust storm anyway."

"Hopefully, they got saddlesore and threw in the towel. Or at least stopped until morning, which would give us a little more time to thumb a ride out of here."

"I'm afraid there doesn't appear to be a truck stop in the vicinity," Pitt replied. He stood and turned the motorcycle handlebars in an arc, shining the headlight across the desert. A high, rocky uplift stretched along their left flank, but the terrain was empty and as flat as a billiard table in the other three directions.

"Personally speaking," Giordino said, "after that

marble-in-a-washing-machine ride down the mountain, a small stretch of the legs sounds glorious. Do you want to keep marching into the wind?" he asked, pointing along the motorcycle's path, which led into the face of the breeze.

"We have a magician's trick to perform first," Pitt said.

"What trick is that?"

"Why," Pitt said with a sly smile, "how to make a motorcycle disappear in the desert."

THE SIX horsemen had quickly given up any effort to keep pace with the faster motorcycle and settled their mounts into a less taxing gait, which they could maintain for hours on end. The Mongol horse was an extremely hardy animal, bred over centuries for durability. Descendants of the stock that conquered all of Asia, the Mongol horse was nail tough. The animals were renowned for being able to survive on scant rations yet still gallop across the steppes all day. Short, sturdy, and, on the whole, mangy in appearance, their toughness was unmatched by any Western thoroughbred.

The tight group of horses reached the base of the mountain, where the lead horseman suddenly held up the pack. The dour-faced patrol leader peered at the ground though the heavy eyelids of a bullfrog. Shining a flashlight, he aimed the beam at a pair of deep ruts cut through the grass, studying them carefully. Satisfied, he stowed the light and spurred his mount to a trot along the trail of ruts as the other horsemen fell in behind.

The commander figured that the old motorcycle could travel no more than another thirty miles. Ahead of them, there was nothing but open steppe and desert, offering few places to hide for over a hundred miles. Conserving the horses, they would track the fugitives down in less than eight hours, he estimated. There was certainly no need to call in mechanized four-wheel drive reinforcements from the compound. It would be a meager challenge for his fellow horsemen. They all grew up learning to ride before they could walk and had the bowlegs to prove it. There would be no escape for the fugitives. A few more hours and the two men who had embarrassed the guards at Xanadu would be as good as dead.

Through the black night they forged on, riding into the blustery winds while tracking the linear trail left by the motorcycle's tires. At first, the taunting sound of the motorcycle's throbbing engine beckoned on an occasional gust of the rustling winds. But the sound soon evaporated over the distant hills, and the riders were left to their own quiet thoughts. They rode for five hours, stopping only once they reached the gravely plain of the desert.

The motorcycle's tracks were more difficult to follow over the hardened desert surface. The riders frequently lost the trail in the dark, halting their progress until the tire marks could be located under the glow of a flashlight. As dawn broke, the buffeting winds that had blinded them with sand the entire journey finally began to diminish. With the morning light, the trail became more visible, and the horsemen hastened their pace. The patrol leader sent a scout ahead, to alert the others in advance if the trail was lost over particularly hard stretches of ground.

The horsemen followed the trail through a sandy wash sided by a rocky bluff. Ahead, the terrain opened into a broad level plain. The motorcycle tracks snaked through the wash then stretched into the distance, clearly rutting the hard, flat surface. The riders began picking up speed again when the commander noticed his scout perched at a stop a few dozen yards ahead. At his horse's approach, the scout turned to him with a blank look on his face.

"Why have you stopped?" the patrol leader barked.

"The tracks . . . have disappeared," the scout stammered.

"Then move ahead and find out where they resume."

"There is no continuation of the tracks. The sand . . . it should show the tracks, but they just end here," the scout replied, pointing to the ground.

"Fool," the patrol leader muttered, then spurred his horse and wheeled to the right. Riding in a huge arc, he circled around the front of his stationary troupe, finally looping his way back to where they stood waiting. Now he was the one with a confused look on his face.

Climbing off his horse, he walked beside the motorcycle's tracks. The heels of his boots pushed easily into a light layer of sand that coated the hard plain. Following the twin trails of cycle and sidecar, he studied the ground until the tracks came to an abrupt end. Scanning the area, he saw that the soft layer of sand covered the ground in all directions. Yet the only visible markings were those made by the guards' horses. There was no continuation of the motorcycle tracks, no human footprints, and no sign of the motorcycle itself.

It was as if the motorcycle and its riders had been plucked off the ground and vanished into thin air.

～ 26 ～

PERCHED LIKE EAGLES HIGH IN a nest, Pitt and Giordino peered down at the proceedings from sixty feet above the desert floor. Cautiously scaling the nearby rocky edifice in the dark, they had discovered a high indented ledge that was perfectly concealed from the ground below. Stretched flat in the hollowed stone bowl, the two had slept intermittently until the horsemen arrived shortly after dawn. Lying to the east of the horsemen, the morning sun aided their stealth, casting their pursuers in a bright glow while they remained nestled in the ridgetop's shadow.

Pitt and Giordino grinned as they watched the horsemen mope in utter confusion around the abrupt end of the motorcycle trail. But they were far from out of the woods yet. They watched with interest as two riders took off ahead, while the other four horsemen split up and searched along either side. As Pitt had hoped, the horsemen focused their search forward of the trail's end, not considering that the two fugitives had backed down the trail before taking to the rocks.

"You realize, Houdini, that you are just going to make them mad at us," Giordino whispered.

"That's all right. If they're mad, then maybe they will be less observant."

They watched and waited for an hour as the horsemen scoured the grounds ahead before regrouping at the trail's end. At the patrol leader's command, the riders spread out along the trail and retraced their original steps backward. Again, a pair of horsemen rode off to either side, with two of the riders approaching the edge of the rock ridge.

"Time to lay low," Pitt whispered as he and Giordino hunkered down into the hollow. They listened as the clip-clop of horse hooves drew closer. The hidden men froze as the sound paused directly beneath them. They had done their best to brush away their tracks before climbing the rock, but it had been done in darkness. And they weren't the only things at risk of exposure.

Pitt's heart beat a tick faster as he heard the riders converse for a moment. Then one of the horsemen dismounted and started climbing up the rocks. The man moved slowly, but Pitt could tell he was moving closer by the sound of his leather boots scuffing against the sandstone boulders. Pitt glanced at Giordino, who had reached over and clasped a baseball-sized stone near his leg.

"Nothing," the man shouted, standing just a few feet

beneath the concealed ledge. Giordino flexed his rock-holding arm, but Pitt reached over and grabbed his wrist. A second later, the mounted horseman shouted up something to the rock climber. By his tone, Pitt guessed he was telling the man to get moving. The scuffle of hard leather on soft rock began to move away, until the man reached the ground a few minutes later and remounted his horse. The clopping hooves echoed again, then gradually faded into the distance.

"That was close," Giordino said.

"Lucky thing our climber had a change of heart. That knuckleball of yours would have left a sting," Pitt replied, nodding toward the rock in Giordino's hand.

"Fastball. My best stuff is a fastball," he corrected.

Gazing off toward the trail of dust kicked up by the horsemen, he asked, "We stay put?"

"Yes. My money says they'll be back for another visit."

Pitt thought back to what he had read about the Mongol conquests of the thirteenth century. A feigned retreat was the favorite battlefield tactic of Genghis Khan when facing a powerful opponent. His army often orchestrated elaborate staged retreats, some lasting several days. The unsuspecting enemy would be drawn to a defenseless position, where a punishing counterattack would destroy them. Pitt knew that taking to the desert on foot would place them at a similarly deadly risk against the mobile horsemen. He wasn't going to take that chance until he was sure they were gone for good.

Crouched in their stone lair, the two men rested from their night adventure while patiently waiting for danger to dissipate on the horizon. An hour later, a sudden rumble shook them awake. The noise sounded like faint thunder, but the sky was clear. Scanning to the north, they saw a high cloud of dust trailing the six horsemen. The horses were galloping at top speed, pounding down the path of the original trail like it was the home stretch at Santa Anita. In seconds, the pack raced past Pitt and Giordino's position until they reached the end of the motorcycle trail. Slowing their pace and splitting up, the horsemen fanned out and searched the area in all directions. The horsemen all rode with their heads hung down, scanning the ground for prints or other clues to Pitt and Giordino's disappearance. They searched for nearly an hour, again coming up empty. Then almost as suddenly as they appeared, the horsemen regrouped and headed back north along the trail, moving at a canter.

"A nice encore," Giordino said as the horses finally disappeared over the horizon.

"I think the party is finally over," Pitt replied. "Time for us to hit the highway and find a burger stand."

The men hadn't eaten since the day before and their stomachs rumbled together in empty harmony. Climbing down the rock ridge, they moved toward the trail, stopping at a clump of tamarisk shrubs growing in thick concentration. Pitt grinned as he eyed the center branch, which was sprouting from the buried shell of the sidecar. A haphazard ring of rocks circled the partially exposed portions of the vehicle, obscuring its sides from the casual observer.

"Not bad for a nighttime camouflage job," Pitt said.

"I think we were a little lucky, too," Giordino added. He patted his coat pocket, which held the horseshoe he had removed from the sidecar's cowling.

Pitt's scheme to make the motorcycle disappear had worked better than he'd expected. After running out of gas, he knew it was just a matter of concealment. Backtracking along their trail on foot, he'd found a hardened gravel gully a few hundred feet behind, then returned to the motorcycle, brushing away the original tire tracks along the way with a thick strand of scrub brush. Then he and Giordino had pushed the motor-cycle and sidecar backward along the same path to the gully, stopping periodically to brush away their foot-prints under the beam of the headlight. To the pursuers following the tracks, there was no way of telling that the motorcycle had actually moved backward from its last marks.

Pitt and Giordino had pushed the motorcycle and sidecar down the gully as far as they could, then set about burying it. Giordino had found a small tool kit beneath the seat of the sidecar. Working under the light of the headlamp, they disassembled the sidecar from the motorcycle. Laying it flat in a nearby hollow, they were able to bury the motorcycle under a few inches of sand. The task was made easier once Pitt fashioned a shovel blade from the seat back. The lightly blowing sand, cursed till now, aided their cause by covering their interment project in a light layer of dust.

The sidecar proved more troublesome to hide once they discovered a hard layer of bedrock lying six inches beneath the surface. Realizing they would never get the sidecar buried without a shovel and pickax, they dragged it to a cluster of tamarisk bushes and buried what they could in the center of the thicket. Giordino stacked rocks around the perimeter while Pitt dug up a thick shrub and planted it on the seat, its droopy branches covering the sides. Though far from invisible, the ad hoc camouflage had done the trick, as evidenced by a set of hoofprints that scratched the sand just a few feet away.

As the midday sun beat down on them, sending a battery of heat waves shimmering off the desert floor, the two men looked nostalgically at the half-buried sidecar.

"Didn't think I'd miss riding in that contraption," Giordino said.

"Not so bad, given the alternative," Pitt replied, scanning the horizon for signs of life. A barren emptiness stretched in all directions, punctuated by an eerie silence.

Pitt brought his left arm up in front of his face, positioning his wrist so that his Doxa watch was flat at eye level. Then he pivoted his body around toward the sun, turning his body until the bright yellow orb was aligned with the hour hand on his watch, which read two o'clock. An old survival trick, he knew that south must be halfway between the hour hand and twelve o'clock if he was standing in the Northern Hemisphere. Peering over his watch at the terrain, he visually lined up one as south, seven as north, and west was between the two at four o'clock.

"We go west," Pitt said, pointing toward some red-hued hills that ambled across the horizon. "Somewhere in that direction is the Trans-Mongolian railway, which runs from Beijing to Ulaanbaatar. If we head west, we'll have to run into it eventually."

"Eventually," Giordino repeated slowly. "Why does that sound like we don't have a clue how far that could be?"

"Because we don't." Pitt shrugged, then turned toward the hills and started walking.

~ 27 ~

THE GOBI DESERT HOSTS SOME of the most hostile temperature extremes in the world. Blistering summertime temperatures of over 110 degrees plummet to minus 40 degrees in the winter months. Even in a single day, temperature swings of 60 degrees are not uncommon. Taken from the Mongolian word meaning "waterless place," the Gobi rates as the world's fifth-largest desert. The arid lands were once an inland sea, and, in later eons, a swampy stomping ground for dinosaurs. The Southwest Gobi still rates as a favorite destination for globe-trotting paleontologists in search of pristine fossils.

To Pitt and Giordino, the vacant undulating plains resembled an ocean, though one made of sand, gravel, and stone. Pink sandstone bluffs and craggy red-rock outcroppings bounded a gravel plain blanketed with brown, gray, and ebony pebbles. Framed against a crisp blue sky, the barren land teemed with its own brand of wasteland beauty. For the two men trekking across the desolate mantle, the scenic environs were a calming diversion to the fact they were in a potential death zone.

The afternoon temperature bounded over the 100-degree mark as the sun seared the rocky ground. The winds had dwindled to a slight breeze, offering all the cooling power of a blowtorch. The two men didn't dare shorten their sleeves or long pants, knowing the ultra-violet ray protection was more important than a slight improvement in comfort. They reluctantly kept their coats as well, tying them around their waists for the chilly night ahead. Tearing a section of the jacket lining out, they fashioned silk bandannas on their heads, which made them look like a pair of wayward pirates.

But there was nothing humorous about the task at hand. On their second day without food or water, crossing a baking desert by day while facing near-freezing temperatures at night, they faced the double dangers of dehydration and hypothermia. Strangely, their hunger pangs had gone away, replaced by an unrelenting and unquenchable thirst. The pounds of dust swallowed during the motorcycle ride had hardly improved matters, adding to their dry, constricting throats.

To survive the desert heat, Pitt knew that conserving their strength was critical. They could survive three days without water, but overexpending themselves in the heat of the day could cut that time in half. Since they were well rested from their morning concealment, they could push their pace for a short while before stopping, Pitt decided. They still had to find civilization in order to survive.

Pitt picked out a physical landmark in the distance, then began walking at a measured pace. Every half hour or so, they would seek out a rock formation that offered shade and rest in the shadows, allowing their bodies to cool. The pattern was repeated until the sun finally dipped toward the horizon and the ovenlike temperatures fell from high to medium.

The Gobi is a large desert and sparsely populated. But it isn't entirely a void. Tiny villages pepper the regions where shallow wells can be dug, while nomadic herders roam the fringes where scrub grass grows. If the men kept moving, they were bound to run into somebody. And Pitt was right. Somewhere to the west was the railroad line from Beijing to Ulaanbaatar and a dusty road that ran parallel to the tracks. But how far was it?

Pitt kept them trudging on a westerly tack, checking their heading with the sun and his watch. As they marched across the flats, they came to a set of ruts running perpendicular to their path.

"Hallelujah, a sign of life on this alien planet," Giordino said.

Pitt bent down and studied the tracks. They were clearly made by a jeep or truck, but the edges of the ruts were dull and caked with a light layer of sand.

"They didn't drive by yesterday," Pitt said.

"Not worth the detour?"

"These tracks could be five days old or five months old," Pitt said, shaking his head. Resisting the temptation to see where they led, the two men ignored the tracks and continued on their heading to the west. They would cross a few more tire tracks that trailed off in different directions to places unseen. Like most of Mongolia, there were few formal roads in the desert. Traveling to a destination was simply a matter of point and go. If a satellite in space ever mapped the myriad of lone tracks and trails across Mongolia, it would resemble a plate of spaghetti dropped on the floor.

As the sun dipped beneath the horizon, the desert air began to cool. Zapped by the heat and lack of fluids, the weakened men were invigorated by the cool air and they gradually picked up their pace across the gravel. Pitt had aimed them toward a rocky three-peaked spire he used as a compass landmark, which they reached shortly after midnight. A clear sky with a bright half-moon had helped illuminate the way under darkness.

They stopped and rested on a smooth slab of sandstone, laying down and studying the stars overhead.

"The Big Dipper is over there," Giordino said,

pointing to the easily identifiable part of the constellation Ursa Major. "And the Little Dipper is visible just above it."

"Which gives us Polaris, or the North Star, at the end of its handle."

Pitt rose to his feet and faced toward the North Star, then raised his left arm out from his side.

"West," he said, his fingers pointing to a dark ridge a few miles away.

"Let's get there before it closes," Giordino replied, grunting slightly as he stood up. The horseshoe in his coat pocket jabbed his side as he rose and he subconsciously patted the pocket with a knowing smile.

With a new compass bearing on the horizon, they set off again. Pitt checked the sky every few minutes, making sure the North Star remained to the right of them. The lack of food and water began to show on the two men, as their pace slowed and casual conversation fell silent. The wound in Pitt's leg began to let itself be known, firing a sharp throb with every step of his left foot. The cool night air soon turned chilly, and the men slipped into the coats they had toted around their waists. Walking kept them warm but consumed crucial body energy that was not being replenished.

"You promised me no more deserts after Mali," Giordino said, harking back to the time they nearly perished in the Sahara Desert while tracing a discharge of radioactive pollutants.

"I believe I said no more sub-Saharan deserts," Pitt replied.

"A technicality. So at what point can we hope that Rudi calls in the Coast Guard?"

"I told him to assemble our remaining equipment off the *Vereshchagin* and, if he could commandeer a truck, then meet us in Ulaanbaatar at the end of the week. I'm afraid our mother hen won't miss us for another three days."

"By which time we will have walked to Ulaanbaatar."

Pitt grinned at the notion. Given a supply of water, he had no doubt the tough little Italian could walk to Ulaanbaatar carrying Pitt on his back. But without a source of water—and soon—all bets were off.

A cold breeze nipped at them from the north as the night temperature continued to plummet. Moving became an incentive to keep warm, though they took satisfaction in knowing the summer nights had a short duration. Pitt kept them heading toward the ridge to the west, though for a time it seemed as if they weren't moving any closer. After two hours of trudging through a valley of loose gravel, they began climbing a series of low rolling hills. The hills gradually grew in size and height until they crested a high bluff, which abutted the base of the target ridge. After a brief rest, they assaulted the ridge, hiking most of the way up before they were forced to crawl on their hands and knees across a rugged section of boulders near the peak. The climb exhausted the men, and they both stopped and gasped for air when they finally reached the top.

A slow-moving cloud blotted the moonlight for several minutes, pitching the ridge top into an oily blackness. Pitt sat down on a mushroom-shaped rock to rest his legs, while Giordino hunched over to catch his breath. While still tough as nails, neither man was the spry stallion of a decade earlier. Each silently coped with a litany of aches and pains that wracked their legs and body.

"My kingdom for a satellite phone," Giordino rasped.

"I'd even consider the horse," Pitt replied.

As they rested, the silvery half-moon slid from behind the cloud, casting their surroundings in a misty blue glow. Pitt stood and stretched, then gazed down the other side of the ridge. A steep incline sloped into some craggy low bluffs that overlooked a bowl-shaped valley. Pitt studied the small basin, detecting what appeared to be several dark round shapes sprinkled across the central valley floor.

"Al. Check my mirage down the way," he said, pointing to the valley floor. "Tell me if it matches yours."

"If it includes a beer and a submarine sandwich, I can already tell you the answer is yes," Giordino replied, standing upright and walking over to Pitt. He took a long patient look down the slope, eventually confirming that he saw nearly two dozen black dots spread about the valley floor.

"It ain't Manhattan, but civilization it appears."

"The dark spots look to be shaped like *ger*s. A small

settlement, or a group of nomadic herders, perhaps," Pitt speculated.

"Big enough that somebody's got to have a coffeepot," Giordino replied, rubbing his hands together to keep warm.

"I'd bank on tea, if I were you."

"If it's hot, I'll drink it."

Pitt glanced at his watch, seeing it was nearly three A.M. "If we get going now, we'll be there by sunup."

"Just in time for breakfast."

The two men took off for the dark camp, working their way cautiously down the short ravine, then snaking their way through the rock-strewn hills. They traveled with a renewed sense of vigor, confident the worst of their ordeal was behind them. Food and water awaited them in the village below, which was now in sight.

Their progress slowed as they wound around several vertical uplifts that were too steep to traverse. The jagged rocks gave way to smaller stands of sandstone that the men could climb over and through. Hiking around a blunt mesa, they stopped and rested at the edge of a short plateau. Beneath them, the black-shadowed encampment sat less than a mile away.

The first strands of daylight began lightening the eastern sky, but it was still too early to offer much illumination. The main structures of the encampment were clearly visible, dark gray shapes against the light-colored desert floor. Pitt counted twenty-two of the round tents he knew to be Mongolian *ger*s. In the distance, they appeared larger than the ones they had seen in Ulaanbaatar and around the countryside. Oddly, there were no lights, lanterns, or fires to be seen. The camp was pitch-black.

Scattered around the encampment, Pitt and Giordino could make out the dark shadows of animals, denizens of the local herd. They were too far away to tell whether the animals were horses or camels. A fenced corral held some of the herd close to the *ger*s, while others roamed freely around the area.

"I believe you asked for a horse?" Giordino said.

"Let's hope they're not camels."

The two men moved easily across the last stretch of ground. They approached within a hundred yards of the camp when Pitt suddenly froze. Giordino caught Pitt's abrupt halt and followed suit. He strained his eyes and ears to detect a danger, but noticed nothing out of the ordinary. The night was perfectly still. Not a sound could be heard but for the occasional gust of wind, and he saw no movement around the camp.

"What gives?" he finally whispered to Pitt.

"The herd," Pitt replied quietly. "They're not moving."

Giordino peered at the host of animals scattered about the darkness, looking for signs of movement. A few yards away, he spotted a trio of fuzzy brown camels standing together, their heads raised in the air. He stared at them for a minute, but they didn't move a muscle.

"Maybe they're asleep," he offered.

"No," Pitt replied. "There is no odor either."

Pitt had visited enough farms and ranches to know that the smell of manure was never far from a herd of livestock. He took a few steps forward, creeping up slowly until he stood alongside the three animals. The creatures showed no fear, remaining still even as Pitt swatted one on its furry rump. Giordino looked on in shock as Pitt then grabbed one of the animals around the neck and shoved. The camel didn't resist at all but keeled stiffly over onto its side. Giordino ran over and stared at the animal, which lay motionless on its back with its legs in the air. Only they weren't legs sticking up but pieces of two-by-fours.

The fallen camel, like the rest of the herd, was made of wood.

— 28 —

DISAPPEARED? WHAT DO YOU MEAN they disappeared?" As Borjin's anger rose, a vein in the shape of an earthworm protruded from the side of his neck. "Your men tracked them into the desert!"

Though he physically towered over Borjin, the gruff head of security wilted like a shrinking violet under his boss's tirade.

"Their tracks simply vanished into the sand, sir. There was no indication they were picked up by another vehicle. They were fifty kilometers from the nearest village, which was to the east as they were traveling south. Their prospects for survival in the Gobi are nonexistent," Batbold said quietly.

Tatiana stood listening at the bar in the corner of the study, mixing a pair of vodka martinis. Handing a glass to her brother, she took a sip from her own drink, then asked, "Were they spies for the Chinese?"

"No," Batbold replied. "I don't believe so. The two men apparently bribed their way onto the Mongolian state security escort. The Chinese delegation seemed not to notice their absence from the motorcade when they departed. It is noteworthy that they also match the description of the two men who broke into our storage facility in Ulaanbaatar two nights ago."

"The Chinese would not have been so clumsy," Borjin commented.

"The men were not Chinese. I saw them myself. They looked Russian. Though Dr. Gantumur at the laboratory claimed they spoke to him in English with an American accent."

Tatiana suddenly choked on her drink, setting the glass down and coughing to clear her throat.

"Americans?" she stammered. "What did they look like?"

"From what I saw out the window, one was tall and lean with black hair while the other was short and robust with dark curly hair," Borjin said.

Batbold nodded. "Yes, that is an accurate description," he mumbled, neglecting to relay how close he was to the two men when he got clobbered by the shovel.

"Those sound like the men from NUMA," Tatiana gasped. "Dirk Pitt and Al Giordino. They were the ones who rescued us from the fishing boat on Baikal. The same men who came aboard the *Primoski* and captured the Russian scientist shortly before we departed Siberia."

"How did they track you here?" Borjin asked sternly.

"I do not know. Perhaps through the lease of the *Primoski*."

"They have stuck their noses where they don't belong. Where did they go in the compound?" he asked, turning to Batbold.

"They drove into the garage with a flat tire, then entered the research facility. Dr. Gantumur phoned security immediately, so they were only in the lab a few minutes. They somehow eluded the responding guards, and were probably examining the residence when you spotted them entering the sanctuary."

Borjin's face flushed with anger, the vein on his neck rising to new heights.

"They are hunting for the oil company employees, I am certain," Tatiana said. "They know nothing of our work. Do not worry, my brother."

"You should have never brought those people here in the first place," he hissed.

"It is your fault," Tatiana roared back. "If you hadn't killed the Germans before they fully assessed the field data, we would not have needed further assistance."

Borjin glared at his sister, refusing to admit the truth

of her words. "Then these oil people must be eliminated, too. Have them accelerate the analysis, I wish them gone by the end of the week," he said, his eyes raging with fire.

"Do not worry. The Americans know nothing of our work. And they will not survive to talk anyway."

"Perhaps you are right," he replied, his temper cooling. "These men of the sea are a long ways from the water now. But just to be sure they stay that way, send the monk down there immediately for insurance," he added, speaking to Batbold.

"A prudent decision, brother."

"To their dry and dusty demise," he mused now, raising his glass and sipping the martini.

Tatiana swallowed the rest of her drink but silently wondered if the demise of the Americans would come as predicted. They were determined men, she had come to realize, who would not face death easily.

IT FELT as though they were walking through the back-lot set of a Hollywood western, only they were surrounded by camels instead of cattle. Climbing through a fenced corral, Pitt and Giordino were amused to see a large trough to water the wooden livestock. The early-morning sun cast long shadows from the large immobile herd that was strategically placed around the village. Pitt gave up counting when he reached a hundred head of the prop camels.

"Reminds me of that guy in Texas who has all those Cadillacs half buried in his yard," Giordino said.

"I don't think these were put out here for art, if that's what you call it."

They made their way to the nearest *ger,* which was more than double the standard size. The circular felt tent was nearly a hundred feet across and stood over ten feet tall. Pitt found a white-painted entry door, which on all Mongol *ger*s faced south. Rapping his knuckles on the doorframe, he shouted a cheery "Hello." The thin doorframe didn't flex at all under his knocking, which echoed with a deep resonance. Pitt placed his hand against the felt wall and pushed. Rather than simply a forgiving layer of canvas over felt, the wall was backed by something hard and solid.

"The big bad wolf couldn't blow this thing down," he said.

Grabbing an edge of the canvas covering, he ripped a small section off the wall. Beneath was a thin layer of felt, which he also tore away. Under the layer of felt he exposed a cold metal surface painted white.

"It's a storage tank," Pitt said, touching the metal side.

"Water?"

"Or oil," Pitt replied, stepping back and eyeing the other phony *ger*s dotting the encampment.

"They may be large by nomadic-tent standards, but they are still relatively small for oil tanks," Giordino remarked.

"I bet we're only seeing the tip of the iceberg. These things might be buried thirty or forty feet down, and we're only seeing the tops."

Giordino scuffed the ground and loosened a small rock, which he picked up and rapped against the tank. A deep empty echo reverberated through the tank.

"She's empty." He took a half step, then lobbed the rock at the next closest *ger*. The stone bounced off the side, producing a similar pinging sound.

"Empty as well," he said.

"So much for your pot of coffee," Pitt replied.

"Why would some empty oil tanks in the middle of nowhere be disguised as a fake village?"

"We may not be far from the Chinese border," Pitt said. "Maybe someone is concerned about the Chinese stealing their oil? I'd guess the target audience is an aerial survey or satellite imaging, at which heights this place would look pretty authentic."

"The wells must not have panned out if these tanks are all dry."

Wandering around the phony village, the men realized there was no food or water to be found and the mystery lost its allure. They worked their way through the string of fake *ger*s, hoping to find some emergency supplies or something more than an empty oil tank. But all the tents were the same, masking large metal tanks half buried in the sand. Only at the very last tent did they find that the door actually opened, revealing a pumping station dug twenty feet into the ground. A maze of pipes led to the other storage tanks, fed from a single four-foot-diameter inlet pipe that protruded from beneath the desert floor.

"An underground oil pipeline," Pitt observed.

"Dug and placed with the help of a tunnel-boring machine?" Giordino posed. "Now, let's see, where have I seen one of those lately?"

"It's quite possible that our friends at Avarga Oil have struck again. May have something to do with the deal they are cooking up with the Chinese, but for what purpose I can only guess."

The two men fell silent again, fatigue and disappointment damping their spirits. Overhead, the rising sun was beginning to bake the sand-and-gravel floor around the mock village. Tired from their all-night trek and weak from lack of food and water, the men wisely decided to rest. Ripping sections of the felt covering from one of the tanks, they bundled a pair of crude mattresses together and lay down in the shade of the pumping house. The homemade beds felt like a cloud to their tired bones and they quickly drifted off to sleep.

The sun was dropping toward the western horizon like a fluorescent billiard ball when the two men finally roused themselves. The sleep break did little to restore their energy levels, however, and they departed the village in a lethargic state. They began hiking with noticeable effort, yet moved at a snail's pace, as if each man had aged forty years in his sleep. Pitt took another bearing with his watch against the sun's rays and led them in a westerly direction again, foregoing any thoughts of trying to trace the underground pipeline. They moved in unspoken unison, willing their bodies forward with each step, as the first hints of delirium began to fog their minds.

The winds gradually began to kick up again, jabbing and swirling in sporadic gusts as a prelude to the force that was to come. The northerly wind brought with it a cold chill. Both men had carried a thin section of felt from the storage tank and wrapped their heads and torsos in the fabric like a poncho. Pitt targeted a distant S-shaped ridge for a bearing as the sun slid away, focusing his efforts on maintaining a straight course. As the winds picked up, he knew his North Star compass would be obscured, and the last thing they needed in their state was to be wandering around in circles.

An annoying mantra, "move or die," began to repeat endlessly in his head, urging him forward. Pitt could feel the swelling in the back of his parched throat and tried to put the unyielding thirst out of his mind. He glanced at Giordino, who bulled ahead with listless eyes. Both their energies and exhausted mental capacities were concentrated on putting one foot in front of the other.

Time seemed to fade away for Pitt, and consciousness nearly as well. He drifted along, then felt his eyes pop open, not sure if he had fallen asleep on his feet. How long he was out, he had no idea, but at least Giordino was still there, trudging along beside him. His mind began to wander, thinking of his wife, Loren, who served in Congress back in Washington. Though lovers for many years, they had only just recently married, Pitt reasoning that his days of globe-trotting adventure were behind him. She'd known the wanderlust would never leave his blood, even if he didn't. Within months of his ascension to the head of NUMA, he grew restless with managing the agency from its Washington headquarters. It was Loren who urged him to take to the field, knowing he was happiest when working with his first love, the sea. Time apart would make their love stronger, she told him, though he doubted she meant it. Yet he wouldn't interfere with her career on the Hill, so he followed her words. Now he wondered if doing so would end up making her a widow.

It was an hour later, maybe two, when the winds decided to make an appearance in earnest, blowing hard from the northwest. The stars above quickly melted away in the dust, obscuring their only source of light. As the blowing dust settled over them in a cottony haze, Pitt's landmark ridge disappeared from view. It was no matter, though, as Pitt stared down at his feet with numb fatigue.

They moved like zombies, lifeless in appearance but unwilling to stop walking. Giordino moved methodically forward alongside Pitt, as if an invisible tether kept the two men linked together. The winds grew intense, stinging their face and eyes with blasting sand that made it painful to see. Still they trudged ahead, though well off their westerly track. The exhausted men began zigzagging to the south, in a subconscious effort to flee the biting wind.

They staggered on in a timeless whirl until Pitt detected Giordino trip over some rocks and fall down next to him. Pitt stopped and reached out to help his friend up. A burly hand rose up and grabbed Pitt's, then yanked hard in the other direction. Pitt sprawled toward Giordino, tripping over him and falling into a bed of soft sand. Lying there dazed, he noticed the blasting sand was no longer peppering his body. Unseen in the turbulent night, Giordino had tripped over a rock piling, behind which lay an indented cove protected from the howling winds. Pitt reached out and touched the rock wall with one hand as he felt Giordino crawl alongside and collapse. With a last ounce of energy, Pitt unwrapped his felt cloth and draped it over both their heads for warmth, then lay back on the soft sand and closed his eyes.

Beneath the screeching desert sandstorm, both men fell unconscious.

~ 29 ~

GIORDINO WAS DREAMING. HE DREAMED that he was floating in a still pond of tropical water. The warm liquid was unusually dense, like syrup, making his movements a slow and laborious effort. The water suddenly lapped at his face in a series of small hot waves. He jerked his head to escape the surf, but the warm moisture followed his motion. Then something about the dream became overly vivid. It was an odor, a very unpleasant one at that. A smell too powerful to reside in a dream. The repulsive aroma finally spurred him awake and he forcefully cocked open a heavy eyelid.

Bright sunshine stung at his eyes, but he could squint enough to see there was no aqua blue water lapping at his body. Instead, a giant pink swab descended on him with a hot wipe across one cheek. Jerking his head away, he saw the pink swab roll behind a picket fence of large yellow teeth housed in a snout that appeared a mile long. The beast exhaled a breath that bathed Giordino's face in a putrid cloud of onion, garlic, and Limburger cheese.

Popping open both eyes and shaking off the cobwebs, he stared past the expansive snout into two chocolate-brown eyes shrouded behind long eyelashes. The camel blinked curiously at Giordino, then let out a short bellow before stepping back to nibble at a fringe of felt protruding from the sand.

Giordino struggled to sit up, realizing the syrupy water in his dream was a layer of sun-warmed sand. A drift of sand nearly a foot thick had piled up in the little cove during the sandstorm the night before. Weakly pulling his arms out of the morass, Giordino nudged the figure next to him similarly buried under felt and sand, then scooped away handfuls of the brown silica. The felt rustled a bit then was thrown back, exposing the drawn and haggard face of Pitt. His face was sunburned, his lips bloated and chapped. Yet the sunken green eyes sparkled at seeing his friend alive.

"Another day in paradise," he rasped through a parched mouth, taking in their surroundings. The overnight sandstorm had blown itself out, leaving them bathed in sunshine under a clear blue sky.

They heaved their bodies upright, the sand falling off them in rivulets. Giordino sneaked a hand into his pocket and nodded slightly in reassurance, finding the horseshoe still there.

"We've got company," he wheezed, his voice sounding like steel wool on sandpaper.

Pitt crawled weakly from under the blanket of sand and peered at the beast of burden standing a few feet away. It was a Bactrian camel, as evidenced by the two humps on his back that sagged slightly to one side. The animal's matted fur was a rich mocha brown, which darkened around its flanks. The camel returned Pitt's stare for a few seconds, then resumed its nibbling on the blanket.

"The ship of the desert," Pitt said.

"Looks more like a tugboat. Do we eat him or ride him?"

Pitt was contemplating whether they had the strength to do either when a shrill whistle blared from behind a dune. A small boy bobbed over the sand, riding a dappled tan horse. He wore a green *del,* and his short black hair was hidden under a faded baseball cap. The boy rode up to the camel, calling it by name as he approached. When the camel popped his head up, the boy quickly looped a pole-mounted lasso around the animal's neck and pulled the rope tight. Only then did he glance down and notice Pitt and Giordino lying on the ground. The startled boy stared wide-eyed at the two haggard men who resembled ghosts in the sand.

"Hello." Pitt smiled warmly at the boy. He climbed unsteadily to his feet as a pool of sand slid off his clothes. "Can you help us?"

"You . . . talk English," the boy stammered.

"Yes. You can understand me?"

"I learn English at monastery," he replied proudly, enunciating each syllable.

"We are lost," Giordino said hoarsely. "Can you share food or water?"

The boy slipped off his wooden saddle and produced a goatskin canteen filled with water. Pitt and Giordino took turns attacking the water, taking small sips at first then working up to large gulps. As they drank, the boy pulled a scarf out of his pocket, which was wrapped around a block of sun-dried curds. Cutting it into small pieces, he offered it to the men, who gratefully split the rubbery milk residue and washed it down with the last of the water.

"My name is Noyon," the boy said. "What is yours?"

"I am Dirk and this is Al. We are very happy to meet you, Noyon."

"You are fools, Dirk and Al, to be in the Gobi without water and a mount," he said sternly. His youthful face softened with a smile, and he added, "You come with me to my home, where you will be welcomed by my family. It is less than a kilometer from here. A short ride for you."

The boy slipped off his horse and removed the small wooden saddle, then prodded Pitt and Giordino to climb aboard. The Mongol pony was not tall, and Pitt easily pulled himself onto its back, then helped hoist Giordino on behind him. Noyon grabbed the reins and led them north across the desert, the roped camel following behind.

They traveled just a short distance before Noyon led them around a thick sandstone ridge. On the opposite side, a large herd of camels were scattered about a shallow plain, foraging for scrub grass that sprouted through the stony ground. In the center of the field stood a lone *ger,* shrouded in dirty white canvas, its southerly door painted a weathered orange. Two poles with a rope tied across acted as an adjacent corral, securing several stout brown horses. A rugged, clean-shaven man with penetrating dark eyes was saddling one of the horses when the small caravan rode up.

"Father, I have found these men lost in the desert," the boy said in his native tongue. "They are from America."

The man took one look at the bedraggled figures of Pitt and Giordino and knew they had flirted with Erleg Khan, the Mongolian lord of the lower world. He quickly helped them down off the horse, returning the feeble shake of the hand offered by each exhausted man.

"Secure the horse," he barked at his son, then led the two men into his home.

Ducking and entering the *ger,* Pitt and Giordino were amazed at the warm décor of the interior, which was in stark contrast to the tent's drab exterior. Brightly patterned carpets covered every square inch of the dirt floor, melding with vibrant floral weavings that covered the tent's lattice-framed walls. Cabinets and tables were painted cheerful hues of red, orange, and blue, while the ceiling support frames were painted lemon yellow.

The interior was configured in a traditional *ger* layout, symbolic of the role superstition plays in daily nomadic life. To the left of the entrance was a rack and cabinet for the man's saddle and other belongings. The right section of the *ger,* the "female" side, held the cooking implements. A hearth and cooking stove was situated in the center, attached to a metal stovepipe that rose through an opening in the tent's ceiling. Three low beds were positioned around the perimeter walls, while the back wall was reserved for the family altar.

Noyon's father led Pitt and Giordino around the left side of the *ger* to some stools near the hearth. A slight woman with long black hair and cheerful eyes tending a battered teapot smiled at the men. Seeing their exhausted state, she brought damp towels to wash their face and hands, then set some strips of mutton to boil in a pot of water. Noticing the bloody bandage on Pitt's leg, she cleaned the dressing as the men downed cup after cup of watery black tea. When the mutton was cooked, she proudly served up a giant portion to each man, accompanied by a tray of dried cheeses. To the famished men, the flavor-challenged meal tasted like French haute cuisine. After devouring the mutton and cheese, the man brought over a leather bag filled with the home-fermented mare's milk, called *airag,* and filled three cups.

Noyon entered the *ger* and sat down behind the men to act as interpreter for his parents, who did not speak English. His father spoke quietly in a deep tone, looking Pitt and Giordino in the eye.

"My father, Tsengel, and my mother, Ariunaa, welcome you to their home," the boy said.

"We thank you for your hospitality. You have truly saved our lives," Pitt said, sampling the *airag* with a toast. He decided the brew tasted like warm beer mixed with buttermilk.

"Tell me, what are you doing in the Gobi without provisions?" Tsengel asked through his son.

"We became separated from our tour group during a brief visit into the desert," Giordino fibbed. "We retraced our steps but got lost when the sandstorm struck last night."

"You were lucky my son found you. There are few settlements in this region of the desert."

"How far arc wc from the nearest village?" Pitt asked.

"There is a small settlement about twenty kilometers from here. But enough questions for now," Tsengel said, seeing the weary look in both men's eyes. "You must rest after your meal. We will talk again later."

Noyon led the men to two of the small beds, then followed his father outside to tend the herd. Pitt lay back on the cushioned bed and admired the bright yellow roof supports overhead before falling into a deep, heavy sleep.

He and Giordino woke before dusk to the recurring smell of mutton boiling on the hearth. They stretched their legs outside the *ger*, walking amid the docile herd of camels that roamed freely about. Tsengel and Noyon soon came galloping up, having spent the afternoon rounding up strays.

"You are looking fit now," Tsengel said through his son.

"Feeling fit as well," Pitt replied. The food, liquids, and rest had quickly revitalized the two men and they felt surprisingly refreshed.

"My wife's cooking. It is an elixir," the man grinned. Tying their horses to the hitching rope then washing at a bucket of soapy water, he led them back into the *ger*. Another meal of mutton and dried cheese awaited them, accompanied by cooked noodles. This time, Pitt and Giordino consumed the meal with much less relish. The *airag* was produced earlier and poured in larger quantities, consumed out of small ceramic bowls that never seemed to empty.

"You have an impressive herd," Giordino remarked, complimenting his host. "How many head?"

"We own one hundred thirty camels and five horses," Tsengel replied. "A satisfactory herd, yet it is a quarter the size of what we once owned on the other side of the border."

"In Chinese Inner Mongolia?"

"Yes, the so-called autonomous region, which has

become little more than another Chinese province." Tsengel looked into the fire with a glint of anger in his eyes.

"Why did you leave?"

Tsengel nodded toward a faded black-and-white photograph on the altar, which showed a boy on a horse and an older man holding the reins. The penetrating eyes of the boy revealed it was a young Tsengel, alongside his own father.

"At least five generations of my ancestors have herded on the eastern fields of the Gobi. My father owned a herd of over two thousand camels at one time. But those days have vanished in the winds. There is no place for a simple herder in those lands anymore. The Chinese bureaucrats keep commandeering the land without regard to its natural balance. Time and again, we have been pushed out of our ancestral grazing lands and forced to drive our herds to the harshest portions of the desert. Meanwhile, they suck the water out wherever they can, for the noble cause of industrializing the state. As a result, the grasslands are disappearing right under their noses. The desert is growing day by day, but it is a dead desert. The fools will not see it until the sands begin to consume their capital of Beijing, by which time it will be too late. For my family's sake, I had no choice but to cross the border. The grazing conditions are sparse, but at least the herder is still respected here," he said proudly.

Pitt took another sip of the bitter-tasting *airag* as he studied the old photograph.

"It is always a crime to take away a man's liveli-hood," he said.

His gaze drifted over to a framed print mounted at the back of the altar. The portrait of a rotund man with a stringy goatee peered back, drawn in an ancient styl-ized hand.

"Tsengel, who is that on the altar?"

"The Yuan emperor, Kublai. Most powerful ruler of the world, yet benevolent friend of the common man," Tsengel replied, as if the emperor were still alive.

"Kublai Khan?" Giordino asked.

Tsengel nodded. "It was a far better time when the Mongol ruled China," he added wistfully.

"It is a much different world today, I'm afraid," Pitt said.

The *airag* was taking its toll on Tsengel, who had consumed several bowls of the potent brew. His eyes grew glassy and his emotions more visceral as the mare's milk disappeared down his throat. Finding the geopolitical conversation becoming a little too sensi-tive for the man, Pitt tried to change the subject.

"Tsengel, we stumbled upon a strange sight in the desert before the sandstorm struck. It was an artificial village surrounded by wooden camels. Do you know the place?"

Tsengel responded by laughing with a throaty guffaw.

"Ah, yes, the richest herdsmen in the Gobi. Only his mares don't produce a drop of milk," he smiled, taking another sip of *airag*.

"Who built it?" Giordino asked.

"A large crew of men appeared in the desert with equipment, pipe, and a digging machine. They dug tunnels under the surface that run for many kilometers. I was paid a small fee to direct their foreman to the nearest well. He told me that they worked for an oil company in Ulaanbaatar, but were sworn not to tell anyone of their work. Several of the crewmen who talked loudly had disappeared suddenly and the rest of the workers were very nervous. They quickly built the wooden camels and large tanks that look like *ger*s, then the men vanished. The tanks in the village stand empty, collecting only dust from the wind. That was many months ago, and I have seen no one return since. It is just like the others."

"Which others?" Pitt asked.

"There are three other camps of metal *ger*s located near the border. They are all the same. They stand empty, but for the wooden camels."

"Are there existing oil wells or oil drilling in the area?" Pitt asked.

Tsengel thought for a moment, then shook his head. "No. I have seen oil wells in China many years ago, but none in this area."

"Why do you think they disguise the storage tanks and surround them with wooden livestock?"

"I do not know. Some say that the metal *ger*s were built by a wealthy herder to capture the rains and that the water will be used to bring back the grasslands. A shaman claims the wooden animals are an homage, placed in appeasement for the desecration of the desert that occurred by their underground digging. Others say it is the work of a tribe of madmen. But they are all wrong. It is simply the work of the powerful, who wish to exploit the wealth of the desert. Why do they disguise their efforts? Why else but to disguise their evil hearts."

The *airag* had nearly finished Tsengel off. He slurped the remains of his bowl, then rose uneasily to his feet and bid his guests and family good night. Staggering over to one of the beds, he collapsed onto the covers and was snoring loudly minutes later. Pitt and Giordino helped the others clean up the remains of the meal, then strode outside for a dose of fresh air.

"It still doesn't make any sense," Giordino said, gazing at the night sky. "Why hide some empty oil tanks out in the desert to collect dust?"

"Maybe there is something more important than the storage tanks that is being hidden."

"What might that be?"

"Perhaps," Pitt replied, kicking his toe into the ground, "the source of the oil."

~ 30 ~

DESPITE TSENGEL'S LOUD SNORING, Pitt and Giordino slept soundly in the *ger*, the boy Noyon giving up his bed to sleep on pillows on the floor. Everyone awoke at sunup and shared a breakfast of tea and noodles. Tsengel had arranged for Pitt and Giordino to accompany Noyon to the nearby village, where the local children were shuttled to a monastery for schooling three days a week. Pitt and Giordino would hop a ride with Noyon to the monastery, where a supply truck from Ulaanbaatar was known to make semiregular visits.

Slipping some dusty bills into her hand, Pitt thanked Ariunaa for the food and comfort, then said good-bye to Tsengel.

"We cannot repay your kindness and generosity."

"The door to a herder's *ger* is always open. Be well in your travels, and think kindly on occasion of your friends in the Gobi."

The men shook hands, then Tsengel galloped off to tend his herd. Pitt, Giordino, and Noyon mounted three of the stout horses and loped off toward the north.

"Your father is a good man," Pitt said as he watched Tsengel's dusty trail disappear over the horizon.

"Yes, but he is sad to be away from the ground of his birth. We are doing well enough here, but I know his heart lies in Hulunbuir, the land to the southeast."

"If he can prosper here, then I'd say he could make it anywhere," Giordino said, eyeing the barren landscape around them.

"It is a struggle, but I will help my father when I am older. I will attend the university in Ulaanbaatar and become a doctor. Then I will buy him all the camels he desires."

They crossed a grainy plain, then threaded their way

through a series of sharp sandstone uplifts. The horses plodded their way along without guidance, following the route the way a Grand Canyon mule knows every step to the Colorado River. It wasn't long before Pitt and Giordino found their backsides chafing in discomfort. The horses were outfitted with the traditional Mongol saddles that were constructed of wood. Like most children of the Mongolian Steppes and desert regions, Noyon had learned to ride before he could walk and grew up accustomed to the hard, unforgiving riding gear. For outsiders like Pitt and Giordino, it was like riding a park bench over an infinite row of speed bumps.

"You sure there's not a bus stop or airport around here?" Giordino asked with a grimace.

Noyon thoughtfully considered the question.

"No bus, other than at the village. But airplane, yes. Not far from here. I will take you to it."

Before Giordino could say another word, Noyon kicked his horse and galloped off toward a ridge to the east.

"That's all we need, an extra side trip," Pitt said. "Shouldn't cost us more than a ruptured spleen or two."

"Who's to say there's not a Learjet waiting for us on the other side of that ridge?" Giordino countered.

They turned toward Noyon's dusty trail and spurred their horses to run, the animals eagerly galloping after the lead horse. They charged up to the base of the ridge, then flanked around its northern tip. The horses' hooves clopped loudly as they crossed a wide section of level sandstone. Winding around some large boulders, they finally caught up with Noyon, who sat waiting in the shadow of a rocky spire. To Giordino's chagrin, there was no jet or airport, or sign of any means of air transportation, for as far as the eye could see. There was just more flat gravelly desert, punctuated by the occasional rocky bluff. At least the boy was truthful in one regard, Giordino thought. They had in fact traveled only a short distance off their original path.

Pitt and Giordino slowed their horses to a walk as they approached Noyon. The boy smiled at them, then nodded toward the back side of the ridge behind him.

Pitt gazed at the ridge, noting only a rocky incline covered in a layer of red sand. A few of the rocks were oddly shaped and seemed to reflect a faint silvery hue.

"A lovely rock garden," Giordino mused.

But Pitt was intrigued and rode closer, noting two of the protrusions were proportionally shaped. As he drew near, he suddenly saw that they were not rocks at all but a pair of partially buried radial engines. One was attached to the blunt nose of an inverted fuselage while the other was mounted to an accompanying wing that disappeared under the sand.

Noyon and Giordino rode up as Pitt dismounted and brushed away the sand from one of the buried cowlings. Looking up with amazement, he said to Giordino, "It's not a Learjet. It's a Fokker trimotor."

~ 31 ~

THE FOKKER F. VIIB LAY WHERE she had crashed, undisturbed for over seventy years. The inverted plane had collected blowing sand by the truckload, until her right wing and most of her fuselage was completely buried. Some distance behind, the port wing and engine lay hidden, crushed against the same rocks that had torn it off during the forced landing. The nose of the plane was mashed in like an accordion, the cockpit filled to the brim with sand. Buried in the dust, the crushed skeletons of the pilot and copilot were still strapped in their seats. Pitt brushed away a thick layer of sand from beneath the pilot's window until he could read the faded name of the plane, *Blessed Betty*.

"Heck of a place to set down," Giordino said. "I thought you said these old birds were indestructible?"

"Nearly. The Fokker trimotors, like the Ford trimotors, were a rugged aircraft. Admiral Byrd used one to fly over the Arctic and Antarctic. Charles Kingsford-Smith flew his Fokker F. VII, the *Southern Cross*, across the Pacific Ocean back in 1928. Powered by the Wright Whirlwind motors, they could practically fly forever." Pitt was well versed about the old airplane—his own Ford trimotor was wedged in with his collection of antique cars back in Washington.

"Must have been done in by a sandstorm," Giordino speculated.

As Noyon watched from a respectful distance, Pitt and Giordino followed the sand-scrubbed belly of the fuselage aft until they found a slight lip on the side. Brushing away a few inches of sand, they could see it was the lower edge of the fuselage side door. Both men attacked the soft sand, scooping away a large hole in front of the door. After several minutes of digging, they cleared away an opening around the door, with room to pull the door open. As Giordino scooped away a last pile, Pitt noticed a seam of bullet holes stitched across the fuselage near the door.

"Correction to the cause of crash," he said, running a hand across the holes. "They were shot down."

"I wonder why?" Giordino mused.

He started to reach for the door handle when Noyon suddenly let out a slight wail.

"The elders say there are dead men inside. The lamas tell us that we must not disturb them. That is why the nomads have not entered the aircraft."

"We will respect the dead," Pitt assured him. "I shall see that they are given a proper burial so that their spirits may rest."

Giordino twisted the handle and gently tugged open the door. A jumbled mass of splintered wood, sand, and broken pieces of porcelain tumbled out of the dark interior, settling into a small pile. Pitt picked up a broken plate from the Yuan Dynasty, which was glazed with a sapphire blue peacock.

"Not your everyday dinnerware," he said, recognizing it as an antiquity. "At least five hundred years old, I'd wager." Though admittedly no expert, Pitt had acquired a working knowledge of pottery and porcelain from his many years of diving on shipwrecks. Often times, the only clues to identifying a shipwreck's age and derivation were the broken shards of pottery found amid its ballast pile.

"Then we have the world's oldest, as well as largest, jigsaw puzzle," Giordino said, stepping back from the doorway to let Pitt peer in.

The interior of the plane was a mess. Mangled and splintered crates lay scattered over every square inch of the main cabin, their shattered porcelain contents strewn across the floor in a carpet of blue-and-white shards. Only a few crates wedged near the tail had survived the violent crash landing intact.

Pitt crawled into the fuselage and waited a moment for his eyes to adjust to the dark interior. The dim cabin and stale dusty air inside lent an eerie feeling to the Fokker's interior, which was augmented by the rows of wicker seats hanging empty from the ceiling of the inverted aircraft. Ducking his head slightly, Pitt turned and moved first toward the intact crates near the tail section. The broken bits of porcelain crunched under each footstep, compelling him to move tentatively through the debris.

He found five crates that were still intact, with FRAGILE and ATTENTION: BRITISH MUSEUM stenciled along the sides. The lid on one crate had been jarred loose, and Pitt grabbed the loose section of wood and pried it open. Inside was a large porcelain bowl wrapped in a loose cloth. Over seven hundred years old, the bowl had a serrated edge and was glazed greenish blue over the white clay base. Pitt admired the floral artistry of the design, then placed the bowl back in the crate. As the debris on the floor seemed to confirm, the plane was carrying a packed cargo of antique ceramics and, thankfully, no passengers.

Pitt moved back up the inverted aisleway, where Giordino joined him at the side door.

"Any clue to the cargo?" he asked in a hushed tone.

"Just that it was headed to the British Museum. A few boxes survived in back. Appears to be all antique porcelain."

Pitt moved forward, creeping past the first row of seats and toward the cockpit bulkhead. Much of the cargo had been thrown forward when the plane crashed, creating a mountain of debris in the front of the cabin. Pitt stepped over a large fractured pot and spotted a dusty leather jacket lying amid some debris on the floor. Stepping around broken shards, he hoisted a broken crate out of the way to take a closer look, then froze in his tracks. Under the dim light seeping in from the doorway, he could see that the jacket was still occupied by its original owner.

The mummified remains of Leigh Hunt lay where he'd expired, decades after he pulled himself out of the crash in agonizing pain from a broken back. His left arm tightly clutched the yellow wooden box while his bony white right hand was wrapped around a small notebook. A wrinkled grimace was etched into Hunt's face, his features well preserved by the dry desert air and a thin layer of silica.

"Poor devil. He must have survived the crash, only to die later," Pitt surmised in a hushed tone.

"That box and notebook evidently meant something to him," Giordino replied.

With an uneasy reverence, Pitt carefully removed the box and notebook from the skeletal grip, handing the wooden box to Giordino. Noticing a dirty worn fedora lying on the floor nearby, he gently placed it over the face of the corpse.

"I don't presume the pilots fared any better," he said, looking forward. Carefully stepping over Hunt's body, he moved to the forward bulkhead and tried to peer through the cutout into the cockpit. The entire compartment was filled with sand, which had blasted through the pilots' windows when the plane crashed.

"It would take the better part of a day to excavate that," Giordino said, looking over Pitt's shoulder.

"Maybe on our next visit," Pitt replied. He had little doubt that the bones of the pilots would be found preserved beneath the heavy layer of sand.

The two men made their way back down the fuselage and climbed out the side door into the bright sunshine. Noyon was pacing back and forth nervously but stopped and smiled with relief when Pitt and Giordino exited the craft. Giordino held the yellow wooden box up for Noyon to see, then gingerly pried off the lid. Inside were the bronze tube and the tightly rolled cheetah skin, in the same pristine condition as when discovered by Hunt.

"Not exactly the crown jewels," he said, eyeing the contents with minor disappointment. Holding the bronze tube up toward the sun, he saw that there was nothing inside.

"This ought to tell us something," Pitt said, holding open the notebook. He flipped open the cover and read the title page aloud. "Excavations at Shang-tu. Commencing May 15, 1937. Field Diary of Dr. Leigh Hunt, Expedition Leader."

"Read on," Giordino said. "I'm dying to know if the cheetah skin was destined as a footstool in Dr. Hunt's library or as a pillow for his mistress's boudoir."

"My friends, we must be on our way if we are to catch the bus to the monastery," Noyon interrupted.

"The mystery will have to wait," Pitt said. He slipped the diary into his shirt pocket, then walked over and closed the Fokker's side door.

"How about our friends inside?" Giordino asked.

"I'll call Dr. Sarghov when we make it back to Ulaanbaatar. He should know who to contact in the Mongolian government to ensure a proper excavation is carried out. We owe it to Dr. Hunt to see that a professional retrieval is made of the artifacts he gave his life for."

"As well as see that he and the pilots are given a proper burial."

Pitt scooped a pile of sand in front of the airplane door to keep it sealed while Giordino stuffed the wooden box into a leather saddlebag. Then they remounted the horses that Noyon had held, settling in to the uncomfortable wooden saddles.

"You sure there weren't any down pillows inside those rear crates?" Giordino asked with a wince.

Pitt just shook his head with a smile. As they trotted toward the village, he turned and gazed a last time at the dusty remains of the old plane and wondered what secrets Hunt's diary would reveal.

An hour's ride took them to the diminutive settlement of Senj. The village, such that it was, would be found on few maps, as it was nothing more than a few *ger*s crowded around a small watering hole. The spring flowed year-round, offering permanent sustenance for the resident herders and their flocks who otherwise would be forced to migrate several times a year in chase of fertile grasslands. As was the usual case in the rural countryside, the camels and horses milling about the village greatly outnumbered the human residents.

Noyon led Pitt and Giordino to a *ger* flying an orange banner, where they tied the horses to a staked rope. Several small children were busy playing chase with one another nearby, stopping for a moment to ogle the strange men before resuming their game. Climbing off his horse, Giordino swayed like a drunken sailor, his legs and rear aching from the hard saddle.

"Next time, I think I'll try the camel and take my chances with the humps."

Pitt was equally sore and glad to be standing on his feet.

"A season with the herd and you'll be riding like an *arat*," Noyon said, referring to the local horsemen.

"A season in that saddle and I'd be ready for traction," Giordino grumbled.

An elderly resident of the village spotted the men and hobbled over on a game leg, speaking rapidly to the boy.

"This is Otgonbayar," said Noyon. "He invites you to visit his *ger* and enjoy a bowl of *airag*."

The low whine of a truck echoed off the surrounding hills, then a small faded green bus crested a ridge and turned toward the village, trailing a cloud of dust. Noyon looked toward the approaching vehicle, then shook his head.

"I'm afraid our bus has arrived," he said.

"Please tell Otgonbayar that we appreciate his invitation but will have to join him another time," Pitt said. He walked over to the old man and shook his hand. The old man nodded and smiled in understanding, exposing a pair of toothless gums.

With a loud squeal of its brakes, the bus ground to a stop and the driver tapped the horn. The playing children ceased their roughhousing and marched single file to the bus, hopping inside after its accordion side door swung open.

"Come on," Noyon said, leading Pitt and Giordino aboard.

The 1980s-era Russian-built bus, a KAvZ model

3976, was a forgotten relic of the Soviet Army. Like many vehicles that ended up in Mongolia, it had been passed along from the old guardian state long after its useful life had been reached. With faded paint, cracked windows, and bald tires, it showed nearly every one of the quarter-million miles that had been placed on her. Yet like an old boxer who refuses to quit, the beaten hulk was patched up and sent back onto the road for another round.

Climbing up the steps after Noyon, Pitt was surprised to find the bus driver was an older Anglo man. He smiled at Pitt through a white beard, his ice-blue eyes sparkling with mirth.

"Hi, boys," he said to Pitt and Giordino. "Noyon tells me that you're from the States. Me, too. Grab a seat and we'll be on our way."

The bus held twenty passengers and was nearly full after scooping up kids from three neighboring encampments. Pitt noticed the seat behind the driver was occupied by a black-and-tan dachshund, stretched out on its side in a deep sleep. The seat opposite the aisle was empty, so he plopped down there, Giordino sliding in beside him. The driver closed the door and quickly wheeled out of the village. Driving clear of the working herd, he mashed the accelerator down as he shifted through the gears. With a shrill whine from its engine, the old bus soon crept up to fifty miles per hour as it bounced over the hard desert surface.

"Bulangiin Monastery ain't exactly a destination resort," the driver said, looking at Pitt and Giordino in the rectangular mirror mounted above his visor. "You boys on one of those horseback adventure tours of the Gobi?"

"You could say that," Pitt replied, "though I hope we're done with the horseback portion of the tour. We are just looking to return to Ulaanbaatar at this point."

"Not a problem. A supply truck from U.B. will be at the monastery tomorrow. If you don't mind spending the night with a cadre of high-rolling monks, then you can hitch a ride on the truck in the morning."

"That would be fine with us," Pitt said as the bus lurched over a rut. He watched in amusement as the dachshund flew into the air, then landed back on the seat, without raising an eyelid.

"If you don't mind me asking, what are you doing out here in these parts?" Giordino asked.

"Oh, I'm helping a private archaeological foundation from the States that is helping rebuild the Buddhist monasteries. Prior to the communist takeover of Mongolia in 1921, there were over seven hundred monasteries in the country. Nearly all of them were ransacked and burned in the 1930s during a devastating purge by the government. Thousands of monks disappeared in the annihilation, either executed on the spot or shipped off to Siberian work camps to die in captivity. Those not murdered were forced to renounce their religion, though many continued to worship in secrecy."

"Must be difficult for them to start anew with their church relics and holy scripts long since destroyed."

"A surprising number of ancient texts and monastery

artifacts were buried by alert monks in advance of the purge. Important relics are turning up every day as some of the old monasteries reopen. The locals are finally becoming comfortable that the government abuses of the past are not going to recur."

"How did you get from laying bricks to driving a school bus?" Giordino asked.

"You have to wear a lot of hats out in the boon-docks," the driver laughed. "The group I'm helping with isn't simply a bunch of archaeologists but also includes carpenters, educators, and historians. Part of our agreement with rebuilding the monasteries is that we also establish schoolrooms for the local children. The structured education available to children of the nomadic herders is pretty spotty, as you can imagine. We're teaching reading, writing, math, and languages, in hopes of giving these rural kids a chance at a better life. Your friend Noyon, for example, speaks three lan-guages and is a whiz at math. If we can offer him accessible schooling for the rest of his childhood, and keep a PlayStation from falling into his hands, he'll probably grow up to be a fine engineer or doctor. That's what we are hoping to offer all of these kids."

The bus crested a blunt ridge, exposing a narrow valley on the other side. At its midpoint, a splash of thick grass dotted with purple shrubs added a sparkle of color to the otherwise monotonous desert. Pitt noticed a cluster of small stone buildings built in the thicket, sided by a handful of white *ger*s. A small herd of camels and goats were corralled nearby, while several small SUVs were positioned at the southern end.

"Bulangiin Monastery," the driver announced. "Home to twelve monks, one lama, seventeen camels, and an occasional hungry volunteer or two from the U.S. of A." He threaded his way down some coarse tire tracks, then pulled the bus to a stop in front of one of the *ger*s.

"School's in," the driver said to Pitt and Giordino as the kids clamored off the bus. Noyon burst by, waving at the two men, before hopping off the bus.

"Afraid I need to go teach a geography lesson," the driver said after all the children had departed. "If you boys head to the large building with a dragon on its eave, you'll find Lama Santanai. He speaks English, and will be glad to look after you for the night."

"Will we be seeing you later?"

"Probably not. After I take the kids home, I promised an overnight stopover at one of the villages to give a talk on western democracy. Was nice chatting with you, though. Enjoy your visit."

"Many thanks for the lift, and for the information," Pitt replied.

The driver scooped up the sleeping dachshund and grabbed a book of world geography from under his seat, then waltzed toward the waiting classroom inside the *ger*.

"Nice fellow," Giordino said as he stood up and then stepped off the bus. Pitt followed, noticing a placard above the driver's visor that read, WELCOME. YOUR DRIVER'S NAME IS CLIVE CUSSLER.

"Yes," Pitt agreed with a searching nod. "But he drives like Mario Andretti."

They made their way across the compound toward three pagoda-shaped buildings whose upturned roofs were layered in an aged blue ceramic tile. The central and largest of the three buildings was the main temple, flanked by a shrine hall and a storeroom. Pitt and Giordino walked up a short flight of steps leading into the main temple, admiring a pair of curvaceous stone dragons that were mounted on the corner eaves, their long tails curving up the steeply angled roof. The two men mindfully entered the temple through an immense open door, where a chorus of low chants greeted them.

As their eyes adjusted to the dim illumination provided only by candlelight, they saw two broad benches that ran lengthwise across the temple, ending near a small altar. A half dozen elderly monks sat on each bench, facing one another across the center aisle. The monks sat cross-legged, dressed in bright saffron robes, their shaved heads held perfectly still as they chanted. Pitt and Giordino tiptoed clockwise around the temple, taking a seat along the back wall and watching the remainder of the mantra.

Tibetan Lamaism is the practiced form of Buddhism in Mongolia, the religious ties between the two countries forged centuries ago. Prior to the government purge, nearly a third of Mongolian males were practicing lamas, living an ascetic existence in one of the many unadorned monasteries scattered around the country. Buddhism nearly vanished during the communist reign, and a whole generation of Mongolians is just now being reacquainted with the spirituality of their ancestors.

Pitt and Giordino could not help but feel the mystique inside the temple as they observed the ceremony, which differed little than that practiced by lamas hundreds of years before. The scent of burning incense enchanted their noses with an exotic aroma. The interior of the ancient temple exuded a warm glow from the candlelight, which flickered off the red-painted ceiling and the bright crimson banners that hung from the walls. Tarnished statues of Buddha in various incarnates dabbled the nooks and altar. Then there was the haunting sound from the lips of the noble lamas.

The craggy-faced monks repeated in unison a line from their prayer books, which lie open in front of them. The mantra slowly grew louder and louder, the voices rising in intensity, until an elderly lama with thick glasses suddenly rapped at a goatskin drum. The other monks joined in the crescendo by ringing tiny brass bells or blowing into large white conch shells until the walls of the temple shook. Then, as if an invisible hand suddenly turned down the volume, the crescendo slowly fell away to complete silence, the monks meditating in quiet for a moment before rising from their benches.

The lama with the thick glasses set down his drum and approached Pitt and Giordino. He was nearly eighty-five yet moved with the strength and grace of a much younger man. His deep brown eyes shined with warmth and intelligence.

"The Americans who wander the desert," he said in heavily accented English. "I am Santanai. Welcome to our temple. We have included a prayer for your safe travels in our worship today."

"Please excuse our intrusion," Pitt said, startled at the lama's knowledge of their arrival.

"The path to enlightenment is open to all," the lama smiled. "Come, let me show you our home." The old lama proceeded to guide Pitt and Giordino around the temple, then led them outside for a walk around the grounds.

"The original monastery dates to the 1820s," he explained. "The occupants were more fortunate than most during the great purge. Government agents destroyed the living quarters and the food stores, then drove away the faithful. For reasons unknown, the temple was left untouched, abandoned to stand empty for many decades. The sacred texts and other articles of worship were secured by a local herdsman and buried in the sands nearby. When the ways of tolerance were resumed by the government, we reopened the temple as the centerpiece of our monastery."

"The buildings look hardly the worse for wear after all those years," Giordino noted.

"Local herdsmen and underground monks secretly maintained the temple during the years of repression. The remote location helped keep the site out of the prying eyes of the most troublesome government atheists. But we have much work yet to do to restore the compound," he said, motioning toward a stack of lumber and building materials. "We live in the *ger*s now, but will someday have a permanent residence structure."

"You and a dozen disciples?"

"Yes, there are twelve monks here plus a visiting aspirant. But we hope to provide housing for an additional ten young men before long."

The lama led Pitt and Giordino to one of the smaller buildings beside the main temple. "I can offer you accommodations in our storeroom. The Western archaeological team visiting us is working at a nearby site for several weeks. They have left behind several cots that you may use. You wish to catch a ride on the supply truck tomorrow?"

"Yes," Pitt replied. "We are anxious to return to Ulaanbaatar."

"It shall be arranged. I must return to the temple for a tutoring session. Please make yourself comfortable, then join us for our evening meal at sunset."

The lama quietly turned and strode to the temple, his loose red robe flapping in the breeze. Pitt and Giordino climbed a short flight of steps and entered the storeroom, which was a narrow windowless structure with a high ceiling. They had to step around a giant iron bell just inside the doorway, a weathered relic in need of a bell tower. Past the bell, they found flour, noodles, tea, and other foodstuffs stacked along one wall. On the opposite side were bins of blankets and furs, stored for the frigid winter months ahead. In the back, they found several canvas cots beneath a painted image of Sakyamuni, the Buddha sitting cross-legged on a lotus-flower throne.

"Odd, that he knew we were in the neighborhood," Pitt said.

"It's a small desert," Giordino replied. "Look on the bright side. We don't have to sleep on the ground and we have plenty of time to relax until our ride shows up. As a matter of fact, I think I'd like to test out our new accommodations straightaway," he said, stretching out on one of the cots.

"I've got some reading to do first," Pitt replied, making his way toward the door before the snoring began.

Taking a seat on the front steps of the storeroom, he gazed in thought at the ancient temple and the dust-strewn valley stretching beyond. Then he pulled open the rucksack and began reading the diary of Dr. Leigh Hunt.

~ 32 ~

GOOD-BYE, DIRK. AND GOOD-BYE TO your friend Al."

Noyon bounded up the steps and bowed. Pitt stood up and shook the boy's hand, marveling at the maturity of the ten-year-old.

"So long, my friend," Pitt replied. "I hope that we shall meet again."

"Yes. Next time, you ride the camels," the boy grinned, then ran down the path toward the waiting school bus at the edge of the monastery. The doors closed behind him and the old bus roared off up the ridge toward the setting sun.

The rumble woke Giordino from his nap and he padded onto the porch, stretching his arms to awaken.

"Noyon and the kids headed home from school?" he asked, catching a glimpse of the bus before it disappeared over the hill.

"He just came by and said farewell. Wanted me to tell you that his best camel is available for riding excursions at any time." Pitt stuck his nose back into Hunt's diary with a mesmerized look on his face.

"How's the kiss-and-tell saga of our petrified archaeologist?"

"One that you won't believe," Pitt said.

Giordino saw the serious look in Pitt's eyes and took a seat on the steps.

"What did you find?"

"Dr. Hunt, his Mongolian assistant, and a team of Chinese laborers were excavating the remains of a vanished city in northern China named Shang-tu."

"Never heard of it."

"You might know it by its more romanticized Western name . . . Xanadu."

"Not another one," Giordino said, shaking his head. "Did it really exist?"

"Most definitely. It was the summer palace of Kublai Khan. He built the joint about one hundred twenty miles northwest of Beijing to get out of the summer heat. It was surrounded by a walled hunting ground and an adjacent village of upwards of one hundred thousand people. By the time Hunt came along, it was no more than a pile of rock and dust on an empty plain."

"So the artifacts on the plane date from Kublai Khan's reign? They must be worth a small fortune. That is, the few items not broken into a thousand pieces during the plane crash."

"Quite possibly. Though Hunt himself was disappointed with the haul. He writes that there was really nothing of significance uncovered until the very last day of the excavation. That's when your wooden box and the cheetah skin were dug up."

Pitt had the open wooden box sitting on the porch, the cheetah skin and bronze tube sitting inside. He pulled out the animal skin first.

"Hunt made little mention of the cheetah skin, but look at this," he said, laying out the fur, then flipping it over. On the skinned side was a series of eight small paintings in separate boxed panels. The first image showed a large Chinese junk sailing down a river trailed by two smaller vessels. The subsequent paintings showed the ships at sea, then anchoring in a small bay. The final panel showed the large ship on fire in the bay. A rippled banner of a blue dog fluttered in flames from the ship's foremast. On the shore, some boxes were stacked near the ship, but they, too, were surrounded by fire. Flames and smoke consumed the land all around the bay.

"Seems to relay a voyage that ended in a firestorm," Giordino said. "Perhaps they ran into some adversaries who were skilled with Greek Fire. Or it looks like they might have moored close to a forest fire ashore and were caught by blowing embers. There was no interpretation by the British archaeologist?"

"None. I wonder if he even examined the back side of the skin before he died."

"Any significance to the box?"

"It wasn't the box that was noteworthy but the bronze tube. Or, rather, something that was inside the bronze tube. A silk scroll of some sort was apparently rolled up inside. Painted on it was a treasure map to an unbelievable find."

"The canister was empty when we found it. Do you suppose it's still with Hunt on the plane?"

"Here, read Hunt's last entries," Pitt said, passing the diary to Giordino. Three brief passages were written on the last page of text.

August 5, 1937. En route to Ulaanbaatar by aircraft. With a heavy heart, I must write of a dreadful discovery. Tsendyn, my loyal associate, partner, and friend, has betrayed me in the end. The silk scroll is gone, stolen from its canister, which I carefully guarded since its excavation. Tsendyn was the only person who could have removed it, striking a dagger in my back before the plane left the ground. With it, the trail to G.K. is lost. I shall endeavor to recall the clues and reconstruct the map by memory. Then I will outfit a small party in U.B. and make the search attempt. Perhaps if nothing else, I will run into Tsendyn on the slopes of Burkhan Khaldun and obtain fair retribution. My only hope

The entry ended midsentence, resumed later in a shaky hand. Giordino noted that the dusty page was stained with drops of blood.

Date unknown. We have crashed in the desert, shot down by a Japanese warplane. Both pilots dead. I fear my back and legs are broken. Am unable to move. Waiting for help. I pray we will be discovered soon. Pain is unbearable.

Then later, in a crude scribble:

Last entry. All hope is gone. My sincere regrets to Leeds at the British Museum, and my love to my dear wife, Emily. God save our souls.

"Poor bugger," Giordino said. "That explains why he was lying atop the debris in the plane. He must have lay there several days before dying."

"His pain must have been all the worse, knowing what he lost."

"So what was the treasure on the silk map? Who or what is G.K.?"

"Hunt describes the silk scroll in an earlier entry, after its discovery. He was convinced, as was his aid Tsendyn, that it depicted the map to a lost tomb. The location in the Khentii Mountains of Mongolia, the royal markings, even a legend about a weeping camel all fit the historical records. The silk map indicated the final burial place of Genghis Khan."

Giordino let out a low whistle, then shook his head. "Genghis Khan, eh? Must have been sold a phony map. Old Genghis has yet to be found. His grave still rates as one of the biggest archaeological mysteries on the planet."

Pitt gazed at a swirling cloud of dust on the horizon, a thousand images running through his mind. Then it was his turn to shake his head.

"On the contrary. His tomb has indeed been found," he said quietly.

Giordino stared at him with a blank look on his face but knew better than to question Pitt's assertion. Pitt flipped through the diary to a page near the beginning and held the passage open for Giordino to see.

"Hunt's assistant from Mongolia, Tsendyn. His last name is Borjin."

"It can't be. His father?"

"If I'm not mistaken, we recently visited the marble tomb of the late Tsendyn Borjin."

"If that was Borjin's father in the stone chapel, then the sarcophagus in the center of the chamber . . ."

"That's right," Pitt said ruefully. "The tomb of Genghis Khan is sitting in Tolgoi Borjin's backyard."

• • •

THEY JOINED the lama and monks at sunset for dinner in one of the *ger*s. Like all their meals of late, it was a simple affair, consisting of a vegetable broth with noodles, washed down with some earthy black tea. The monks ate in silent reverence, nodding only in reply to the lama's occasional spoken word. Pitt casually studied the faces of the wizened monks who moved with stoic grace. Most were older than sixty, their studious brown eyes peering from crevice-lined faces. All wore their hair shaved close to the head but for one younger man with a thick build. He quickly gulped down his meal, then turned and grinned incessantly at Pitt until the others were finished.

After the meal, Pitt and Giordino observed an evening prayer in the temple, then retired to the storeroom. The revelation about Genghis Khan in Hunt's diary consumed Pitt's thoughts, and he was more anxious than ever to return to Ulaanbaatar. As they prepared to turn in, he dragged one of the cots over near the entryway.

"Can't sleep under a closed roof anymore?" Giordino chided.

"No," Pitt replied. "Something's bothering me."

"The lack of a decent meal in nearly a week is bothering me," Giordino said, crawling under a blanket.

Pitt pulled down an open box from the shelf that contained incense, beads, and other accoutrements of Buddhist prayer. After rummaging around a few minutes, he turned out the kerosene lamp and joined Giordino in counting sheep.

● ● ●

THE PROWLER came after midnight, silently opening the storeroom door just enough to let himself and a sliver of moonlight through the crack. Hesitating a moment to let his eyes adjust to the dark interior, he moved slowly toward the cot near the entry. Stepping toward the bed, his foot grazed a small prayer bell left on the floor. As the soft metallic ring echoed through the still room, the intruder froze, halting even his breathing. As the seconds ticked away, his ears strained to detect movement or stirring in the room, but all remained quiet.

Steady on his feet, the man knelt to the floor, locating the bell with a soft hand and gently sliding it out of his path. His knuckles grazed a second bell, which he cautiously moved before inching closer to the cot. He could just make out the sleeping body that lay still under a blanket. Standing above it, he raised a glistening double-edged sword toward the rafters with both hands, then swung the blade down in a lethal slash. The razor-sharp blade struck just below the pillow, where the sleeper's neck would be.

But something was wrong. There was no knotty resistance of the blade cutting through bone, no splash of blood or gasp of breath from the dying victim. The sword instead cut through without resistance down to the cot, the blade driving deep into the wooden frame. A startled confusion came over the would-be assassin before the sudden realization that he'd been had. But by then it was too late.

Pitt was already charging from his cot at the back of the room. The sliver of light creeping through the open door perfectly backlit the would-be killer hunched over the entryway cot, giving Pitt a clear target. In his hands, Pitt carried a wooden-handled shovel that he had borrowed from the excavation area and stashed under his bed. A step away from the cot that was stuffed with pillows, he pulled the shovel over his shoulder and swung at the black silhouette.

The intruder did his best to recover. Hearing Pitt's footsteps approach, he pulled the sword out from the cot and wielded it over his head. Feeling rather than seeing Pitt draw near in the dark, he thrust the sword toward him in a wide arc.

But Pitt's movements were already ahead of him. The blade of the shovel materialized out of the darkness and smashed into the intruder's hand as he started his downswing. The crunching sound of knuckles mashed on metal was quickly followed by a bloodcurdling cry of agony that echoed across the compound.

The sword flew out of the assassin's hand and clattered across the hardwood floor. Not interested in a duel, he grasped his mangled hand and staggered back toward the doorway. Pitt made another swing with the shovel from his left side but the intruder lurched out of harm's way. The cot was situated between the two men and Pitt made one more lunge across the empty bed. He swung hard and low as he saw the intruder turn toward the door. The shovel head clipped the back of the man's leg just below the calf.

Another shot of pain seared through the assassin's body as he lost all balance and tumbled hard to the floor. Still clutching his mashed hand, he failed to brace himself as he fell. Unseen in the dark, the heavy iron bell clipped him at the hairline as he went down. Pitt heard a cracking sound like a shattering baseball bat, followed by the secondary thud of the man's body hitting the floor.

Giordino materialized at Pitt's side, then stepped around the cot and kicked the door fully open. Under the full glow of the moon, they could see the intruder's lifeless body lying on its side, the head tilted at an unnatural angle.

"Snapped his neck," Giordino said, bending over the still form.

"A kinder treatment than he had in mind for us," Pitt said, leaning his shovel against the wall and picking up the sword.

Lights appeared on the porch, then the lama and two monks entered the room, each carrying a kerosene lantern.

"We heard a scream," the lama said, then looked down at the body near his feet. The bright red robe worn by the victim shined brightly under the lanterns. Even Giordino was startled by seeing that the intruder was dressed in attire associated with the nonviolent Buddhist monks. The lama looked at the short black hair and youthful face with immediate recognition.

"Zenoui," the lama said without emotion. "He's dead."

"He tried to kill us," Pitt said, holding up the sword and displaying the sliced blankets on the cot. "I tripped him with the shovel, and he fell on the bell and broke his neck. I suspect you will find additional weapons on his body."

The lama turned to one of the monks and spoke in Mongolian. The underling knelt down and patted the robes on the corpse. Lifting a section of red cloth, he revealed a belt that held a dagger and a small automatic pistol.

"This is not the way of the dharma," the lama said with shock.

"How long has he been at the monastery?" Pitt asked.

"He arrived just the day before you. He said he hailed from the northern state of Orhon but that he was crossing the Gobi in search of inner tranquillity."

"He's found it now," Giordino said with a smirk.

The lama contemplated an earlier conversation, then gazed suspiciously at Pitt and Giordino. "He asked about two foreigners crossing the desert when he arrived. I told him we knew nothing of you but that there was a good chance you might appear here, as the weekly supply truck is the most reliable means to Ulaanbaatar in the vicinity. After telling him this, he expressed the desire to prolong his stay."

"That explains your knowledge of our arrival," Pitt said.

"But why the attempt on your lives?"

Pitt briefly explained their visit and escape from

Borjin's compound while in search of the missing oil survey team. "This man was likely an employee of Borjin."

"Then he is not a monk?"

"I would say that was not his primary calling."

"He was indeed ignorant of many of our customs," the lama said. His face burrowing, he added, "A killing at the monastery, I fear, may cause us great trouble with the state authorities."

"His death was in fact an accident. Report it as such."

"We can certainly do without a state inquisition," Giordino muttered.

"Yes," the lama agreed, "if that is the truth, then it will be reported as an accident. After you have departed." The lama had the other two monks wrap the body in a blanket and move it to the temple.

"I regret your lives were placed in peril while visiting our enclave," he said.

"We regret attracting such trouble to your monastery," Pitt replied.

"May the rest of your stay be enjoyed in peace," the lama said, then he drifted off to the temple, where a brief prayer was held for the dead intruder.

"Nice bit of detective work," Giordino said, closing the door and bracing the damaged cot behind it. "How did you know there was a phony monk in the deck?"

"Just a hunch. He didn't seem to have the ascetic air of the other devout monks, plus he kept looking us over at dinner like he knew who we were. It didn't seem a stretch that Borjin would still have someone on the prowl for us, even someone disguised as a monk."

"I hope he didn't bring any friends with him. I guess that means I owe you now," Giordino said.

"Owe me what?"

"Shovel duty for the rest of the night," he said, sliding the dented spade under his cot before burrowing under the covers.

THE SUPPLY truck arrived late the next morning, offloading several crates of vegetables and dry goods into the storeroom. After helping unload the truck, the monks congregated in the temple for a period of meditation. The lama lagged behind, chatting with the truck driver as Pitt and Giordino prepared to depart.

"The driver welcomes your company in the cab. He says it will be a five-hour trip to Ulaanbaatar."

"Our sincere thanks for your hospitality," Pitt said. He gazed toward the temple, where the wrapped body of the assassin lay on a bench. "Has anyone come looking for your other visitor?"

"No," the lama said, shaking his head. "He will be cremated in four days, but his ashes will not remain in the compound. He did not carry the spirit of Sakyamuni in his heart," he said, referring to the historical Buddha. The old lama turned back toward Pitt and Giordino. "My heart tells me that you are men of honor. Travel in wisdom and strength of spirit and you shall find what you seek."

The lama bowed deeply, and Pitt and Giordino

returned the gesture before climbing into the truck. The driver, an old Mongolian with several missing front teeth, smiled broadly, then started the truck and drove slowly out of the compound. The lama stood motionless, his head down, until the truck was out of sight, its settled trail of dust coating the old man's robe and sandals.

Pitt and Giordino sat silently as the truck bounced over the desert, both reflecting the parting words of the lama. It seemed as if the wizened old man knew what they were after, and had given them the green light.

"We have to go back," Pitt finally muttered.

"To Xanadu?" Giordino asked.

"To Xanadu."

PART III

TREMORS

~ 33 ~

THE BLUE-SPOTTED GROUPER CAST a steely eye at the large figure swimming toward him. It moved too slowly to be a shark, and the neon-blue skin was too dazzling to be a dolphin. And it propelled itself in an odd manner by yellow appendages where the tail should be. Deciding the figure was neither friend nor foe, the grouper eased out of the way and headed for another section of the reef to scour for food.

Summer Pitt paid scant attention to the big fish as it darted into the blue murk. Her focus was on a yellow nylon line stretched across the seafloor that she followed like a marked trail. Her lithe body moved gracefully through the water at a steady pace, skimming just a foot or two above the gnarled heads of the coral reef. A digital video camera was clasped in her hands, capturing the colorful images of the reef on either side of the yellow line.

Summer was documenting the reef as part of a NUMA project assessing the health of coral reefs in the Hawaiian Islands. Sedimentation, overfishing, and algae outbreaks due to pollution and global warming had wreaked a slow and steady degradation of coral reefs around the world. Though the reefs of Hawaii had mostly been spared, there was no guarantee they would not succumb to the severe bleaching and mass mortality that had been witnessed in reefs surrounding Australia, Okinawa, and Micronesia. By monitoring the health of the reefs, the influence of man-made activities could be detected and addressed proactively.

The methodology was remarkably simple. Video frames from a surveyed reef were compared with sample images taken months or years earlier at the same locale. A count of the fish and "benthic," or seafloor, organisms provided a scientific snapshot of the reef's relative health. Dozens of reefs around the islands were targeted by the NUMA project to provide an assessment of the entire region's waters.

Summer kicked lazily along the track line until reaching the end point in a sand gully, marked by a stainless steel pin driven into the seafloor. A plastic card marked in grease pen was attached to the pin. Summer reached down and turned the card toward the camera, filming the designated line and waypoint before turning the camera off. As she let go of the placard, something in a nearby burrow of sand caught her eye. Kicking her yellow fins in short scissors kicks, she glided over to a cluster of small rocks. A small octopus was sliding about the rocks, puffing its body up and down as it drew water through its gills. Summer watched the intelligent invertebrate as it changed color, turning nearly translucent as it expanded its mantle before squirming away toward the reef. Gazing back at the rocks, she noticed a small round object protruding from the nearby sand. A miniature face seemed to smile up at Summer, as if happy to be discovered. Summer fanned away a light layer of sand, then plucked up the object and held it in front of her mask.

It was a tiny porcelain figurine of a maiden, wearing a flowing red robe, her black hair rolled high in a bun. The statuette's plump cheeks were tinged with red like a cherub while the narrow eyes were unmistakably Asian. The artistic handiwork was somewhat crude, and there was an ancient look to the dress and pose. Just to assure herself, Summer flipped the figurine over, but found no MADE IN HONG KONG stamp on the bottom. Sifting her free hand through the soft sand, she found no other buried objects nearby.

A few yards away, the silvery air bubbles from another diver caught her attention. It was a man, kneeling on the edge of the reef taking a sediment sample. Summer swam over and hovered in front of the other diver, then held up the porcelain figure.

The bright green eyes of her brother Dirk glistened in curiosity as he studied the object. Lean and tall like the father he shared names with, Dirk secured the sediment sample in a dive bag, then stretched out his legs and motioned for Summer to show him where she found it. She led him away from the reef and across the sandbar to the gravelly patch where she had spotted the

410

smiling face. Dirk pulled alongside, and the two of them swam in a wide circle around the sandbar, gliding a few feet off the bottom. The undulating field of sand abruptly ended in a gnarled bed of lava as they circled toward the shore. Moving away from the shoreline, the sand bed dropped away in a steep incline that didn't reach bottom for another fifteen thousand feet. A small patch of coral appeared in the middle of the sand field, which Dirk swam down to examine.

The coral stretched in a linear path for ten feet before disappearing under the sand. Dirk noticed the sand appeared darker along a continuing line before meeting the lava wall. Summer swam toward a small round clump that rose from the bottom, then waved Dirk over to take a look. Dirk kicked over to what appeared to be a large rectangular stone nearly six feet across. He dove down and felt its hard growth-encrusted edge with a gloved hand, then probed along its surface. The hardness gave way as his fingers pressed into a dense growth of sea urchins at its center. Nodding his head with interest, Summer moved in with her video camera and filmed a close-up shot of the object. The two divers then abandoned the item and completed their circular sweep, finding no other objects. Reaching a drop line near where they started, they kicked to the rippling surface thirty feet above.

Their heads bobbed up in the sapphire blue waters of a large cove near Keliuli Bay on the southwest shore of Hawaii's Big Island. A few hundred yards away, the surf crashed into a rocky shoreline, which rose steeply to encircle the cove in high cliffs of black lava. The crash of the waves striking the rocks reverberated off the steep walls in a thunderous roar as a ring of white foam settled on the surface.

Dirk swam over to a small inflatable boat tethered to the drop line and bellied himself over the side. Unfastening his tank and weight belt, he reached over the side and helped pull his sister aboard. Summer spat out her regulator, barely catching her breath.

"What do you make of that coral outcropping in the middle of the sandbar?" she asked.

"It showed some linearity."

"I thought so, too. I'd like to excavate some of the sand around its fringes and see if there's anything there not devoured by the coral."

She pulled the porcelain figurine from her dive bag and studied it under the sunlight.

"You think you've got a shipwreck in the coral, eh?" Dirk chided, releasing the bowline and starting a small outboard motor.

"This had to come from somewhere," she said, holding up the figurine. "How old do you think it might be?"

"I haven't a clue," Dirk replied. "For my money, the rectangle stone is much more intriguing."

"You have a theory?"

"I do," he said, "but I don't think I'll make any outlandish claims until I've had a chance to peruse the ship's research computers."

Dirk gunned the throttle and the small boat leaped over the waves toward a ship moored in the distance. The NUMA research vessel was painted a bright turquoise blue, and as they approached from the stern the black-lettered MARIANA EXPLORER could be read on the transom. Dirk idled the boat to the port side, drifting beneath a small crane that hung over the water dangling a strand of cables. As Dirk and Summer attached the cable ends to D hooks mounted to the rubber boat, a man's torso leaned over the rail. With a muscular build, thick mustache, and steely blue eyes, the man could have been the incarnate of Wyatt Earp, reborn with a Texas accent.

"Hang on to your pants," he shouted, pressing the controls on the hydraulic winch. In an instant, Jack Dahlgren raised the boat out of the water and deposited it on the ship's deck. As he helped rinse off and stow the dive equipment, he asked Summer, "Did you capture the final reef here? The captain wants to know if he can pick up and move to the next survey area, Leleiwi Point, on the east side of the island."

"The answer is yes and no," Summer replied. "We've completed the data collection, but I'd like to make another dive on the site."

Dirk held up the porcelain figure. "Summer thinks she has a treasure wreck on her hands," he grinned.

"Cultural treasure would be just as fine with me."

"What signs of a wreck did you find?" Dahlgren asked.

"Nothing obvious, but Summer did find an interesting stone object," Dirk offered. "We need to go look at the videotape."

Dirk and Summer showered and dressed, then met Dahlgren in one of the research ship's laboratories. Dahlgren had hooked the video camera to a monitor and was replaying the images over the large screen. When the rectangular stone appeared, Dirk reached over and pressed the PAUSE button.

"I've seen something like that before," he said, then sat down at an adjacent computer and began tapping the keyboard. "It was at an underwater archaeology conference, from a paper presented on a wreck discovered in Malaysia."

After a few moments of searching, he located a website that contained a copy of the scientific paper, along with photographs of the excavation. Dirk scrolled through the images until he stopped at an underwater photograph of a stone slab. It was a rectangular piece of granite, tapered on one end, with a pair of holes carved through the center.

"Clear away the growth and I'd say you have a close match to the object in Summer's video," Dahlgren asserted, comparing images.

"Yes, not only the same shape but the same relative size," Dirk noted.

"Okay, I'll bite," Summer said. "What is it?"

"An anchor," Dirk replied. "Or, rather, the stone weight that fitted into a wooden grappling anchor. Before the days of lead and iron, it was a lot simpler to construct an anchor from wood and stone."

"You're talking the ancient days of sail," Dahlgren said.

Dirk nodded. "That's why it is intriguing. Summer's anchor looks to be an identical match for this one," he said, pointing to the screen.

"We all agree on that," Summer said. "But what's it from? What kind of wreck did they excavate in Malaysia?"

"Well," Dirk said, scrolling down the screen to a computerized drawing of a four-masted sailing ship. "Would you believe a thirteenth-century Chinese junk?"

— 34 —

THE AIR OVER KHARG ISLAND was hazy brown. Oily smoke spewed up by the holocaust at Ras Tanura a week before still choked the skies over the Persian Gulf. Even at Kharg Island, a rocky limestone spit on the Iranian side of the gulf one hundred eighty miles from Ras Tanura, taking a breath of the thick polluted air left the greasy taste of petroleum in one's mouth.

The toxic air was an environmental match to the waters east of the small island, which were topped with a perpetual layer of oil. The water pollution was home-grown, however, in the form of leaks and spills from the adjacent crude oil transport facility. A huge T-shaped jetty on the east side of the island held berths for up to ten tankers. Off the west coast, a man-made island could fill the bellies of several Ultra Large Crude Carrier supertankers, fed by gravity from an assortment of storage tanks built on the central heights of the island. Though just a tiny land mass, Kharg Island is Iran's largest oil export terminal, as well as one of the biggest oil transport facilities in the world.

Dusk was approaching when a battered black drill ship chugged past the fleet of tankers aligned in a row along the eastern terminal. Angling north, the drill ship turned and approached the island, mooring close to the bluffs at the tip of the northern coast. An Iranian military boat patrolling the coastal waters cruised by but paid no thought to the old ship, which flew the flag of India.

None of the oil workers ashore paid much attention either, especially after night fell. But that's when the drill ship quietly sprang to life. The ship moved slowly back and forth, surveying the black waters before settling on a desired spot. Fore, aft, and side thrusters were activated, gluing the ship to a stationary point despite the effect of wind and current. Under low-wattage deck lighting, the ship's crew scurried about wearing black jumpsuits. A short drill string was assembled beneath the derrick and lowered through an open moon pool. The end of the drill string didn't hold the usual roller cone drill bit for oil drilling, but rather an odd trio of oblong cylinders bound in a tripod fashion.

The tripod was lowered to the bottom, then the deck crew slowly disappeared and the ship grew quiet. But twenty minutes later, an explosive boom emanated from beneath the ship. A loud but muffled clap was all that could be heard on the surface, barely discernible to the neighboring ships and island workers. But fifty feet beneath the ship, a high-powered sound wave was blasted into the gulf floor. The downward-directed seismic wave bounced and refracted harmlessly through the earth's crust. Harmless, except for a single point of convergence from the three oblong cylinders, which focused their blast of sound at the exact depth and position of a marked fault line.

The brief acoustic burst was followed by a second discharge, then a third. The concentrated acoustic blasts bombarded the subterranean fault line with vibrating seismic waves until it reached a point of irreversible stress. Like Ella Fitzgerald shattering a glass with her voice, the pounding acoustic vibrations fractured the fault located a half mile beneath the surface.

The rupture reverberated to the surface with a savage shake. The U.S. Geological Survey would clock it at 7.2 on the Richter scale, a killer quake by all accounts. Loss of life was minimal, with major damage limited to just a few Iranian coastal villages near Kharg Island. Since the Persian Gulf waters were too shallow for a tsunami to form, the damage was restricted almost entirely to a section of Iranian shoreline near the gulf's tip. And to Kharg Island.

On the tiny oil-pumping island, the damage was catastrophic. The whole island shook as if a nuclear bomb had detonated beneath it. Dozens of oil storage tanks ruptured like balloons, spilling their black contents in rivers that slopped down the hillside and into the sea. The huge fixed oil terminal off the eastern shore broke into several free-floating pieces that battered and punctured the moored tankers. The supertanker terminal on the western side of Kharg Island disappeared altogether.

The small black drill ship didn't wait around to survey the damage, instead steaming south in the early hours of the morning. The flurry of helicopters and rescue ships streaming to the rocky island took little notice of the old vessel headed away from the destruction. Yet in its wake, the drill ship had single-handedly devastated Iranian oil exports, jolting the global petroleum market once again while plunging China into a state of chaos.

～ 35 ～

To the teetering oil futures market, the report of the destruction at Kharg Island hit like an atomic blast, unleashing a fear-driven free-for-all. Frenzied traders jumped over the oil futures contracts, bidding the price of sweet crude up to a stratospheric one hundred fifty dollars per barrel. On Wall Street, the Dow headed in the opposite direction. A reeling stock market was forced to shut down early as trading curbs halted activity after a massive sell-off erased twenty percent of the market's value in half a day.

Across the U.S., anxious motorists reacted to the news by racing to the nearest gas station to fill their cars up on cheaper fuel. The stampede buying quickly exhausted the thin margin of surplus refined gasoline and fuel shortages soon sprouted across every state. Sporadic violence flared over the waning supply in some regions as a sense of panic gripped the country.

At the White House, the president called an emergency meeting of his top security and economic advisers in the Cabinet Room. A no-nonsense populist elected from Montana, the president listened quietly as his chief economic adviser recounted a litany of disastrous consequences resulting from the oil shock.

"A near doubling of oil prices in less than a month will produce unprecedented inflationary pressures," touted the adviser, a balding man with thick glasses. "Aside from the obvious distress to the entire transportation sector, there are countless industrial and manufacturing bases that rely on petroleum content. Plastics, chemicals, paint, textiles . . . there's hardly an industry that is not directly impacted by the price surge. The dramatic rise in oil costs will have to be passed on to the consumer, who is already suffering from shock at the gas pump. An immediate recession is a foregone conclusion. My fear is that we are standing at the precipice of a deep and prolonged economic depression of global proportions."

"Isn't this price hike a knee-jerk reaction?" the president asked. "After all, we don't import a drop of oil from Iran."

"There is a major element of panic, no doubt about it. But the damage to Kharg Island disrupts the global supply of oil, which impacts the price in the U.S. even if our own import supply remains steady. Of course, we are already seeing a shortfall in imports from the destruction at Ras Tanura. As a result, the markets are on edge. The anxiety is partly being fueled by rumors, one of which says that a terrorist element was responsible for the damage to both Persian Gulf facilities."

"Anything to those claims?" the president asked his national security adviser, a studious man with a lean face.

"None that we've ascertained," the man replied in a staid voice. "I'll task Langley with a further look, but all evidence points to naturally occurring earthquakes. The fact that two damaging rattles took place in close relative proximity appears to be a fluke of nature."

"Fair enough, but let's not take chances with any homegrown fanatics who want to capitalize on the situation here for a headline. Dennis, I'd like Homeland Security to elevate the terrorist threat advisory for all seaports. Let's make sure surveillance is boosted at our oil terminals, particularly along the Gulf Coast."

"Consider it done, Mr. President," replied the director of homeland security, seated opposite of the chief executive.

"Garner, I think a quick means to quell the public hysteria would be to immediately release some stocks from the Strategic Petroleum Reserve." The suggestion came from Vice President James Sandecker, a retired admiral and former head of NUMA. He was a small but intense man with blazing eyes and a fiery red Vandyke beard. An old friend of the president, he seldom addressed his boss by title. "The oil markets should cool down over time. Releasing a portion of the reserves should dampen the immediate public fear of an outright oil shortage, and perhaps boost confidence in the markets."

The president nodded. "Write up a Presidential Order to that effect," he barked at an aide.

"A sales pitch from the bully pulpit might not hurt, either," Sandecker added, glancing toward a large portrait of Teddy Roosevelt hanging on a side wall.

"I'll do my part," the president agreed. "Contact the networks and schedule a televised address for tonight," he directed. "I'll advocate voluntary gas rationing for the next thirty days. Might help the refineries catch up on supplies. We'll get the public calmed down first, then try to figure a way out of this mess."

"There must be some options to consider," mused the chief of staff. "Temporary price freezes and mandatory fuel rationing could be instituted quickly."

"Might be wise to promote some conservation measures publicly while privately twisting some arms," Sandecker said. "We can probably entice some of our other foreign suppliers to boost oil production. Maybe our domestic producers can help as well, though I understand the Alaska Pipeline is now operating at capacity again."

"Yes, the arctic drilling has increased production,"

the economic adviser confirmed. "We would otherwise be in a lot worse shape right now. But that just means the upside from our present condition is limited. The measures mentioned are all fine and good, but they will only have a minor effect on domestic demand. The ugly reality is that they will have almost no impact on the global markets. A major supply fix is what's needed and that will take months for Saudi Arabia and Iran to sort out. I'm afraid to say, there is very little we can do right now to impact the global price of oil in a meaningful manner."

The dire assessment silenced the room. Finally, the president spoke.

"All right, gentlemen, put everything on the table. I want to look at all options and every worst-case scenario. And I suspect we'll have to move fast. With the oil price holding at the current level, exactly how much time do we have before completely losing the economy?" he asked, his dark eyes boring into the economist.

"Difficult to say," the adviser replied nervously. "Perhaps a thirty-day window before we see the first major work stoppages and associated layoffs. Once the markets have digested this initial shock, the price pressure may abate. But we'll need to see a price retreat of at least thirty to forty dollars to avoid a severe recession. The flip side is that the markets are in a very tenuous state. Another shock of any sort and we could have a global calamity on our hands."

"Another shock," the president said softly. "God help us from that."

THE EMPTY PATCH OF SAND that yielded Summer's porcelain figurine now looked like an underwater construction site. Aluminum grids and yellow ropes stretched in all directions across the seabed, punctuated by tiny orange flags staked into the ground. What had started as a sample test pit dug near the rocky outcropping had grown into a full-blown excavation project after Dirk and Summer uncovered a large framing timber buried two feet under the sand. Additional test pits confirmed that the porcelain figure and stone anchor were no random objects tossed over the side but part of an entire wreck buried between the two coral reefs.

Beautifully crafted blue-and-white porcelain plates and bowls, along with votives and carvings of jade, all hinted at a wreck of Chinese origin. Portions of the ship's frame also correlated with the design of a massively sized Chinese junk. To Summer's amazement and chagrin, the potential discovery of an early Chinese ship in Hawaiian waters had caused a sensation. Media representatives from around the world descended on her like vultures to capture the story. After a slate of repetitive news interviews, she was only too happy to slip on a tank and fins and escape the bedlam underwater. The newshounds would lose interest in the story quick enough, she knew, and then the excavation could be resumed uninterrupted.

Summer floated over the grids and past a pair of divers blowing sand away from a large timber believed to be the sternpost. A few yards away, manual probes driven into the sand had detected another large section of wood that might be the rudder. Gliding to the edge of the work site, she kicked toward the surface alongside a drop line, holding a balled fist over her head until she broke the surface.

A brown metal barge was now moored over the site, and Summer swam the few yards over to its side ladder. Tossing her fins onto the deck, she climbed up and onto the small barge. It was little more than an open deck, with a dingy tin hut constructed at one end. A wall rack full of dive gear hung against the side of the hut, while the deck rail was lined with a generator, water pump, and several compressors. A pair of surfboards lying on the tin shack's roof offered the only hint of frivolity to the work site. The boards belonged to Dirk and Summer and were deemed standard equipment whenever they worked in Hawaii.

"How's the water?" drawled the voice of Jack Dahlgren. He was hunched over one of the compressors, screwdriver in hand, as Summer stowed her tank and dive gear.

"It's Hawaii," she smiled. "Always a delight." She toweled her hair off, then walked over to Dahlgren.

"Be up and running soon?" she asked.

"Just waiting for a final fuel and supply drop from the *Mariana*. We've got one compressor to run an airlift and another to provide surface-supplied air. They'll make diving in these purty waters a breeze."

"I'm more excited about applying the airlift to the last few buried areas."

The airlift was little more than a hollow tube with compressed air fed into the lower end. The pressurized air ascended up the tube, producing a vacuum effect ideal for sucking away sand and loose debris from a wreck site.

"*Mariana Explorer* to *Brown Bess*," crackled a hand-held radio strung to the side rail. Dirk's voice was instantly recognized on the other end.

"*Bess* here. Come on back," Dahlgren replied.

"Jack, we've got the fuel and hot dogs and are ten miles away. The captain says we'll tie up on your lee-ward side to off-load the fuel."

"We'll be waiting." Dahlgren peered across the horizon, spotting a turquoise dot cruising toward the barge. Then the radio crackled once more.

"And tell Summer that she has yet another visitor who would like to talk to her about the wreck. *Explorer* out."

"Not another reporter," Summer cursed, rolling her eyes in disgust.

"Summer says she'll be happy as a clam to host another interview. *Bess* out," Dahlgren replied into the microphone, laughing at Summer's taciturn look.

The NUMA vessel arrived within the hour and tied up alongside the barge. While Dahlgren oversaw the loading of a fifty-five-gallon drum of gasoline,

Summer climbed aboard the *Mariana Explorer* and made her way to the wardroom. There she found Dirk having coffee with a dark-skinned Asian man wearing slacks and a navy polo shirt.

"Summer, come meet Dr. Alfred Tong," Dirk said, waving her over.

Tong stood up and bowed, then shook Summer's outstretched hand.

"A pleasure to meet you, Miss Pitt," he said, looking up into the gray eyes of the taller woman. He had a powerful grip, she noted, and skin like her own that had seen much of the sun. She tried hard not to stare at a prominent scar that ran down his left cheek, instead gazing at his intense walnut-colored eyes and jet-black hair.

"Thank goodness," Summer blushed. "I was expecting another TV reporter."

"Dr. Tong is a conservator with the National Museum of Malaysia," Dirk explained.

"Yes," Tong said and nodded, then continued in choppy English. "I was attending a seminar at the University of Hawaii when I heard of your discovery. An associate at the university put me in touch with a local NUMA representative. Your captain and brother were kind enough to invite me out for the day."

"The logistics were well timed," Dirk explained. "The *Mariana Explorer* happened to be in Hilo picking up fuel and supplies for the barge and will be returning that direction this evening."

"What is your interest in the wreck?" Summer asked.

"We have a sizeable collection of Southeast Asian artifacts in the museum, as well as an extensive exhibit from a fourteenth-century Chinese vessel excavated from the Straits of Malacca. Though it is not my specific area of expertise, I have some knowledge of Yuan and Ming dynasty pottery. I am interested in what you have retrieved, and thought I might offer assistance in identifying the age of the vessel through its artifacts. I, like many others, would revel in the discovery of a thirteenth-century Chinese royal vessel in the western Pacific."

"Identifying the age of the vessel is a key question," Summer replied. "I'm afraid we've uncovered just a limited number of ceramic artifacts. We sent a sampling to the University of California for analysis, but I'd be happy to let you examine the remaining items."

"Perhaps the context of the artifact finds will be useful. Can you share with me the condition and configuration of the wreck?"

Dirk unrolled a large script of paper sitting on the table. "I was just going to walk you through the excavation profile before Summer walked in."

They all took a seat at the table and examined the chart. It was a computer-aided diagram of the wreck site from an overhead view. Sections of timbers and scattered artifacts were displayed in a horseshoe-shaped region next to the lava bed. Tong was surprised by the tiny amount of remains and artifacts documented in the drawing, hardly indicative of a large sailing vessel.

"We've worked with the archaeologists from the University of Hawaii to excavate nearly all of the accessible portions of the wreck. Unfortunately, we are only seeing about ten percent of the entire vessel," Dirk said.

"The rest is under coral?" Tong asked.

"No, the wreck actually lies perpendicular to two reefs under a sandbar, with her nose to the shore," Summer said. She pointed to the diagram, which showed two coral mounds on either side of the excavation field. "The sand has protected the existing artifacts from consumption by the coral. We think this section of sand may have been a natural channel cut through the reef eons ago when the seas were lower."

"If the coral has not imprisoned the wreck, then why are there not more remains visible?"

"In a word, lava." Summer pointed to the closed end of the horseshoe, which showed a rocky bed that ran off the chart in the direction of the shoreline. "If you look out the window, you can see that this section of coastline is one big lava field. The rest of the wreck, I'm sorry to say, is buried under a bed of lava rock."

"Remarkable," Tong said with a cocked brow. "So the rest of the wreck and its cargo is intact under the lava?"

"The rest of the ship is either under the lava or was consumed by it. If the ship sank and was buried under sand before the lava flow arrived, then it may well be preserved intact beneath the lava field. The timbers we've found adjacent to the lava field are well buried, which suggests that the rest of the ship may indeed still be there."

"The upside is that we may be able to use the lava to help age the wreck," Dirk said. "We have a local volcanologist studying the historical record of volcanic eruptions and associated lava flows on this part of the island. So far, we know that there has been no volcanic activity in this immediate area for at least two hundred years, and possibly much longer. We hope to receive more definitive information in a few days."

"And what of the actual ship have you identified?"

"Just a few pieces, which appear to be from the stern section. The timbers are thick, indicating a potentially large ship, perhaps even two hundred feet or more. Then there is the anchor stone, which is consistent with known Chinese design, and also indicative of a size-able vessel."

"A vessel that size and age would most certainly be Chinese," Tong said.

"Yes," Dirk replied, "the European vessels of the day were half as large. I've read of the legend of the Chinese admiral Zheng He, who purportedly sailed around the world with his massive Treasure Fleet in 1405. This is no six-masted, five-hundred-foot behemoth, though, like Zheng He supposedly sailed, if such massive ships even existed."

"History tends to exaggerate," Tong said. "But crossing half the Pacific a hundred years before Zheng He's purported voyage would be an astounding accomplishment."

"The ceramic artifacts recovered present the most intriguing evidence that the wreck is that old," Summer said. "We've found comparable design patterns in our research which suggest the ship may date to the thirteenth or fourteenth centuries. Perhaps you can confirm our assessment with an examination of the ceramics?"

"I am most interested to see what you have recovered."

Summer led them down a flight of stairs to a brightly illuminated laboratory. Racks of plastic bins lined the back bulkhead, all filled with various artifacts recovered from the wreck and now soaking in fresh water.

"Most of the items recovered were fragments of the actual ship," she explained. "The cargo holds and living quarters must all be under the lava, as we recovered few personal artifacts. We did find a few everyday cooking utensils and a large pot," she said, pointing to an end rack, "but you will probably be most interested in these."

She pulled two trays off one of the racks and set them on a stainless steel table. Inside the trays were several plates, a bowl, and numerous fragments of porcelain. Most of the items were sugary white in color, though the bowl was made of black clay. Tong's eyes lit up as he slipped on a pair of reading glasses and began examining the artifacts.

"Yes, very nice," he muttered as he quickly ran through the inventory.

"What can you tell us about the design?" Summer asked.

"The patterns and material are consistent with the product of the Chinese kilns at Jingdezhen and Jianyang. The overall quality appears less advanced than the work produced during the later Ming Dynasty. The fish emblem here," he said, holding up one of the plates. "I have seen this before on a Yuan-period bowl. I would concur with your assessment, these ceramics are characteristic of items manufactured in the Song and Yuan dynasties of the twelfth and thirteenth centuries."

A broad smile crossed Summer's lips and she gave a happy wink to Dirk. Tong reached over and pulled the last artifact from the tray, a large teal-and-white plate with a pie-slice section missing from the platter. The glazed image of a pcacock strutted across the center, while smaller images of a cheetah chasing a herd of deer circled the plate's perimeter. Tong studied the plate with a renewed intensity, looking again and again at the ornate glazing and animal portrayal.

"One of the lab conservators found a similar design in the database used by Yuan royalty," Dirk said.

"Yes, it is," Tong muttered, then put the plate down and backtracked. "Similar, that is, but surely not made for royalty. A close design used for trade, most likely," he added. "But I would agree that it is from the Yuan era, which, as you know, lasted from 1264 to 1368. Well ahead of Admiral Zheng."

"That's what we believe, remarkable as it is to think a ship of that era found its way to Hawaiian waters."

The door to the lab opened and in walked the *Mariana Explorer*'s captain. A towering sandy-haired man, Bill Stenseth commanded the respect of the entire ship by his quiet intelligence and his good-natured sense of fair play.

"Dahlgren has completed loading the fuel and supplies onto your floating hotel. Whenever you two are set to jump ship, we'll be on our way."

"We're about finished, Captain. Dirk and I will get our things and join Jack on the barge."

"You are still working on the wreck?" Tong asked.

"We have a final section of timber to uncover, which we believe may be part of the rudder post," Summer explained. "If so, it will give us a better idea of the ship's dimension. The *Mariana Explorer* needs to continue a reef survey project on the other side of the island, so Dirk, Jack Dahlgren, and I are going to camp out on the barge for a few days and complete the excavation work."

"I see," Tong replied. "Well, thank you for sharing the recovered artifacts with me. When I return to Malaysia, I will research our museum's records and see if I can't provide you some additional information about the ceramics I have seen today."

"Thank you for taking the time to visit us and share your insights. We are excited that you have confirmed our initial assessment of the ship's age and possible ancestry."

Dirk and Summer quickly threw together a few personal belongings and jumped onto the barge, where Dahlgren was busily removing the ship's mooring lines. With a blast of the horn, Captain Stenseth backed the *Explorer* away from the barge and in a short while the turquoise ship disappeared around the jagged coastline heading toward Hilo.

"Well, what did you two find out about our Chinese lava ship?" Dahlgren asked, digging into a large cooler for a drink.

"Dr. Tong agrees that the age of the ceramics matches our initial readings, which put the wreck at seven to eight hundred years old," Summer replied.

"The good doctor seemed mighty interested in the plate our lab boys thought had royal markings, though he wasn't willing to bite," Dirk said.

"Professional jealousy, I think," Summer grinned. "It's a royal ship, I just know it."

"Royalty," Dahlgren said, plopping into a canvas chair with a can of beer and hoisting his feet to the side rail. "Now, don't that beat all?"

~ 37 ~

FIVE THOUSAND MILES TO THE east, Pitt and Giordino tramped into the lobby of the Continental Hotel in Ulaanbaatar looking like a pair of worn saddlebags. Their wrinkled clothes were laden in dust, which permeated their hair, skin, and shoes. Sunbaked blisters tainted the portion of their faces where scraggly growths of beard failed to sprout. All that was missing was a circle of flies buzzing around their heads.

The hotel manager looked down his nose with disdain as the two stragglers approached the front desk with bleary eyes.

"Any messages for rooms 4024 or 4025?" Pitt asked, his white teeth sparkling brightly behind his blistered lips.

The desk manager raised a brow in recognition, then briefly retreated to a small side room.

"One message and a delivery, sir," he said, handing Pitt a slip of paper and a small box plastered with overnight-shipping labels.

Pitt took the message and handed the package to Giordino while stepping away from the desk.

"It's from Corsov," he said quietly to Giordino.

"Pray tell, what does our favorite KGB agent have to say?"

"He was called away to a Foreign Ministry conference in Irkutsk. Sends his regards, hopes our foray south was productive. He'll contact us in a few days when he gets back to town."

"Very polite of him," Giordino said with a touch of sarcasm. "I wonder if Theresa and Jim will have the luxury of awaiting his return." He ripped open the overnight package, revealing an old leather book and a heavy jar of vitamins. A small card fell out, which he picked up and handed to Pitt.

"From the wife?"

Pitt nodded, silently reading the handwritten note inside.

Your favorite book, along with some extra vitamins to keep you healthy. Please use sparingly, my love.
   The kids send their best from Hawaii. They have created quite a stir by discovering an old wreck. Washington is a bore without you, so hurry home.
   Loren

"A book and vitamins? Not very romantic of Mrs. Pitt," Giordino chided.

"Ah, but it is my favorite story. Always packs a wallop." Pitt held up the leather-bound novel, displaying the spine to Giordino.

"Melville's *Moby-Dick*. A tasteful choice," Giordino said, "though the adventures of Archie and Veronica work fine for me."

Pitt opened the book and flipped through the pages until a cutout section revealed itself. Buried in the center of the mock book was a Colt .45 automatic.

"I see she comes with a harpoon, Ahab," Giordino whispered, letting out a low whistle.

Pitt popped open the vitamin bottle cap, displaying a dozen or so .45 caliber rounds that matched the Colt.

"Wouldn't a congresswoman get in a bit of trouble for shipping firearms around the world?" Giordino asked.

"Only if she got caught," Pitt smiled, sealing the bottle and closing the book.

"With a little canned heat, there's no sense in waiting for Corsov," Giordino urged.

Pitt shook his head slowly. "Nope, I think we make for a quick turnaround. It probably wouldn't be safe lolling about here for long anyway, once Borjin fails to hear back from his Buddhist hit man."

"A shower and a beer should aid the planning process."

"First some facts," Pitt said, walking to a cramped business center off the main lobby. He fished into his pocket and pulled out the silver pendant taken from Borjin's lab and laid it on a copy machine. He scribbled a note on the resulting photocopy, then fed it through an adjacent fax machine, dialing up a long-distance number by rote. He then fed the pages from the seismic-imaging manual through the fax, dialing a second number.

"That ought to keep a few pair of idle hands out of the devil's workshop," he said to himself as he made his way up to his room.

THE EXTERIOR of the Georgetown carriage house looked like any other upscale residence in the swanky quarter of Washington, D.C. The weathered-brick structure had freshly painted eaves, its nineteenth-century glass windows were sparkling clean, and the small surrounding yard was neatly manicured. It was a stark contrast to the home's interior, which resembled the book depository for the New York Public Library. Polished wooden bookshelves lined nearly every wall in the house, each packed to the brim with historical books on ships and seafaring. More books littered the dining table and the kitchen counters, in addition to strategic stockpiles at various locales on the floor.

The home's eccentric owner, St. Julien Perlmutter, wouldn't want it any other way. Books were a major passion for one of the nation's preeminent maritime historians, who had assembled a reference collection that librarians and private collectors salivated over. Generous with his archives, he gladly shared his knowledge and resources with those like him who had a love of the sea.

The beep and whir of a fax machine startled Perlmutter awake from an overstuffed leather chair, where he had fallen asleep while perusing the ship's log from the famous ghost ship *Mary Celeste*. Hoisting his rotund, nearly four-hundred-pound frame from the chair, he walked to his den and retrieved the fax. He stroked a thick gray beard as he read the brief note on the cover page:

St. Julien,
A bottle of fresh brewed airag for you, if you can identify this.
Pitt

"*Airag?* That's bloody blackmail," he muttered with a grin.

Perlmutter was a grand gourmand who loved rich and exotic food, as evidenced by his immense belly.

Pitt had touched a culinary nerve with a bribe of the Mongolian fermented mare's milk. Perlmutter closely examined the following fax pages, which showed the front and back side of a silver pendant.

"Dirk, I'm no jeweler, but I know who just might peg this," he said aloud. Picking up a telephone, he dialed a number and waited for a voice to answer.

"Gordon? St. Julien here. Say, I know we had lunch scheduled for Thursday but I could use your help on something. Could you meet today instead? Fine, fine, I'll take care of the reservation and see you at noon."

Perlmutter hung up the phone and gazed again at the image of the pendant. Coming from Pitt, that meant there was probably a wild tale behind it. Wild and dangerous.

THE MONOCLE near Capitol Hill was bustling with a workday lunch crowd when Perlmutter walked in the door. A popular haunt of Washington politicians, the restaurant was filled with senators, lobbyists, and Hill staffers. Perlmutter quickly spotted his friend Gordon Eeten in a side booth, as he was one of the few occupants not wearing a blue suit.

"St. Julien, good to see you again my friend," Eeten greeted. A large man himself, Eeten had a humorous demeanor mixed with the observant eye of a detective.

"I see I have some catching up to do," Perlmutter grinned, eyeing a nearly empty martini glass on the table.

Perlmutter hailed the bartender for a Sapphire Bombay Gibson, then the two men ordered lunch. As they waited for the meal, Perlmutter handed Pitt's fax to Eeten.

"Business before dining pleasure, I'm afraid," Perlmutter said. "A friend ran across this brooch in Mongolia and would like to know its significance. Can you shed any light?"

Eeten studied the photocopies with a poker face. As an antiquities appraiser with the famed auction house of Sotheby's, he had assessed literally thousands of historic artifacts before they were put up for public auction. A childhood friend of Perlmutter's, he regularly tipped off the marine historian when a pending auction contained items of maritime interest.

"Difficult to gauge the quality," Eeten prefaced. "Hate to give an estimate over a fax copy."

"Knowing my friend, he could care less about its value. I believe he is more interested in its age and historical context."

"Why didn't you say so in the first place?" Eeten replied, visibly relaxing.

"So you know what it is?"

"Yes, I believe so. I've seen something similar in a lot we auctioned a few months ago. Of course, I would have to examine the piece in person to verify its authenticity."

"What can you tell me about it?" Perlmutter asked, taking notes in a small book.

"It appears to be Seljuk in origin. The double-headed

eagle, a very unique motif, was a favored symbol of the dynasty."

"If my memory serves, the Seljuks were a band of Turkish Muslims who briefly controlled a large chunk of old Byzantium," Perlmutter said.

"Yes, they overran Persia around 1000 A.D., but their power peaked about two hundred years later, before they were crushed by the rival Khwarezmid Empire under Ala ad-Din Muhammad. The Seljuks were fine artisans, particularly in carving stone, but were also skilled in metallurgy. They even minted coins of silver and copper for a time."

"So this pendant is within their skill base."

"Absolutely. The minute calligraphy is consistent with a Seljuk practice of inscribing an Islamic prayer or dedication on their later metalwork. There's a professor at Columbia who could translate the inscription for you, which is probably written in Kufic. Who knows, perhaps it is a personal inscription to a sultan."

"Royalty implications?"

"Yes. You see, the Seljuks seldom used silver and gold in their artwork. The materials were regarded as luxury items and therefore inconsistent with the Islamic ideal of simplicity. Of course, the rules didn't necessarily apply to the sultans, some of whom hoarded the stuff. So if this pendant is made of silver, which it appears to be, then there's a strong likelihood of a sultan connection."

"So we are talking Seljuk manufacture, dating approximately 1100 to 1200 A.D., and possibly sultan pedigree," Perlmutter summed up, scribbling in his book.

"Most likely. The items we examined and auctioned recently were part of a cache linked to Malik Shah, a Seljuk sultan who died in 1092. It is interesting that your friend found this piece in Mongolia. As I mentioned, the Seljuks were sacked by the forces of Ala ad-Din Muhammad, who in turn was defeated by Genghis Khan around 1220. This may well have been one of the spoils of war brought home by the armies of Genghis Khan."

A waiter arrived and set their lunches on the table, a rib-eye steak for Eeten and an order of calf's liver for Perlmutter.

"Some remarkable insights, Gordon. I don't suppose a great deal of twelfth- and thirteenth-century Asian artifacts reach the marketplace very often."

"It's a funny thing. We seldom used to see artifacts from that era. But about eight or nine years ago, we were contacted by a broker in Malaysia who had a consignment to sell and he has provided us a steady stream of artifacts ever since. I bet we have sold over one hundred million dollars' worth of similar goods in that time. And I know Christie's has been auctioning similar quantities."

"My word. Any idea of the source of all those relics?"

"I could only speculate," Eeten said, chewing on his steak. "The Malaysian broker is a most secretive fellow and refuses to divulge his sources. I've never even been allowed to meet the man face-to-face. But he has never shipped us anything phony. Every consignment has contained the genuine article from top to bottom."

"Seems a little odd that kind of volume emanates from Malaysia."

"True, but the goods could be routed from anywhere. He's just a broker. Neither he nor his firm's name even sounds Malaysian."

"What's that?" Perlmutter asked, finishing his meal.

"An odd name. It's called the Buryat Trading Company."

～ 38 ～

THERESA FELT A SLIGHT sense of relief when the door to her room opened and a guard motioned for her to step into the hallway. If they were going to kill her, then so be it, she thought. It would be better than an endless confinement in fearful anticipation.

It had been two days since she was first locked in the room without explanation. There had been no contact by anyone, save for the occasional tray of food shoved in the room. Though she knew nothing of the visit by the Chinese delegation, she had heard the caravan of cars arrive and depart. Of greater mystery was the heavy gunfire that had erupted from the rear of the compound. She strained to peer out the tiny window at the back of her room but could see little more than swirling dust. Idly staring out the window again the next day, she had observed the horse guards on patrol trotting by, though their numbers seemed smaller.

Now walking out her door, she was glad to see Wofford standing in the hall, leaning on a cane. He flashed her a warm smile.

"Vacation's over," he said. "Guess it's back to work."

His words proved prophetic, as they were escorted back to the study. Borjin sat waiting for them, inhaling a thick cigar. He appeared more relaxed than the last time they saw him, his effusion of arrogance stronger than ever.

"Come sit, my friends," he said, waving them over to his table. "I hope you enjoyed your time off from work."

"Sure," Wofford said. "Staring at four walls was most relaxing."

Borjin ignored the comment and pointed to a fresh stack of seismic reports.

"Your work here is nearly complete," he said. "But there is some urgency in the appropriate selection of well sites in this region." He unfurled a topographic map covering a two-hundred-square-mile area. Theresa and Wofford could see from the markings that it encompassed an area of the Chinese Gobi Desert just southeast of the Mongolian border.

"You have already provided inputs on a number of detailed sites within this region. I must say, your assessments have been most insightful," he said with a patronizing tone. "As you can see, the blocks you have

443

already examined are marked on this regional map. I ask that you evaluate those blocks in relation to the entire region and identify a prioritization of test-well sites to maximize potential production."

"Aren't these sites located in China?" Wofford asked, pressing the point.

"Yes, they are," Borjin replied matter-of-factly, offering no further explanation.

"You know that the potential reserves are rather deep?" Wofford asked. "Probably why they have been overlooked in the past."

"Yes. We have the appropriate equipment to drill to the required depths," Borjin replied with impatience. "I need to have two hundred high-producing wells in six months. Locate them."

Borjin's arrogance finally rankled Wofford. Theresa could see from the rising flush of red to his face that he was about to tell the Mongolian to shove it. She quickly beat him to the punch.

"We can do that," she blurted. "It will take us about three or four days," she added, stalling for time.

"You have until tomorrow. My field manager will meet with you in the afternoon for a detailed briefing on your analysis."

"Once completed, will we be free to return to Ulaanbaatar?" she asked.

"I will arrange a vehicle to transport you the following morning."

"Then we better get down to work," Theresa replied, grabbing the folder and spreading its contents across the table. Borjin nodded with an untrusting grimace, then stood up and left the room. As he disappeared down the corridor, Wofford turned to Theresa and shook his head.

"That was quite the show of cooperation," he whispered. "Turning over a new leaf?"

"Best that he thinks we believe him," she replied, holding a report in front of her mouth. "Plus, I didn't want you to deck him and get us both killed."

Wofford smiled sheepishly, realizing how close she was to the mark.

Still wary of the security camera, Theresa pulled a map out from the bottom of the file and casually flipped it over while scattering some other reports about. On the blank back side, she took a pen and wrote "Ideas for Escape." Jotting a few notes beneath it, she slid it across the table to Wofford. He picked the chart up and studied Theresa's comments with interest. While he was holding it up to his eyes, Theresa noticed the map on the reverse side depicted the Persian Gulf. A series of red jagged lines were imposed across various sections of the map. Theresa saw that a red circle was drawn at two points over a couple of the heavier lines. One circle, she noticed, was around the city of Ras Tanura, and the other around a small island off the coast of Iran.

"Jim, look at this map," she interrupted, flipping the chart over for him to see.

"It's a fault map," Wofford said after studying the colored lines. "It shows a tectonic plate boundary run-

445

ning right along the Persian Gulf and major fault zones running off it."

Isolated since their abduction, neither knew anything about the devastating earthquakes that had recently struck the gulf. While Wofford studied the two red circles, Theresa rummaged through the rest of the file and produced two similar maps. The first was an enlarged view of Lake Baikal in Siberia.

"My word, look at this," she said, holding up the map. Her finger pointed to the top of the blue-colored lake. Just beyond her fingertip, at the lake's northern shoreline, was a large fault line circled in red. A newly constructed oil pipeline was also marked on the map, running just a mile or two north of the lake.

"You don't suppose they did something around the fault that triggered the seiche wave on the lake?" she asked.

"Short of setting off a nuclear device, I don't see how," Wofford replied, though his voice was thin on conviction. "What's on the other map?"

Theresa slid the other map to the top of the pile. They both immediately recognized it as a map of the Alaskan coastline, running from Anchorage down to British Columbia. Highlighted in yellow was the Alaska Pipeline, which stretched inland from its end point at the port city of Valdez. The four-foot-thick pipeline carried crude oil from the rich Prudhoe Bay fields on Alaska's North Slope, supplying a million barrels a day to the U.S. domestic market.

With a growing apprehension, Theresa pointed to a

thick fault line marked on the map running just off the coastline. A dark red circle was drawn around a point on the fault, directly off the port of Valdez.

In silent dread, they both stared at the mark, wondering what Borjin had in store for the Alaska Pipeline.

~ 39 ~

HIRAM YAEGER WOLFED DOWN A grilled-chicken sandwich with green tea, then excused himself from his cafeteria companions. The head of NUMA's computer resource center seldom left his precious bay of processing hardware for long and quickly headed back to his lair on the tenth floor of the Washington headquarters building. Exiting the cafeteria, he smiled to himself as a pair of visiting politicians in blue suits gave the fiftyish man in the Rolling Stones T-shirt a slanted look.

The lanky computer whiz flaunted his nonconformity by dressing in jeans and cowboy boots while wearing his long hair tied in a ponytail. His skill had overshadowed his appearance, as indicated by the massive computer center he had built and managed from scratch. Within its databases was the world's most exhaustive collection of research related to oceanography and underwater studies, as well as real-time sea and weather conditions processed from hundreds of monitoring stations around the world. Yaeger found the computer center a double-edged sword, however.

Its vast computing power spurred a constant demand by NUMA's array of research scientists eager to apply its horsepower to the latest pet project. Yet Yaeger was never known to turn down a request for computer time within the agency.

As the elevator doors opened on the tenth floor, Yaeger walked into his cavernous computer lab, fronted by a large horseshoe-shaped console. A solid, slightly balding man with a friendly face sat waiting in one of the swivel chairs that lined the console.

"I can't believe it," the man smiled. "I actually caught you away from the roost."

"Unlike my beloved computers, I've still got to eat," Yaeger replied. "Good to see you again, Phil," he added, shaking hands. "How are things down in the gravel pit?"

Dr. Phillip McCammon chuckled at the reference. As head of NUMA's Department of Marine Geology, McCammon was the resident expert in the study of undersea sediments. As it happened, the department was located in one of the underground levels of the headquarters building.

"We're still pounding rocks," McCammon said. "I could use your help with some computing resources, however."

"My kingdom is at your disposal," Yaeger replied, waving a hand at the computer center around him, which represented the processing power of nearly a half dozen supercomputers.

"I won't need to monopolize the castle for long. I received an unofficial request from an associate at

Langley to take a look at some seismic data. I guess the CIA is interested in the two recent earthquakes that have pulverized the Persian Gulf."

"It is an interesting coincidence that there were two big quakes so close to each other and they both put a crimp on the oil supply. If there are any more spikes in the price of gas, I'll soon be riding my bicycle to work," Yaeger griped.

"You and a lot of other people."

"So, what can I do to help?"

"They have arranged for the National Earthquake Information Center in Golden, Colorado, to transfer a copy of their complete historical record on global seismic activity for the last five years," McCammon said, handing Yaeger a sheet of paper with the relevant contact information. "One of my analysts has written a software program to evaluate the specific characteristics of the Persian Gulf quakes. Those parameters will then be run against the global seismic database to see if there are any other similar profiles."

"You think there might be something to it?"

"No, I can't imagine how there could be. But we'll help our friendly neighborhood spooks by covering the bases."

Yaeger nodded. "Not a problem. I'll have Max pull the data in from Golden this afternoon. Send up your software program and we'll have some answers for you in the morning."

"Thanks, Hiram. I'll get the program to you straight-away."

As McCammon headed toward the elevator, Yaeger turned to a keyboard and monitor and began typing in a string of commands. He stopped tapping when he noticed a multipage fax lying in his in-basket. He groaned when he spotted that it originated from the Continental Hotel in Ulaanbaatar.

"When it rains, it pours," he muttered as he skimmed over the fax. Then he set it down and resumed his key-strokes.

In an instant, a beautiful woman materialized on the opposite side of the console. She wore a sheer white blouse and a pleated wool skirt that fell to her knees.

"Good afternoon, Hiram. I was beginning to wonder if you were going to call today."

"You know I can't keep away from you, Max," he replied. A mirage of sorts, Max was in fact a holographic image created by Yaeger as a user-friendly interface to his computer network. Modeled after Yaeger's wife but with the perpetual figure of a twenty-year-old, Max had become very real to Yaeger and others in the NUMA building who relied upon her artificial intelligence for solving complex problems.

"Compliments will get you everywhere," she cooed slyly. "What is it today? Big problem or little?"

"Some of both," he replied. "You might be pulling an all-nighter tonight, Max."

"You know I never sleep," she replied, rolling up the sleeves on her blouse. "Where do we begin?"

"I guess," he said, pulling the fax in front of him, "we better start with the boss."

T HE TROPICAL SUN CLIMBED SLOWLY over the hills of lava and coconut palm trees until it bathed the anchored barge in rays of golden light. On board the craft, the rhythmic sounds of a Hawaiian steel guitar band bellowed from a boom box, masking the background hum of a portable generator.

Summer, Dirk, and Dahlgren had already risen from their cots in the small covered shack and were preparing for a long day's work underwater. As Dirk topped up the gas tanks on a pair of compressors, Summer finished eating her breakfast of fresh papaya and bananas, washed down with a glass of guava juice.

"Who's on first?" she asked, gazing at the calm morning seas surrounding the barge.

"I believe Captain Jack has assembled a work schedule," Dirk said, nodding toward Dahlgren.

Dressed in swim shorts, flip-flops, and a faded Hawaiian shirt, Dahlgren was bent over inspecting the regulators on a pair of lightweight dive helmets. The captain moniker derived from a tired blue hat he wore on his head. It was the classic captain's hat favored by rich yachtsmen, sporting crossed gold anchors on its prow. Dahlgren's hat, however, looked like it had been run over by an M-1 tank.

"Aye," Dahlgren barked in a gravelly voice. "We'll work ninety-minute shifts below, two divers at a time, then rotate after a break. Dirk and I will take the first shift, then you can join me below for the second shift while Dirk works on his tan," he said, nodding toward Summer.

"That reminds me, I didn't see a blender on board this plank," Dirk said with disappointment.

"I am sorry to report that the last of the rum rations disappeared last night anyway. For medicinal purposes," Dahlgren added.

As a panicked look crossed Dirk's face, Summer rolled her eyes with a "Why me?" look. "All right, my future AA recruits, let's get to work. If by luck we have found the rudder, then we have a lot of excavating to do. We still need to disassemble and stow away the grid markers, and I'd like to leave some time before the *Mariana Explorer* returns to survey some additional areas."

Dahlgren stood up and took off his captain's hat and flung it across the deck. The hat spiraled perfectly, striking Summer square in the chest. Reacting with a start, she managed to catch the hat after a bobble.

"There," Dahlgren said. "You make a far better Bligh than I do."

As Dirk laughed, Summer blushed, then retorted, "Careful or I might accidentally cut your surface air while you are downstairs."

Dirk fired up the two air compressors then joined Dahlgren in slipping on a warm-water wet suit. They would dive sharing surface-supplied air from one of the compressors. Eliminating the cumbersome air tanks made it easier to work, while extending their bottom time. Since the water depth was only thirty feet at the wreck site, they could theoretically work all day underwater without fear of the bends.

Summer gathered up the airlift and lowered the big piece of PVC pipe over the side. A hose from the second compressor was attached to the business end of the airlift, which provided the air feed through a controllable valve. Summer slowly lowered the pipe via the air hose till it struck the bottom and the tension slacked on the line.

Dirk slipped on his fins, then glanced at his watch. "See you in ninety minutes," he said to Summer, then pulled his dive helmet over his head.

"I'll leave the lights on," Summer replied, shouting over the drone of the compressors. She moved to the rail and sorted a trio of air lines that would tail the underwater operation. Dirk threw her a wave then stepped off the side of the barge, followed by Dahlgren a second behind.

The bellow of the compressors evaporated as Dirk struck the surface and he submerged into the turquoise water. Clearing his ears, he thrust his head down and kicked to the bottom, quickly locating the airlift. Grabbing the pipe, he chased after Dahlgren, who was swimming toward deeper water. They stopped at a pair of small orange flags that poked up from the sandy bottom. Dirk lifted the airlift, standing it on end, then flipped the control lever to the air line. A rush of compressed air burst into the lower end of the pipe, then gurgled up toward the surface, drawing sand and water with it. Dirk swung the base of the airlift back and forth above the seabed, digging a small hole as he cleared away sand around the marker.

Dahlgren watched for a moment, then took up position a few feet away. In his hands, he carried a stainless steel shaft with a cross handle at one end. He began twisting the metal probe into the sand, driving it down nearly two feet until it struck something solid. His experienced hands could tell by the vibration that the probe had struck wood. Yanking the probe out, he moved over another foot and repeated the process. After a few more probes, he began marking the perimeter of the buried object with small orange flags.

The hole created by the airlift in Dirk's hands grew slowly. He had worked his way down to a flat surface that was heavily encrusted. Looking at the outline of marker flags Dahlgren had started laying down, he realized the object was of an immense size. If it was indeed a rudder, they might have to rethink the entire scale of the remaining ship.

On the deck of the barge, Summer checked the compressors once more, then took a seat in a beach chair across the deck but within sight of the air lines. A cool offshore gust blew across the barge, sending a shiver up her spine. She was thankful the morning sun was quickly warming up the deck.

She happily soaked in the surrounding environment, admiring the rugged Hawaiian coast and delicious smells of the nearby flora that wafted from the lush island. Gazing seaward, the rolling Pacific waters seemed to shine with an exotic intensity from its blue depths. Absently noting a black ship steaming in the distance, she took a deep breath of the fresh sea air and leaned back in her chair.

If this is work, she thought amusedly, then they can keep my vacation pay.

～ 41 ～

P ITT WAS ALREADY AWAKE AND dressed when an early-morning knock sounded on his hotel-room door. Opening it with some trepidation, he was relieved to find a smiling Al Giordino standing in the doorway.

"I found this vagrant panhandling in the lobby," he said, jerking his thumb over his shoulder. "I thought you might know what to do with him."

A tired and disheveled Rudi Gunn peeked behind Giordino's thick frame with a look of relief on his face.

"Well, my long-lost deputy director," Pitt grinned. "We thought perhaps you had found yourself a nice babushka and taken up residence in the wilds of Siberia."

"I was only too happy to depart the wilds of Siberia. However, I would have stayed had I known that Mongolia was twice as uncivilized," Gunn harangued, entering the room and falling into a chair. "Nobody told me that there isn't a paved road in the entire country. Drove all night on something I'm not even sure was a road. I feel like I hopped on a pogo stick from New York to L.A."

Pitt handed him a cup of coffee from an in-room pot. "You were able to bring our search gear and dive equipment with you?" he asked.

"Yes, I got it all onto a truck that the institute was kind enough to loan me, or sell me, I'm still not sure. It cost me every ruble I had to grease the palms of the Russian border guards to let me into Mongolia. I'm sure they think I'm CIA."

"Your eyes aren't beady enough," Giordino muttered.

"I guess I can't complain," Gunn said, looking at Pitt. "Al told me about your traipse across the Gobi Desert. Didn't sound like any picnic."

"No, but a great way to see the countryside," Pitt smiled.

"This nutcase at Xanadu . . . he's still holding the oil survey team?"

"We know Roy is dead. We can only presume the others are there and still alive."

A ring of the telephone interrupted the conversation. Pitt answered and spoke briefly, then slid the phone toward the center of the room and activated the speakerphone. Hiram Yaeger's easygoing voice boomed from the speaker.

"Greetings from Washington, where the local bureaucracy is beginning to wonder what has become of their favorite gurus of the deep," he said.

"Simply busy enjoying the delightful underwater treasures of greater Mongolia," Pitt replied.

"As I suspected. Of course, I'm sure you had a hand in the breaking political news coming from your part of the world."

The three men in the hotel room looked at each other blankly.

"We've been a little preoccupied," Pitt said. "What news?"

"China declared this morning that they are acceding the territorial lands of Inner Mongolia to the country of Mongolia."

"I noticed a gathering of people in the square down the street who looked like they were headed for a celebration," Gunn said. "I thought it might be a local holiday."

"China is playing it up as a friendly diplomatic gesture to their old neighbor, and has garnered all kinds of accolades from the United Nations and Western government leaders. Underground movements have been afoot for years to seek independence for Inner Mongolia, or reunification with Mongolia proper. It has been a point of embarrassment with the Chinese for years. Privately, analysts are saying it was less about politics and more about economics. Some have speculated that it involved a pipeline deal and trade agreement to provide oil or other resources needed to keep China's economy growing, though no one seems to think Mongolia actually holds much in the way of oil reserves."

"That's exactly what it is about. I guess you could say Al and I were indeed a part of the negotiations," Pitt said, glancing at Giordino with a knowing look.

"I knew you must have had something to do with it," Yaeger laughed.

"It has a lot more to do with the Avarga Oil Company and Tolgoi Borjin. Al and I saw some of his resources. He's got storage facilities already in place along the border."

"Pretty remarkable that he got hold of the keys to the castle so quickly," Giordino said. "He must have had some pretty good bargaining chips."

"Or misinformation. Hiram, were you able to track down any of the info that I faxed you?" Pitt asked.

"Max and I pulled an all-nighter, digging up what we could. This guy and his company are quite an enigma. Well funded, but operating in an almost clandestine fashion."

"A local Russian contact confirmed similar findings," Giordino said. "What did you make of his oil holdings?"

"There is no record of the Avarga Oil Company actually exporting any oil from Mongolia. But then, there isn't much to export. They are known to operate only a handful of active wells."

"So they are not pumping enough volume sufficient to make a dent in China's demand, or anybody else's, for that matter?"

"There is no evidence of it. Funny thing is, we uncovered a number of sizeable contracts with a couple of Western oil field equipment suppliers. With oil prices surging over one hundred fifty dollars a barrel, there has been a mad rush for new exploration and drilling. The oil equipment suppliers have huge backlogs. Yet Avarga was already at the front of the line. They have apparently been purchasing a massive amount of specialized drilling and pipeline equipment for the last three years, all shipped to Mongolia."

"We found some of it here in Ulaanbaatar."

"The only item that was amiss was the tunnel-boring device. We found only one record of that model being shipped out of the country and it was exported to Malaysia."

"Perhaps a front company for our friends at Avarga Oil?" Pitt ventured.

"Probably. The particular model you saw is designated for shallow earth pipeline installations. Perfect, in other words, for burying an oil pipeline in the soft sands of the Gobi Desert. What I haven't been able to decipher is how this Borjin has obtained the resources to acquire all this equipment without any visible revenue stream," Yaeger said.

"Genghis Khan is picking up the tab," Pitt replied.

"I don't get the joke."

"It's true," Giordino said. "He's parked in the guy's backyard."

While Giordino told Gunn and Yaeger about the existence of the tomb in Borjin's sanctuary and the later discovery of Hunt's diary in the crashed trimotor,

Pitt pulled out a ten-page fax he had received back from Perlmutter.

"St. Julien has confirmed as much," Pitt said. "Sotheby's and the other major auction houses have had a steady stream of consignments for the past eight years of major twelfth- and thirteenth-century mainland Asian art and artifacts."

"Loot buried with Genghis Khan?" Gunn asked.

"To the tune of over one hundred million dollars. Perlmutter verified that the artifacts have all been consistent with the geographic regions of Genghis Khan's conquests up to the date of his death. The pattern fits, as does the source. The artifacts have all been consigned from a shadowy Malaysian company named the Buryat Trading Company."

"That's the same firm that purchased the tunnel borer," Yaeger exclaimed.

"Small world, eh? Hiram, when we are finished perhaps you and Max can take a closer look at this Malaysian front company."

"Sure thing. I guess we should also talk about that bit of German strudel you sent me."

"Ah yes, the documents written in German. Did you and Max come up with anything?"

"Not much on the documents per se. Just as you noted, they read like the first pages of a technical operator's manual. You found them with a large electrical device?"

"A room full of computing equipment, powering a three-legged tubular device that stands ten feet high.

Any idea what it might be?"

"There wasn't enough data to determine its exact function. The pages were simply operator's instructions for an acoustic seismic array."

"Care to try that again in English?" Giordino asked.

"Mostly the stuff of lab experiments. Von Wachter evidently succeeded in taking the technology a leap forward."

"Who's von Wachter?" Pitt asked.

"Dr. Friedrich von Wachter. An eminent electrical engineering professor from the University of Heidelberg. Well known for his research in acoustics and seismic imagery. Max made the link between von Wachter and the acoustic seismic array. One of his last papers discussed the theoretical application of a parametric acoustic array for subsurface imagery."

Gunn helped himself to more coffee as the men in the hotel room listened attentively to Yaeger's voice on the speakerphone.

"Though the facts are murky, it appears that Dr. von Wachter developed a working model for acoustic seismic imagery," he said. "As you know, in the oil exploration business seismic imagery usually relies on a mechanical explosive, such as dynamite or a thumper truck, to send a shock wave into the earth. The refracted seismic waves are then recorded and processed by computer modeling to develop a subsurface image."

"Sure. The marine survey ships use an air gun to generate the shocks," Giordino said.

461

"Von Wachter apparently eliminated the explosives by developing an electronic means of producing the shock wave. The acoustic array, if I understand it correctly, transmits a high-frequency sound burst, which converts to seismic waves under the surface."

"Our experience with survey sonar systems is that high-frequency waves don't provide adequate penetration to 'see' very far beneath the surface," Giordino stated.

"That's true. Most of the waves are easily refracted near the surface. Apparently, von Wachter's concentrated burst allows a greater bombardment, if you will, of sound waves, ensuring that a useful percentage of waves penetrate deeply. From the preliminary data in the manual and your visual description of the device, it sounds as if von Wachter uses three rather large arrays to transmit the sound waves."

"I'll bet that is how they found Genghis," Pitt remarked. "His tomb was supposedly buried in a hidden location in the mountains, along with Kublai Khan and other related royalty."

"And they're obviously using it to hunt for oil," Gunn added.

"A valuable technology that the oil companies would pay dearly for. Dr. von Wachter must be a rich man," Giordino said.

"I'm afraid he's a dead man. He and his team of German engineers were killed in a landslide in Mongolia a little over a year ago."

"Why does that sound suspicious?" Giordino added.

"Need I add that they were working for the Avarga Oil Company at the time," Yaeger said.

"More blood on the hands of Borjin," Pitt said without surprise. The ruthlessness of the Avarga Oil empire and its head, Tolgoi Borjin, was becoming old news.

"None of it adds up," Giordino said. "A seismic survey team murdered, another abducted. A tunnel borer, specialized drilling equipment, a vast disguised storage facility in the middle of the desert. One of several, according to our camel herder friend, Tsengel. All tied in to a system of underground pipelines running hidden across an empty desert. Yet no visible sign of output. Why?"

The room fell silent for a moment, the turning gears in everyone's heads nearly audible. Then a knowing look spread across Pitt's face.

"Because," he said slowly, "they have been unable to drill where the oil is."

"Borjin has probably greased enough wallets to drill anywhere he wants to in Mongolia," Giordino countered.

"But suppose the oil isn't in Mongolia?"

"Of course," Gunn said, the answer suddenly apparent. "He's found oil in China, or Inner Mongolia to be precise. How he convinced the Chinese to turn the land over, that's what I'd like to know."

"They're in a bad way," Yaeger said. "Because of the earthquakes in the Persian Gulf and the fire at their main oil import terminal near Shanghai, China has lost more than half of its oil imports overnight. They're in a desperate situation and liable to act a little irrational in order to find a quick fix."

"It would explain the storage facilities located by the border. They might already have some secret wells in Inner Mongolia pumping to one of the other storage sites," Pitt speculated. "The Chinese would only see the end product shipped from Mongolia and not know the oil originated in their own yard."

"I wouldn't want to be on this side of the Great Wall when they figure that scam out," Gunn said.

"It might explain why Borjin abducted the oil survey team from Baikal," Giordino said. "He probably needs their expertise to pinpoint the drill sites and get the oil out of the ground quickly."

"Seems like he could have hired that expertise on the open market," Yaeger said.

"Perhaps. But he probably didn't want to risk leaking the secret of where the oil deposits are located."

"Maybe he'll release them, now that he's got his deal with the Chinese," Gunn said.

"Not likely," Pitt replied. "They already murdered Roy and tried to kill us. No, I'm afraid they are as good as dead once Borjin has the information he wants out of them."

"Have you contacted the local American embassy yet? We need to get the political forces working to save them," Gunn said.

Pitt and Giordino looked at each other in affirmation.

"Diplomacy ain't going to work in this case, Rudi,"

Giordino said. "Borjin is too well protected. Our Russian friends have been trying that route to no avail, and they've got a lot more clout in this part of the world than we do."

"We've got to do something," he countered.

"We are," Pitt said. "We're going in after them."

"You can't do that. Going in under the name of the U.S. government might create an international incident."

"Not if the U.S. government doesn't know anything about it. And by the way, it's not just Al and me going in. You're coming with us."

A sick feeling struck Gunn in the stomach and he could feel the color drain from his face.

"I knew I should have stayed in Siberia," he muttered.

~ 42 ~

DR. McCAMMON ENTERED THE NUMA computer center just as Yaeger hung up the phone to Mongolia. On the opposite side of the console, the holographic image of Max turned toward the marine geologist and smiled.

"Good evening, Dr. McCammon," she said. "Working late?"

"Uh, good evening," McCammon replied, not sure if he should feel foolish for conversing with a computerized image. He nervously turned and greeted Yaeger.

"Hello, Hiram. Long day?" he asked, noting that Yaeger was dressed in the same clothes he wore the day before.

"Very," Yaeger replied, suppressing a yawn. "A late request from the boss yesterday kept us busy. We expected to see you hours ago."

"Some unexpected meetings managed to kill most of my day. I understand if you didn't get a chance to retrieve the data from the earthquake center," McCammon offered.

"Nonsense," Yaeger replied, as if insulted. "Max can multitask with the best of them."

"Yes," Max replied. "And at least some of us keep our demeanor in the process."

"We pulled in the data last night," Yaeger continued, ignoring the comment, "and ran your program early this morning. Max," he said, facing the image of his wife, "please print Dr. McCammon a copy of the program results. And while that is running, why don't you give us a verbal overview of your findings."

"Certainly," Max replied. A large laser printer at the side of the room immediately began humming with the printed output while Max chose her words.

"The data received from the National Earthquake Information Center reflected global seismic activity for the last five years, including the two large quakes that just recently struck the Persian Gulf. I ran your software program, which analyzed the two earthquakes, then filtered their key commonalties against the entire database. Interestingly, there were several unique characteristics associated with the two earth-quakes."

Max paused for effect, then stepped closer to Yaeger and McCammon before continuing.

"Both events were classified as extremely shallow earthquakes, as their epicenters were less than three kilometers beneath the surface. This compares to most shallow-focus earthquakes, which are typically in the five- to fifteen-kilometer depth range."

"That's a meaningful difference," McCammon said.

"Of less significance, both were tectonic quakes rather than volcanic in origin. And, as you know, both were large quakes, measuring over 7.0 on the Richter scale."

"Isn't that quite rare to have a pair of quakes with that magnitude?" Yaeger asked.

"It's a little unusual but not unheard of," McCammon said. "An earthquake of that size in Los Angeles would capture plenty of attention, but the fact is there is a 7.0 magnitude or greater earthquake occurring on average once a month somewhere around the world. Since they mostly strike in nonpopulated areas or under the sea, we don't hear much about them."

"That is correct," Max said. "Though there is a statistically significant anomaly in that the two quakes of that magnitude struck in such close proximity."

"Any other similarities, Max?" Yaeger asked.

"Yes. Though difficult to quantify, it appears that the damage produced by these earthquakes was not commensurate with their size. Significant structural damage was recorded at both sites, which exceeded the norm for similarly sized earthquakes. The actual damage was more reflective of what an 8.0 magnitude quake would produce."

"The Richter scale is not always an accurate measure of an earthquake's destructive power," McCammon noted, "particularly for shallow-focus events. In this case, we had two shallow quakes that proved highly damaging. The intensity on the ground was likely much higher than the magnitude rating indicated."

Max frowned briefly as she rifled through her databases, then nodded at McCammon.

"You are absolutely correct, Doctor. The primary seismic waves were much smaller in magnitude than the surface waves for both quakes."

"Anything else, Max?" McCammon asked, finally finding a comfort level with the image.

"Yes, one final aspect. In both earthquakes, there was a record of low-magnitude P-waves registering before the actual quake-induced waves occurred."

"Foreshocks, I suppose," McCammon said. "Not at all unusual."

"Will somebody kindly explain all this surface wave and P-wave business?" Yaeger asked tiredly.

Max shook her head. "Must I teach you everything? Elementary seismology. The slippage from a common tectonic earthquake generates three types of seismic energy releases, or shock waves, if you will. The initial wave is called the primary, or P-type wave. It has similar properties to a sound wave, able to travel through

468

solid rock and even the earth's core. A slower and hence secondary wave is called an S-wave. The S-waves are capable of shearing rock sideways to the direction of travel and produce the damaging vertical and horizontal movement of the ground when they reach the earth's surface. As both types of waves approach the surface, they refract to produce additional surface waves, which create the bulk of the shaking that is felt on the ground."

"I see," said Yaeger. "So they are essentially different frequencies sent out from an earthquake's epicenter."

"That's right," McCammon said.

"Is there a large fault line in the area where the two earthquakes struck?"

"The Persian Gulf actually lies near the boundary of two tectonic plates, called the Arabian and Eurasian. Nearly all the seismic activity that takes place around the world is in narrow zones surrounding the plate boundaries. The large earthquakes we've seen historically in Iran, Afghanistan, and Pakistan would suggest that these two quakes in the gulf were not extraordinary but for their proximity."

"I guess your friend at Langley won't have too much to chew on," Yaeger said.

"I can't imagine," McCammon replied. "But thanks to Max, he'll have plenty of data to peruse."

As McCammon walked to the printer to retrieve the output, Yaeger threw one more question at the computer.

"Max, when you ran Phil's filter program did you

match any other earthquakes to the same parameters?"

"Why, yes. It would be easier for me to show you graphically, so feast your eyes on the video board."

A large white screen behind Max was suddenly illuminated with a color map of the world. Two flashing red dots appeared in the Persian Gulf, marking the recent earthquakes. A few seconds later, a flurry of red dots erupted in several clusters, concentrated in an area of Northeast Asia. They were followed by a lone flashing dot slightly north of the others. McCammon set down his reports and approached the map in curiosity.

"A total of thirty-four seismic events were identified from the National Earthquake Information Center's data as matching the characteristics of the two sample earthquakes. The most recent occurred just over a week ago in Siberia," Max said, pointing to the lone red dot.

Yaeger's bleary eyes widened in shock. "And the locations of the other events?" he asked.

"Primarily Mongolia. Fifteen events occurred in the mountains east of the capital of Ulaanbaatar, ten in the southern Mongolian province of Dornogov, and another nine in an area just across the border in China. There was also one event in Siberia, at Lake Baikal."

"Mongolia," Yaeger muttered, shaking his head in disbelief. Slowly rising to his feet and rubbing his tired eyes, he turned to McCammon.

"Phil," he said, "I think you, me, and Max are going to need some coffee."

L ISTENING TO THE LATEST Nils Lofgren CD on a
portable MP3, Summer hummed along happily as
she monitored the tension on the air lines snaking over
the side of the barge. Boredom was just beginning to
set in, and she found herself looking forward to getting
back into the water and working the other end of the
line. Standing up and stretching, she gazed seaward
and caught sight of the black ship she had noticed earlier, now rounding Kahakahakea Point. Something
nagged at the back of her brain as she watched the ship
turn and aim its bow directly at the NUMA work barge.

"Please, no more media hounds," she said aloud,
hoping it was not another boatload of reporters. But
her deepening suspicions rang louder, and, as she
studied the ship, she realized what it was.

The approaching vessel was a drill ship. Small by
most drilling standards at less than two hundred fifty
feet, the ship was at least thirty years old and had
clearly seen better days. Rust appeared to grow from
the ship's scuppers, while its deck and forecastle were
stained with dirt and grease. It was less the appearance
than the function of the ship that troubled Summer.
What was a drill ship doing in Hawaiian waters?
There were no oil deposits in the Hawaiian Islands to
speak of, and the surrounding ocean depths quickly
drop to over ten thousand feet, making any offshore

drilling efforts a costly proposition.

Summer watched as the old ship continued churning directly for her, frothy sprays of white foam creasing away from its weathered bow. The ship was less than a mile away now and showed no signs of decreasing speed. When it closed to within a quarter mile still at speed, Summer glanced at a makeshift flagpole erected over the barge's sleeping shack. A large red diver's flag with the cautionary white slash across the middle fluttered in the morning breeze.

"I've got divers in the water, you idiot," she cursed as the ship continued its beeline track. The vessel was close enough that Summer could make out a couple of figures standing on the ship's bridge. She quickly walked to the facing rail then turned and waved an arm at the dive flag. Summer detected the ship finally starting to slow, but it was approaching without caution. It was clear by now that the drill ship intended to moor alongside the barge.

Summer hustled to the shack, where a marine radio was mounted to the wall. Spinning the dial on the VHF set to channel 16, she spat into the microphone.

"Approaching drill ship, this is NUMA research barge. We have divers in the water. I repeat, we have divers in the water. Please stand off, over."

She waited impatiently for a reply but there was none. With a greater urgency in her voice, she repeated the call. Again, there was no answer.

By now, the drill ship was only a few yards away. Summer returned to the rail and yelled at the ship while pointing to the dive flag. The ship started to turn, but, by its angle, Summer could see it was only preparing to pull alongside. Half expecting to see a horde of seasick reporters and cameramen lining the rail, she was surprised to find the ship's starboard and stern decks empty. A slight chill ran up her spine at seeing no one on deck, the men in the forecastle remaining concealed on the bridge.

With an experienced helmsman's touch, the drill ship glided alongside the barge until its starboard rail hung just above the lower side rails of the barge. The drill ship's multiple positioning thrusters were activated and the ship hung precisely in place as if physically moored to the barge.

The vacant ship stood perfectly still for a minute, Summer watching with a mixture of curiosity and concern. Then a faint yell erupted from inside the ship and a half dozen men came storming out of a bulkhead door. Summer took one look at the men, all tough-looking Asians, and shivered with fear. As they scrambled to the ship's rail and began leaping onto the barge, Summer turned and sprinted back to the sleeping shack. She could feel somebody chasing her but didn't look back as she tore into the shack and grabbed the radio.

"Mayday, mayday, this is . . ."

Her voice withered away as a pair of thick-callused hands reached into the shack and tore the radio off the wall, ripping the microphone clutched in Summer's hands out of the socket. With a perverse grin on his face, the man took a short step and hurled the radio over the side rail, watching as it splashed into the water. Turning back toward Summer with a thin smile that revealed a set of dirty yellow teeth, it was his turn for a shock. Summer took a step toward him and let loose with a powerful kick to his groin.

"Dirty creep," she cursed as the man fell to one knee in agony. His eyes bugged out of his head, and Summer could tell he was teetering with dizziness. She quickly stepped back and swung her leg in another kick, delivering a roundhouse blow to the side of the man's head. The assailant crumpled to the deck, where he rolled about in obvious pain.

Two of the other boarders witnessed the takedown and quickly charged Summer, grabbing her arms to restrain her. She struggled to free herself until one of the men pulled out a knife and held it to her throat, grunting into her ear with stale breath. The other man found a section of rope and hastily tied her hands and elbows together in front of her.

Gripped with fear but helpless to act, Summer studied her assailants with deliberation. To a man, they were short in stature yet bullish in build. They were of Asian descent, but had high cheekbones and more-rounded eyes than the classic Chinese profile. Each was dressed in black T-shirt and work pants, and all looked like they were accustomed to hard work. Summer guessed they were Indonesian pirates, but what they wanted with a sparse work barge was beyond her guess.

Gazing at the opposite end of the barge, Summer felt her stomach suddenly tightened into a knot. Two of the boarders had carried axes with them and were now swinging them through the air, cutting into the stern mooring lines. With a few quick swings, they severed the lines, then walked toward the bow to repeat the act. A third man stood overseeing the work with his back to Summer. His profile looked familiar, but it wasn't until he turned around and exposed the long scar on his left cheek that she recognized him as Dr. Tong. He walked slowly toward Summer, surveying the equipment on the deck as the two hatchet men went to work on the forward anchor lines. When he came near, she shouted to him.

"There are no artifacts here, Tong," she said, figuring he was no doctor but simply an artifact thief.

Tong ignored her, staring at the running equipment with annoyance. He turned and barked an order to the man Summer had kicked, who was now limping around the deck trying to walk off the blow. The injured man limped to the shack, where the small portable generator was humming. As he had done with the radio, he hoisted the generator up in the air and shoved it over the side. The machine gurgled as it slipped under water, silencing the small gas motor. The man then set his sights on the two air compressors. Limping to the nearest one, he looked it over, searching for the kill switch.

"No!" Summer shouted in protest.

Finding the STOP button, the injured man turned to

Summer and gave her a twisted smile, then pressed his thumb against the switch. The compressor immediately wheezed to a stop.

"There are men below on those air lines," Summer pleaded.

Tong ignored her, instead nodding to his minion. The man hobbled over to the second compressor and, with another smile directed at Summer, punched STOP. As the roar of the dying compressor fell away, Tong walked over and stuck his face close to Summer's.

"I hope your brother is a good swimmer," he hissed.

A well of fury burned within Summer, replacing her fear. But she said nothing. The man holding the knife at her throat pulled tighter, then spoke to Tong in a foreign tongue.

"Shall I kill her?"

Tong glared at Summer's fit tan body lasciviously. "No," he replied, "take her aboard."

The two axmen finished cutting the bow anchor lines and walked toward Tong with their hatchets over their shoulders. The barge was now drifting freely, the current pushing it out to sea. On board the drill ship, the helmsman manually engaged the positioning thrusters and backed the ship in reverse to stay alongside the moving barge. Absent a fixed target, the drill ship had to bob and weave to keep from colliding with the free-floating barge. Several times they nudged sides, the barge slapping against the bigger drill ship with a clang.

"You—incapacitate the rubber boat," Tong barked to

one of the men holding an axe. "Everybody else, back on the ship."

A small Zodiac had been secured to the bow of the barge, in case the NUMA team needed to go ashore. The ax bearer walked over and with a few quick swings cut loose the securing lines. He then pulled a knife from his belt and wedged it into the inflated pontoon in several spots, producing a loud rush of escaping air. For good measure, he stood the boat on end, then flipped it over the side rail. The deflated rubber boat bobbed on the surface for several minutes until a wave swamped its sides and sent it to the bottom.

Summer witnessed little of the sabotage as the thug at her side shoved her roughly to the rail. A thousand thoughts were surging through her mind. Should she risk trying to fight back with a knife to her throat? How could she help Dirk and Jack? Would anything good come from stepping aboard the drill ship? Every query led down a short path to something bad. There might be one chance, she decided, and that was if she could get into the water. Even with her hands tied, outswimming these roughnecks would likely be no problem, she figured. If she could jump into the water, she could easily swim under the barge to the other side. Maybe it would be enough of an annoyance to let her go. And maybe she could then help get Dirk and Jack aboard and mount a stronger defense. That is, if they were all right.

Summer feigned a lack of resistance and followed

the other men as they climbed on top of the rail and pulled themselves onto the deck of the drill ship. The knife wielder gave her a boost, holding her elbows as she stepped onto the rail. One of the men on the ship knelt down and reached over to help pull her up. Summer reached up but pretended to slip before she could reach the man's hands. She then flung her right foot backward, striking the knife holder flush in the nose with her heel. By the sound of the muffled crunch, she knew she had broken his nose but didn't turn to see the blood rushing out of his nostrils. Instead, she ducked her head forward and dove for the thin patch of water between the two vessels.

She floated weightless for a fraction of a second, awaiting the splash of the cool water. But it never came.

Seeming to materialize out of thin air, a pair of hands sprung over the rail and clasped the back of her shirt and the cuff of her shorts. Instead of falling vertically, she felt herself flung sideways, bouncing harshly over the side rail before falling hard to the deck of the barge. She had hardly hit the ground when the same pair of hands jerked her to her feet. The hands belonged to Tong, who showed remarkable strength for a man who stood nearly a foot shorter than Summer.

"You will be going aboard," he spat.

The blow came from her left side and Summer was a hair late warding it off. Tong's fist struck her on the side of the jaw and she immediately buckled to her knees. A flurry of stars danced before her eyes but she didn't pass out. In a dazed stupor, she was yanked aboard the drill ship and dragged up to the bridge, where she was locked in a small storage room at the back of the wheelhouse.

Resting on a large coil of rope, it seemed to Summer that the whole world was spinning around her head. A wave of nausea swept over her until she threw up into a rusty bucket in the corner. She immediately felt better and pulled herself up to a small porthole. Sucking in fresh air, her vision gradually cleared until she could see that the drill ship was positioned in the cove over the same spot where the barge had been moored.

The barge. She craned her neck, finally spotting the brown barge drifting out to sea, already more than a mile away. Squinting to try to improve her blurry vision, she fought to make out signs of Dirk and Jack aboard. But they were nowhere to be seen.

The empty barge was drifting out to sea without them.

~ 44 ~

DIRK'S ARMS HAD BEGUN TO feel like spaghetti. The airlift had to be constantly wrestled into place against the invisible push of the surrounding waters. Though Dahlgren had relieved him a few times, he had been toting the pressurized tube for over an hour. The work had been made more strenuous by the building currents of an outgoing tide, which pushed the surface water seaward at nearly two knots. The current was much lighter on the bottom, but manhandling the wavering airlift over the dredge site was like balancing a flagpole on the head of a pin.

Dirk glanced at his dive watch as he wrestled the airlift over a few inches. Only fifteen minutes to go till the end of the shift, then a break from the monotonous work. Progress was slower than he had hoped, but he had still uncovered a rough square about six feet across. The encrusted wood was thick but flat, consistent with the shape of a ship's rudder. Only the size was a little perplexing. Dahlgren's probe marks had encompassed an object nearly twenty feet long, an enormous dimension for a sailing ship rudder.

Following the ascent of his air bubbles as they rose to the surface, he gazed again at the undersides of the large black ship moored next to the barge. He and Dahlgren had heard the rumble of the ship's engines underwater as it drew near and they watched with curiosity as the dark shape brazenly drew alongside the barge. They had watched the positioning thrusters engaged and felt a slight assurance that the fool wasn't going to drop anchor on them. Another well-financed video documentary group, Dirk surmised. There would no doubt be an array of underwater photographers descending on them shortly. Hooray, he thought sarcastically.

He shook off the annoyance and refocused on driving the airlift into the fine sand. Pushing the lip toward a small mound, he noticed that no sand was being sucked up, then realized that the vibration and whooshing noise of the compressed air had ceased. Summer must have shut off the airlift, which meant she was signaling them back to the barge for some reason or the compressor just ran out of gas. He sat for a moment, deciding to wait a minute or two before surfacing to see if Summer restarted the motor.

A few yards away, Dahlgren was driving his probe into the sand. Out of the corner of his eye, Dirk noticed him suddenly rise off the bottom. Something about the movement didn't seem right and Dirk looked over to see that his instincts were right. Dahlgren had let go of the probe and had his hands wrapped around his faceplate and air line, while his legs hung loose beneath him. He was being yanked off the bottom, Dirk realized, like a puppet on a string.

He had no time to react, for an instant later the airlift was ripped from his own hands, sailing off through the water in the direction of Dahlgren. Dirk looked up just in time to see his own air line pull taut in the water and then jerk him up off the seafloor.

"What the . . ." he started to mouth, but the words fell away as he tried to draw a breath of air. He inhaled a slight puff and then there was nothing. The compressor supplying the air lines had been cut off, too. Like Dahlgren, he found himself grabbing hold of the air line to control his movements and not rip the connection from his dive helmet. Beside him, the airlift swung wildly in the water like a pendulum out of control. The big plastic pipe came barreling at him, slamming into his leg before bouncing off in another direction. Out of air, yanked like a rag doll, and pummeled by the airlift, Dirk faced enough sensory obstacles to drive most people to panic. From there, it would be just a short step to drowning.

But Dirk didn't panic. He had spent the better part of his life scuba diving. Technical failures underwater were nothing new to him. He had sucked a tank of air dry on shallow-water dives many times. The key to surviving an emergency, underwater or elsewhere, he told himself, was to remain calm and think logically.

Air was the first necessity. His natural inclination was to kick to the surface, but that wasn't necessary. While working on surface-supplied air, the divers all carried a small emergency bottle of air. Slightly larger than a thermos, the thirteen-cubic-foot bailout bottle, called a "pony tank," provided about ten minutes of air. Dirk let go of the air line with one hand and reached under his left arm, where the bottle was attached to his buoyancy compensator. Twisting the valve on the top of the tank, he immediately drew in a breath of air through the regulator. After a couple of deep draws, he could feel his heart begin to slow its racing beat.

His thoughts ran to Dahlgren, who was on the shared line of surface air. Thirty feet ahead, he saw a purge of exhaust bubbles rise from Dahlgren's helmet and knew that he was breathing off his emergency air as well. The dangling airlift had ventured over toward

Dahlgren and was gyrating in the water close behind him. The airlift pipe was being dragged by its flexible outlet hose secured to the barge, which created an elastic springing action like a rubber band. The hose would stretch under the drag of the water-filled tube, then snap back, whipping the tube forcefully through the water. Dirk saw that the tube was pulled taut in a precarious position behind Dahlgren and he waved to get his friend's attention. The Texan was busy pulling himself up the air line and didn't see the airlift or Dirk's warning. A second later, the outstretched tube burst forward, launching straight toward Dahlgren. To Dirk's horror, the tube shot up like an arrow and struck the back of Dahlgren's head just beneath his dive helmet. As the airlift fluttered off, Dahlgren's body went limp.

Dirk cursed to himself as he felt his heart race faster again. He noticed that the seafloor had dropped away beneath them and that they were being pulled more forcefully through the water. On the surface, an off-shore breeze had joined forces with the island currents to push the stubby barge along at over four knots. Under the waves, Dirk wondered why in blazes the barge was drifting and where Summer was. Then he turned toward Dahlgren. There was no thought of sur-facing yet. He had to reach Dahlgren and make sure he was still breathing.

With a frantic determination, Dirk began reeling himself up the air line to close in on Dahlgren. His tired arms ached in pain with each pull, made harder by the thirty-five-pound weight belt strapped around his midsection. He didn't dare jettison the belt yet, as he needed to stay at the same submerged depth as his friend.

Pulling himself up like an underwater mountaineer, he clawed his way to within ten feet of Dahlgren when his old nemesis reappeared. The dancing airlift came rushing toward him, swinging past just out of arm's reach. The big tube swung toward Dahlgren, flexed a moment, then reversed direction and bounded back. This time, Dirk stuck out an arm and caught hold of the tube as it swung by. The heavy mass of the water-filled tube nearly jerked him out of his fins as he straddled his legs around it and bounced through the water. Riding it like a bucking bronco, he carefully shimmied up to the top of the tube, where it was clasped to the thick rubber hose. Pulling out a small dive knife that was strapped to his leg, Dirk lunged at the hose with the blade and began sawing through it. The tube whipped violently beneath him as he muscled the knife through to sever the hose. The heavy plastic tube snapped away with the last cut and sank to the depths as Dirk slid off and gave it a farewell kick.

Free of the mad battering ram, Dirk turned his attention back to Dahlgren. Dirk's fight to rid himself of the airlift had caused him to lose his place on the air line and he found himself trailing Dahlgren by thirty feet again. His friend looked like a wet mop, towed through the water by the line from his neck. With his tired arms stinging, Dirk pulled himself up the line again, fighting foot by foot until he was even with Dahlgren. He coiled his own air line around his waist in a bowline knot, then kicked and swam his way over to his friend. Reaching over and grabbing Dahlgren's BC, Dirk pulled himself up and peered into his face mask.

Dahlgren was unconscious with his eyes closed. He was breathing lightly, though, as evidenced by a small stream of exhaust bubbles that floated out of his regulator every few seconds. Grabbing Dahlgren with one hand, Dirk reached down and unbuckled his own weight belt, then reached up to his buoyancy compensator and hit the button on the inflation hose. What little air was left in his emergency pony bottle surged into his vest, filling it half full before running out of compressed air. It was more than enough to propel them to the surface, with Dirk kicking his legs hard to accelerate the ascent.

No sooner did they break the surface then they were dragged forward, yanked under the water like a fallen water-skier who forgets to let go of the rope. A second later, they would resurface for a moment, then get pulled under again. As they bounded up and down, Dirk reached down and ditched Dahlgren's weight belt, then managed to twist off his own dive helmet. Grabbing gulps of air when they popped to the surface, he grasped the manual inflation tube to Dahlgren's BC. While pushed under the surface, he opened the thumb valve and exhaled into it. In a few cycles, he had Dahlgren's vest fully inflated, which helped reduce the duration of their immersions.

Fearful that his friend's head or neck might get injured by the tug of the air line, Dirk cinched up a few inches of the line and ran it through a D ring on Dahlgren's BC, then tied it in a knot. As long as the line didn't snap, he would safely be towed by his vest.

With his buddy mostly afloat, Dirk let go of him to grab his own air line again. He had to get aboard the barge now and began pulling himself hand over hand toward the moving platform. There was more than forty feet of line ahead of him, and he was already heavily fatigued from his time in the water. With his strength diminished, his progress slowed to just inches at a time. He repeatedly had to will himself to shake off the pain and a creeping urge to just let go. Instead, he reluctantly placed one hand ahead of the other and pulled, repeating the process without stopping.

For the first time, he looked up at the barge, hoping to see Summer standing at the rail. But there was no sign of her or anyone else on the open deck. Dirk knew his sister would never willfully abandon him. Something had happened when the black ship came alongside and Dirk was afraid of the prospects. A renewed sense of urgency mixed with anger surged through his body, and he hauled himself up the last few feet of line in a possessed fury.

Finally reaching the side of the barge, he yanked himself up and through the railing and collapsed on the deck. He afforded himself just a few seconds of rest, then ripped off his dive gear and scanned the deck for Summer, shouting her name. Met with a silent response, he stood up and grabbed Dahlgren's air line and began reeling him toward the barge. The Texan disappeared under the water for several seconds before reappearing, as larger ocean-borne waves rolled over him. He had regained consciousness and slowly kicked his legs and arms in a mostly futile attempt at propulsion. With his arms fatigued nearly to the breaking point, Dirk pulled him alongside the barge, then tied off the air line on the rail. Reaching into the water, he grabbed Dahlgren by the collar and hoisted him aboard.

Dahlgren rolled onto the deck, then teetered to a sitting position. He clumsily pulled off his dive helmet and gazed at Dirk with blurry eyes. Rubbing the back of his neck with one hand, he winced as his fingers rolled over a baseball-sized lump.

"What in blazes happened down there?" he asked in a slurred voice.

"Before or after the airlift used your skull for batting practice?" Dirk replied.

"So that was the sucker that hit me. I remember getting yanked off the bottom, then my air went dry. I hit my pony tank and was preparing to ascend when the lights went out."

"Lucky thing you cranked on your emergency air. It took me a few minutes to ditch the airlift and get you to the surface amid the tow ride."

"Thanks for not throwing me back," Dahlgren smiled, his senses slowly returning. "So where's Summer? And why are we twenty miles from shore?"

he asked, noting the rugged coast of Hawaii receding in the distance.

"I don't know," Dirk said solemnly.

As Dahlgren rested, Dirk searched the shack and examined the rest of the barge for signs of Summer's disappearance. When he returned, Dahlgren could tell by the look on his face that the news was not good.

"Radio is gone. Zodiac is gone. Generator is missing. And all of our mooring lines were cut at deck level."

"And we're drifting to China. Pirates in Hawaii?"

"Or treasure hunters thinking we had a gold ship." Dirk stared back toward the island. He could no longer see the cove but knew the black ship was still there.

"The ship we heard roll in?" Dahlgren asked, his vision too fuzzy to see for himself.

"Yes."

"Then Summer must be aboard her."

Dirk silently nodded. If she was on the ship, then she might be all right. It was something to hope for. But hope was fleeing his grasp by the minute as they moved farther and farther away from land. They had to help themselves before they could help Summer. Drifting across the middle of the Pacific Ocean on a powerless barge, they could float for weeks before approaching a passing ship. Hope, Dirk thought grimly as he watched the island shrink in size, was for a quick means back to shore.

45

T HE LAST PLACE IN THE world that Rudi Gunn
wanted to be was back in the Russian-built truck
bouncing over a rough dirt road. But that's exactly
where he found himself. His back, rear, and legs all
ached from the constant jarring. With every rut and
pothole sending his teeth chattering, he was convinced
that the truck manufacturer had neglected to install
shocks and springs on the vehicle.

"The suspension on this thing must have been
designed by the Marquis de Sade," he grimaced as they
rolled over a harsh bump.

"Relax," Giordino grinned from behind the wheel.
"This is the smooth section of the highway."

Gunn turned a lighter shade of pale, observing that
the highway consisted of a weathered pair of dirt
tracks through the high steppe grass. They had
bounced across the open lands since midday, en route
to Borjin's compound of Xanadu. They had to rely on
Pitt and Giordino's collective memory to find their
way there and several times were forced to guess
which of the myriad of tracks to follow over the
rolling hills. Familiar landmarks confirmed they were
on the right route as they approached the small mountain range to the southeast that they knew housed the
estate.

"Another two hours, Rudi," Pitt said, gauging the

distance out the windshield, "and your troubles will be over."

Gunn silently shook his head, having the distinct feeling that his troubles were just beginning. A follow-up phone call from Hiram Yaeger before they departed Ulaanbaatar had added a new sense of urgency and gravity to their mission. The revelation that an odd series of earthquakes had been occurring in Mongolia was impossible to ignore.

"We're just scratching the surface on establishing a correlation, but this much we know," Yaeger said in a weary voice. "A series of earthquakes have rocked several areas in north-central Mongolia, as well as a dispersed area in and around the southern border of China. The earthquakes are unique from the norm in that their epicenters are relatively close to the surface. They mostly have been moderately sized quakes, as measured on the Richter scale, yet have produced high-intensity surface waves, which can be particularly destructive. Dr. McCammon has discovered that the foreshocks that preceded each quake are nearly uniform in intensity, which is inconsistent with a naturally occurring earthquake."

"So you think there is some sort of man-made activity that is inducing the earthquakes?" Pitt asked.

"As unlikely as it sounds, the seismological records seem to indicate as much."

"I know that oil drilling sometimes generates earthquakes, and underground nuclear testing has suspected links. I recall that when the old Rocky Flats Arsenal near Denver began injecting contaminated water deep into the ground, earthquakes shook the surrounding area. Have you determined if there is some sort of major drilling operation going on? Or perhaps some nuclear testing by Mongolia's neighbor to the south?"

"The epicenters in the northern part of the country have been located in a mountainous region east of Ulaanbaatar, a remote and rugged area, from what we've been able to determine. And a drilling-induced quake would not show the uniform preshock seismicity, according to Max. As far as the southern-area quakes, we would see it in the seismic profiles if a nuclear test blast had occurred."

"Then let me take a guess and say that brings us to the late Dr. von Wachter."

"Give that man a cookie," Yaeger said. "When Max told us that von Wachter had been killed in a landslide in the Khentii Mountains east of Ulaanbaatar, the light went on. The coincidence was too great. We concluded that his acoustic seismic array, or an offshoot of the technology, must have something to do with the earthquakes."

"That doesn't seem possible," Gunn said. "You would need a tremendous shock wave to set things off."

"That's the general perception," Yaeger replied. "But Dr. McCammon, working with Max and some other seismologists, has a theory on that. We spoke to a colleague of von Wachter's, who had been told by the doctor of his success at reflection imagery. The secret of his detailed imaging, if you will, was the ability to condense and packet the acoustic waves emitted into the ground. Normally transmitted sound waves behave like a pebble thrown into a pond, rippling out in all directions. Von Wachter developed a means of packeting the waves so that they remained concentrated in a narrow band as they penetrate the earth. The resulting waves, as they reflect back to the surface, apparently produce a crisp, detailed image far beyond any existing technology. Or so the colleague stated."

"So how do you get from a seismic image to an earthquake?" Gunn persisted.

"By two leaps of faith. First, that von Wachter's system produces a detailed image that visibly identifies active subterranean faults and fault lines. That is hardly a stretch of the imagination for shallow faults, which existing technologies can already detect."

"Okay, so von Wachter's seismic array can accurately pinpoint active faults beneath the surface," Gunn said. "You would still need to disturb those pressure points in some manner, say by drilling or with explosives, in order to produce a rupture and subsequent earthquake."

"That's our second leap. You are correct, the fault would need to be disturbed in order to trigger an earthquake. But a seismic wave is a seismic wave. The fault doesn't care if it comes from an explosion . . ."

". . . or an acoustic blast," Pitt said, finishing Yaeger's sentence. "It makes sense. The ten-foot hanging tripod is a transducer array system that generates the acoustic blast. From the size of the transducers and the power supply that goes with it, it looked to me like they could generate a sonic boom."

"If the acoustic blast is pinpointed at a fault line, the resulting vibrations from the seismic waves could induce a fracture, then, bammo, instant earthquake. It's just a theory, but McCammon and Max both agree it could work. Perhaps von Wachter's imaging technology was never intended as such but was discovered as an inadvertent side effect."

"Either way, it is in the hands of Borjin now. We've got to assume he possesses the technology and the ability to use it," Pitt said.

"You've already seen the effects up close," Yaeger said. "One of the quakes that matched the profile was at Lake Baikal. Perhaps by accident, it set off the underwater landslide, which created the seiche wave that nearly killed you. We now suspect their real target was an oil pipeline at the northern end of the lake, which they succeeded in rupturing."

"That explains why they tried to sink the *Vereshchagin* and destroy our computers. We told Borjin's sister, Tatiana, of our seismic studies in the lake. She must have realized that our equipment would have detected the man-made signals that preceded the earthquake," Giordino said.

"Signals that we could have traced to a vessel on the lake . . . the *Primorski*," Pitt added.

"So they've already put the technology to destructive use," Gunn said.

"It's worse than you think. We don't know the purpose or motivation behind the earthquakes in Mongolia and China. But the characteristics of those quakes exactly match the two recent Persian Gulf earthquakes that have devastated oil exports from the region."

The men in the hotel room were shocked. That the technology existed to induce an earthquake was startling enough. More unbelievable was that it was being used to instigate a near-global economic collapse, and that the trail led to the enigmatic mogul who lived in the hinterlands of Mongolia. Borjin's games of deception and destruction were becoming clearer to Pitt now. With his apparent discovery of oil reserves in Inner Mongolia, he was positioning himself to become the de facto oil king of East Asia. Pitt doubted his ambitions would end there.

"Has this been elevated?" Pitt asked.

"I've been in touch with Vice President Sandecker and have a briefing scheduled with him. The old bull wants to see something concrete. He promised he would have the president convene a National Security Council special session if the facts warrant immediate attention. I told him of your involvement, and he asked that you provide proof that the earthquakes can be specifically linked to Borjin." Admiral James Sandecker, now Vice President Sandecker, was Pitt's former boss at NUMA and still maintained a close relationship with Pitt and his staff at the marine agency.

"The proof," Pitt said, "is in the laboratory on Borjin's compound. He's got a seismic array sitting there, though I don't think it is the same one used at Baikal."

"Perhaps the Baikal device was flown to the Persian Gulf. We have to assume that there are at least two of the devices at large," Yaeger said.

"Three might be a safer bet. I guess you've proven by the Baikal and gulf quakes that they can trigger the device aboard a ship."

"Yes. The epicenters of both Persian Gulf quakes were located offshore."

"The ships might be the link," Pitt noted. "The vessel at Baikal had a moon pool and a derrick on the stern deck. You might start the hunt in the Persian Gulf for a similar utility or research vessel."

"It's a frightening prospect that they might be able to set off earthquakes all over the globe," Yaeger replied. "You boys be careful. I'm not even sure what the vice president can do to help you in Mongolia."

"Thanks, Hiram. You just track those ships down and we'll see about putting the finger on Borjin."

PITT DIDN'T wait to hear the results of Yaeger's briefing with Sandecker. He knew there was little that could be done in the short term. Though Mongolia and the U.S. had strong developing ties, it would take days, if not weeks, to generate government intervention. And the evidence against Borjin himself was circumstantial at best.

With the lives of Theresa and Wofford at stake, Pitt instead formulated a plan of infiltration with Giordino and Gunn, then set off for Xanadu. Borjin certainly wouldn't be expecting visitors, he knew. With a little stealth, and a large dose of luck, they just might be able to free Theresa and Wofford and escape with incriminating proof against Borjin.

The dust-caked truck crested a small hill, then Giordino applied the brakes as they approached a side road. The smoothly grated lane, fronted by a small gate, signaled the entryway to Borjin's retreat.

"The happy trail to Xanadu," Giordino stated.

"Let's hope the opposing traffic is light today," Pitt grimaced.

Dusk was drawing near, and Pitt figured it wasn't likely that anybody would be departing the compound late in the day, with Ulaanbaatar a four-hour drive away. There was still the risk that one of Borjin's horse-mounted patrols would be making the rounds beyond the gates, but there was little they could do about that.

Giordino turned onto the side trail and followed the empty road as it wound up and into the heart of the mountain range. After cresting a steep summit, Giordino slowed the truck as the river appeared alongside the road. An unusually strong summer rainstorm had just struck the mountaintop and the river raged with its powerful runoff. After days of encountering dry dust, Giordino was surprised to find the road turned muddy from the recent rains.

"If my memory serves, the compound is roughly two miles from the point here where the river first makes an appearance," Giordino said.

"It's the aqueduct we need to keep a sharp lookout for," Pitt replied.

Giordino drove on slowly, all eyes keeping a sharp lookout for both the aqueduct and wandering security patrols. Pitt finally spotted a large pipe sprouting from the river, which fed into the concrete-lined aqueduct. It was the landmark they were looking for that told them they were within a half mile of the compound.

Giordino found an opening off the road and pulled the truck into a strand of pine trees, then shut off the motor. The dust and mud-splattered truck blended well into the surroundings, and it would take an observant eye to spot them from the road.

Gunn looked nervously at his watch, noting it was a little before eight o'clock.

"What now?" he asked.

Pitt pulled out a thermos and poured a round of coffees.

"Relax and wait until dark," he replied, sipping at the steaming brew, "till it's time for the bogeymen to come out."

46

T HE STEADY TROPICAL BREEZE BLEW briskly across the barge as Dirk and Dahlgren stripped off their wet suits, shook off their fatigue, and set about getting back to land.

"This tub's too unwieldy to try and sail, even if we had a mast and sailcloth," Dahlgren said.

"Which we don't," Dirk replied. "First things first. Let's see if we can at least slow our drift rate."

"A sea anchor?"

"That's what I was thinking," Dirk said, walking over to one of the air compressors.

"A rather expensive anchor," Dahlgren noted, gathering up sections of their mooring lines.

They fashioned a thirty-foot line to the compressor, tying the opposite end to a stern bollard. Together they muscled the compressor to the side rail and dumped it over the edge. Dangling under the surface, the compressor would act as a makeshift sea anchor, partially slowing the wind-borne portion of their drift.

"One bite into that baby ought to keep the sharks away, too," Dahlgren joked.

"That's the least of our problems," Dirk replied. He scanned the horizon, searching for another vessel that they might be able to attract. But the seas around the far southwest end of the Hawaiian Island chain were completely empty.

"Looks like we're on our own."

The two men turned to the equipment on board the barge. With the Zodiac gone, there was no apparent means of ditching the barge and sailing to shore. A remaining compressor and water pump, plenty of dive gear, and some food and clothing were all they had left aboard.

Dahlgren rapped a knuckle against the side of the shack. "We could build a raft out of this," he said. "We've got some tools and plenty of rope."

Dirk considered the idea without enthusiasm. "It would take us a day to build, and we would have a pretty tough go running it against the wind and current. We're probably better off staying put and waiting for a passing vessel."

"Just trying to think of a way to get to Summer."

The same thought was on Dirk's mind. There was no question of their survival. They had plenty of food and water aboard. Once the *Mariana Explorer* returned to the cove and found the barge missing, an all-out search-and-rescue operation would ensue. They would be found inside of a week, he was certain. But how much time did Summer have?

The thought made him sick with dread, wondering what kind of people had abducted her. He cursed their predicament, sitting powerless as they drifted farther and farther away from shore. Pacing the deck, he caught sight of Summer's surfboard atop the shack and felt an added pang of helplessness. There had to be something they could do.

Then the light went on. It was right there in front of him. Or maybe Summer had willed him the answer.

A knowing beam crossed his face as he turned to Dahlgren.

"Not a raft, Jack," he said with a confident smile. "A catamaran."

THE GRAY-AND-WHITE herring gull flapped off the water with a loud squawk, angry at nearly being run over. Circling overhead, the bird warily eyed the offending watercraft skimming along the surface, then flew down and settled in its wake. The bird had never seen a sailing craft quite like it before. Nor had many people, for that matter.

Dirk's brainchild had been to construct a catamaran from his and Summer's surfboards, and the two men turned the crackpot idea into a workable design. The buoyant fiberglass boards made for a perfect pair of pontoons. Dahlgren came up with the idea of using their sleeping cots to attach as cross-members. Stripped of their fabric covering, two of the aluminum frames were laid crossways and secured to the boards with looped ropes, then sealed in duct tape for good measure.

"If we could drill or knock a small hole in the center of the boards, we could run a safety line through to ensure that the cross-members don't go dancing off in the first head wave," Dahlgren suggested.

"Are you crazy? These are vintage Greg Noll boards. Summer would kill us both if we damaged her board."

They took the third cot frame and rigged it into a mast supported by several guylines. Along with the fabric from the first two cots, they fashioned a sail from the bright blue material. In less than two hours, they had completed a miniaturized, bastardized version of a sailing cat.

"I wouldn't take her on the Sydney-to-Hobart yacht race, but I do believe she'll get us back to the Big Island," Dirk said, admiring the finished product.

"Yep," Dahlgren drawled. "Ugly as sin, yet perfectly functional. You have to love it."

The two men slipped back into their wet suits and attached a satchel of food and water to the mast, then launched the craft over the side. Cautiously climbing aboard, they checked its stability, then Dahlgren let loose a towline to the barge. The barge quickly floated away as the two men kicked their feet to angle the cat's sail against the wind. Dirk pulled the makeshift sail taut and tied it down to the rear cross-member. To his surprise, the tiny little craft nearly jumped ahead through the waves under the force of its rectangular blue sail.

The men each lay on one of the surfboards until they were satisfied that the cot frames would hold fast. Their rope work had been effective and the two boards attacked the waves as one, while the cross-members showed very little movement. Rising to a sitting position on each board, the men still got doused by the head waves.

"Feels like I'm water-skiing in a lawn chair,"

Dahlgren grinned as a large wave rolled over them.

The little cat held steady and skimmed quickly along, held true in part with the aid of a paddle that Dirk had rigged to the stern member as a rudder. Steering was limited, however, so they held a steady line for an hour or two before tacking. Dirk would drop the sail and then the two men would kick the nose of the craft around ninety degrees, then pick up the breeze on the opposite side of the sail.

"You might want to rethink that Sydney-to-Hobart race, ol' buddy. She sails like a dream," Dahlgren chided.

"True enough. Though I think I might want to pack a dry suit for that run."

They were both amazed at the crude efficiency of the craft. It wasn't long before the barge had completely disappeared from sight, while the Big Island appeared to grow larger on the horizon. As they settled in for the ride, Dirk's thoughts returned to Summer. As fraternal twins, they shared a close-knit bond that most siblings couldn't grasp. He could almost feel her presence, and he knew with certainty that she was alive. *Just hang on,* he silently willed her. *Help will soon be on the way.*

THE DARK lava slopes of Mauna Loa shimmered purple in the setting sun as they drew near the southwest shoreline of Hawaii. The jagged section of coast was largely uninhabited, the lava cliffs too foreboding for sea access but for the occasional black sand beach. Dahlgren pointed to a rocky point a mile or two to their south that protruded into the Pacific like a balled fist.

"Isn't that Humuhumu Point?"

"It sure looks like it," Dirk agreed, trying to identify the landmark in the fading light. "Which means Keliuli Bay is not far around the other side. We nearly hit the coast at the point we departed."

"A fine bit of surfboard navigation," Dahlgren said. He then peered up the coastline in the other direction. "That means that the nearest spot to pull in and contact the authorities would be Milolii."

"Which is roughly six miles away."

"A healthy ride. Unless one is of the mind to go the other direction and visit the boys that sent us on our merry ride."

Dahlgren knew the answer from the gleaming look in Dirk's eyes. Without saying a word, they tacked the catamaran to the southeast and headed down the coast toward Keliuli Bay.

～ 47 ～

TRAPPED INSIDE THE TINY STOREROOM, Summer languished as the afternoon crept by at a snail's pace. After scouring the room unsuccessfully for any tools or objects that might aid an escape, there was little to do but sit and wonder about the fate of Dirk and Jack. She finally pushed an empty crate beneath the porthole and fashioned a crude chair out of the rope coil, which allowed her to gaze out to sea in some comfort while capturing the ocean breeze on her face.

From her nook, she could detect a flurry of activity on the ship's stern deck. A rubber boat was lowered over the side, and she watched as several divers investigated the wreck site. Summer took small satisfaction in knowing they wouldn't procure any artifacts from the exposed portion of the wreck, which had already been picked clean during the survey and excavation.

After the divers returned to the ship, she saw and felt the drill ship be repositioned. Then around sundown the activity picked up again, as shouting voices and the whir of a crane drifted up from the deck below. She was startled when the door to the storeroom suddenly burst open and she was greeted by a bullnecked thug with crooked teeth. At his prodding, Summer followed him onto the bridge and over to a chart table, where Tong was examining a diagram under a bright swivel light. He looked up and gave her a condescending sneer as she approached.

"Miss Pitt. My divers have confirmed that your excavation was most thorough. And you did not lie. Most of the ship lies under the lava. There is work ahead to confirm her true designs."

He waited for a response, but Summer just gave him a cold stare, then raised her hands, still tied together at the wrist.

"Ah, yes. Very well, I suppose there is no place for you to run now," he said, nodding at Bull Neck. The underling pulled out a knife and quickly sliced through the ropes. Rubbing her wrists, Summer casually looked around the bridge. A lone helmsman stood by the forward window, gazing at a radarscope. The rest of the bridge was empty, save for her two immediate companions. Tong motioned for her to take a seat next to him, which she did hesitantly.

"Yes," Summer spoke quietly. "As we told you aboard the *Mariana Explorer*, which is due back any minute now, we have removed all of the artifacts from the lava-free sections of the wreck, which were in fact a fairly small quantity."

Tong smiled at Summer, then leaned over and put his hand on her knee. She wanted to slap him and run from the table, but she did neither. Instead, she just gave him an icy glare, fighting her hardest to hide her fear and revulsion.

"My dear, we passed the *Mariana Explorer* outside of Hilo," he leered. "She should be near her destination of Leleiwi Point by now, on the opposite side of the island," he added, laughing with a wicked grin.

"Why is this wreck so important to you?" she asked, hoping to steer his attention away from her.

"You really have no idea, do you?" he replied incredulously. Then he removed his hand from her knee and turned back to the chart of the table. It was a sonar image of the seabed, showing the site of the wreck excavation and the adjacent lava field. An X was marked on the chart near the center of the lava flow.

"Have you penetrated the lava field in your excavations?" he asked.

"No, of course not. I don't know what you are after,

Dr. Tong. The artifacts have been removed and the rest of the wreck is sealed under lava. There is nothing you or anyone else can do about that."

"Oh but you see there is, my dear, there is."

Summer stared at Tong with fear and curiosity, wondering what these mercenary looters had up their sleeve.

Tong left Summer under the guard's eye and marched onto the bridge wing and down a flight of stairs. Moving aft, he opened a side hatch and entered a large open bay. Racks of computers and electronic panels lined the walls, in a quantity that duplicated the test chamber at the family compound in Mongolia. A short man with steely eyes stood next to a large desk lined with color monitors, gazing over the shoulder at the chief operator's display. He was the same man who had headed up the aborted search efforts in the Khentii Mountains after killing the Russian seismic survey team. He nodded as Tong approached.

"We have identified a minor fault and have the coordinates targeted," he said in a husky voice. "It is in close proximity, but may not be sufficient to create the desired fissure in the lava field. What you ask for is an impossible request, I'm afraid. We should not waste time here but proceed to Alaska as your brother requested."

Tong did not let the affront bother him. "A day or two's delay is worth the gamble. If we are successful and it is in fact the royal Yuan vessel, then the mission to Alaska will appear a mere trifle in comparison."

The short man nodded in deferral. "I recommend four or five incremental detonations, then send the dive team down to check the results. That should tell us if there is any hope of rupturing the lava."

"Very well, proceed with the acoustic bursts. We will work through the night. If there is no success, then we will abandon the site in the morning and proceed to Alaska."

Tong stood back and let the technicians take over. As in the Persian Gulf, a seismic acoustic array was lowered through the ship's moon pool to the lava field below, where the framed and weighted device stood upright on the seafloor. A nearby subterranean fault was pinpointed and targeted, then the computer processors and signal amplifiers activated. With a click of the computer, the first massive electrical pulse went shooting through the three transducer arrays five fathoms below. A second later, the muffled blast of the acoustic shock wave resonated up to the ship with a subtle vibration.

Tong stood watching the blast with an expectant grin, hoping the voyage would bring two successes.

A MILE away, the low-riding catamaran skirted into the cove under a black nighttime sky. Dirk and Dahlgren resumed their prone positions on the surfboards and paddled their way along the high rocky shoreline. Spotting a shallow ledge just above the water level, they ground the boat beneath a nearly vertical wall of lava. Dirk stood and eyed the bright lights of the nearby drill ship, then dismantled the mast and sail to improve their stealth profile.

The two men sat and rested as they studied the ship, spent from their long day on the water. They were close enough to see a dozen or so men scurrying about the derrick on the illuminated stern deck. They watched as a tall tripod device was lowered through the deck into the water.

"Do you think they're actually trying to drill through the lava to get to the wreck?" Dahlgren postulated.

"Can't imagine what they would expect to recover that way."

The two men downed their supply of food and water and stretched their tired limbs. Slightly refortified, they were contemplating a plan of attack when a low-pitched rumble sounded near the ship. It was a muffled noise, as if emitted from deep within the ship or beneath it.

"What the Sam Hill was that?" Dahlgren drawled.

"Underwater explosion?" Dirk muttered. He looked at the water surface surrounding the ship, anticipating a rising burst of spray and bubbles, but nothing appeared. The surface water in the cove showed barely a ripple.

"Odd that it didn't affect the water. Must have come from within the ship," he said.

"Doesn't seem to be causing any excitement aboard," Dahlgren replied, noting that the deck crew had mostly disappeared and that the ship appeared calm. "How's about we take a closer look?'

They started to drag the catamaran back into the water when a second muffled boom erupted. Like the first, it made no impact to the waters in the middle of the cove. As the two men contemplated the strange detonation, a new, more thunderous noise began rumbling beneath their feet. The noise rose up as the ground began shaking violently, nearly knocking them off balance. Small chunks of loose lava and debris began raining down from the steep cliff face above them.

"Watch out!" Dirk shouted, spotting a nearby boulder break free and slide toward them. The two men barely dove out of the way as the rock rolled past them and over a corner of the catamaran before splashing into the water.

The ground vibrated for several more seconds before fading away. A few frothy waves stirred up by the earthquake slapped violently against the cliffside, then the waters of the cove fell calm.

"I thought the whole cliffside was going to drop on us," Dahlgren said.

"Might well yet," Dirk replied, eyeing the towering wall of lava warily. "Let's not hang around to find out."

Dahlgren stared toward the drill ship. "They created that earthquake," he said matter-of-factly. "It was triggered by the detonation."

"Let's hope it was accidental. They must be trying to rip up the lava field to get to the wreck."

"They can have it. Let's find Summer and get out of

here before they bring the whole island down on our heads."

They quickly threw the catamaran in the water and shimmied aboard. Quietly paddling away from the rocks, they moved cautiously toward the drill ship. Dahlgren eyed the board in front of him and noticed that the tip was flattened to the thickness of a pancake.

He didn't have the heart to tell Dirk it was his surfboard that was smashed by the falling rock.

~ 48 ~

SUMMER SAT AT THE WHEELHOUSE chart table contemplating a possible means of escape when the first acoustic blast was triggered. The muffled thump sounded directly beneath the ship, and she assumed like Dirk that it was some sort of explosion. The criminals must be trying to blast the lava off the wreck, she figured.

Bull Neck stared at her malevolently from across the table, baring a thin smile at the look of confusion and anger in Summer's face. His tobacco-stained teeth glared wider when a second underwater blast reverberated through the bridge a few minutes later.

Though Summer was repulsed by her captors, she became intrigued by their actions. Resorting to murder and wanton destruction of the wreck site meant they thought there was something of great value in her holds. Summer recalled Tong's interest in the porcelain plate and its possible royal markings. But he was interested in something more than pottery if he was blasting away lava to reach it. Gold or gemstones must their objective, she surmised.

As the second shock sent a slight vibration through the bridge, her thoughts turned again to escape. Getting off the ship was the first order of business if she was to have any chance at survival. Summer was a strong swimmer. If she could get into the water, she could easily make it to the rocky rim of the cove. Moving inland or down the coast would be no picnic, given the steep and jagged shoreline, but perhaps she could simply hide in the rocks until the *Mariana Explorer* returned. Whatever the difficulties, it was a better prospect than a continued voyage with the ship of thugs.

Alone on the bridge with just the helmsman and her brutish escort might be the best chance she got, she decided. The helmsman appeared to be little threat. He was nearly a boy, slight in stature and had a subservient look about him. He continually gawked at the six-foot-tall Summer as if she were Aphrodite.

She turned her attention to Bull Neck across the table. That's where the trouble lay. Violence was clearly no stranger to the brute with bad teeth. He had a look about him that said he would enjoy hurting a pretty woman and she shuddered at the thought. She would have to take him at his own game, but at least potentially she had the element of surprise on her side.

Mustering up the nerve, she finally told herself it was

now or never. Rising slowly from the table, she casually strode toward the front of the bridge as if stretching her legs and admiring the black view out the window. Bull Neck immediately mimicked her movements, stopping a few feet behind her.

Summer lingered a moment, taking a deep breath to relax, then turned toward the portside bridge wing. With a long stride, she quickly paced toward the open door as if catching an elevator. The guard immediately grunted at her to stop but she ignored the command. Striding light on her feet, she nearly made it out the door. The surprised thug jostled to catch up, bounding forward and placing a grimy hand on Summer's shoulder to stop her. The speed of her counter reaction surprised even herself.

Fully anticipating his lunge, she reached up and grabbed the man's wrist with both of her hands. She immediately spun to the side while shoving his wrist up and jamming his open palm backward toward the ground. Summer then backed into the man a step and dropped to one knee. The thug anticipated the attempted judo drop and hopped to the side, but she had him in a pain-inducing wristlock and could snap the bone with a flick of her hands. The angered man flailed with his free arm to strike Summer, but his blows lacked any leverage, only bruising her on the back. In response, she rose back to her feet and drove the heavier man backward with another twist to his hand. The man gasped in agony and flailed at Summer uselessly with his left arm. But the searing pain was too much and he finally staggered back. He crashed into the forward console near the helm, then fell to his knees incapacitated. As long as Summer maintained her grip, the burly thug was helpless.

A red light quickly flashed on the console as a slight shudder vibrated from the bowels of the ship. In his collision with the helm, Bull Neck had fallen against a button that deactivated the automatic ship thrusters, releasing them for manual control. The young helmsman, shocked at Summer's physical dominance over the larger man, backed away from the helm but chattered excitedly in Mongolian while pointing at the flashing light. With her heart pounding from the short engagement, Summer took a breath and glanced at the console.

The ship's controls were all inscribed in Mandarin, but beneath the factory markings somebody had taped plastic label translations in English. Summer glanced at the light and read the English translation below, which read, "Manual Thruster Control." An idea quickly chimed in Summer's head.

"Slight change of plans," she muttered to the uncomprehending helmsman. "We're going for a little ride first."

Summer scanned the adjacent controls until spotting a pair of dials marked PORT THRUSTER FORE and PORT THRUSTER AFT. She reached over with her free hand and turned the dials down to zero. Almost simultaneously, a third burst erupted beneath them as the acoustic array was triggered again. The blast was good timing,

Summer considered. The eruption masked the sound of the changing thrusters. With luck, the crew might not notice that the ship was now moving laterally across the cove. It would take only a few minutes until the ship would collide with the lava rocks lining the cove. The ensuing confusion ought to give her ample opportunity to escape.

"Back off," she barked at the nervous helmsman, who had crept closer to the controls. The young man jumped back from the helm, eyeing with fright the twisted look of agony on Bull Neck's face.

The drill ship moved quietly and smoothly across the cove, pushed evenly by the bank of starboard thrusters. Summer thought she heard a minor clunk near the waterline, but the ship continued on its sideways path through the dark, the black night offering little in the way of visibility. If she could just hold on a little longer, she thought, as her grip on the thug's hand grew weary.

She nervously counted the seconds, waiting for the grinding impact of the ship's hull against lava. But her heart sank when a different sound emerged from the open doorway. It was the sound of a man's voice.

"What is this, now?" the voice grumbled.

Turning with dread, she saw it was Tong. And in his hand, he held an automatic pistol aimed at Summer's heart.

49

THEY HAD KICKED AND PADDLED the mastless catamaran to within a hundred yards of the drill ship,
circling in toward the port bow in order to avoid the
glaring spotlights that illuminated the stern deck. As
they scanned the ship for nearby crewmen or lookouts,
Dahlgren suddenly leaned toward Dirk and whispered.

"Take a look at the bridge. Quick."

Dirk glanced up at the ship's forward superstructure.
Through the open side wing door, he caught a brief
glance of a person stepping by. A tall person with
flowing red hair that fell beneath the shoulders.

"Summer."

"I'm sure it is her," Dahlgren said.

A wave of relief fell over Dirk at seeing his sister still
alive. With renewed vigor, he kicked the catamaran
harder toward the ship. "Let's get aboard and find out
what's going on."

It was a task easier said than done. The ship's lowest
deck was still ten feet above them. And with the ship
held in position by its thrusters, there was no anchor
line in the water. Dirk hoped there might be an
imbedded steel ladder on the ship's stern, a feature not
uncommon on utility vessels.

They reached the bow and were quietly paddling aft
when the third detonation erupted below them. They
could feel a minor vibration from the ship and noticed

a few ripples in the water, but still no boiling torment of an underwater explosion. The lights around the moon pool illuminated the underside of the ship, and they could see a string of cables running down to the tripod device, which stood upright on the sea bottom.

They moved a few more feet down the ship's side when Dirk realized that the rumble of the nearby side thrusters had fallen silent. Before he knew what was happening, the ship's side hull smacked into the catamaran with a bang, then jerked the craft up on a building wave of water. The entire ship was moving laterally into them and quickly building speed. Sitting atop the side thrown high, Dirk could see that the catamaran was going to flip. The low surfboard was being pushed down and it was just a matter of seconds before the whole craft got sucked under the moving ship.

"Get off the board," Dirk yelled at Dahlgren.

He prepared to roll off the side himself when he caught sight of a line over his head. It was an unused mooring line that looped over the side of the ship, dangling down a few feet below the deck. With a desperate lunge, Dirk sprang up and off the twisting catamaran, barely grasping the rope with his left hand. Pulling his body around, he grabbed on with both hands, the line dropping taut under his weight to within a yard of the water.

He looked back to see the catamaran tumble down and under the advancing ship, swallowed beneath its side. Dahlgren was farther back, riding atop the cresting wave and swimming like a madman.

"Over here. I've got a line," Dirk implored in a low voice, hoping not to draw attention to their plight.

It was loud enough for Dahlgren to hear. He fought his way toward Dirk at a frantic pace that both men knew he could not sustain for long. The water seemed to swirl in all directions off the flat side of the ship, tugging Dahlgren one way, then another. When he finally surged close, Dirk reached out and grabbed a handful of his wet suit and yanked with all his strength. He pulled him far enough out of the water that Dahlgren was able to hook an arm over the line. He hung limp for a minute, catching his breath from the exertion.

"That was exciting," he muttered.

"And also the second time today that I've had to fish you out of the water," Dirk said. "If this continues, I must insist that you go on a diet."

"Ah'll take that under advisement," Dahlgren panted.

Resting for a moment, they proceeded to climb up opposite ends of the rope, emerging on deck a few yards apart. Though faint voices told them that a few crew members were on the stern, they were able to regroup undetected on the port beam. Dirk took a quick glance toward the high wall of lava that was quickly approaching in the darkness. There was clearly something amiss in the wheelhouse, as the ship was on a collision course and nobody seemed to be aware of it.

"Let's move," Dirk whispered. "I have a feeling we're not long aboard this ship."

As they started to move forward, another deep rumble began to sound in the distance. This time, the noise came from the shore.

FIVE THOUSAND miles away, the elevator doors opened on the tenth floor of the NUMA headquarters building and a sleepy-eyed Hiram Yaeger eased toward his computer room toting a thermos of Sumatra-blend coffee. His eyes widened at the sight of Dr. McCammon seated at the console, an anxious look on his face.

"You got the jump on me again, Phil?" Yaeger asked.

"Sorry for the early intrusion. Something just came over the wire from the National Earthquake Information Center that looks important."

He spread a seismogram across the table as Yaeger slid into an adjacent swivel chair.

"A large quake struck the Big Island of Hawaii just moments ago," McCammon said. "A little over 7.0 magnitude. And it was a shallow quake. Its epicenter was just a mile off shore, in a place called Keliuli Bay."

"What do the foreshocks look like?"

McCammon crinkled his brow. "Very similar to the ones we've seen before. Man-made in appearance. I just fed the data to Max for assessment. Hope you don't mind me taxing her talents while you were away," he added.

Max was standing near a computer bank with her arms crossed, looking deep in thought. She turned and smiled at McCammon.

"Dr. McCammon, I am delighted to assist you at any time. It is a pleasure to work with a gentleman," she added with a slight tweak of her nose in Yaeger's direction.

"Good morning to you, too, Max," Yaeger said. "Have you completed the analysis for Dr. McCammon?"

"Yes," Max nodded. "As Dr. McCammon can show you, there were two primary foreshocks recorded before the quake. Each had nearly identical seismic readings, though there was a slight increase in intensity with the second foreshock. And both foreshocks appear to have originated near the surface."

"How do they compare to the foreshocks recorded before the two Persian Gulf earthquakes?" Yaeger asked.

"The foreshocks show near identical signal characteristics to those that preceded the earthquakes at Ras Tanura and Kharg Island. Like those shocks, they originated near the surface."

Yaeger and McCammon looked at each other with grim silence.

"Hawaii," Yaeger finally said. "Why Hawaii?"

Then with a shake of the head, he added, "I think it's time we contact the White House."

50

SUMMER KEPT HER HANDS GRIPPED around Bull Neck's wrist, despite staring down the barrel of a Glock automatic pistol. Tong stood still in the doorway, trying to assess the situation. Behind him, a deep rumbling echoed across the water, but he ignored the sound while silently admiring Summer's skill at subduing one of his toughs.

On the opposite side of the bridge, the helmsman regained his tongue and nerve, while keeping a safe distance from Summer.

"The port thrusters are disabled," he shouted at Tong. "We will strike the rocks." Waving animatedly, he pointed toward the lava cliffs now materializing off the port beam.

Tong listened without quite comprehending, then followed the helmsman's motions and looked out the bridge wing. As he turned, an unseen pair of thick arms, clad in the black neoprene rubber material of a wet suit, reached out of the darkness and grabbed Tong around the torso. The Mongolian instinctively squeezed the trigger on his pistol, but the shot fired harmlessly through the roof of the bridge. Tong then turned to fight off his attacker by whipping the gun around as a club. But his movements came too late. His assailant had already taken a step forward, pitching Tong off balance. Tong staggered forward, trying to stay on his feet, but only added momentum to his captor. The assailant capitalized on the momentum with a gyrating lift, sweeping Tong completely off his feet. With a staggering lunge, he heaved Tong up and over the side railing, then let go. The stunned Mongolian let out a shriek as he disappeared over the side, his scream ending with a loud splash when he struck the water below.

On the bridge wing, the ex–calf roper Jack Dahlgren turned back toward the wheelhouse and gave Summer a quick wink and a grin. An instant later, Dirk rushed past him onto the bridge, wielding a gaff he had snared off the lower deck.

"You're all right," Summer gasped at the sight of the two men.

"Alive but soggy." Dirk smiled.

A jovial reunion was cut short by a jarring crash that knocked everyone to the deck. The four-thousand-ton drill ship, driven by the unabated power of its starboard thrusters, smashed broadside into the edge of the cove. The grinding impact of lava against steel echoed up from the waterline. The sharp volcanic rock sliced easily through the ship's hull, penetrating the lower hold in more than a dozen places. Seawater flooded in like a sieve, quickly tilting the ship to a port list. Somewhere in the darkened waters beneath the ship, the lifeless body of Tong swirled about, having found himself at the unfortunate point of impact between ship and shore.

The young helmsman was the first to find his feet,

striking a ship's alarm bell, then fleeing out the starboard wing. Summer finally let go of Bull Neck's wrist, but the thug was in no mood to fight when Dirk jabbed the pike into his ribs and prodded him out the port wing door. Outside, the sound of men's shouts competed with the continued rumbling.

"Why did I have a feeling you had a hand in piloting the ship?" Dirk asked his sister with a grin.

"Desperate measures," Summer replied.

"Company on the way," Dahlgren said, peering off the bridge wing. Two flights down, a band of armed men were rushing toward the bridge.

"Can you handle a swim?" Dirk asked, leading the way up the sloping deck toward the starboard wing.

"I'm fine," Summer replied. "A dip was actually on my agenda before you arrived."

The threesome quickly scrambled off the bridge and down to the lower deck, where yells and shouts from the crew peppered the night air. On the bow, several crewmen were preparing to lower a lifeboat, though the water was already washing over the deck of the listing port side. On the opposite beam, Summer wasted no time in further encounters with the crew, climbing over the rail and sliding down the angled ship's flank until plunging into the water. Dirk and Dahlgren followed her in and quickly swam away from the ship.

The rumbling from the shoreline intensified until yet another earthquake rocked the ground. Stronger than the prior jolt, the quake rattled the unstable sections of the lava cliff face. All along the cove, chunks of lava were jarred free, tumbling down the cliffsides and crashing into the water with explosive eruptions of sea and foam.

The cliff towering above the drill ship shared in the instability, the quake carving out a large slice of volcanic rock. The huge piece tumbled once, bounding out from the cliff in free space before dropping directly onto the ship. The spire sliced through the rear of the bridge, collapsing the deck onto the computer room below. The base of the rock mashed into the port beam amidships, flattening a wide section of the ship. Panicked crewman dove into the water to escape the carnage, while the lone lifeboat finally broke free of the bow.

The rumbling from the quake finally fell away, and, with it, the crashing of the loosened rocks. The night air was now ruffled by the gurgling sounds of the dying drill ship, punctuated by the occasional shout of a crewman. A hundred yards away, Dirk, Summer, and Dahlgren treaded water while watching the old vessel's final minutes.

"She'll make for a nice reef," Dahlgren noted as the ship tilted lower into the water. A few moments later, the drill ship slowly rolled to her side, sliding off the rocks and disappearing under the waves to the seafloor seventy feet below. Only her tall derrick, sheared off during the roll and lying against the cliff wall, gave a clue to the ship's final resting spot.

"What did they hope to extract from the wreck?" Dirk asked.

"I was never able to find out," Summer replied. "But they were going to the extreme of ripping open the lava field to get to it."

"While generating a couple of earthquakes in the process," Dahlgren added. "I'd like to know what kind of black box they were using for that."

"I'd just like to know who they are," Summer said.

The drone of an airplane approached from up the coast and shortly banked over the cove. It was a low-flying Coast Guard HC-130 Hercules turboprop, with its landing lights glaring brightly across the ocean's surface. The plane began circling overhead, buzzing the lifeboat and the mangled derrick, before expanding its search for survivors in the water. A few minutes later, a pair of Hawaii Air National Guard F-15s from Hickam Field on Oahu screeched by at low altitude, then lazily circled overhead in support of the Hercules. Unbeknown to the NUMA crew in the water, Hiram Yaeger had persuaded the vice president to investigate the scene when evidence of the second earthquake appeared. An immediate military sortie had been ordered to the site of the earthquakes' epicenter.

"That's a sight for sore eyes," Summer said as the Hercules continued to circle overhead. "I don't know why they're here, but I'm sure glad they are."

"I bet a cutter and some choppers are already on the way," Dirk said.

"Heck, we don't need a darn cutter to pick us up," Dahlgren suddenly said and chuckled. "We've got our own rescue vehicle."

He swam off toward a nearby object floating in the water, then returned a minute later. Behind him, he towed the mangled but still intact catamaran.

"The cat. It lives," Dirk said in astonishment.

Summer looked at the object, then declared with a frown, "My surfboard. What's it doing here?"

She looked quizzically at a mangled aluminum frame that was roped to Dirk's surfboard, which she noticed was pummeled in several places.

"And what happened to your board?"

"Sis," Dirk said with a shrug, "it's a long story."

~ 51 ~

THE HANDS OF THE CLOCK had stopped. Or so it seemed to Theresa. She knew that the constant glances at the ornate timepiece on the wall of Borjin's study only acted to slow its movements. The pending attempt at escape was making her nervous until she finally willed herself to stop staring at the clock and at least pretend to focus on the geological report in front of her.

It was the second straight day they had worked into the night, sequestered in the study with only a break for meals. Unbeknown to their captors, Theresa and Wofford had actually completed the drilling analysis hours before. They feigned continued work in hopes that their evening escort would be just one guard, as occurred the night before. One of the two guards stationed at the door had disappeared after their dinner was cleared away, raising their prospects for escape.

Theresa glanced at Wofford, who was digesting a seismic-imaging report with an almost-happy glow. He had marveled at the detailed imaging that von Wachter's technology had produced and devoured the profiles like a hog at Sunday brunch. Theresa quietly wished she could push the fear out of her mind as easily as Wofford seemed to.

The clock's hands were creeping past nine when Tatiana entered the study, dressed in black slacks and a matching light-wool sweater. Her long hair was combed neatly, and she wore a dazzling gold amulet around her neck. Her attractive external appearance, Wofford judged, was not enough to mask the cold and emotionless personality that ticked within.

"You have completed the analysis?" she asked bluntly.

"No," Wofford replied. "These additional profiles have impacted our earlier assumptions. We need to make further adjustments in order to optimize the drilling prospects."

"How long will this take?"

Wofford yawned deeply for effect. "Three or four hours should put us pretty close."

Tatiana glanced at the clock. "You may resume in the morning. I will expect you to complete the assessment and brief my brother at noon."

"Then we will be driven to Ulaanbaatar?" Theresa asked.

"Of course," Tatiana replied with a thin smile that bled insincerity.

Turning her back, she spoke briefly to the guard at the door then vanished down the hallway. Theresa and Wofford made a slow show of restacking the reports and cleaning up the worktable, stalling for time as best they could. Their best chance, perhaps their only chance, was if they remained alone and unseen with the guard.

After stalling as long as they dared without appearing obvious, they stood up and stepped toward the door. Wofford scooped up a stack of files to take with him, but the guard pointed at the reports and shook his head. Dropping the reports on the table, Wofford grabbed his cane and hobbled out the door with Theresa, the guard following on their heels.

Theresa's heart was racing as they walked down the long corridor. The house was quiet and the lights were turned low, lending the appearance that Tatiana and Borjin had retired to their private quarters in the south wing. The emptiness was broken when the short doorman popped out of a side room, holding a bottle of vodka. He gave a haughty glance to the captives, then scurried off toward the stairwell and the servants' quarters downstairs.

Wofford hobbled along with exaggerated effect, playing the role of harmless invalid to full effect. Reaching the end of the main corridor, he slowed at the turn, quickly scanning the side passages to ensure there were no other guards or servants about. Passing through the foyer, Wofford waited until they were close to their rooms along the north hall before making his move.

By all appearances, it was simply a careless act. He poked his cane forward and a little out of line, tapping the ground in front of Theresa's right foot. Stepping forth, she caught her foot on the cane and lurched forward in a fall worthy of a Hollywood stuntman. Wofford followed suit, staggering forward as if to fall, then kneeling down on his good leg. He looked over at Theresa, who was sprawled flat on the floor, barely moving. It was up to the guard now.

As Wofford had predicted, the Mongolian guard proved himself more gentleman than barbarian and reached down to help Theresa up. Wofford waited until the guard grabbed Theresa's arm with both hands, then he sprang like a cat. Driving off his good leg, he jumped up and into the guard, whipping his cane up by the stock in a pendulum motion. The curved handle of the cane struck the guard flush under the chin, popping his head back. The force of the blow snapped the wooden cane in two, the loose handle clattering across the marble floor. Wofford watched as the guard's eyes glazed over before he tumbled backward to the ground.

Theresa and Wofford remained motionless in the still household, nervously waiting for a charge of guards down the corridor. But all remained quiet, the only sound in Theresa's ears being the loud thumping in her chest.

"You all right?" Wofford whispered, bending over to help Theresa to her feet.

"I'm fine. Is he dead?" she asked, pointing with a tentative finger at the prone guard.

"No, he's just resting." Wofford pulled out a drapery cord he had purloined from his room and quickly bound the guard's hands and feet. With Theresa's help, he dragged the man along the polished floor to the first of their rooms and across the threshold. Yanking a pillowcase off the bed, he gagged the guard's mouth with it, then closed the door and locked him inside.

"You ready to earn your pyromania stripes?" he asked Theresa.

She nodded nervously, and together they crept to the main foyer.

"Good luck," he whispered, then slipped behind a side column to wait.

Theresa had insisted that she return to the study alone. It made more sense, she convinced Wofford. He moved too slow and noisily on his game leg, which placed them both in greater jeopardy.

Hugging one wall, she scurried down the main corridor as quickly as she dared, stepping lightly on the stone floor. The hallway was still empty and quiet, save for the ticking pendulum of an old clock. Theresa quickly reached the study and ducked through its open door, thankful the guard had turned the lights off on the way out. The dark room gave her cover from the illuminated hallway, and she allowed herself a deep breath to help reduce the anxiety.

Feeling her way across the familiar room, she reached the rear bookcase. Grabbing a stack of books at random, she knelt down and began quietly tearing the pages out in handfuls, crumpling the sheets as they broke free of the bindings. Accumulating a small mound of kindling, she then built a pyramid-shaped stack of books around it, cracking open the spines and facing the loose pages inward. When she was satisfied with her handiwork, she stood and probed around the back of the study until finding a small corner table. Perched on the tabletop was a cigar humidor and a crystal decanter filled with cognac. Theresa grabbed the decanter and began pouring its contents around the room, dumping the last quarter's worth onto her paper pyramid. She returned to the table and opened the humidor, feeling around inside until she found a box of matches that Wofford had discovered earlier. Gripping the matches tightly, she tiptoed to the front of the room and carefully peeked out the door. The main corridor was still quiet.

Creeping back to the book pile, she leaned over, lit one of the matches, and tossed it onto the cognac-soaked papers. There was no explosive ball of fire or immediate inferno, but just a small blue flame that traveled across the cognac-stained carpet like a river.

"Burn," Theresa urged aloud. "Burn this bloody prison down."

T HEY LOOKED LIKE BOGEYMEN, black-rubbery-
skinned ogres moving ghostlike through the trees.
Moving in silence, the three dark figures crossed the
road in a cumbersome gait, then inched their way up to
the side of the aqueduct. A few yards away, the rushing
waters of the mountain river echoed across the hillside
with a pounding fury. One of the figures stuck an arm
into the aqueduct, then flicked on a small penlight. The
clear water swirled past at an easy current, unlike the
raging river beyond. Pitt turned off the light, then
nodded at his companions.

They had waited an hour after sundown, until the
forested hilltop was nearly pitch-black. A late-rising
moon would allow them plenty of darkness for at least
another hour or two. Climbing into the back of the
truck with Giordino and Gunn, Pitt found their gear
orga-nized into three stacks.

"How deep is the aqueduct?" Gunn asked as he
slipped into a black DUI neoprene dry suit.

"No more than six feet," Pitt replied. "We could
probably get by with snorkels, but we'll use the
rebreathers in case we need to stay under a bit longer."

Pitt had already zipped up his dry suit and was slipping on a Dräger rebreather harness. Weighing just
over thirty pounds, the system allowed a diver to
breathe a contained supply of purified air recirculated

with carbon dioxide scrubbers. Replacing the large steel air tank with a small tank and pack, the rebreather nearly eliminated visible exhaust bubbles as well. Pitt strapped on a weighted dive belt, then attached a waterproof dive bag. Inside he had placed his shoes, two handheld radios, and his Colt .45. Climbing out of the truck, he surveyed the perimeter area, then ducked his head back into the rear.

"You gentlemen ready for a midnight swim?" he asked.

"I'm ready for a warm bath and a glass of bourbon," Gunn said.

"All set, just as soon as I load up my breaking-and-entering tools," Giordino replied. He rummaged around a toolbox until producing a hacksaw, monkey wrench, crowbar, and portable underwater torch, which he clipped to his belt, then hopped out the back. Gunn followed him out of the truck with an earnest look on his face.

The men made their way to the aqueduct in their black dry suits, each carrying a pair of lightweight dive fins. At the side of the V-shaped channel, Pitt took a final look around. The moon had yet to appear, and visibility under the partly cloudy skies was no more than thirty feet. They would be virtually undetected in the aqueduct.

"Try to keep your speed down. We'll pull out under the small bridge just inside the compound wall," Pitt said, pulling on his fins. He checked his regulator, then pulled down his mask and gently rolled into the aqueduct. Gunn splashed in a few seconds behind, then Giordino slipped in to follow from the tail position.

The bone-chilling river water would have frozen an unprotected man in minutes, but for Pitt in his dry suit, it felt like only a cool breeze. He'd nearly overheated hiking to the aqueduct in the insulated dry suit and was actually thankful for the cooling effect, despite the bitter chill around his mouth and face mask.

The gravity-induced water in the aqueduct flowed faster than he expected, so he shifted his feet forward and lay prone on his back. Lazily kicking his fins against the downward flow, he was able to slow his speed to a walking pace. The aqueduct followed the winding course of the road, and Pitt felt himself snake from one side to the other as he descended. The concrete channel was coated with a thin layer of algae, and Pitt bounced and slipped easily off its slimy walls.

It was almost a relaxing ride, he thought, gazing up at the sky overhead and the thick pine trees lining the bank. Then the trees gradually fell away, and the aqueduct channel straightened as it flowed through an open clearing. The dim glow of a light shined ahead, and Pitt could just make out the top of the compound wall rising in the distance.

There were actually two lights, one mounted atop the compound wall and another glowing from the interior of the guard hut. Inside the hut, a pair of duty guards sat chitchatting in front of a large video-monitor board. Live video feeds ran from nearly a dozen cameras mounted around the perimeter grounds, including one directly above the aqueduct. The grainy green night-vision images captured the occasional wolf or gazelle but little else in the remote setting. The studious guards refrained from the natural urge to sleep or play cards in order to relieve the boredom, knowing that Borjin had zero tolerance for indolent behavior.

At the sight of the compound, Pitt purged a shot of air from his dry suit, sinking his body a few inches below the surface. He craned his neck just before going under, spotting the dark image of Gunn floating a few yards behind him. He hoped Gunn would take the cue and submerge as well.

The water was clear enough that Pitt could easily detect the glow of the entry lights and the looming edifice of the compound wall. As he glided closer, he flattened his feet and bent his knees to brace for a possible impact. He wasn't disappointed. As he whizzed past the lights on his right, his finned feet collided with a metal grate that filtered large debris, and intruders, from passing through the aqueduct into the compound. Pitt quickly kicked to one side, then dropped to his knees and looked upstream. A black object quickly loomed up in front of him, and Pitt reached out and grabbed the murky Rudi Gunn a second before he collided with the grate. Not far behind, Giordino appeared, halting against the grate with his feet as Pitt had.

Inside the guard hut, the two security men sat oblivious to the three intruders in the aqueduct just a few feet away. Had they been monitoring the overhead video camera closely, they might have detected several dark objects in the water and gone to investigate. Had they even stepped outside their warm hut and listened attentively, they might have heard a muffled grinding noise coming from under the water. But the guards did neither.

The grate proved an easier obstacle than they expected. Rather than a tightly latticed plate that they would have had to cut through, the grate was a simple strand of vertical iron bars six inches apart. Feeling the way with his hands, Giordino grabbed the center bar and pulled himself to the bottom, where he attacked the base with his hacksaw. The bar was well rusted, and he was able to slice through it with only a few dozen strokes. He moved to the adjacent bar and cut through it with little additional effort. Bracing his feet on the floor of the aqueduct, he grabbed both bars just above the cuts and pulled up. With a burst from his burly thighs, he bent both bars up and away from the grate, creating a narrow passageway at the bottom of the aqueduct.

Gunn was resting on his knees when Giordino grabbed his arm and guided him to the access hole. Gunn quickly felt his way around the opening, then kicked through, twisting sideways to slip past the remaining bars. He turned and kicked against the flowing water until he detected the shapes of Pitt and Giordino slip through, then he relaxed and let the current pull him. They drifted through a concrete pipe passing under the compound wall, gliding through total darkness, until they spilled into the open aqueduct on the other side.

Gunn lazily kicked to the surface just in time to see the small footbridge passing over his head. He struggled to stop as an arm reached out of nowhere and yanked him to the side.

"End of the line, Rudi," he heard Pitt's voice whisper.

The steep and slippery sides of the aqueduct made for a difficult exit, but the men were able to pull themselves out by the bridge supports. Sitting in the shadow of the small bridge, they quickly stripped out of their dry suits and stashed them under the bridge footing. A scan of the compound revealed all was quiet, and no horse patrols were visible in the immediate area.

Gunn unzipped his dive bag and pulled out his glasses, shoes, and a small digital camera. Beside him, Pitt had retrieved his .45 and the two handheld radios. He made sure the volumes were turned down low, then clipped one to his belt and handed the other to Gunn.

"Sorry we don't have enough weapons to go around. You get in a bind, then give us a call," Pitt said.

"Believe me, I'll be in and out of there before anyone has a chance to blink."

Gunn's task was to sneak into the lab and photograph the seismic device, grabbing any documents he could along the way. If there were workers about, then he had Pitt's order to abandon the effort and wait by the bridge. Pitt and Giordino had the stickier objective of entering the main residence and locating Theresa and Wofford.

"We'll try to rendezvous here, unless one of us doesn't make it out cleanly. Then we'll head for the garage and one of Borjin's vehicles."

"Take this, Rudi," Giordino said, handing Gunn his crowbar. "In case the door is locked . . . or an over-inquisitive lab rat gives you trouble."

Gunn nodded with a humorless grin, then grabbed the crowbar and skulked off in the direction of the laboratory. He wanted to curse Pitt and Giordino for bringing him here, but he knew it was the expedient thing to do. They had to try to rescue Theresa and Wofford. And to simultaneously document the seismic array meant it was a three-man job. Heck, it was a hundred-man job, Gunn thought, glancing skyward in hopes that a company of special operations forces would magically parachute into the compound. But the heavens only offered a few scattered stars, struggling to twinkle through a light haze of clouds.

Gunn shook off the prayer and moved quickly across the open compound, dashing from shrub to shrub where cover availed itself. Only while crossing the entryway road did he slow down, crawling across the gravel road at nearly a snail's pace so as not to create an audible crunch underfoot. He followed Pitt's directions, moving past the illuminated open garage. The tinkling sound of banging tools told him that at least one person was up performing late-night mechanical duties.

He moved on toward the adjacent lab when the sudden braying of a horse froze him in his tracks. He could detect no movement around him and finally decided that the sound came from the horse stables at the end of the building. He studied the lab and was relieved to see only a few dim lights turned on on the lower level. Some brighter lights glimmered from the upstairs windows, and he heard the faint sound of music coming from above. The living quarters for the scientists who worked in the lab obviously were upstairs.

Checking again to see that no horse patrols were nearby, he crept to the glass entry door and pushed. To his surprise, the door was unlocked and opened into the test bay. He entered quickly and closed the door behind him. The bay was illuminated by a few desk lamps and buzzed with the hum of a dozen oscilloscopes but was otherwise empty. Gunn noticed a coatrack near the entrance and grabbed one of several white, long-sleeved lab coats hanging on the hooks, which he slipped over his own dark jacket. Might as well look the part, he thought, figuring it might be enough to deceive someone looking in from outside.

He walked to the main corridor, which stretched the length of the building, and noticed the lights were turned on in a few scattered offices. Fearful of being caught in the open hallway, he hesitated only a second, then stormed down the hall. He walked as fast as his legs could move without breaking into a run, keeping his eyes forward and face down. To the three other people still working at the late hour, he was just a quick blur past the window. All they could tell was that it was someone in a white lab coat, one of their comrades, probably on the way to the bathroom.

Gunn quickly reached the thick door at the end of the hall. With heavy breath and heart pounding, he flipped the latch and shoved. The massive door swung open quietly, revealing the huge anechoic chamber inside. Towering in the center of the room under a bright circle of overhead lights was von Wachter's acoustic seismic device, just as Pitt and Giordino had described it.

Thankful to find the chamber empty, Gunn climbed through the door and up onto the catwalk.

"We're halfway home," he muttered as he pulled out the digital camera. Noting the handheld radio on his belt, he silently wondered how Pitt and Giordino were faring.

— 53 —

IF YOU CAN PROVIDE A distraction from the front, then I should be able to slip around and surprise them from the side," Pitt whispered, studying the two guards standing like bookends on either side of the main residence door.

"A visit from my pet monkey should do the trick," Giordino replied, patting the heavy red pipe wrench dangling from his belt.

Pitt lowered his head then released the safety on his Colt. That they would have to subdue the front-entry guards in order to gain entry to the residence was a given. The challenge would be to do so without firing a shot and alerting the small army of security forces that Borjin kept on the compound.

The two men moved quietly along one of the reflecting canals that flowed toward the house, advancing in short quick bursts. They dropped to the ground and crawled to a rose bed that circled around the residence's main covered entryway. They were within clear sight of the guards as they peered through a bed of ivory yellow Damask roses.

The guards stood leaning against the residence in a relaxed state, accustomed to the uneventful grind of the night shift. Save for an evening walk or a late return from Ulaanbaatar, neither Borjin nor his sister were seldom seen after ten o'clock.

Pitt motioned for Giordino to stay put and give him five minutes to reposition himself. As Giordino nodded and hunkered down in the rose bed, Pitt silently looped his way around toward the far side of the entrance. Following the rose bed, he reached the entry drive and, as Gunn had done, gently stepped his way across the crushed gravel. The grounds were open from the road to the house, and Pitt moved quickly across the area, running low to the ground. The front face of the house was dotted with shrubs, and he ducked behind a large juniper bush, then peeked through it to the front porch. The guards stood as they were, oblivious to his movements in the dark just a few dozen yards away.

Creeping forward, he picked his way bush by bush

until reaching the edge of the covered portico. He kneeled to the ground, tightened his grip on the .45, and waited for Giordino to start the show.

Seeing no suspicious activities by the guards, Giordino gave Pitt an extra minute before moving from the rose bed. He had noted that the column supports for the portico roof offered a perfect blind spot from which to approach the porch. He inched to one side until one of the columns blocked his view of the guards, then stepped out of the rosebushes.

As he figured, if he couldn't see the guards, then they couldn't see him, and he angled his way right up to the back side of the column. The front door was less than twenty feet away, and he would have a clear shot at either guard. Without saying a word or making a sound, he casually stepped from behind the column, took aim at one of the guards, then hauled back and flung the pipe wrench like a tomahawk.

Both guards immediately saw the squat Italian step into view, but both were too startled to react. They stared in disbelief as a red object tumbled through the air at them, smashing one of them in the chest, cracking his ribs and knocking the breath out of him. The buffeted guard fell to his knees, wheezing a moan of shock and pain. The other guard instinctively stepped to his aid, but, seeing that his partner was not injured seriously, stood up to charge after Giordino. Only Giordino was no longer there, having ducked back behind the column. The guard stumbled toward the column, then stopped when he detected footsteps behind him. He turned in time to see the butt of Pitt's .45 strike his temple just beneath his helmet.

As the lights went out, Pitt managed to slip his hands under the man's arms and catch him before he collapsed to the ground. Giordino popped from behind the column and approached as Pitt dragged the unconscious guard toward some bushes. Pitt noticed a sudden glint in Giordino's eyes just before he yelled, "Down!"

Pitt ducked as Giordino took two steps and leaped directly toward him. Giordino stretched out and soared up and over Pitt, flying toward the first guard who now stood behind Pitt. The injured man had shaken off the blow from the wrench and staggered to his feet with a short knife, which he'd been preparing to plunge into Pitt's back. Giordino whipped his left arm forward midair, knocking the guard's knife to the side before tumbling into him with his full weight. They fell hard to the ground together, Giordino driving his weight into the man's chest. The pressure on the guard's broken ribs was unbearable and the wincing man gasped as he tried to suck in air. Giordino's right fist beat out the cry, crashing into the side of his neck and knocking him out before another warble left his mouth.

"That was a little close," Giordino gasped.

"Thanks for the leap of faith," Pitt said. He stood up and surveyed the compound. The grounds and house appeared quiet. If the guards had triggered an alarm, it wasn't apparent.

"Let's get these guys out of sight," Pitt said, dragging

his victim again toward the bushes. Giordino followed suit, grabbing his guard by the collar and pulling him backward.

"Hope the next shift change doesn't arrive soon," he huffed.

As Pitt deposited his body by the bushes, he turned to Giordino with a twinkle in his eye.

"I think it may arrive sooner than you think," he said with a knowing wink.

~ 54 ~

THERESA WATCHED AS THE TINY flames gobbled up the torn pages, then slowly grew higher and brighter as the fire danced over the open books. When it was clear that the fire would sustain itself, Theresa moved quickly to the study doorway, grabbing the file of reports that Wofford had earlier tried to take. Inside were samples of von Wachter's detailed imaging, along with the seismic fault maps and their unsettling red markings, including the chart of Alaska. Casting a glance back at the glowing yellow blaze beginning to erupt at the back of the room, Theresa turned and bolted down the corridor.

She moved in a shuffling run, fleeing as fast as she could without pounding the marble floor with a loud patter. Nervous adrenaline pumped through her veins as she dashed along, the prospect of escape at last a reality. The plan was simple. They would hide off the foyer until the fire drew the response of the front-entry guards. Slipping outside, they would try to commandeer a vehicle in the ensuing chaos and make a break at the front gate. The fire was now set, and Theresa felt a glimmer of confidence that their humble escape plan might actually work.

She slowed to a walk as she approached the foyer, searching for Wofford's hiding spot. He stood where she left him, standing beside a large fluted column. Seeing her approach, he looked at her with dread in his eyes. Theresa smiled in return, indicating with a nod that she had been successful. The normally jovial Wofford stood stone-still, his face in a tight grimace.

Then Tatiana stepped out from behind Wofford's shadow, waving a small automatic pistol at his back. With a menacing smile, she hissed at Theresa. "A beautiful evening for a walk, no?"

Theresa gasped as a chill ran down her spine like the Polar Express. Then seeing the wicked smile on Tatiana's lips, her fear was replaced with anger. If her time was at hand, she decided, then she wasn't going to go down meekly.

"I could not sleep," she tried bluffing. "We are so close to finishing the analysis. I convinced the guard to let us retrieve some of the reports so that we could work in our rooms," she said, holding up the file under her arm.

It was a game effort, but Theresa could see by the look in Tatiana's eyes that she was buying none of it.

"And where is the guard?"

"He is closing down the study."

A conveniently timed tumbling of books sounded from down the corridor, the work of the fire burning through a lower bookshelf. An inquisitive look crossed Tatiana's face and she took a step toward the center of the foyer to peek down the hall, keeping the gun pointed at Wofford. He glanced at Theresa, who nodded slightly in return.

As if in a rehearsed move, Theresa flung her bundled papers at Tatiana's face while Wofford lunged for her right arm, the one holding the pistol. With a snakelike quickness that surprised them both, Tatiana instantly spun in a half circle, sidestepping Wofford's reach as the tossed files bounced harmlessly off the back of her head. Spinning forward, she stepped toward Theresa and jammed the gun in her cheek while the cloud of papers was still fluttering to the ground.

"I should kill you now for that," she hissed into Theresa's ear while waving Wofford back with her other hand. "We shall see what other tricks you have been up to."

Prodding Theresa across the foyer with the muzzle of the gun, a Makarov PM automatic, she led her to the front door. Reaching around with her free hand, Tatiana flung the door open.

"Guards," she barked. "Come assist me."

The two guards on the porch, dressed in Mongol warrior attire with their tin helmets pulled low, burst through the door and quickly sized up the situation. The first guard stepped toward Wofford and produced a handgun, which he jammed into the geophysicist's ribs. The second guard, a shorter man, stepped up to Theresa and grabbed her tightly by the arm.

"Take her," Tatiana ordered, pulling the gun away from Theresa's face. The guard obliged by roughly jerking her away from Tatiana. A wave of hopelessness fell over Theresa as she looked at Wofford with despair. Oddly, the look of gloom had passed from Wofford's face and he looked at her with a gaze of hope. Then the viselike grip around her arm suddenly eased. In an unexpected move, the guard let go of Theresa's arm and suddenly grasped Tatiana by the wrist. With the flick of his powerful hand, he twisted Tatiana's wrist while applying a pincerlike squeeze to her hand. The gun slipped from her hand before she realized what was happening, the pistol clanging across the marble floor. The guard then jerked her wrist again and shoved, sending Tatiana sprawling to the floor with a shriek of pain.

"What on earth are you doing?" she cried, rising to her feet while cradling her bent wrist. For the first time, she looked earnestly at the guard, noticing that his sleeves dangled from a shirt two sizes too large. He smiled at her with a somehow-familiar grin that seemed out of place. She turned toward the other guard and saw that his uniform was way too small for his tall frame. And the gun he was holding was now aimed at her. Looking into the face, she gasped at the pene-trating green eyes that stared back at her with morbid delight.

"You!" she rasped, losing her voice in shock.

"You were expecting Chicken Delight?" Pitt replied, holding the .45 aimed at her belly.

"But you died in the desert," she stammered.

"No, that would be that phony monk friend of yours," Giordino replied, picking up the Makarov. Tatiana seemed to shrivel at the words.

"Al, you came back," Theresa said, nearly welling up at the turn of events. Giordino squeezed her hand.

"Sorry to rough you around on the way in," he said. Theresa nodded her head in understanding and squeezed his hand back.

"We are sure glad to see you, Mr. Pitt," Wofford said. "We had little hope of getting out of here in one piece."

"We saw what they did to Roy," Pitt said with a cold eye to Tatiana. "This place isn't exactly a Girl Scout camp. All the same, you saved us the trouble of trying to find you in this palace."

"I think it might be a good time to make an exit, before any real palace guards show up," Giordino added, escorting Theresa toward the door.

"Wait," she said. "The seismic reports. We found evidence that they may try to disrupt tectonic fault zones in the Persian Gulf and Alaska."

"This is absurd," Tatiana declared.

"No one is talking to you, sister," Giordino replied, pointing the Makarov in her direction.

"It's true," Wofford said, bending down and helping Theresa scoop up the papers that littered the floor. "They designated the destruction of the oil pipeline at the northern end of Lake Baikal that somehow triggered the seiche wave. They've also targeted specific faults in the Persian Gulf, and one near the Alaska Pipeline as well."

"They've already struck the gulf successfully, I'm afraid," Pitt said.

"The data should fill in nicely with the photos that Rudi is taking as we speak," Giordino added.

Pitt saw the quizzical looks on Theresa and Wofford's faces.

"An acoustic seismic array sits in the lab across the way. Used to trigger earthquakes, we believe, which have already created extensive damage to oil port facilities in the Persian Gulf. Your documents would appear to support the contention. We didn't know Alaska was next on the hit list."

Theresa stood up with an armload of documents when a deafeningly shrill pierced the hallway. The growing blaze of burning books had finally triggered a smoke detector outside the study, its alarm echoing throughout the residence.

"We set fire to the study," Theresa explained. "Hoped to use it as a diversion for Jim and I to escape."

"Maybe we still can," Pitt replied, "but let's not wait for the fire brigade to arrive."

He quickly stepped through the open door as Theresa and Wofford followed behind. Tatiana edged toward the back wall, trying to slip behind in the mass exit. Giordino smiled at her attempt, walking over and grabbing a fistful of her sweater.

"I'm afraid you'll be leaving with us, darling. Do you care to walk or fly?" he asked, shoving her roughly toward the door. Tatiana turned and snarled at him, then begrudgingly moved through the doorway.

Outside, Pitt quickly led the group across the portico to the outlying support columns, then stopped. The sound of galloping horse hooves far to his right told him a patrol near the northern edge of the residence had heard the alarm and was charging toward the entrance. Ahead and to his left, a yelling and commotion was erupting near the stables and security quarters. Pitt could see lanterns and flashlights hurrying toward the residence, carried by guards woken by the alarm and rushing there on foot.

Pitt silently cursed that Theresa had set fire to the residence. If they had gotten away a few minutes earlier, the confusion might have played into their hands. But now the entire security force was roused and rushing toward their position. Their only option was to lay low and hope the guards surged past them.

Pitt motioned toward the rosebushes behind the columns. "Everybody get down flat. We'll wait for them to enter the house, then we'll move on," he said in a low voice.

Theresa and Wofford quickly dove to the ground and slithered behind a row of the thorny flowers. Giordino shoved Tatiana behind a budding bush, then clasped a hand over her mouth. With his other hand, he motioned the Makarov's barrel to his lips and said, "Shhh."

Pitt kneeled down and pulled the handheld radio

from his belt then held it to his lips.

"Rudi, can you hear me?" he said quietly.

"I'm all ears," came an equally hushed reply.

"We're on our way out, but there's a party starting up. We'll have to meet up on the fly, in about five or ten minutes."

"I'll wrap up and head toward the garage. Out."

Pitt hit the ground as a trio of guards from the stables approached. Running on foot, they bolted by a few feet from Pitt, barely noticing that the entry guards were nowhere in sight before rushing into the residence. Only a few dim lights were turned on near the door, leaving Pitt and the others hidden in the covering darkness.

The horse patrol was still fifty yards away. Pitt contemplated moving past the rosebushes and into the compound grounds before they got closer, then thought better of it. The horse patrol wouldn't expect anyone lying around the entrance. With luck, Theresa's fire would be raging sufficiently that they would all be pressed into firefighting duty.

The horse patrol, numbering eight men, had been galloping fast toward the front entry when they suddenly pulled up hard on their reins as they reached the gravel drive. An uneasy feeling came over Pitt as he watched the horsemen fan out in a large semicircle at the edge of the portico, then stop. Two of the horses snorted in uneasiness as the riders held them still. Inside the residence, the ringing alarm suddenly fell silent as four additional guards approached on foot from the opposite side and stopped short of the drive. The fire was either raging out of control, or as Pitt feared, it had been contained before it could spread.

The answer came with a blinding glare of white light. With the flick of a switch, a dozen floodlights mounted in the portico's rafters popped on in a bright burst. The light from the halogen bulbs spilled over onto the surrounding grounds. Clearly illuminated under the glare were the bodies of Pitt and the others, stretched out beneath the rosebushes.

Pitt tightened the grip on his .45 and casually took aim at the nearest horseman. The guards on foot were positioned farther away and did not appear to be armed. It was a different story with the horsemen. In addition to their lethal bows and arrows, Pitt was chagrined to see they all carried rifles, now shouldered and aimed in their direction. Though he noticed Giordino now had the Makarov aimed at a horseman as well, their odds were not at all attractive.

The gunfight became moot when a flurry of footsteps echoed from the marble foyer and four bodies burst onto the porch. The three guards who had rushed across the compound took a few steps out, then stopped and stared at Pitt and the others. Smoke and ashes blackened their bright orange tunics, but there was no panic in the men's eyes. Of more concern to Pitt were the AK-74 assault rifles they now cradled in their arms.

Busting past the gunman was the fourth man, who charged to the center of the driveway as if he owned it, which he well did. Borjin was dressed in a blue silk robe, which contrasted with his beet red face flush with anger. He glared to the side bushes, where the stripped and unconscious bodies of the door guards lie visible under the bright lights. Borjin turned to Pitt and the others with an apoplectic gaze. Then in a measured voice, he growled, "I will have retribution for this."

— 55 —

A WAVE OF CURIOSITY REPLACED the fear surging through Gunn's body when he entered the anechoic chamber. He had seen soundproof test chambers before, but none filled with the array of high-powered electronic gear packed into this high-ceilinged compartment. Row after row of computers and power racks lined the outer platform, reminding him of the computer-processing equipment jammed into a Trident submarine. Of greater interest was the odd appendage in the middle of the room, the three conjoined tubes that towered ten feet high. Gunn stared at the acoustic transducers, a chill running through him at the thought of Yaeger's assertion that it could create an earthquake.

The chill quickly turned to sweat as he realized the temperature in the chamber was about 100 degrees. He was surprised to find that the equipment in the chamber was on and running, engaged in a preprogrammed test of some sort. The heat generated from the assembly of power supplies running the electronics had turned the chamber into a dry sauna. Stripping off his borrowed lab coat and black foul-weather jacket beneath, he pulled out the digital camera and climbed up onto the center platform. Starting at the far end, he hurriedly began photographing each piece of equipment. Sweating profusely, he stepped to the entrance and opened the door, allowing a blast of cool air to gush through. Knowing he could better hear approaching footsteps, and also receive calls on his radio, he left the door open and resumed his photography.

Gunn stopped when he reached a large console fronted by a plush leather chair. It was the system operator's control station for activating the seismic array. Gunn slipped into the chair and studied the brightly colored flat-screen monitor that faced him. A pop-up message was centered on the screen with the words TEST RUNNING flashing in German. Gunn had a rudimentary knowledge of German, having spent several months with a German research team studying the sunken World War II liner *Wilhelm Gustloff*, and deciphered the ongoing software test. He clicked on a box marked ABORT and a vivid abstract image suddenly popped onto the screen.

The monitor showed a three-dimensional image of sediment layers, each colored in a different shade of yellow-gold. A scale to one side indicated five hundred meters, and Gunn correctly guessed that it was a stratigraphic image of the sediment directly beneath the lab. Gunn reached for a trackball mouse on the table and slid it toward him. As the cursor moved on the screen, a loud ticking noise emitted from the towering transducers a few feet away. The ticking quickly stopped as the monitor readjusted to a new subterranean image. Gunn noticed that the side scale now read five hundred fifty meters.

Von Wachter had indeed perfected his seismic-imaging system to a remarkable degree. Gunn wheeled the mouse back and forth, admiring a crystal clear image of the sedimentary layers hundreds of feet below him. Alongside him, the acoustic array ticked away as an electric motor rotated the mechanism and its changing angle of penetration. Like a kid with a computer game, Gunn became temporarily engrossed in the images produced by the device, studying the aberrations in the ground layers. He barely noticed when Pitt called him on the radio, jolting him to rush toward the open chamber door so as not to lose the signal inside the protected chamber.

Signing off the radio, he took a quick peek down the hallway. Seeing no signs of life, he scurried back to the platform and finished taking pictures of the seismic array and ancillary equipment. He slipped on his jacket and started to leave, then rummaged through some documents and papers he saw on the console. He found what appeared to be the operator's manual, a thick booklet clamped to a miniature stainless steel clipboard. The front pages were missing, presumably torn off by Pitt on his last visit. Gunn stuffed the manual and clipboard into a zippered chest pocket on his jacket, then made for the door. He was just about to exit when a voice erupted from his radio.

His heart dropped when he realized the voice was not Pitt's. And what it had to say meant that all was lost.

— 56 —

PITT ROSE SLOWLY TO HIS feet, the Colt held down at his side so as not to incite any trigger-happy fingers from Borjin's machine-gun-toting guards. He waited until Giordino jerked Tatiana to her feet and turned her toward her brother, the Makarov held clearly visible against her ear. Tatiana tried futilely to break away from his grip but to no avail.

"Let me go, you pig. You are all dead men," she hissed.

Giordino simply smiled as he grabbed a fistful of her hair and forced the muzzle of the Makarov deeper into her ear. Tatiana winced with pain, then gave up the struggle.

With all eyes on Tatiana, Pitt slowly raised the Colt until it was pointed at Borjin's midsection. With his left hand, he unobtrusively brushed the TRANSMIT button on his radio, hoping to clue Gunn in to their predicament.

Borjin gazed at his sister's peril with a look of mild disinterest. When he studied Pitt and Giordino with a closer scrutiny, his eyes suddenly flared in recognition.

"You," he cried, then regained his composure. "You

survived your ride in the desert to trespass on my property again? Why do you risk such foolishness? Simply for the lives of your friends?" He nodded toward Theresa and Wofford, who had wisely moved behind Tatiana.

"We came to put an end to your earthquakes and your murdering rampage for oil," Pitt replied. "We came for our friends. And we came for Genghis."

Pitt's reference to the earthquakes barely registered a reaction. But his mention of the Mongol warlord's name nearly sent a tremor through Borjin. His eyes creased together as his face turned red, and Pitt half expected flames to spring from his lips.

"Death will greet you first," he spat, nodding at the guards surrounding him.

"Perhaps. But you and your sister will accompany me on the journey."

Borjin took a hard look at the rugged man who threatened him so boldly. He could tell by the steely resolve in Pitt's eyes that he had stared down death many times before. Like his own idol, Genghis, he showed no apparent fear in battle. But he suspected Pitt had a weakness, one that he could play to his advantage to be rid of him once and for all.

"My men will cut you down in an instant," he threatened back. "But I do not wish to see my sister die. Release Tatiana, and your friends are free to go."

"No," Theresa protested, stepping in front of Giordino. "You must let us all go free." Then in a whisper to Giordino, she said, "We will not allow you to stay behind and be murdered."

"You are in no position to make demands," Borjin replied. He pretended to pace back and forth, but Pitt could tell he was trying to remove himself from the field of fire. Pitt tightened the grip on his .45 as Borjin stepped behind one of the guards, then halted.

The boom erupted like a sledgehammer to an iron kettle only with an explosive echo. But the blast didn't originate from any of the weapons pointed around the entryway. Instead, the sound rumbled from across the compound, in the direction of the laboratory. Twenty seconds crept by with everyone frozen in confusion when a second boom erupted, identical to the first. Tatiana was the first to recognize the sound. With a foreboding sense of dread in her voice, she shouted to her brother.

"It is von Wachter's device. Someone has activated it."

Like the thundering crash of a temple gong, a third boom erupted, drowning her words as the echo shook from the laboratory.

GUNN HAD shown remarkable cool under pressure. He knew Pitt would have wanted him to take the photographic evidence and escape the compound, contact the authorities, and expose Borjin to the court of world opinion. But he just couldn't walk away and leave his friends to die. Armed with nothing more than a crowbar, he also knew that rushing to their side would result in little more than his own death. But perhaps he thought, just perhaps, he could turn Borjin's demon against its master.

Gunn stepped back into the anechoic chamber and pulled the door shut behind him, then raced to the console. He was at once thankful that the system had been left on and that he had taken a few minutes earlier to joyride with the controls. Jumping into the operator's seat, he grabbed the trackball mouse and quickly scrolled down, searching for an image he had seen earlier. As the tripod device ticked and hummed to follow the commands, Gunn frantically bounced the cursor about. Finally, he eyed the stratum that he was looking for. It was an odd jump in the sedimentary line, dividing two layers of sediment with a distinct cut. Around the cut were a dozen or so round blemishes, which were actually cracks in the rock. He had no idea if it was actually a fault, or even if there was any pressure built up at the point. Perhaps with the acoustic seismic array, it didn't really matter anyway. Gunn didn't have the answers but rationalized it was the best prospect he had, under the circumstances.

He guided the cursor to the crown of the sedimentary cut and clicked the button. An illuminated crosshair began flashing over the indicated point as the tripod ticked again. Gunn rolled the cursor to the top of the screen and quickly scrolled through a series of drop-down menus. Sweat began dripping off his forehead as he worked frantically in the hot chamber. Each new command was in German, the software having been created by von Wachter and his team. Gunn desperately tapped the recesses of his brain, trying to resurrect forgotten words and phrases. He recalled Yaeger's report that von Wachter was using concentrated packets of high-frequency waves in his imaging, so he selected the highest-frequency setting. He guessed WEITE meant amplitude, and chose the highest power level, then selected a repetitive cycle interval of twenty seconds. A flashing red box appeared with AKTIVIEREN in bold letters. Gunn mentally crossed his fingers and clicked the button.

At first, nothing happened. Then a long sequence of software script rolled across the monitor at rapid speed. It might have been Gunn's heightened senses, but the power amplifiers and computers physically seemed to come alive in the chamber, bursting with a low hum. Wiping his brow, he was certain the room temperature had increased by at least ten degrees. He noticed the tripod was ticking again, but at a higher crescendo. Then with a flicker of the lights, an explosive boom erupted from the inverted tip of the tripod. It felt like a bolt of lightning had struck just inches away. The acoustic blast shook the building, nearly tossing Gunn from his chair. He staggered toward the door with his ears ringing, then stopped and gazed at the room in dismay.

The anechoic chamber. It was designed to absorb sound waves. Even the concentrated blasts erupting from the acoustic array would be seriously diluted by the sound-deadening floor panels. His effort at activating the system was for naught.

Gunn jumped off the catwalk onto the foam floor and vaulted over to the base of the tripod. He anticipated the next blast and covered his ears as a second acoustic burst was fired from the transducer tubes, expounding with a deafening bang.

The thunderclap knocked Gunn to his knees, but he quickly recovered and crawled to the base of the tripod. Frantically tearing at the foam floorboards beneath the device, he counted out loud to twenty in anticipation of the next blast. Luck was on his side, as the foam panels were not attached to the floor and lifted off easily in large sections. Beneath the foam, the floor appeared tiled, but Gunn saw from the dull silver finish that the tiles were made of lead as an extra sound deadener. Gunn was at the count of eleven when he lunged at the console and grabbed the crowbar he had left on the table. Jamming its blade into a floor seam, he quickly pried up one of the heavy tiles and muscled it aside. Ignoring his count of eighteen, he dove down and quickly ripped away three other lead plates, which together with the first had formed a square beneath the business end of the acoustic array.

Gunn had counted too fast during his adrenaline rush to clear the floor and stepped back just as the third acoustic blast fired. Jamming his palms to his ears, he looked down as saw that the device was now firing through a thin layer of concrete that had formed the foundation for the building.

"Nothing I can do about that," he muttered after the

blast passed, and he made his way to the door.

Tugging open the heavy door, he half expected to face a legion of armed guards waiting for him to exit. But the guards had all rushed to the residence, at least temporarily. Instead, he saw a small group of scientists, some in pajamas, swarming at the opposite end of the hallway. Stepping through the chamber door, Gunn was met by a yell from one of the scientists, spurring the angry mob to charge toward him. With just a few yards of leeway, Gunn rushed to the nearest office on his right and stepped in.

Like most of the offices in the lab building, it was sparsely decorated, with a gray metal desk centered on one wall and a lab table covered with electronics to the side. None of the furnishings mattered to Gunn. The only thing of importance was the small picture window that faced the compound grounds. Stepping to the window, he silently thanked Giordino for loaning him the crowbar now gripped tightly in his hands. With a powerful thrust, he jabbed the blunt end of the bar into a corner of the window, shattering the glass. Scraping the broken shards off the sill, he dove out the window. His body barely hit the ground when the fourth and final blast emitted from the acoustic array, the impact much less violent to Gunn now that he was outside the building.

A chorus of frantic yells could be heard through the broken window as the scientists ignored Gunn and rushed into the chamber. He knew they would deactivate the system before another blast would strike. His rash gamble at inducing an earthquake was finished. So too, he thought with dread, was his chance at saving the lives of Pitt and Giordino.

∽ 57 ∽

WHEN THE SOUND OF THE second blast echoed across the compound, Borjin ordered two of the mounted guards to go investigate. They quickly galloped across the darkened compound as a slight rumble echoed in the distance. The deep boom of a third seismic blast quickly drowned out their pounding hoofbeats and the faraway rumble as well.

"You have brought friends as well?" Borjin sneered at Pitt.

"Enough to close you down for good," Pitt replied.

"Then they shall die with you."

A crash of shattering glass sounded from the laboratory, followed by the fourth detonation of the acoustic seismic array. Then all fell silent.

"It would appear that your friends have been introduced to my guards," Borjin smiled.

The sneer was still on his face when another distant rumble reverberated off the hills like the sound of approaching thunder. Only this time, the rumble continued to resonate, growing with the intensity of an approaching avalanche. Outside the compound walls, a pack of wolves nearby began howling in mournful unison. The horses inside the compound picked up the cue and began neighing loudly, in nervous anticipation of the pending cataclysm that their human counterparts could not foresee.

A thousand meters below the surface, a trio of condensed sound waves, fired from the three transducers, converged at the angled fracture targeted by Gunn. The sedimentary cut was indeed an ancient oblique fault. The first two blasts of the seismic array, dissipated by the chamber's shielding, had struck the fault with only a minor pulse. The third blast, however, hit with the full power of the convergent shock waves. Though the sediment held firm, the seismic waves rocked with a vibrating force that rattled the fault line. When the fourth blast arrived, it would prove enough to break the camel's back.

A fault line, by nature, is a rock fracture prone to movement. Most earthquakes are the result of energy released from a slippage in a fault zone. Pressure builds up at a point along the fault due to underlying tectonic movement until a sudden slippage relieves the strain. The slippage reverberates to the surface, sending out a variety of shock waves that create a surface-rattling earthquake.

For the fault beneath the Mongolian mountainside, the fourth and final barrage of acoustic waves struck like a torpedo. The seismic vibrations jolted the fracture, causing it to slip in both vertical and horizontal directions. The buckle was small, just a few inches spread across a quarter-mile rift, but because it was close to the surface the wave impact was dramatic.

The shock waves burst through the ground in a sinister turmoil of vertical and horizontal shaking. By the Richter scale, the resulting quake would measure a 7.5 magnitude. But the scale didn't reflect the true intensity on the surface, where the shaking felt ten times more powerful to those standing on the ground.

For Pitt and the others, the motion was preceded by the low rumble, which grew in intensity until it sounded as if a freight train was rumbling by underground. Then the shock waves reached the surface and the ground beneath their feet began to gyrate. At first, the ground shook back and forth. Then it seemed to break loose in all directions, steadily increasing in force.

Pitt and the guards eyed each other warily as the quake started, but the violent shaking soon tossed everyone off their feet. Pitt watched as one of the guards fell backward onto the porch steps, his machine gun sprawling at arm's length. Pitt didn't fight to stay standing but instead dove to the ground, throwing his arms and the .45 out in front of him. The smaller, lighter weapon gave him a sudden advantage over the guards, and he zeroed in on the closest man still standing and squeezed the trigger. Despite the vibration, Pitt hit his target, and the man sprawled backward to the ground. Pitt quickly swept his gun toward the second guard, who was crouching on his knees to stabilize himself. Pitt fired three times in succession as the guard let loose a return burst from his AK-74. Two of Pitt's three shots struck home, killing the guard instantly while the guard's errant burst peppered the ground to Pitt's left side.

Pitt immediately swung his muzzle toward the first guard, who had fallen down just in front of Borjin. The Mongolian tycoon had scrambled up the steps at the first gunshot and ducked behind the door as Pitt turned in that direction. The guard was scrambling after Borjin and just reached the doorstep when Pitt fired once. Another shot rang out behind him, fired by Giordino after he body-slammed Tatiana to the ground. The shaking was at its zenith and proved too great for either man to aim accurately. With a staggering lunge, the guard dove through the residence door unscathed.

At the other end of the driveway, the mounted guards had been of little concern. A chorus of snorts and whinnies still blared from the horses, who had no conception of why the ground was shaking beneath their hooves. Three of the terrified horses reared repeatedly, their riders clutching the reins for dear life. A fourth horse up and bolted, galloping full tilt across the drive, stomping the bodies of the dead guards as it streaked petrified toward the horse corral.

The violent bucking lasted for nearly a minute, making the prone observers feel as if their bodies were being tossed into the air. Inside Borjin's residence, there was a chaotic crashing of glass and fixtures as the lights began flickering out. Across the compound, a lone alarm wailed feebly from inside the lab building.

And then it ended. The rumbling ceased, the shaking gradually fell away, and an eerie calm fell over the compound. The lights around the portico had fallen dead, casting Pitt and the others in a thankful darkness. But he knew the gun battle was far from over.

Gazing at the others, he saw Theresa and Wofford were unhurt, but that a streak of red flowed down Giordino's left leg. Giordino perused the wound with a look of minor inconvenience.

"Sorry, boss. Caught a ricochet from Machine Gun Kelly. No bones, though."

Pitt nodded, then turned toward the horsemen, whose mounts were now quieting.

"Take cover behind the support columns. Quick," Pitt directed. He barely spoke the words when a rifleshot rang out from one of the horsemen.

With a slight limp, Giordino dragged Tatiana to the base of one of the columns while Theresa and Wofford hunkered down behind an adjacent column. Pitt fired a covering round in the general direction of the shooter before scrambling behind a third column. Tucked behind the marble columns, they were at least temporarily clear of the line of fire from both the residence and the horsemen.

With their horses settled, the five remaining mounted guards could freely open fire and randomly peppered the three columns. But while their quarry was now hidden from view, they stood exposed on open ground. In a quick lunge, Giordino leaned around his column and let loose two quick shots at the nearest horseman, then ducked back behind cover. The targeted guard took a hit to the leg and shoulder as his comrades returned fire, chipping the stone column concealing Giordino. The wounded rider dropped his rifle and made a hasty retreat toward some bushes behind the drive. With Giordino drawing fire, Pitt took a turn, leaning out and firing two shots, nicking one of the other guards in the arm. The patrol leader barked a command and the remaining horsemen bolted toward the rear bushes.

Giordino turned toward Pitt's position. "They'll be back. A dollar says they're dismounting and will counterattack on foot."

"Probably trying to flank us as we speak," Pitt replied. He thought of Gunn and reached down for his radio, but it wasn't there. It had been knocked off during the earthquake and lay somewhere in the dark.

"Lost the radio," he said, cursing.

"I doubt Rudi can do anything more to help us. I've only got five shots left," he added.

Pitt had only a few rounds left in his Colt as well. With Wofford and Giordino both hobbled, they couldn't move far in a hurry. The guards were no doubt forming a noose around the compound and would close in from three sides. Pitt looked to the open front door and decided the residence might be the best option for a defensive stand. It had been strangely silent. Perhaps he and Giordino had hit the guard after all and only Borjin was hiding inside.

Pitt rose to a knee and prepared to lead the others toward the entry when a shadow flashed by the doorway. In the faint light, Pitt detected what appeared to be the muzzle of a gun poking out. A sudden rustle in the rosebushes to his back told him it was too late. The trap had been set with no means of escape. Outgunned, outmanned, and with nowhere to hide, they would have to make a final stand alone where they stood.

Then a deep rumble echoed off the hillsides. It was similar, but strangely different, to the roar that had preceded the earthquake. And with it came a new and unexpected cataclysm of death.

— 58 —

PITT LISTENED, AND NOTED THAT the rumble originated up the mountain rather than beneath the ground. It was a thundering noise that refused to wane, growing louder each second. The tone seemed to transform from a rumble to a rush as it drew closer. Everybody in the compound stared toward the main entrance, where the sound seemed to be heading. Unbelievably, the rushing noise grew still louder till it matched the roar of a dozen 747 jumbo jets blasting down a runway in unison.

Over the din, a pair of panicked shouts burst forth near the compound entrance. Unseen outside the walls, the two front-entry guards hurried to open the heavy iron gate. Their cries and bid to escape vanished under the crushing face of a giant wall of water.

A quarter mile upstream, the earthquake had triggered a deep chasm perpendicular to the riverbank. The raging river waters swirled in a confused vortex as the force of gravity led it in a new direction. Near the mouth of the aqueduct, the entire river shifted laterally, staking a new course alongside the elevated dirt road.

The river had rushed toward Borjin's compound before pooling in a large depression. A high berm, built as an equipment causeway between the road and the aqueduct, created an unintended dam within sight of the compound. The surging waters filled the depression, turning it into a large reservoir before the surplus flow began dribbling over the top. The overflowing water cut a crack in the dirt wall that quickly expanded to its base. In a flash, the entire berm collapsed under its own weight, releasing a surging wall of water.

The accumulated pool of icy black water burst toward the compound in a ten-foot-high wave. The front guards, oblivious to the approaching floodwaters until it was too late, were crushed by the wave as it smashed into the gate and gushed over the compound walls. The torrent lost little momentum before ripping away the front gate while also breaching a large hole through the wall above the aqueduct. The two swells of water merged forces inside the compound and surged toward the residence in a six-foot-high rolling wave.

Pitt gazed at the approaching wall of water and knew there was no chance of them outrunning it, especially Giordino and Wofford. Sizing up the surroundings, he saw one chance at survival.

"Grab hold of the columns and hang on," he shouted.

The Doric marble columns supporting the portico were deeply fluted, allowing a firm grasp to be made on the vertically cut edges. Theresa and Wofford stretched their arms completely around a column and linked hands. Giordino reached a thick arm around his column, keeping the Makarov held tight in his other hand. Tatiana abandoned her fright of getting shot and fearfully wrapped her arms around Giordino's waist in the face of the watery onslaught. Pitt barely had time to lie flat, grab the column, and hold his breath before the deluge hit.

But the shriek of men's voices arrived first. Encircling the drive in stealth, the guards were caught flat-footed by the floodwaters. The men were swept off their feet and devoured by the wave as it rolled toward the residence. Pitt heard the agonized cry of one guard just a few feet away as he was propelled toward the house by the surge.

The wave followed the path of least resistance, rolling across the northern part of the compound and mostly bypassing the lab and garage. Accompanied by a deep rumble, the advancing wave slammed into the residence with a crash. As Pitt had hoped, the marble columns took the brunt of the impact, but his legs were still ripped off the ground and pulled toward the house. He gripped the column tightly as the initial surge passed over and then the forceful tug of the water gradually receded. The initial fear of being battered and washed away by the flood was supplanted by the shock of the icy water. The bitter-cold water sucked the air out of his lungs and stung his skin like a thousand sharp needles. Grabbing the column, he pulled himself to his feet, finding the floodwaters had dropped to thigh level. At the adjacent column, he saw Giordino pull Tatiana up from under the water, the Mongolian woman coughing and sputtering. A second later, Theresa and Wofford emerged at the next column, gasping from the cold.

The wall of water had barreled into the house on its quest for a new pathway down the mountainside. Though two feet of water swirled through a crater-sized opening that had been the front door, the bulk of the floodwaters had been repelled from the heavy structure. The tormented waters finally surged around the northern end of the residence, pouring over the back-side cliff in a wide waterfall. Faint screams echoed above the river's rumble from scattered men who had survived the impact only to be washed down-stream. Nearby, a loud splash pronounced that the northern tip of the residence had crumbled under the force of the rushing waters.

The surge and current eased at the front of the house, and Pitt waded toward the others congregating at Giordino's column. He grimly noted the stiff bodies of several guards floating about the driveway. Reaching the column, he found Theresa staring at him through glazed eyes while shivering uncontrollably. Even the rocklike Giordino appeared numb, the effect of the gunshot wound with the icy immersion sending him on a path to shock. Pitt knew they would all be facing hypothermia shortly if they didn't escape the freezing water.

"We need to get to dry ground. This way," he said, motioning toward the lab, which stood on a slightly elevated rise. Wofford helped guide Theresa while Pitt made sure Tatiana didn't stray from Giordino. He need not have worried, as Borjin's sister was quietly subdued from the icy bath.

The diverted river had settled into two main channels through the compound. The primary flow ran from the front gate to the northern edge of the residence, where the waters continued to gnaw at the collapsing walls. A secondary flow swirled toward the laboratory before angling back to the residence's portico. A portion of the waters rolled through the house, while the rest rejoined forces with the main flow wrapping around the side.

It was the secondary swirl that encapsulated Pitt and the others. He quickly guided the group out of the deepest section, but they still faced ankle-deep flows of the chilly water in all directions. Around them, shouts and yelling echoed across the grounds as the scientists tried to prevent the waters from flooding the laboratory. Inside the garage, somebody shouted as a car was heard starting up. Further chaos ensued outside. The guards' horses had escaped the corral during the earthquake and the frightened herd stampeded back and forth across the compound in nervous confusion.

Pitt had his own problems to contend with. Watching

Theresa fall to her knees, he rushed to aid Wofford helping her up.

"She's fading," he whispered to Pitt.

Pitt looked in her eyes and saw a vacant stare. The uncontrollable shivering had continued unabated, and her skin was pale and clammy. She was on the verge of hypothermia.

"We need to get her warm and dry, pronto," Wofford said.

Standing in the middle of the flooded compound, their options were limited. They suddenly got worse when a vehicle in the garage came barreling out the bay doors with its lights ablaze.

Nearly a foot of water covered the ground around the garage, but the car plowed through it like a tank. Pitt watched anxiously as the vehicle turned in their direction, heading toward the residence's entry. The driver flashed on his high beams, then began weaving back and forth like a drunken snake. In less than a minute, the bright headlights flared across Pitt and the others and the driver suddenly ceased swerving and accelerated straight for their position.

The frozen group had stopped in a broad patch of open ground. There was nowhere to hide within easy reach. The black water swirling about their ankles prevented a quick escape, even had there been some nearby cover. Pitt calmly eyed the approaching vehicle, then turned to Wofford.

"Hold on to Theresa for a moment," he said, slipping her arm off his shoulder. He then raised his .45 and took aim at the car's front windshield and unseen driver behind the wheel.

Pitt held the gun steady, his fingers tightening on the trigger. The driver ignored the threat, charging forward, while streams of water gushed off the front bumper and fender wells. As the car drew nearer, it gradually drifted to one side, then started to slow. Pitt held his fire as the car, a jet-black supercharged Range Rover, cut a wide turn, then sloshed to a stop just a few yards in front of him. Pitt adjusted his aim to the driver's side window that now faced him and took a step forward with the Colt extended at arm's reach.

The car sat idling for a moment, hissing small clouds of steam that bubbled up from the vehicle's hot underside. Then the black-tinted driver's window rolled quietly down to the sill. From the dark interior of the car, a familiar bespectacled face popped through the window.

"Somebody call for a taxi?" Rudi Gunn asked with a grin.

— 59 —

PITT PLACED THERESA IN THE backseat of the Range Rover as Giordino shoved Tatiana in, then climbed in beside Theresa. Wofford took to the front passenger's seat as Gunn turned the heater up high, quickly roasting the interior. Giordino stripped off

Theresa's shoes and outer clothing, as his own shivering finally abated. The warm interior revived them all, and Theresa soon surprised everyone by sitting up and helping bandage Giordino's leg.

"Do we have you to thank for shaking up Borjin's abode?" Pitt asked of Gunn while he stood leaning on the driver's open window.

"Dr. von Wachter, actually. His seismic device is for real, and very user-friendly. I took a gamble and pressed the button and the next thing you know, instant tremor."

"Without a moment to spare, I might add."

"Nice shake, Rudi," Giordino grunted from the backseat, "but we could probably have done without the ice-water bath."

"I can't really take responsibility for the bonus elements of fire and flood," Gunn replied with feigned humility.

Pitt turned toward the laboratory and noticed for the first time a billow of smoke and flames pouring out the second-story windows. Somewhere in the building, a broken gas line had ignited, sending a fireball through the structure. A disheveled band of scientists were desperately pulling out equipment, research materials, and personal belongings before the whole building went up in flames.

Rid of her chill by the car's warm interior, Tatiana suddenly regained her feistiness.

"Get out," she hissed suddenly. "This is my brother's car."

"I thought it a nice choice as well," Gunn replied. "Remind me to thank him for leaving the keys in the ignition."

Gunn opened the door and started to climb out of the driver's seat. "You want to drive?" he asked Pitt. "I'll climb in back with the wildcat."

"No," Pitt said, gazing toward the residence. "I want Borjin."

"Go ahead," Tatiana cursed, "so he can kill you dead."

Giordino had enough. With a quick jab, he rocked Tatiana's jaw. The screeching died as she melted onto the seat unconscious.

"I've been wanting to do that for some time," he said somewhat apologetically. He then turned to Pitt. "You'll need backup."

"Not one with a bad wheel," he replied, nodding toward Giordino's bandaged leg. "No, you'd better support Rudi in getting everyone out of here, in case there's more trouble. I just want to make sure that our host hasn't disappeared."

"You can't last much longer in that icy water," Gunn said, noting a shiver from Pitt. "At least take my coat," he offered, slipping off his heavy jacket. "Not that you should cover up that fancy costume." He grinned at the soggy orange *del* Pitt was wearing. Pitt stripped off the waterlogged outfit and gratefully zipped up Gunn's dry jacket in its place.

"Thanks, Rudi. Try to get off the grounds before the whole place slides off the mountain. If I don't find you within an hour, then hightail it to Ulaanbaatar without me."

"We'll be waiting."

Gunn jumped back into the Range Rover and jammed it into drive, sloshing toward the compound entrance. The original gate and a twenty-foot section of adjoining wall had been toppled by the floodwaters, littering the grounds with chunks of concrete and debris. Pitt watched as Gunn guided the Rover to the large gap in the wall, then bounced the four-wheel-drive vehicle over the debris until its taillights vanished outside the compound grounds.

Wading toward the dark and flooded residence, Pitt suddenly felt alone and very cold as he wondered what Borjin might have in store for him.

～ 60 ～

THOUGH THE WORST OF THE flooding had subsided, there was still a half foot of water seeping though the residence when Pitt waded up the front steps. He stopped in front of the open front door, spotting a body lying facedown in the water, its legs wedged behind a large planter. Pitt moved closer and examined the man. He wasn't one of the gunmen Pitt had shot at but apparently another guard drowned by the floodwaters. Pitt noted that the man still clutched a wooden spear in one hand, his fingers clenched in a rigid grip. Pitt bent down and ripped the orange tunic from the man's body, then pried the spear from his left hand. He drove the spear tip through the armholes of the tunic and let it drape down as if hung from a hangar. A fool's bait, he thought, but it was all he had to counter those lying in wait inside.

Crouching at the doorway, he quickly slipped into the residence, rotating his .45 in an arc around the foyer. The entrance was empty and the entire house quiet, save for the steady rush of water cascading down a distant stairwell. The electricity had long since been extinguished, but a handful of emergency red lights dotted the hallway ceiling, powered by a remote generator. The lights provided little illumination, casting only patches of crimson shadows through the empty corridors.

Pitt peered down the three separate hallways. He could see out the open end of the northern corridor, where the gushing river was continuing to wash away the end of the wing. Borjin couldn't escape that way unless he had a kayak and a death wish, he thought. Pitt recalled Theresa indicating that the study was down the main corridor, so he slowly moved off in that direction.

Pitt hugged the side wall, his Colt aimed ahead in his right hand. He brought up the spear and tucked it under his elbow, bracing the tip at an outward and forward angle with his left hand. The ripped orange tunic, acting as Pitt's point man, marched a few feet ahead of Pitt, dangling in the center of the corridor.

Pitt moved slowly, shuffling his feet so as not to

splash the water and provide an auditory warning of his arrival. He actually had little choice, as his feet were so numb from the frigid river water that he felt like he was walking on stumps. There would be no high-speed foot chases from him, as he fought to maintain a precarious sense of balance.

He moved with measured patience, passing by several small side rooms without entering. He would stop past each doorway and then wait several minutes to ensure no one crept up behind him. A fallen credenza and some broken statuettes blocked his path and he temporarily moved to the center of the hallway. Approaching the residence kitchen, he melded back to the side wall, letting the dangling tunic lead the way down the center of the corridor.

Numbed by the icy water, Pitt concentrated on keeping his visual and auditory senses on high alert. When his ears detected a faint swishing sound, he froze, straining to determine if the noise was something in his imagination. Standing still, he slightly jiggled the wooden spear back and forth.

The burst came from the kitchen, a deafening blast of automatic gunfire that echoed off the walls. In the faint red light, Pitt could see the orange tunic shredded by the burst, as the bullets continued their path and slammed into the corridor wall just a few feet in front of him. Pitt calmly swiveled his .45 toward the open kitchen door, took aim at the muzzle flash, and squeezed the trigger three times.

As the Colt's booming report receded down the

hallway, Pitt heard a weak gurgled gasp wail from the kitchen. It was followed by the metallic clang of a machine gun banging against steel pans, then a loud splash as the dead guard tumbled to the floor.

"Barsijar?" shouted the voice of Borjin from down the hallway.

Pitt grinned to himself as he let the query be met with silence. He had the distinct feeling that there were no more henchmen between himself and Borjin. Dropping the spear and tunic, he moved aggressively toward the sound of Borjin's voice. His deadened feet felt as if they had lead weights tied to them. Almost hopping through the water, he brushed his free hand along the wall to keep balanced. Ahead of him, he could hear the splashing footsteps of Borjin suddenly dissipate at the end of the corridor.

A loud crash echoed from the side of the house as another chunk of the north wing crumbled under the river's surge. The whole residence shook under the rapid erosion, which ate closer and closer to the center of the house. Perched as it was on the side of a cliff, Pitt knew there was a real danger of the whole structure sliding down the mountain. But he dispelled any notion of turning and heading for the exit. Borjin was close now and he could take him alive.

Pitt moved quickly past a few small side rooms then hesitated as he reached the fire-blackened study. He shook off a freezing shiver from the cold and wet and willed himself to focus on the environment around him rather than his own discomfort. A steady murmur of rushing water had grown louder as he neared the end of the hall. Under the dim glow of an emergency light, he saw that it was the floodwaters cascading down a stairwell just past the study. Faint though they were, Pitt could also see a pair of wet prints leading into the dry conference room at the hall's end.

Pitt moved slowly past the stairwell and out of the draining water, thankful to at last remove his feet from the icy runoff. He cautiously approached the jamb of the conference-room door and peered inside. The late-rising moon had crept over the horizon and cast a bright silvery beam through the conference room's high glass windows. Pitt strained to discern Borjin's presence in the cavernous room, but all was still. He quietly stepped in, the muzzle of his Colt moving with his eyes.

Borjin's timing was impeccable. The Mongolian popped up from behind the end of the conference table while Pitt was facing the opposite side of the room. Too late, Pitt turned toward the movement as a loud twang erupted from the spot. Off balance and wheeling around on numb feet, Pitt fired a single shot toward Borjin but missed wide, the bullet shattering the glass window behind him. Borjin's aim was to prove more accurate.

Pitt saw but a fleeting glimpse of the feathered arrow before it struck his chest just below the heart, pene-trating with a dull thud. It struck with a powerful impact, knocking him right off his feet. Thrown back-ward to the floor, Pitt caught a lasting image of Borjin standing with a crossbow cradled in his arms. The moonlight sparkled off his sharp teeth, which were bared in a satisfied, murderous grin.

～ 61 ～

AFTER SLOGGING THE FOUR-WHEEL DRIVE through fallen bits of the entry wall, Gunn turned the Range Rover toward a small rise outside the compound and clawed his way to the top. He swung the vehicle around on the summit, then turned off the headlights. From the elevated perch, they had a perfect view of the disintegrating compound below. The raging mountain runoff pounded through the shattered entrance wall and rippled around the main residence, while smoke and flames grew higher from the laboratory on the opposite side.

"I'd be happy if there's not a cinder left of that place," Wofford remarked, eyeing the destruction with satisfaction.

"Seeing how we're one hundred fifty miles from the nearest fire department, there is probably a pretty good chance of that," Gunn replied. Sweating from the blasting car heater that was drying and thawing the others, he climbed out of the car. Giordino hobbled out behind him, watching the devastation below. The sound of gunfire echoed from somewhere inside the residence, and then, a few minutes later, a single gunshot was heard.

"He shouldn't have gone back alone," Giordino said, cursing.

"Nobody could have stopped him," Gunn said. "He'll be all right."

But a strange feeling in his stomach said otherwise.

BORJIN PLACED the medieval crossbow back among his collection of antique weaponry, then stepped to the cracked window and took a hurried look outside. A torrent of water rained down in back of the house, gathering on the rear ledge before tumbling over the cliffside in a wide waterfall. Of greater concern to Borjin was the growing pool of water accumulating in the courtyard and approaching the sanctuary. He gazed with distress at the stone structure. The main edifice was still intact, but the arched entryway had been shaken to bits during the earthquake.

Ignoring Pitt's prone body on the opposite side of the room, Borjin rushed out of the conference room and waded down the adjacent stairwell. The cascading water surged at the back of his legs, and he hung tightly to the banister as he moved down the steps. He stopped only momentarily to gaze at the dark portrait above the midlanding, nodding faintly at the painting of the great warrior khan. The rising water was nearly waist-high on the lower level, until he unbolted the side door and released an icy torrent onto the court-yard. Stumbling like a drunken sailor, he staggered across the flooded yard to the shattered entrance of the sanctuary. Stepping over a pile of fallen stones, he entered the torchlit interior and was relieved to find only a few inches of water running across the built-up floor.

After checking to see that the tombs were undamaged, he surveyed the walls and ceiling. Several large cracks stretched across the domed ceiling like a giant spiderweb. The old structure was in a perilous state from the rattling earthquake. Borjin nervously gazed from the ceiling to the center tomb, considering how best to protect his most prized possession. He never noticed a shadow flickering by one of the torches.

"Your world is crumbling down around you, Borjin. And you with it."

The Mongolian spun around, then froze as if he had seen a ghost. The specter of Pitt standing on his feet across the room, the crossbow arrow protruding from his chest, was unearthly. Only the Colt .45 in his hand, held rock steady and aimed at Borjin's chest, dispelled any notion of supernatural rejuvenation. Borjin could only stare back in disbelief.

Pitt edged toward one of the marble tombs at the side of the chamber, pointing at it with the barrel of his gun. "Nice of you to keep the relatives around. Your father?" he asked.

Borjin silently nodded, trying to regain his composure at the sight of a talking dead man.

"It was your father who stole the map to Genghis Khan's grave from a British archaeologist," Pitt said, "but that still wasn't enough to locate it."

Borjin raised a brow at Pitt's comment. "My father

acquired information as to the general location. It required the use of additional technologies to find the specific grave site."

"Von Wachter's acoustic seismic array."

"Indeed. A prototype discovered the buried grave. Additional improvements to the instrument have proven most remarkable, as you have witnessed." The words dripped with irony, as Borjin's eyes scoured the room for a means of defense.

Pitt moved slowly to the center of the room and placed his free hand on the granite tomb displayed on the pedestal. "Genghis Khan," he said. Weary and frozen as he was, he still felt an odd reverence in the presence of the ancient warlord. "I suspect the Mongolian people won't be too thrilled to learn you've been keeping him in your backyard."

"The people of Mongolia will revel in a new dawn of conquest," Borjin replied, his voice rising in a shrill cry. "In the name of Temujin, we will rise against the fools of the world and take our place in the pantheon of global supremacy."

He barely finished the raving when a deep rumble echoed through the floor. The rumble grew for several seconds until resounding in a loud crash as the entire north wing of the residence, or what was left of it, broke free of its foundation and slid unceremoniously down the hillside.

The resulting impact shook the grounds all around the estate, jarring the remaining residence structure as well as the sanctuary. The mausoleum floor visibly vibrated under the feet of Pitt and Borjin, throwing them off balance. Wobbly and exhausted from the cold, Pitt grabbed hold of the tomb in order to keep his gun trained on Borjin.

Borjin fell to a knee, then stood as the rumble and shaking subsided. His eyes widened as a sharp cracking sound rippled from overhead. He looked up to see a huge chunk of the ceiling come hurtling toward the ground beside him.

Pitt flattened himself against the side of the tomb as the rear of the sanctuary collapsed on itself. A barrage of stones and mortar smashed to the ground, raising a thick cloud of blinding dust. Pitt could feel chunks of the ceiling smack the top surface of the tomb beside him, but none of the stones struck him directly. He waited several seconds for the dust to clear, as he felt the cool night wind rustling on his skin. Standing in the remains of the now-darkened sanctuary, he could see that half the ceiling and the entire back wall had collapsed under the shifting ground. Through the piles of stones, he could see cleanly to the corral in back and the old car parked inside.

It took him a few moments to spot Borjin in the debris. Only his head and part of his torso were exposed from a mound of stones. Pitt walked near as Borjin's eyes fluttered open, dull and listless. A trickle of blood streamed from his mouth, and Pitt noticed the Mongol's neck seemed unnaturally distorted. His eyes gradually focused on Pitt and flashed with a glint of anger.

"Why . . . why won't you die?" Borjin stammered.

But he never heard the answer. A muted choke grumbled from his throat and then his eyes glazed over. His body crushed by his own monument to conquest, Tolgoi Borjin died quickly in the shadow of Genghis Khan.

Pitt stared at the broken body without pity, then slowly lowered the Colt still gripped in his hand. He reached down and unzipped the large pocket on the front of his jacket, then used the moonlight to peek inside. The heavy seismic array operator's manual with metal clipboard was right where Gunn had placed it. Only it was now perforated by a crossbow arrow that penetrated each and every page. The arrow had even dinged the metal clipboard, which had prevented it from ripping into Pitt's heart and killing him instantly.

Pitt walked over to Borjin and looked down at the lifeless body.

"Sometimes, I'm just lucky," he said aloud, answering Borjin's final query.

The collapse of the residence's northern wing had funneled more water into the courtyard. A heavy rush of water now flowed along the perimeter of the sanctuary and threatened to pour into the disintegrating structure. It was just a matter of time before the floodwaters would weaken the ground beneath the sanctuary and wash it down the mountainside. The tomb of Genghis Khan would be destroyed in the carnage, his bones lost for good this time.

Pitt turned to make his escape before any more walls

toppled, but hesitated as he glanced through the open rear wall at the corral in back. He turned and gazed again at the tomb of Genghis, which had miraculously survived the collapsing sanctuary intact. For an instant, Pitt wondered if he would be the last man to see the tomb. Then it hit him. It was a crazy idea, he thought, and he couldn't help but grin through a cold shiver.

"All right, old boy," he muttered at the tomb. "Let's see if you've got one more conquest left in you."

～ 62 ～

T HE FEELING WAS JUST RETURNING to Pitt's feet with a painful tingle as he climbed out the back of the sanctuary and into the corral. He staggered to the side and quickly yanked several timbers off the wooden fence to clear an opening. Tossing boxes and crates aside, he burrowed a wide path through the junk and debris until he reached his objective, the dust-laden old car.

It was a 1921 Rolls-Royce Silver Ghost open tourer, with a custom body by the English coachmaker Park Ward. Decades of dirt and grime covered a unique eggplant purple body paint. Long since faded, the color once complemented the car's burnished aluminum hood and wheel covers. More familiar on the streets of London, Pitt wondered how such a grand auto had ended up in Mongolia. He then recalled that T. E. Lawrence had acquired a Rolls-Royce armored car built on a 1914 Silver Ghost chassis, which he used in his desert campaign against the Turks in Arabia. Pitt wondered if the car's reputation for durability in the desert had reached the Gobi years before. Or perhaps a car built before the Mongolian revolution was the only vehicle of opulence that the Communist Party would allow Borjin's family to own.

None of that mattered to Pitt. What did matter was that the Rolls had a silver-handled crank protruding from its snout. Equipped as a backup for the early electric starters, the crank gave Pitt a small hope that he could start the car, even with a long-dead battery. Provided, that is, that the engine block wasn't frozen solid.

Pitt opened the right-side driver's door and placed the gearshift in neutral, then stepped to the front of the car. Leaning down and grabbing with both hands, he pulled up on the crank, driving with his legs. The crank held firm, but Pitt grunted out a second effort and the handle inched upward. He rested for a second, then gave another heave. The crankshaft broke free with the extra push, driving the six pistons up and down in their cylinders.

With his own small collection of antique cars at home in Washington, Pitt was well versed with the intricacies of starting up a vintage vehicle. Climbing back into the driver's seat, he adjusted the throttle, spark, and governor controls, which were set by movable levers mounted on the steering wheel. He then opened the hood and primed a tiny pump on a brass canister, which he hoped contained gasoline. He then returned to the crank and proceeded to manually turn the engine over.

Each pull of the crank led to a series of rasps as the old motor tried to suck in air and fuel. Zapped by exposure to the cold, Pitt's strength waned on every pull. Yet he willed himself to keep trying in the face of each dying wheeze from the engine. Then on the tenth pull, the motor coughed. Several more pulls produced a sputter. With his feet frozen, yet beads of sweat on his brow, Pitt heaved again on the crank. The crankshaft spun, the air and fuel ignited, and with a put-put-put sound, the engine labored to life.

Pitt rested briefly as the old car warmed up, spouting a thick cloud of black smoke out its rusty exhaust pipe. Rummaging around the corral, he found a small barrel filled with chains, which he tossed in the backseat. Taking his place in the driver's seat, he slipped the car into gear, released the clutch with his numb left foot, and drove the Rolls shakily out of the corral.

～ 63 ～

IT'S BEEN WELL OVER AN hour," Gunn remarked, looking glumly at his watch.

He and Giordino stood on the rise, watching the scene of devastation below. The laboratory fire burned in a blazing tempest, consuming the entire building and adjacent garage. Black smoke and flames leaped high into the sky, casting a yellow glow over the entire compound. Across the landscaped grounds, a large chunk of the residence was missing, replaced by rushing water where the northern wing of the house previously stood.

"Let's take a quick drive down," Giordino said. "Maybe he's injured and can't walk out."

Gunn nodded. It had been almost an hour since they heard the automatic fire from inside. Pitt should have made it out long ago.

They started to walk toward the car when a low rumble shook from below. No earthquake this time, they knew, but rather the erosive effects of the flooding waters. They stopped and stared, dreading what they knew was next. From their vantage, it resembled a collapsing house of cards. The northern end of the structure began toppling one wall at a time. The structural failure seemed to build momentum, moving across the residence in a rippling wave of destruction. The central section of the residence simply folded in on itself with a grinding crash, then disappeared under the water. The large white spire over the entrance melted away, disintegrating into a thousand bits under the floodwaters. Gunn and Giordino could only see chunks of debris poking through the water as the bulk of the residence slid off its ledge and washed down the mountain. In just a few seconds, it was gone. Only a small section of the southern wing survived, standing next to a wide flow of water where the rest of the house had once stood.

With the destruction of the house, all hopes for

finding Pitt alive had vanished. Gunn and Giordino knew that no one in and around the residence could have survived. Neither man said a word nor made a move. Together, they stood and solemnly stared at the altered river as it glided over the foundation of the house and roared down the cliffside beyond. The rushing of the wild waters competed with the crackling from the lab fire to disrupt the otherwise quiet late-night hour. Then Gunn's ears detected another sound.

"What's that?" he asked. He pointed a finger toward a small chunk of the southern wing, which stood on dry ground and had survived the collapse of the main residence. The whirring pitch of a high-revving engine rumbled from the hillside behind. The motor sporadically coughed and stuttered but otherwise sounded like it was operating at its redline. The roar grew louder until it was matched with a pair of lights that slowly crept over the hill.

Through the smoke and flames of the burning laboratory, the object appeared like a giant primordial bug crawling out of a hole in the ground. Two round but dimly illuminated lamps probed the night like a pair of large yellow eyes. A shiny metallic body followed behind, clouded by dirt and dust kicked up by its clawing rear appendages. The living beast even breathed vapor, a white cloud of smoke rising from its head.

The creature, lurching with great effort, finally clamored over the hill, seeming to fight every step of the way. A sharp gust of wind suddenly blew the smoke and dust away, and, under the light of the burning fire, Gunn and Giordino could see that it was no overgrown insect but the antique Rolls-Royce from the corral.

"Only one guy I know would be driving an old crate like that at a time like this," Giordino shouted with a whoop.

Jumping into the Range Rover, Gunn charged the car down the hill and stormed back into the compound. Shining their headlights onto the Rolls, they saw that the old car was still struggling to lurch forward, and had a line of chain stretched taut off the rear bumper. The old beast was trying desperately to pull something up the side of the hill.

Inside the Rolls, Pitt threw a thankful wave toward the approaching Range Rover, then turned back to coaxing the old auto forward. His numb right foot held the accelerator to the floor while the gearshift lever was still locked in first gear. The rear wheels spun and clawed at the ground, the worn, airless tires gamely trying to find a grip. But the weight behind was too great, and the big car seemed to be losing the battle. Under the hood, the overworked engine began to protest with loud knocks. What little coolant that existed in the block and radiator had nearly all boiled away, and Pitt knew it wouldn't be long before the engine seized.

With a surprised look, he suddenly saw Giordino appear and grab hold of the doorpost with a wink and a smile. Bandaged leg and all, he threw his weight into pushing the car forward. Gunn, Wofford, and even

Theresa appeared, taking up spots around the vehicle and pushing with all their might.

The extra manpower was just enough to propel the car in its last gasp. With a sudden lunge, the big car lurched forward. Thirty feet behind, a large block of granite teetered over the edge of the hill, then skidded forward easily under the car's newfound momentum. Chugging forward to a safe, dry spot, Pitt killed the engine under a whoosh of white steam.

As the vapor cleared away, Pitt saw that he was surrounded by a dozen scientists and technicians, along with a guard or two, who had given up fighting the lab fire to investigate his appearance. He cautiously climbed out of the Rolls and walked to the rear of the car. Giordino and the others had already gathered around and confirmed that the chained item had survived Pitt's tow intact.

Fearing for their safety, Pitt gripped his .45 as the crowd surged close to them. But he need not have worried.

At seeing that the sarcophagus of Genghis Khan had been rescued from the flood, the guards and scientists broke into a cheer and applauded him.

A VOYAGE
TO
PARADISE

~ 64 ~

THE U.S. NAVY CRUISER *Anzio* turned north from her station off the United Arab Emirates, a hundred miles inside the Strait of Hormuz, and headed on a dissecting path across the Persian Gulf. Though far from being the largest ship in the gulf, the Ticonderoga-class Aegis cruiser was easily the most deadly. With its phased array radar system housed in the ship's boxy superstructure, the ship could detect and target enemy craft on land, sea, and air within a two-hundred-mile radius. At the push of a button, one of one hundred twenty-one Tomahawk or Standard missiles could be dispatched from its vertical launch system housed belowdecks, obliterating the offending target within seconds.

The high-tech arsenal was managed by the Combat Information Center, a dark control room in the depths of the ship. Under its dim blue overhead lights, Captain Robert Buns studied one of several large projection screens mounted on the wall. The surrounding region of the gulf was displayed in multiple colors, overlaid with various geometric shapes and symbols that danced across the screen in slow motion. Each symbol represented a ship or aircraft tracked by the radar system. One shape, a highlighted red ball, was inching toward the Strait of Hormuz from left to right across the ship's path.

"Twelve miles to intercept, sir," reported a nearby sailor, one of several electronics experts seated at computer stations around the bay.

"Steady as she goes," Buns replied. A studious but witty line officer highly admired by the crew, Buns had enjoyed his current tour of duty in the gulf. Aside from missing his wife and two children, he found gulf duty to be an invigorating challenge, enlivened with occasional danger.

"We'll cross Iranian waters in three miles," warned a youthful tactical operations officer standing at his side. "They are clearly tracking the Iranian coast for safety."

"After Kharg Island, I don't think the Iranians are up for harboring these guys," Buns replied. "Pat, I think I'll watch the show from the bridge. You have the CIC."

"Aye, Captain. We'll be dialed in just in case."

Buns made his way out of the darkened command center and up to the bridge, which was bathed in bright sunlight reflecting off the gulf's waters. A dark-haired officer stood near the helm with a pair of binoculars to his eyes, observing a black vessel on the water ahead.

"Is that our target, commander?" the captain asked.

Commander Brad Knight, the *Anzio's* chief operations intelligence officer, nodded in reply.

"Yes, sir, that's the drill ship. Air recon has confirmed she's the *Bayan Star*, out of Kuala Lumpur. The same vessel that our satellites pegged at Ras Tanura and Kharg Island prior to the earthquakes."

Knight gazed down at the cruiser's forward deck, spotting a contingent of Marines in assault gear, prepping a pair of Zodiac boats.

"Boarding party looks to be in order, sir."

"Well, let's see if the *Bayan Star* will play ball."

Buns stepped to a seated radio communications officer and issued a command. The cruiser began hailing the drill ship, first in English, then in Arabic, ordering the vessel to stop and heave to for boarding and inspection. The drill ship ignored the calls in both languages.

"No change in speed," a radar operator reported.

"Can't believe those Hornets didn't get their attention," Knight said. A pair of F/A-18s from the aircraft carrier *Ronald Reagan* had tracked the drill ship for the prior hour, buzzing it constantly.

"Guess we'll have to do things the old-fashioned way and fire a shot across their bow," Buns said. The cruiser had a pair of five-inch guns capable of such a shot, and much more.

The cruiser closed to within two miles of the drill ship when the radar operator barked, "She's slowing, sir."

Buns leaned over and watched the radar screen,

seeing the drill ship's blip cease movement on its southwesterly course.

"Bring us alongside. Have the boarding party stand by."

The sleek gray cruiser angled to the northeast, pulling even with the drill ship with a half mile of water separating the two vessels. The Marines were quickly loaded into the Zodiacs and lowered over the side. As they began motoring toward the drill ship, Knight suddenly alerted Buns. "Captain, I see two boats in the water off the enemy's stern. I think the crew is abandoning ship."

Buns picked up a pair of binoculars and gazed at the drill ship. Two lifeboats filled with crewmen in black fatigues were making their way from the ship. Buns swung his binoculars toward the dilapidated vessel just in time to spot several puffs of white smoke rise from the lower levels.

"They mean to scuttle her," he said. "Call back the boarding party."

As the *Anzio*'s crew watched with surprise, the drill ship quickly began settling low in the water. In just a few minutes, the salty waters of the Persian Gulf began washing over the ship's bow. As the bow sunk lower, the stern rose higher into the air, until the flooded ship knifed to the bottom with a sudden whoosh.

Knight shook his head as he watched the trail of bubbles and foam dissipate over the ship's grave.

"Pentagon's not going to like that. They were eager for us to capture her intact. Had some big-time intel curiosity about the technology aboard."

"We still got her crew," Buns said, nodding toward the two lifeboats, which were headed willingly toward the cruiser. "And the Pentagon can still have the ship if they want her. She's just three hundred feet deep in Iranian waters," he added with a grin.

— 65 —

A CRISP BREEZE RIPPLED ACROSS the lower slopes of Burkhan Khaldun, snapping taut the multitude of blue-and-red Mongolian state flags fluttering high overhead. The largest of the flags, a mammoth banner fifty feet wide, wavered above a large granite mausoleum whose carved façade had been hastily completed by local craftsmen just days before. The empty mausoleum was surrounded by a large crowd of dignitaries, VIPs, and news reporters, who talked quietly among themselves while waiting for the future occupant to arrive.

A rush of excited whispers swirled through the crowd, then all fell silent as the sound of marching boots drew near. A company of Mongolian Army soldiers appeared through the pines, marching up a slight incline toward the waiting assembly. They were the first in a long procession of military honor guards escorting the remains of Genghis Khan to his final resting place.

Genghis had been engaged in a battle siege near

Yinchuan in northwest China when he'd fallen off his horse and died a few days later from his injuries. A secret funeral procession had brought his body back to Mongolia and the slopes of Burkhan Khaldun for burial in 1227, but history doesn't record the details of the cortege. Desiring to keep their enemies unaware of his death, as well as keep his burial spot secret for all eternity, his warrior comrades likely returned his casket in a nondescript, perhaps even covert, procession before burying him in an unmarked location. Nearly eight centuries later, there would be nothing covert about his reburial.

The Mongol warrior's body had lain in state in Ulaanbaatar for a week, drawing visits from over two million people, incredibly more than two-thirds the population of the entire country. Pilgrimages from all corners of the country were made by the thousands to lay eyes on his coffin. A three-day funeral procession to his grave site in the Khentii Mountains drew an equally impressive number of well-wishers, who lined the route holding flags and images of the ancient leader. Women and children waved and cried when the caisson rolled by, as if it was a favored relative who had just passed away. A national day of mourning, and future holiday of remembrance, marked the third leg of the procession. On this day, the caravan climbed up a makeshift road to a peaceful spot near the base of Burkhan Khaldun, where the warlord was said to have been born.

Pitt, Giordino, and Gunn, with Theresa and Wofford alongside, sat in the front row of dignitaries, just a few seats down from Mongolia's president and parliament leaders. Pitt turned and winked at a young boy seated behind him as the funeral procession drew near. Noyon and his parents, special guests of Pitt's, looked on at the surroundings with awe, the boy's eyes widening in wonder as the Khan's caisson finally appeared.

In a splendor worthy of the greatest conqueror the world has ever known, Genghis Khan's body was carried on a mammoth wooden caisson painted bright yellow. A magnificent team of eight snow-white stallions pulled the funeral cart, seemingly dropping their hooves in perfect unison. Atop the caisson was the granite tomb Pitt had saved from the floodwaters, now covered in fresh lotus blossoms.

A troupe of aged lamas wearing bright red robes and arched yellow hats quietly took up position in front of the tomb. Down the hill, a pair of monks blew into their *radong*s, enormous telescopic horns that emitted a deep baritone hum heard all down the valley. As the low resonations wafted in the breeze, the lamas launched into a lengthy funeral prayer, incorporating drums, tambourines, and burning incense. At the completion of the ceremony, the lamas quietly filed off to the side as an old shaman took to the stage. The age of Genghis Khan was filled with mysticism, and shamanism played an important role in the nomadic lifestyle. The grizzled shaman, who had a flowing beard and was dressed in caribou skins, danced and chanted around a large fire containing sheep bones. With a shrieking moan, he blessed the Khan's remains, imparting them from the land of the eternal blue sky to an afterlife of conquering the heavens.

When the service was completed, the granite sarcophagus was rolled into the mausoleum, then sealed with a six-ton slab of polished stone lowered by a crane. The spectators would later all swear they heard a distant clap of thunder at the precise moment the tomb was sealed, even though there was not a cloud in the sky. Genghis Khan was at rest again in his beloved homeland mountains, and his tomb would stand forever as a cultural mecca for tourists, historians, and all the peoples of Mongolia.

As the crowd began filtering out, Ivan Corsov and Alexander Sarghov approached from the rear, where they had been seated with the Russian ambassador.

"I see you are as adept at sniffing out historic treasures on land as at sea," Sarghov laughed, giving Pitt and Giordino a friendly bear hug.

"Simply a bonus for figuring out why somebody tried to sink the *Vereshchagin*," Pitt replied.

"Indeed. By the way, we still have our joint research project to complete on Lake Baikal. The *Vereshchagin* will be repaired and ready to go next season. I hope you both will join us."

"We'll be there, Alexander."

"Just as long as there are no more seiche waves," Giordino added.

Corsov sidled up, his usual ear-to-ear grin in full display.

"An impressive demonstration of undercover work,

my friends," he said. "You should join the Russian Federal Security Service, there is a need for men of your talents."

"I think my boss might have a thing or two to say about that," Pitt laughed.

The president of Mongolia approached with a small entourage. Sarghov said a quick farewell, as Pitt slyly noted Corsov melding away into the exiting crowd. A short, polished man of forty-five, the president spoke nearly flawless English.

"Mr. Pitt, on behalf of the people of Mongolia I wish to thank you and your NUMA team for rescuing Genghis for all posterity."

"A giant of history deserves to live forever," Pitt replied, nodding toward the mausoleum. "Though it is a shame that the riches of the tomb have all been lost."

"Yes, it is a tragedy that the treasures of Genghis were dispersed to collectors around the world simply to enrich the pockets of Borjin and his siblings. Perhaps our country will be able to buy back some of the antiquities from our newfound oil revenues. Of course, the archaeologists all believe that a greater trove lies with Kublai Khan, whose grave Borjin was thankfully unable to find. At least Kublai and his treasure still reside undisturbed in Mongolia, buried somewhere beneath these hills."

"Kublai Khan," Pitt muttered, staring at the mausoleum of Genghis. On its granite façade, he noted an engraving of a lone wolf, whose outline figure was painted blue.

"Yes, that is the legend. Mr. Pitt, I wish to also personally thank you for exposing the corrupt activities of the Borjin family and helping put a stop to their lawlessness. I have initiated an investigation into my own government to determine the extent of the influence-peddling on their behalf. The remnants of their actions will be buried with the body of Borjin, I promise."

"I hope that Tatiana is proving to be a cooperative witness."

"Most assuredly," the president replied with a furtive grin. Tatiana, he knew, was being held at a less-than-comfortable security site. "With her help, and the continued assistance of your oil industry companions," he said, nodding toward Theresa and Wofford, "we shall be able to exploit the discovered oil reserves for the good of a new Mongolia."

"China isn't going to renege on acceding Inner Mongolia?" Gunn asked.

"It's too politically dangerous for them to do so, both internationally and within the confines of Inner Mongolia, whose occupants largely favored secession from China. No, the Chinese will be happy enough, as we've agreed to sell them oil at a favorable price. That is, until our pipeline to the Russian port of Nakhodka is completed." The president smiled and waved at the Russian ambassador, who stood a few yards away chatting with Sarghov.

"Just ensure that the oil revenues go to the people who need it most," Pitt requested.

"Indeed, we've taken a lesson from your own state of

Alaska. A portion of the revenues will be distributed to every man, woman, and child in the country. The remainder will support the state's expansion of health, education, and infrastructure. Borjin has taught us that not a dime of profits will end up in the hands of an individual, I can assure you."

"That is good to know. Mr. President, I have one favor to ask of you. We discovered a plane crash in the Gobi Desert."

"My director of antiquities has already informed me. We'll be sending a research team from the National University of Mongolia right away to excavate the aircraft. The bodies of those aboard will be returned to their homes for proper burial."

"They deserve that."

"It was a pleasure, Mr. Pitt," the president said, as an aide tugged at his sleeve. He turned and started to walk away, then stopped.

"I almost forgot," he said to Pitt. "A gift from the people of Mongolia to you. I understand you have an appreciation for such objects."

He pointed down the hill to a large flatbed truck that had discreetly followed the funeral procession up the mountainside. A large covered object sat upright on the truck's bed. As Pitt and the others watched with curiosity, two workmen climbed up and pulled back the canvas covering. Underneath sat the dust-covered Rolls-Royce from Borjin's compound.

"Should make for a nice restoration project on the weekends," Wofford said, eyeing the decrepit car.

"My wife Loren will love that," Pitt replied with a devious grin.

"I'd love to meet her sometime," Theresa said.

"Next time you are in Washington. Though I take it you'll be working in Mongolia for some time to come."

"The company gave us three weeks of paid leave for our ordeal. We are both hoping to go home to rest and recuperate before Jim and I come back."

From the look she gave Giordino and the tone in her voice, it was clear that the "we" was not referring to Wofford.

"I don't suppose you could take it upon yourself to nurse a rabid old sea dog like Al back to health during that time," Pitt offered.

"I was rather counting on it," she said coyly.

Giordino, leaning on a crutch with his lower leg heavily bandaged, smiled broadly.

"Thanks, boss. I've always wanted to see the Zuider Zee."

As the friends parted company, Pitt strolled down the hill toward the flatbed truck. Gunn joined him as he approached the old Rolls.

"The Mongolian energy minister just told me that the price of oil is down another ten dollars today," he said. "The markets are finally accepting the news that the Avarga Oil Company has been put out of business for good and the destructive earthquakes are finished. Combined with the news of the oil reserves in Inner Mongolia, the experts predict that the price will soon drop to levels below those seen before the Persian Gulf disruption."

"So the oil panic has subsided and a global depression averted. Maybe the economic powers that be will finally learn the lesson and focus on developing renewable energy sources in earnest."

"They won't until they absolutely have to," Gunn said. "Incidentally, I was told that the Pentagon was none too happy that all three of von Wachter's seismic devices were completely destroyed, after the last-known device was sunk in the Persian Gulf."

"NUMA can't take responsibility for that one."

"True. It was a lucky stroke that Summer and Dirk stumbled upon Borjin's brother and the second device in Hawaii. Or he stumbled upon them. Had the ship traveled on to Valdez and damaged the Alaska Pipeline as planned, there would have been real pandemonium."

"It was the Chinese wreck Summer found. It drew them there for some reason," Pitt said. A faraway look crossed his face as he mentally searched the clues. Then his green eyes suddenly sparkled in enlightenment.

Gunn was oblivious to the mystery, focused instead on the immediate demands of his government.

"Not only were all of the seismic devices destroyed, but von Wachter's research materials as well. Apparently, Borjin had all of the professor's data in the laboratory building, which is now a pile of charcoal. There's nothing left for anyone to be able to resurrect the technology."

"Is that a bad thing?"

"I suppose not. Though I'd feel better if I knew the knowledge was in our hands and not the likes of Borjin."

"Just between you, me, and the car," Pitt said, "I happen to know that the operator's manual you lifted from the lab survived the flood and fire."

"The manual survived? It would give a big leg up to anyone trying to duplicate von Wachter's work. I hope it's secure."

"It's found a safe and permanent home."

"You sure about that?" Gunn asked.

Pitt walked to the rear of the Rolls and opened a large leather trunk mounted to the car's luggage rack. Lying at the bottom of the musty interior was the seismic array operator's manual, with the shaft from the crossbow arrow still protruding from its cover.

Gunn let out a low whistle, then put his hands over his eyes and turned away.

"I never saw it," he said.

Pitt latched up the trunk, then casually inspected the rest of the car. Overhead, a bank of dark gray clouds began moving in rapidly from the west. The remaining mourners milling about the tomb quickly headed toward their vehicles parked below to avoid the pending deluge.

"I guess we better be on our way," Gunn said, steering Pitt toward their rented jeep down the hill. "So, it's back to Washington?"

Pitt stopped and stared at the mausoleum of Genghis

Khan one last time. Then he shook his head.

"No, Rudi, you go on ahead. I'll catch up in a few days."

"You staying here a bit longer?"

"No," Pitt replied with a faraway twinkle in his eye. "I'm going to hunt a wolf."

— 66 —

THE TROPICAL SUN BEAT WARMLY on the deck of the *Mariana Explorer* as she rounded the rocky lava finger of Kahakahakea Point. The NUMA ship's captain, Bill Stenseth, slowed the vessel as it entered the mouth of the now-familiar cove in Keliuli Bay. Ahead and to his left he noted a red marker buoy bobbing on the surface. Seventy feet beneath it lay the mangled remains of the Avarga Oil Company drill ship, partially buried under a pile of loose lava rock. With the depths shallowing, Stenseth took the research ship no farther, stopping engines and then dropping anchor.

"Keliuli Bay," he announced, turning toward the rear of the bridge.

Seated at a mahogany chart table, Pitt was examining a coastal chart of Hawaii with a magnifying glass. Unfurled beside the map was the cheetah skin he had retrieved from Leigh Hunt's crashed Fokker in the Gobi Desert. Pitt's children, Dirk and Summer, stood nearby, looking over their father's shoulder with curiosity.

"So, this is the scene of the crime," the elder Pitt said, rising from the table and peering out the window. He stretched his arms and yawned, tired from his recent flight from Ulaanbaatar to Honolulu, via Irkutsk and Tokyo. The warm humid air felt refreshing on his skin, after leaving Mongolia during a late-summer cold snap that had snow flurries in the air when he boarded his flight.

Pitt's return to Hawaii brought with it a certain melancholy, which deepened during his layover in Honolulu. With a three-hour wait for his commuter flight to Hilo, he rented a car and drove across the Koolau Mountains to the east shore of Oahu. Off a side road near Kailua Beach, he wandered into a tiny cemetery that overlooked the ocean. It was a small but well-maintained patch of green surrounded by lush foliage. Pitt sauntered methodically through the grounds, examining the assorted tombstones. Beneath the shadowy branches of a blossoming plumeria tree, he found the grave site of Summer Moran.

His first and deepest love, and the mother of his children, Summer Moran had died only recently. Pitt had not known she was alive and living in seclusion after a disfiguring accident, believing that she had died decades earlier. He had lived the years trying to purge her memory from his mind and heart, until the sudden arrival of his two grown children on his doorstep. A flood of emotions returned, and he painfully wondered how his life would have been different, had he known she was alive and raising their twin children. He had forged a close bond with the kids now, and he had the love of his wife Loren. But the feeling of loss remained, tinged with anger at losing the time he could have spent with her.

With heaviness in his chest, he gathered up a handful of the fragrant plumeria blossoms and sprinkled them gently over her grave. For a long while, he stood wistfully by her side, staring out at the ocean. The gentle rolling waves from his other love, the sea, helped wash away the pain he felt. He finally stepped from the cemetery tired and drained, but with a renewed sense of hopefulness.

Standing on the bridge now with his children, he felt a warm glow, knowing a part of Summer still lived. The adventuresome spirit rekindled, he refocused on the mystery Chinese shipwreck.

"The marker buoy is where Summer laid waste to the drill ship." Dirk smiled, pointing out the window. "The Chinese wreck site is almost in the dead center of the cove," he said, swinging his arm around to the right.

"The artifacts have all dated to at least the thirteenth century?" Pitt asked.

"Everything has indicated as much," Summer replied. "The ceramic pieces recovered date from the late Song to the early Yuan dynasties. The wood samples came up elm and date to approximately 1280. The famed Chinese shipyard of Longjiang used elm and other woods in their ship construction, which is another piece of confirming evidence."

"The local geological records don't hurt either," Dirk

said. "Since the wreck was devoured by a lava flow, we checked the known history of volcanic eruptions on the Big Island. Although Kilauea is the best-known and most-active volcano, Hualalai and Mauna Loa also have a recent history of activity. The closest to our spot here, Mauna Loa, has erupted thirty-six times in the last one hundred fifty years. She's had an untold number of lava releases in the centuries prior. Local geologists have been able to radiocarbon-date charcoal samplings recovered from beneath the lava flows. One lava sample study, from neighboring Pohue Bay, dates around eight hundred years old. We don't know for sure if the lava flows that washed into the cove and buried our ship were from that same eruption, but my money says it was. If so, then our ship would have arrived no later than 1300 A.D."

"Does anything correlate with your cryptic cheetah skin?" Summer asked.

"It is impossible to date, but the voyage depicted shows some interesting similarities," Pitt replied. "The lead vessel is a mammoth four-masted junk, which seems to match the size of your wreck, based on the rudder uncovered by Dirk and Jack. Unfortunately, there was no narrative accompanying the images. Only a few decipherable words appear on the skin, which translates as 'A lasting voyage to paradise.'"

Pitt sat down and studied the two-dimensional artistry on the animal skin again. The series of draw-ings clearly showed a four-masted junk at sail with two smaller support ships. Several panels depicted a long ocean voyage until the ships arrived at a cluster of islands. Though crudely marked, the islands lay in the same relative position as the largest of Hawaii's eight islands. The large junk was shown landing on the biggest island, anchoring near a cave at the base of a high cliff. The final panel was what most intrigued Pitt. It showed the moored ship near some crates at the base of the cliff. Fire and smoke enveloped the ship and the surrounding landside. Pitt studied a flag burning on the ship's mast with particular interest.

"The volcanic eruption fits like a glove," he said. "The flames in the drawing look like a brush fire, but that's the secret. It wasn't a fire at all but a volcanic eruption."

"Those crates," Summer said. "They must contain some sort of treasure or valuables. Tong, or Borjin, as you've said his real name is, knew something about the ship's cargo. That's why they were trying to open up the lava field with a directed earthquake."

"I guess the laugh is on them," Dirk said. "The treasure, or whatever it is, wasn't even on the ship. If the drawing is correct, then the cargo was taken ashore and destroyed by the lava flows."

"Was it destroyed?" Pitt asked with a wily grin.

"How could it have survived the lava flows?" Summer asked. She picked up the magnifying glass and studied the last panel. Her eyebrows arched just a trace as she studied the crates surrounded by black stone. The image showed no flames on or about the crates.

"They are not on fire in the picture. Do you really think they could have survived?"

"I'd say it is worth a look. Let's go get wet and find out for sure."

"But would it have to be buried in lava?" Dirk protested.

"Have a little faith in the old man," Pitt smiled, then headed off the bridge.

With a high degree of skepticism, Dirk and Summer followed their father to the rear of the ship and assembled three sets of dive gear. Loaded into a Zodiac, they were lowered over the side of the ship by Jack Dahlgren.

"I'll have a tequila waiting for the first person who finds a Ming vase," he joked as he cast off the rubber boat.

"Don't forget the salt and lime," Summer shouted back.

Pitt steered the Zodiac toward the shore, angling to one side of the cove before killing the motor a few yards from the surf line. Dirk tossed an anchor over the side to secure their position, then the threesome slid into their dive gear.

"We'll run parallel to shore as close to the surf line as we can get," Pitt instructed. "Just watch out for the breakers."

"And what exactly are we looking for?" Dirk asked.

"A stairway to heaven." His father smiled cryptically, then pulled his mask down over his face. Sitting on the edge of the boat, he leaned over backward and dropped into the water, disappearing under a small wave. Dirk and Summer quickly adjusted their masks and regulators, then followed him over the side.

They converged on the bottom, less than twenty feet below, in water that was dark and turbid. The crashing surf roiled the water with foam and silt, reducing the visibility to just a few feet. Summer saw her father nod at her then turn and head into the murk. She quickly followed behind, knowing her brother would take up the rear.

The bottom surface was a bed of craggy black lava that rose up sharply to her left. Even underwater, she was pushed strongly from the side by the incoming waves and she frequently turned seaward and kicked hard with her fins to avoid being body-slammed into a rising mount of lava.

She followed her father's fins and trail of bubbles for twenty minutes before he finally disappeared for good into the dark waters ahead of her. She figured they were roughly halfway across the cove's landfall shore. She would swim another ten minutes, she decided, then surface and find out exactly where she was.

Following the surf line, she felt herself being carried close to a lava rise by a large wave. Turning to kick away, she was surprised by a second, more powerful wave, which pushed her forcefully toward shore. The wave quickly overpowered her, and she slammed backward into the lava wall, her steel air tank grinding against the rock.

Unhurt by the collision, she remained pinned against

the lava until the wave rolled past. She started to move away when she noticed a dark spot on the rocks above her head. Pulling herself closer, she peered into a black tube that angled slightly upward and toward the shore line. She couldn't tell in the murky water whether it was just a hole in the rocks, so she pulled out a flashlight and reached inside. The beam of light faded in the water, not detecting an opposing wall to reflect. The opening clearly traveled for some distance.

Her heart skipped a beat as she realized that this was what her father was searching for. She braced herself by the opening as another large wave passed by, then reached around and banged the flashlight against her dive tank. A metallic clanging echoed through the water.

Almost immediately Dirk appeared, looking at Summer quizzically, then eyeing the opening with surprise as she pointed the way. A minute later her father swam up, playfully patting Summer on the head after spotting the tunnel. Flicking on his own flashlight, he swam into the tube, his kids following behind.

Pitt immediately recognized the opening as a lava tube. Its cylindrical-shaped walls were almost perfectly formed, rounded and smoothed as if made by a machine. But the passage was actually the result of a steady flow of hot lava cooling on the surface and creating an outer crust. The liquid center ultimately flowed out, leaving a hollow tube. Lava tubes have been found that stretch fifty feet wide, while a few run several miles long. Summer's tube was relatively small, stretching about six feet in diameter.

Pitt followed the tube for thirty feet, noticing a gradual ascent on his depth gauge. The tube suddenly flared wide, and he noticed a reflection from his flashlight just before his head broke the surface of a calm pool of water. Bobbing on the surface, he turned the light around him. Steep black walls of lava fell vertically to the water on three sides. The fourth side, however, opened to a wide, rocky clearing. Pitt kicked lazily toward the landing as the underwater lights of Summer and Dirk surfaced near him. They all swam to the rocks and climbed out of the water before anyone spat out their regulators and spoke.

"It's amazing," Summer said. "An underground cavern fed from a flooded lava tube. Though it could use a little air-conditioning." The air in the cave was dank and musty, and Summer contemplated keeping her tank and regulator on.

"It was likely a much deeper cave at one time, but became sealed off by the lava flows gushing down the mountainside," Pitt said. "It's a fluke that a lava tube happened to form at its entrance."

Dirk dropped his tank and weight belt, then flashed his light around the clearing. Something caught his eye in the rocks.

"Summer, behind you."

She turned and gasped at the sight of a man standing just a few feet away. She stifled a cry at realizing that the man wasn't real.

"A clay warrior?" Dirk asked.

Summer shined her light and noticed another figure standing nearby. They were both life-sized figures, with painted uniforms and sculpted swords. Summer crept closer, eyeing the artisans' detail. They were soldiers, and each had braided hair, and a stringy mustache beneath almond-shaped eyes.

"Emperor Qin's terra-cotta warriors of Xian?" Pitt said. "Or perhaps a thirteenth-century facsimile."

Summer looked at her father quizzically. "Thirteenth century? What are they doing here?"

Pitt stepped up to the two figures and noticed a small path that ran between them, cut through the lava.

"I think they are guiding us to the answer," he said. Stepping between the clay sculptures, he followed the path, with Dirk and Summer in tow. The worn trail twisted around several walls of lava, then suddenly opened into a wide, cavernous room.

Pitt stood at the threshold with his two children, shining their flashlights in awe. The huge chamber was filled with an army of clay figures flanking the walls. Each wore a heavy necklace of gold or an amulet studded with gemstones. Positioned inside the clay warriors was another ring of sculptures, mostly scale figures of animals. Some were carved jade or stone, while others were gilded with gold. Deer grazed fearlessly next to large falcons. A pair of prancing white mares was showcased near the center of the room.

Interspersed with the sculptures were dozens of small lacquered cabinets and tables covered in dust. On a large teak table, Summer noticed an elaborate place setting that shone under her light. The plates, flatware, and goblets sitting atop a silk mat were all cast in gold. Adjacent to the table was an assortment of silver and gold ornaments, some adorned with Arabic lettering and literary Chinese script. Other tables held mirrors, boxes, and art objects glistening with decorative gemstones. Summer crept to a nearby cabinet covered with scenes of battle painted in bright colors and pulled open a drawer. Inside, trays of amber, sapphires, and rubies filled the silk-lined case.

The sculptures and jewels didn't interest Pitt. He stared past the artifacts toward the centerpiece of the entire chamber. On a raised stone platform in the middle of the room stood a long wooden box. It was painted bright yellow and featured detailed carvings on each panel. Pitt stepped closer and shined his light at the top of the box. A stuffed cheetah, its teeth bared and a clawed paw scratching the air, seemed to hiss back at Pitt. He lowered his light to the top surface of the box and smiled at the image. A large wolf, painted blue, was emblazoned across the surface.

"May I present the late emperor of the Yuan Empire, Kublai Khan," he said.

"Kublai Khan," Summer whispered in reverence, her eyes wide. "It can't be."

"I thought he was buried somewhere near Genghis," Dirk said.

"According to popular legend. But the tale just didn't seem to add up. Borjin was able to locate the grave of Genghis Khan with his seismic device, but he never found Kublai. They should have been buried in the same ballpark. Then your Dr. Tong appears here, sidestepping a mission to disrupt the Alaska Pipeline in order to visit a shipwreck? There was obviously a greater draw, something only the Borjins could appreciate. I suspect they may have found an empty tomb for Kublai in Mongolia, or discovered some other clue that he was buried elsewhere."

"I still don't see how that leads here," Summer said.

"The story is in the cheetah skin. It was discovered at Shang-tu, so it had an original link with Kublai. The emperor was known to possess trained cheetahs used for hunting, so the skin may have even come from one of his pets. More relevant was that the cheetah skin was unearthed together with a silk map that purportedly showed the location of Genghis Khan's tomb. Borjin's father acquired the silk map, and Borjin himself admitted that it helped lead to the grave site. For some reason, the significance of the cheetah skin paintings was overlooked when first found. The blue wolf was the trigger for me."

"What blue wolf?" Summer asked.

"A design motif," he said, pointing to the image painted on the elevated wooden coffin. "It was a known emblem for the imperial khans, originated by Genghis. If you look at the cheetah skin closely, you can see a banner of a blue wolf flying on the mast of the burning junk in the last painting. It wouldn't be flown except in the presence of a khan. Your wreck, which matched the depiction of a royal vessel departing China on the panels, was dated fifty years after the death of Genghis. Too late for him to be taking a cruise. No, the dates align with the era when Kublai ruled. And died. The secret of the cheetah skin is that it shows the final voyage of Kublai Khan."

"But why was he brought to Hawaii?" Summer asked, passing her light across the length of the sarcophagus. She held the beam momentarily on a twisted wooden staff that leaned against one end of the tomb. She noted curiously that a shark-tooth necklace dangled from its worn grip.

"His last years were difficult ones. Perhaps his 'voyage to paradise' was a plan to spend eternity on a faraway shore."

"Dad, how did you know his tomb survived the volcanic blast and that we could find it?" Dirk asked.

"Whoever painted the cheetah skin had seen the tomb and treasures and had known they survived the lava flows, otherwise they would have been depicted in flames as well. I took a gamble on the entrance. The sea levels are higher than they were eight hundred years ago, so I figured the entrance might now be underwater."

"The treasures here must represent the riches accumulated during his lifetime of conquest," Dirk said, stunned at the sheer volume around him. "Perhaps some of the items were amassed during the reign of Genghis as well. It must be worth an untold fortune."

"The Mongolian people were cheated out of Genghis Khan's treasure. It would only be fitting if they secure the riches of Kublai Khan. I trust they will find a more appropriate burial spot, on Burkhan Khaldun, where Kublai can spend eternity."

The wonder of the hidden tomb played heavily on their inner thoughts, and the trio found themselves whispering as they roamed through the ancient treasures. Illuminated by just the glow of their flashlights, the shadowy chamber teemed with the mystery and aura of the Middle Ages. As the beams of light played off the glistening walls, Pitt was reminded of the real Xanadu, and the haunting poem by Samuel Coleridge.

" 'The shadow of the dome of pleasure / Floated midway on the waves,' " he recited in a low voice. " 'Where was heard the mingled measure / From the fountain and the caves.' "

Summer approached her father and squeezed his hand. "Mom always told us you were a hopeless romantic," she smiled.

Their lights running low, Pitt and Summer moved together toward the passageway. Dirk sidled up as they took a last look around the chamber.

"First you save the tomb of Genghis. Now you discover Kublai Khan and the treasures of his empire," he said with awe. "That's one for the ages."

Summer nodded in agreement. "Dad, sometimes you are just amazing."

Pitt reached his arms out wide and gave both his kids an affectionate hug.

"No," he replied with a broad grin. "Sometimes, I'm just lucky."

7

Center Point Publishing

600 Brooks Road ● PO Box 1
Thorndike ME 04986-0001 USA

(207) 568-3717

US & Canada:
1 800 929-9108